ZOMBIES from the PULPS

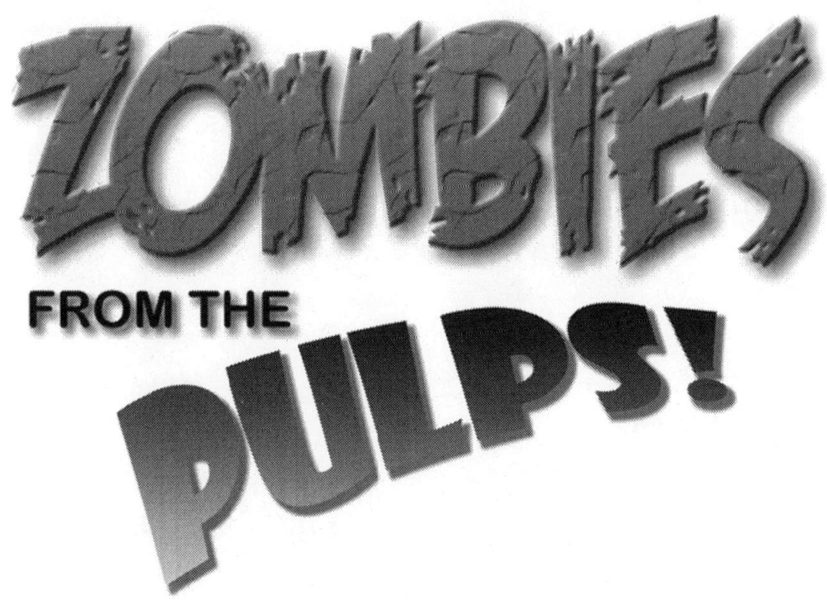

Twenty Classic Tales of the Walking Dead

Edited with an Introduction by

Jeffrey Shanks

SKELOS PRESS

Published by Skelos Press
www.skelospress.com

First Trade Edition

This volume was previously published in a limited signed & numbered edition of 50 copies.

ISBN-13: 978-1495236044

For Claudia, Alex, and Sage

Table of Contents

List of Illustrations

Publication History

"Herbert West—Reanimator" was originally serialized in six parts in the February through July 1922 issues of the magazine *Home Brew*

"Jumbee" was originally published in the September 1926 issue of *Weird Tales.*

"The Corpse-Master" was originally published in the July 1929 issue of *Weird Tales.*

"Dead Girl Finotte" was originally published in the January 1930 issue of *Weird Tales.*

"Salt is Not for Slaves" was originally published in the August-September 1931 issue of *Ghost Stories.*

"The Dead Who Walk" was originally published in the September 1931 issue of *Strange Tales of Mystery and Terror.*

"The House in the Magnolias" was originally published in the June 1932 issue of *Strange Tales of Mystery and Terror.*

"The Empire of the Necromancers" was originally published in the September 1932 issue of *Weird Tales.*

"The Devil's Dowry" was originally published in the February 1935 issue of *Terror Tales.*

"The Walking Dead" was originally published in the November 1935 issue of *Spicy Mystery.*

"The Graveyard Rats" was originally published in the March 1936 issue of *Weird Tales.*

"The Grave Gives Up" was originally published in the August 1936 issue of *Thrilling Mystery.*

"Zombie" was originally published in the November 1936 issue of *Spicy Mystery.*

"Revels for the Lusting Dead" was originally published in the July-August 1937 issue of *Terror Tales.*

"Corpses on Parade" was originally published in the April 1938 issue of *Dime Mystery.*

"Pigeons from Hell" was originally published in the May 1938 issue of *Weird Tales.*

"The Man Who Loved a Zombie" was originally published in the May-June 1939 issue of *Terror Tales.*

"While Zombies Walked" was originally published in the September 1939 issue of *Weird Tales.*

"The Song of the Slaves" was originally published in the March 1940 issue of *Weird Tales.*

"The Forbidden Trail" was originally published in the April 1941 issue of *Unknown.*

Acknowledgements

The idea for this book came from several pulp cover images posted by a fellow collector on an internet forum which I frequent. One of these was the cover to the November 1938 issue of Thrilling Mystery. The image, from which the front cover of this volume is derived, was by Rafael DeSoto and showed a tough-looking hero with a .45 defending a chained woman from a horde of zombie-like individuals. As a fan of the modern zombie genre, seeing these pulp zombies from eight decades ago piqued my interest considerably.

Because of my previous research, I was well-aware of the early contributions of Robert E. Howard, H. P. Lovecraft, Clark Ashton Smith and some of the other Weird Tales writers to the zombie genre, but I had little knowledge of the numerous zombie and quasi-zombie stories in the shudder pulps. As I began to delve into them I learned much more about the fascinating historical and social context in which this first "zombie boom" in the 1930s developed and that drove me to put together this collection of remarkable stories.

I am greatly indebted to my fellow pulp enthusiasts Glenn Goggin, Todd Warren, David Saunders, and Mark Finn who provided crucial information, scans, and images—and without whom this book would not have been possible. I would also like to thank Jay Zetterberg of Robert E. Howard Properties, Inc. for permission to reprint "Pigeons from Hell," and also legendary editor and pulp scholar Robert Weinberg of Argosy Communications, Inc. for permission to reprint stories from *Terror Tales* and *Dime Mystery*.

Finally, I would like to thank my family, particularly my wife Claudia and my children Alex and Sage, for their patient forbearance in allowing me to devote time to this project. Like many people today, my kids take for granted the presence of zombies as a commonplace element in entertainment (perhaps too much—is it bad for a six-year old to know the meaning of "double tap"?), and so I hope that this volume will help introduce new fans like them to the early days of the genre and its fascinating origins in the pulps.

Jeffrey Shanks
January 2014

Introduction:

Dawn of the Zombie Genre

By Jeffrey Shanks

ZOMBIES ARE everywhere! Zombies—shambling, crawling, and swarming after their human prey—have become a ubiquitous part of the popular culture landscape. Wildly-successful multimedia properties like *The Walking Dead* and *World War Z* demonstrate the continuing popularity of the zombie trope through films, television shows, books, graphic novels, and video games. Zombies regularly cross into other genres creating new hybrids like zombie westerns and zombie romances. We have even seen "zombified" versions of ostensibly unrelated cultural icons like Marvel superheroes and Jane Austen's *Pride and Prejudice*.

The public's current fascination with zombies is generally seen as the peak of a cultural trend that began with George Romero's *Night of the Living Dead* (1968), continued through the 1970s and early 1980s with several sequel films and various knock-offs, faded somewhat in the 1990s, only to reemerge stronger than ever after the turn of the millennium. But there was an earlier "zombie boom" that predates the current fad, predates Romero's groundbreaking film, and even predates the undead-filled EC horror comics of the 1950s. Zombies first entered the American public consciousness in the late 1920s and early 1930s, and for a little over a decade they were a frequent element in horror fiction both on the silver screen, on the stage, and in print, before fading into relative cultural obscurity until Romero reimagined the trope over two decades later.

This anthology collects a number of these early zombie stories from one of the most popular entertainment mediums of the time: the pulp magazines. Taking their name from the cheap pulpwood paper from which they were made, the pulps were periodicals containing popular fiction in the form of short stories or serialized novels. Considered inexpensive, disposable entertainment, the pulps were aimed at the general reader, and the aspirations of the writers, editors, and publishers were generally more commercial than literary (with some notable exceptions).

The zombies that appeared in these early pulp stories are often quite different from the flesh-eating, apocalypse-causing zombies of modern fiction. Rather, they are depicted as the product of Haitian voodoo (or, more properly, *Vodou*) and black magic—corpses brought back to life by a *bokor* or witch doctor and used for slave labor. Undead creatures like vampires and ghouls have, of course been a part of European and Near Eastern myth and folklore for centuries, and the best-known fictional animated corpse, the monster of Mary Shelly's *Frankenstein*, first appeared in 1818; but it was the voodoo zombie that so attracted the American public's fascination in the years between the world wars. It was a fascination that had its origins in the colonialist anxieties and racial tensions that were permeating American society at the time and, as we will see, those anxieties were expressed in the popular fiction of the period.

IN 1915, the United States military invaded Haiti and began an occupation of the tiny island nation that would last for nearly two decades. Ostensibly, the occupation was a reaction to fears of German-instigated political instability in the country, but the controversial enterprise continued long after the end of the First World War, becoming a true colonist endeavor with paternalistic overtones. The United States oversaw a massive infrastructure improvement campaign: constructing roads, bridges, canals, hospitals, and schools—but much of this was accomplished using forced local conscription labor. Tensions between the Haitian population and the American occupiers led to violent protests and revolts, ultimately making it an untenable situation. The United States began its withdrawal by the early 1930s with the last troops leaving Haiti in 1934.

As American troops, missionaries, and expatriates began to return home from Haiti they brought with them tales of strange voodoo ceremonies and mysterious *bokors* and even rumors of zombies. These stories began to appear occasionally in print in both fictional and nonfiction formats.

The most famous of these publications, and the one that was most responsible for introducing the American public to the concept of the zombie, was William B. Seabrook's 1929 travelogue of Haiti, *The Magic Island*. Seabrook's book was a best-seller and his chapter on zombies, "Dead Men Working in the Cane Fields," has been reprinted many times. In it he describes seeing three glassy-eyed zombie laborers, though he surmised they were not animated corpses, but rather mentally-disabled individuals. He also mentions that the Haitian penal code has an unusual and very specific law against administering a drug that simulates death—suggesting for the first time that the origin of the zombie might be pharmacological rather than supernatural. This idea was given widespread currency years later by ethnobotanist Wade Davis in his 1985 bestseller *The Serpent and the Rainbow* and its 1998 film adaptation by Wes Craven.

It is Seabrook's book that gives us some of the basic characteristics of the voodoo zombie that we see in the fiction of the time: the *bokor* or *houdun* who makes the zombies by robbing the graves of the recently deceased, the use of zombies as slave labor, and the fact that if a zombie tastes salt it will realize that it's dead and return to its grave.

The numerous illustrations in the book by Austrian artist Alexander King (such as the illustration reproduced at the beginning of this introduction) would have been the first visual representations many Americans would have had of Haiti and its culture, of Vodou, and of zombies. King's illustrations have frequently been vilified by scholars of Haitian culture as "emblematic of European- and American-centric representations of Haiti at their most exoticizing, titillating, and racist extreme."[i] As we will see, the works of pulp fiction that were heavily influenced by Seabrook's book and King's illustrations would, for the most part, fit that description as well.

The Magic Island created something of a minor sensation. It inspired writer Garnett Weston (under the pseudonym G. W. Hutter) to pen the short story "Salt Is Not for Slaves" for the pulp magazine *Ghost Stories* (reprinted in this volume). Weston was then chosen to write the screen play for what would become the first motion picture in the genre, *White Zombie* (1932), starring Bela Lugosi and directed by Victor Halperin. Legosi, coming off his break-out performance in *Dracula* (1931) the previous year, plays a zombie-master who uses his voodoo knowledge to enslave an American woman visiting Haiti with her fiancé, turning her into a zombie.

White Zombie was soon followed by the voodoo thriller *Ouanga* (1935) and then *Revolt of the Zombies* (1936), the latter also by Halperin. Several years later, *King of the Zombies* (1941) featured Nazis using an army of zombie slaves. Then, former SF pulp writer Curt Siodmak and partner Ardel Wray wrote the screenplay for the classic *I Walked with a Zombie* (1943). The cinematic portion of the early zombie fad finally came to an end with lesser efforts such as *Revenge of the Zombies* (1943), *The Voodoo Man* (1944), *Isle of the Dead* (1945), and *Valley of the Zombies* (1946).

Several novels and a number of short stories about zombies were published during this time as well. The popular cocktail known as "The Zombie" also appeared in the 1930s. The zombie had stumbled out of Haitian religion and folklore and into American popular culture. But in truth the pop culture zombie had little to do with true Haitian or African folklore or the actual religion of Vodou. Rather, it was a reflection of white America's distorted vision of Afro-Caribbean spirituality and mysticism, filtered through the lens of a crumbling colonialist and racist system.

The basic premise of *White Zombie*, i.e. the threat of becoming enslaved, was one of the primary plot devices of early zombie fiction, both in cinema and in the pulps. This is quite different than the threat posed in modern zombie fiction. The real fear in these early stories is often not of being attacked or eaten by zombies, but rather of *becoming* a zombie. The voodoo zombie then is not merely the embodiment of racial oppression and enslavement, but represents the potential for a reversal of the racial status quo and the loss of white privilege. It presents the reader or viewer with the possibility of the enslaver becoming the enslaved; it exploits the subconscious fears and anxieties inherent in a society stratified by race and gender and it threatens to undermine that social hierarchy.

Not all of the stories of the living dead in the pulps are based on the voodoo-type zombie. Some harken back to *Frankenstein* with animated corpses given the semblance of life though scientific means. Others, perhaps more fantasy than horror, use ancient necromantic sorcery to raise up undead creatures. Some zombies are not dead at all, but are living people who have been drugged or hypnotized by an evil zombie-master. But the majority of the zombie stories from this time are based on some variation of the voodoo-style of the walking dead.

Because of this, it should not be surprising that many of the zombie stories from this period, including some of the ones in this collection, contain depictions of race and ethnicity that are highly-problematic and often patently offensive. This includes the use of racist stereotypes and language that was unfortunately commonplace in early 20th century America. Other stories have depictions of women that are clearly misogynistic and sexually exploitive. Despite the ofttimes cringeworthy material in some of these stories, I have kept my editorial interventions to a minimum, confining the edits to punctuation and grammar for the most part. I have left the content of the stories unchanged—warts and all—as I view these works as popular artifacts from which we can learn quite a bit about our shared cultural history—even the ugly parts—and come away with a better understanding of the historical context and social milieu in which the zombie genre first appeared and thrived.

MOST OF these stories could be found in two types of pulp magazines: the weird fiction pulps and the shudder pulps. The primary weird fiction pulp of the day was the legendary *Weird Tales,* first published in 1923. *Weird Tales* was one of the earliest magazines to specialize in supernatural fiction and it was in its pages that the modern American horror and fantasy genres were developed and refined by authors like H. P. Lovecraft and Robert E. Howard. Other weird fiction pulps included *Strange Tales of Mystery and Terror* (often shortened to just

Strange Tales) and John W. Campbell's *Unknown*. Authors like Ray Bradbury, Robert Bloch, and Tennessee Williams got their start in these weird fiction periodicals and it was in magazines like *Weird Tales* and *Unknown* that pulp fiction often came closest to transcending its sub-literary status.

The shudder pulps or 'weird menace' pulps, on the other hand, have a notorious reputation that is well-deserved. A sort-of spin-off of mystery fiction, weird menace stories featured seemingly supernatural threats that ultimately turn out to have a rational explanation. With titles like *Dime Mystery*, *Terror Tales*, and *Thrilling Mystery*, they are known for their lurid covers depicting scantily-clad women being attacked or tortured by hideous villains. The stories, which took their cue from the gory and violent content of the French Grand Guignol Theater, relied far more on shock value and gratuitous, sexualized violence than on literary merit or narrative complexity to appeal to their readers. The shudder pulps could be said to occupy a similar place in the pulp canon that the low-budget exploitation films of the 1970s hold in cinema (and perhaps also their 21st century "torture porn" descendants such as *Saw* (2004), *Hostel* (2005), *The Human Centipede* (2010) and the like). It's difficult for most people to understand the appeal of such material, but there is no doubt that there was a market for these magazines and they were certainly a hotbed for zombie stories.

The initial entry in this collection, "Herbert West—Reanimator," appeared first, not in a pulp, but in an amateur literary magazine, *Home Brew*, in 1922. Its author H.P. Lovecraft is, however, one of the best-known and most influential of all pulp writers and is considered to be one of the most important pioneers of the modern horror genre. The story, which was ultimately reprinted in *Weird Tales* two decades later, is not a voodoo zombie tale, but instead features a doctor who brings corpses back to a semblance of life through strange scientific means. The story was made famous decades later by its loose adaption into the feature film *Re-animator* (1985) directed by Stuart Gordon. There are several Lovecraft stories that could have qualified as zombie tales, including "The Outsider" and "Pickman's Model," but I selected this one as a prime example of the type of *Frankenstein*-inspired tale of animated corpses that could be found prior to the explosion of Haitian zombies in the 1920s and 1930s.

Pulp writer Henry S. Whitehead was a regular contributor to *Weird Tales* who served as a missionary in the Virgin Islands during the 1920s. There he heard tales of voodoo and zombies and wrote several stories that incorporated these elements. He is an excellent example of one of the Caribbean travelers of the period who brought tales of island folklore back to America. His story "Jumbee" published in *Weird Tales* in 1926 is rare example of a voodoo zombie story before the publication of Seabrook's *The Magic Island*.

"The Corpse-Master" by Seabury Quinn, on the other hand, may be the first zombie story that *was* directly inspired by *The Magic Island*. Published in the July 1929 issue of *Weird Tales*, "The Corpse-Master" is one the prolific Quinn's many stories of the occult detective Jules de Grandin. The influence of Seabrook's just-released book can be seen in the mention of salt making a zombie return to its grave, as well as a final scene in which de Grandin expounds on the nature of zombies in a passage lifted almost verbatim from *The Magic Island*.

The January 1930 issue of *Weird Tales* saw the publication of "Dead Girl Finotte" by Henry De Vere Stacpoole, which may be the first pulp zombie story to directly mention Seabrook's book by name, thus indicating an expectation of at least some familiarity with the work on the part of the reader. A former ship's doctor from Ireland, Stacpoole was already an established novelist by the time he appeared in *Weird Tales*, and was best known for his tales of the South Seas. His most famous work, the 1908 novel *The Blue Lagoon* was adapted to the silver screen on multiple occasions.

Garnett Wilson was another writer heavily inspired by Seabrook's work. He wrote a review of *The Magic Island* and followed it up with the story "Salt is not for Slaves," published in the August-September 1931 issue of the pulp *Ghost Stories* under the pen name G. W Hutter ('Hutter' being his wife's maiden name). As noted above, it was this story along with his review of *The Magic Island* that got the attention of director Victor Halperin and landed Wilson the job of screenwriter for *White Zombie*.

September 1931 saw the debut of *Strange Tales*, a competitor to *Weird Tales*, which specialized in the same type of stories and often hired the same writers as its older weird fiction counterpart. That first issue contained a zombie story from Ray Cummings, one of the great pioneers of early modern science fiction. Not a voodoo story, "The Dead Who Walk" begins with a scene of a walking corpse in a cemetery, not unlike the opening sequence of Romero's *Night of the Living Dead*. Given his background it should not be a surprise that Cummings relies on a scientific or, more properly, a science fiction explanation for his zombies.

August Derleth is best-known today as the founder of Arkham House, the publishing company responsible for reprinting and popularizing the works of H. P. Lovecraft and his *Weird Tales* contemporaries long after the magazine's heyday. Derleth, along with his childhood friend and sometime-collaborator Mark Schorer, produced a classic zombie story for the June 1932 issue of *Strange Tales* entitled "The House in the Magnolias." Set in a mysterious old plantation house on the outskirts of New Orleans, the story can be described as early example of the Southern Gothic genre. Once again we see salt used as the method of eliminating the zombies, with a means of delivery—pistachio candies—again, lifted straight from *The Magic Island*.

The next story in this collection is a bit of a departure from the other entries. "Empire of the Necromancers" by Clark Ashton Smith is a fantasy story set on a dying Earth far in the future where modern civilization and science have been replaced by ancient technology and sorcery. The protagonists are two necromancers who raise an army of the undead to serve them. Here we see zombies used in much the same that they are in modern fantasy role playing games like *Dungeons and Dragons* (this is not a coincidence—Smith, and his fellow members of the *Weird Tales* "Triumvirate," Howard and Lovecraft, were major influences on the seminal RPG). Smith's natural talent as a poet, his love of baroque language, and his visionary imagination gave his prose a unique and surreal flavor that was unlike anything else his contemporaries in the pulps were doing.

With "The Devil's Dowry," published in the February 1935 issue of *Terror Tales*, we have our first entry from the shudder pulps. Author Ben Judson (a pseudonym for Judson Benjamin) penned a handful of weird menace stories in the 1930s, but he also wrote for the western pulps. This story features a Haitian voodoo master practicing his arts in a modern American city and with its theme of "white slavery" and racist overtones (typical of these kinds of stories) it seems to take much of its inspiration from *White Zombie*.

Like several of the authors in this collection, E. Hoffmann Price was a frequent contributor to *Weird Tales* and the weird fiction pulps. He was also a correspondent and one-time collaborator with Lovecraft. But Price wrote stories for a number of publications during his career, from high-end pulps like *Argosy* to the lowly shudder pulps. Like many of his contemporaries (including Cave and Howard) he also tried his hand writing for the "spicies"—pulps that were essentially the soft-core erotica of the day (though in truth, they were quite tame by modern standards). There were "spicy" versions of most of the popular genres including *Spicy Western, Spicy Detective,* and *Spicy Mystery.* It was in the November 1935 issue of the latter title that Price's zombie tale "The Walking Dead" appeared. Containing several of the voodoo tropes we have seen before, the story takes its cue (as many did) from *The Magic Island,* though Price, a native of New Orleans, places the story in the Mississippi Delta.

Henry Kuttner was one of the more influential writers of SF and fantasy in the 1940s and 1950s, often collaborating with his wife and fellow author, Catherine L. Moore. His professional career officially began, however, with the story "The Graveyard Rats," published in the March 1936 issue of *Weird Tales.* The tale revolves around a grave-robbing cemetery caretaker in Salem, whose illegal resurrectionist activities are being complicated by a plague of oversized rats. When he finds himself in the rodents' burrows, however, he discovers an undead threat far worse than the bothersome rodents.

D. L. Champion, using the pseudonym Jack D'Arcy, began his career writing for *Ghost Stories* in the early 1930s, but is best known for creating the Phantom Detective character for Ned Pines' Thrilling Publications. The second hero pulp after *The Shadow, The Phantom Detective* debuted in 1933, with Champion writing the first dozen stories under the house name "G. Wayman Jones." When Pines decided to get in on the shudder pulp fad by launching *Thrilling Mystery,* Champion resumed his old Jack D'Arcy pen name in order to try his hand at the weird menace genre. "The Grave Gives Up" from the August 1936 *Thrilling Mystery* begins with the protagonist receiving a phone call from his recently-deceased lover that sends him on a search for the truth and bringing him face-to-face with the living dead.

Another contribution from *Spicy Mystery,* the simply-titled "Zombie" in the November 1936 issue was written by Edwin Truett Long under one of his many pennames, "Carl Moore." A native of Texas,

Long contributed a number of racy stories to the spicies in the 1930s, before breaking into the Munsey detective pulps with his tales of the crime-fighting snake oil salesman, Thaddeus "Doc" Barker. "Zombie" is one of the more explicitly racist and misogynistic stories in this collection with its negative portrayal of both miscegenation and female sexuality. While it makes for uncomfortable reading, it exemplifies many of the attitudes that were unfortunately common in white America at the time.

Arthur Leo Zagat gave up his law practice to become a full-time writer. After beginning his career with a series of SF stories co-written with Nat Schrachner, Zagat spent several years writing for the shudder pulps before moving on to the more-upscale *Argosy*. He wrote several stories with undead menaces, but "Revels of the Lusting Dead" is certainly one of the most interesting. Published in the August 1937 issue of *Terror Tales*, the story pushes far past the boundaries of good taste with scenes of torture, bondage, sadomasochism, violent cat-fighting, and the threat of zombie rape! As offensively misogynistic as it is, the story serves as an excellent example of what makes the shudder pulps so notorious.

Another interesting contribution from the shudder pulps is "Corpses on Parade" by husband-and-wife team Edith and Ejler Jacobson. Published in the April 1938 issue of *Dime Mystery*, the story features New York City socialites being turned into living zombies by a mysterious menace—a plot device which perhaps contains a bit of rudimentary commentary on issues of class. The Jacobsons went on to create some notable pulp characters, including the hemophiliac detective Nat Perry, as well as The Skull, the protagonist of the one-shot villain pulps *The Octopus* and *The Scorpion*.

The creator of such legendary characters as Conan the Cimmerian, Solomon Kane, and Kull of Atlantis, Texas writer Robert E. Howard was one of the giants of the pulp magazines. Though best known as the father of sword and sorcery, Howard wrote stories in many different genres including horror, westerns, boxing, historical adventure, and hardboiled detective stories. He also wrote a number of Southern Gothic horror stories, among which was the zombie story "Pigeons from Hell" published in the May 1938 issue of *Weird Tales*—a story Stephen King once claimed was one of his favorites. Based on stories told to him as a child by his African American housekeeper, "Pigeons from Hell" features a new type of creature, the *zuvembie*—a female zombie that has the power to create new zombies. The story was adapted for the television show *Thriller* (hosted by Boris Karloff) in 1961 and is one of the series' most famous episodes.

Bruno Fischer was a regular contributor to the shudder pulps, often under the pseudonyms Russell Gray or Harrison Storm. Fischer was a prolific writer for four decades, authoring several well-received crime and suspense novels after his pulp career ended. He was also very active in left-leaning political circles for many years and ran as the Socialist party candidate for the New York state senate in 1938. Written under his Russell Gray pen name, "The Man Who Loved a Zombie," was published in the June 1939 issue of *Terror Tales*. The story makes use of a typical Fischer plot device, in which a regular "everyman" protagonist is put in a tricky situation which tests his moral fiber. In the case of this story, the tricky situation is an army of menacing zombies that includes his fiancée.

Thorp McCluskey was fiction writer and journalist who contributed several notable stories to *Weird Tales*, among which was "While Zombies Walked" in the September 1939 issue. The story borrows some elements from *White Zombie*, particularly the concept of a Caucasian zombie-master. Ironically, McClusky's story seems to have been the inspiration for the later film *Revenge of the Zombies* (1943) though it was not credited as such.

One of the most-talented authors to emerge from the pulps, Manly Wade Wellman beginning his career writing for *Weird Tales*, *Wonder Stories*, and *Astounding*. He had great success in later years as a writer of science fiction and horror, and, in particular, with his Silver John series about a backwoods minstrel who encounters supernatural threats in the Appalachians. "Song of the Slaves," published in the March 1940 issue of *Weird Tales*, hints at Wellman's interest in both music and folklore. It is also a bit different than some of the other stories in this collection, in that it subverts the role of the zombies in the narrative, making them the sympathetic characters. While it still makes use of some of the typical racial stereotypes of the time, Wellman's story could be considered somewhat progressive for its day, particularly with its harsh critique of the Atlantic slave trade.

The fantasy pulp *Unknown* was launched in 1939 by legendary editor John W. Campbell as a sister publication to his successful SF magazine *Astounding*. In addition to encouraging "higher-brow" fantasy fiction, Campbell also introduced a number of new female authors, among them Jane Rice. Rice was a favorite of Campbell and would become a regular contributor to *Unknown*. She went on to write for other SF publications in the 1950s including *The Magazine of Science Fiction &*

Fantasy under the pseudonym Mary Austin. Her zombie story "The Forbidden Trail" was published in the April 1941 issue of *Unknown* and features some of the wonderful touches of ironic humor that characterized many of the stories published under Campbell's editorship.

IT IS my hope that the pulp stories in this collection will give the reader not only a few hours of creepy entertainment, but also a better understanding of the historical roots of the zombie genre. The modern zombie craze is only the latest expression of our fascination with the walking dead. While the zombie's appeal and its role as a reflection of the *zeitgeist* have evolved and changed over the decades—along with our society—it still remains a symbol of our mortality and reminder of the fragility of our social structure. From its birth in the anxieties of America's pre-WW II imperialist adventures in the Caribbean to Romero's critique of modern consumerism in the 1970s and 1980s to the 21st century fears of societal breakdown and the apocalyptic collapse of civilization, the zombie has fascinated us for generations and will no doubt continue to fascinate us for decades to come.

---

[i] Twa, Lindsay. "The Black Magic Island: The Artistic Journeys of Alexander King and Aaron Douglas from and to Haiti." In Carlage, et al. (eds.) *Haiti and the Americas*. Jackson, MS: University Press of Mississippi, 2013, 133.

Bibliography and Suggested Reading:

Bishop, Kyle William. *American Zombie Gothic: The Rise and Fall (and Rise) of the Walking Dead in Popular Culture*. Jefferson, NC: McFarland and Company, 2010.

Carlage, Carla, Raphael Dalleo, Luis Duno-Gottberg, Clevis Headley. (Eds.) *Haiti and the Americas*. Jackson, MS: University Press of Mississippi, 2013

Chester, Tony. "Zombies Before Romero." *The Science Fact & Science Fiction Concatenation*. August 29, 2011. www.concatenation.org.

Jones, Robert Kenneth. The Shudder Pulps: A History of the Weird Menace Magazines of the 1930's. West Linn: Collector's Editions, 1975.

Moreman, Christopher M. and Cory James Rushton, eds. *Race, Oppression and the Zombie: Essays on Cross-cultural Appropriations of the Caribbean Tradition*. Jefferson, NC: McFarland and Company, 2011.

Renda, Mary. *Taking Haiti: Military Occupation and the Culture of U.S. Imperialism, 1915-1940*. Chapel Hill: University of North Carolina Press, 2001.

Schmidt, Hans. *United States Occupation of Haiti (1915-1934)*. New Brunswick, NJ: Rutgers University Press, 1995.

Weinberg, Robert. *The Weird Tales Story*. West Linn, OR: Fax Collector's Editions, 1977.

Herbert West: Reanimator

By H. P. Lovecraft

Part I: From the Dark

OF HERBERT WEST, who was my friend in college and in after life, I can speak only with extreme terror. This terror is not due altogether to the sinister manner of his recent disappearance, but was engendered by the whole nature of his life-work, and first gained its acute form more than seventeen years ago, when we were in the third year of our course at the Miskatonic University Medical School in Arkham. While he was with me, the wonder and diabolism of his experiments fascinated me utterly, and I was his closest companion. Now that he is gone and the spell is broken, the actual fear is greater. Memories and possibilities are ever more hideous than realities.

The first horrible incident of our acquaintance was the greatest shock I ever experienced, and it is only with reluctance that I repeat it. As I have said, it happened when we were in the medical school where West had already made himself notorious through his wild theories on the nature of death and the possibility of overcoming it artificially. His views, which were widely ridiculed by the faculty and by his fellow-students, hinged on the essentially mechanistic nature of life; and concerned means for operating the organic machinery of mankind by calculated chemical action after the failure of natural processes. In his experiments with various animating solutions, he had killed and treated immense numbers of rabbits, guinea-pigs, cats, dogs, and monkeys, till he had become the prime nuisance of the college. Several times he had actually obtained signs of life in animals supposedly dead; in many cases violent signs but he soon saw that the perfection of his process, if indeed possible, would necessarily involve a lifetime of research. It likewise became clear that, since the same solution never worked alike on different organic species, he would require human subjects for further and more specialised progress. It was here that he first came into conflict with the college authorities, and was debarred from future experiments by no less a dignitary than the dean of the medical school himself—the learned and benevolent Dr. Allan Halsey, whose work in behalf of the stricken is recalled by every old resident of Arkham.

I had always been exceptionally tolerant of West's pursuits, and we frequently discussed his theories, whose ramifications and corollaries were almost infinite. Holding with Haeckel that all life is a chemical and physical process, and that the so-called "soul" is a myth, my friend believed that artificial reanimation of the dead can depend only on the condition of the tissues; and that unless actual decomposition has set in, a corpse fully equipped with organs may with suitable measures be set going again in the peculiar fashion known as life. That the psychic or intellectual life might be impaired by the slight deterioration of sensitive brain-cells which even a short period of death would be apt to cause, West fully realised. It had at first been his hope to find a reagent which would restore vitality before the actual advent of death, and only repeated failures on animals had shewn him that the natural and artificial life-motions were incompatible. He then sought extreme freshness in his specimens, injecting his solutions into the blood immediately after the extinction of life. It was this circumstance which made the professors so carelessly sceptical, for they felt that true death had not occurred in any case. They did not stop to view the matter closely and reasoningly.

It was not long after the faculty had interdicted his work that West confided to me his resolution to get fresh human bodies in some manner, and continue in secret the experiments he could no longer perform openly. To hear him discussing ways and means was rather ghastly, for at the college we had never procured anatomical specimens ourselves. Whenever the morgue proved inadequate, two local negroes attended to this matter, and they were seldom questioned. West was then a small, slender, spectacled youth with delicate features, yellow hair, pale blue eyes, and a soft voice, and it was uncanny to hear him dwelling on the relative merits of Christchurch Cemetery and the potter's field. We finally decided on the potter's field, because practically everybody in Christchurch was embalmed; a thing of course ruinous to West's researches.

I was by this time his active and enthralled assistant, and helped him make all his decisions, not only concerning the source of bodies but concerning a suitable place for our loathsome work. It was I who thought of the deserted Chapman farmhouse beyond Meadow Hill, where we fitted up on the ground floor an operating room and a laboratory, each with dark curtains to conceal our midnight doings. The place was far from any road, and in sight of no other house, yet precautions were none the less necessary; since rumours of strange lights, started by chance nocturnal roamers, would soon bring disaster on our enterprise. It was agreed to call the whole thing a chemical laboratory if discovery should occur. Gradually we equipped our sinister haunt of science with materials either purchased in Boston or quietly borrowed from the college—materials carefully made unrecognisable save to expert eyes—and provided spades and picks for the many burials we should have to make in the cellar. At the college we used an incinerator, but the apparatus was too costly for our unauthorised laboratory. Bodies were always a nuisance—even the small guinea-pig bodies from the slight clandestine experiments in West's room at the boarding-house.

We followed the local death-notices like ghouls, for our specimens demanded particular qualities. What we wanted were corpses interred soon after death and without artificial preservation; preferably free from malforming disease, and certainly with all organs present. Accident victims were our best hope. Not for many weeks did we hear of anything suitable; though we talked with morgue and hospital authorities, ostensibly in the college's interest, as often as we could without exciting suspicion. We found that the college had first choice in every case, so that it might be necessary to remain in Arkham during the summer, when only the limited summer-school classes were held. In the end, though, luck favoured us; for one day we heard of an almost ideal case in the potter's field; a brawny young workman drowned only the morning before in Summer's Pond, and buried at the town's expense without delay or embalming. That afternoon we found the new grave, and determined to begin work soon after midnight.

It was a repulsive task that we undertook in the black small hours, even though we lacked at that time the special horror of graveyards which later experiences brought to us. We carried spades and oil dark lanterns, for although electric torches were then manufactured, they were not as satisfactory as the tungsten contrivances of today. The process of unearthing was slow and sordid—it might have been gruesomely poetical if we had been artists instead of scientists—and we were glad when our spades struck wood. When the pine box was fully uncovered, West scrambled down and removed the lid, dragging out and propping up the contents. I reached down and hauled the contents out of the grave, and then both toiled hard to restore the spot to its former appearance. The affair made us rather nervous, especially the stiff form and vacant face of our first trophy, but we managed to remove all traces of our visit. When we had patted down the last shovelful of earth, we put the specimen in a canvas sack and set out for the old Chapman place beyond Meadow Hill.

On an improvised dissecting-table in the old farmhouse, by the light of a powerful acetylene lamp, the specimen was not very spectral looking. It had been a sturdy and apparently unimaginative youth of wholesome plebeian type—large-framed, grey-eyed, and brown-haired—a sound animal without psychological subtleties, and probably having vital processes of the simplest and healthiest sort. Now, with the eyes closed, it looked more asleep than dead; though the expert test of my friend soon left no doubt on that score. We had at last what West had always longed for—a real dead man of the ideal kind, ready for the solution as prepared according to the most careful calculations and theories for human use. The tension on our part became very great. We knew that there was scarcely a chance for anything like complete success, and could not avoid hideous fears at possible grotesque results of partial animation. Especially were we apprehensive concerning the mind and impulses of the creature, since in the space following death some of the more delicate cerebral cells might well have suffered deterioration. I, myself, still held some curious notions about the traditional "soul" of man, and felt an awe at the secrets that might be told by one returning from the dead. I wondered what sights this placid youth might have seen in inaccessible spheres, and what he could relate if fully restored to life. But my wonder was not overwhelming, since for the most part I shared the materialism of my friend. He was calmer than I as he forced a large quantity of his fluid into a vein of the body's arm, immediately binding the incision securely.

The waiting was gruesome, but West never faltered. Every now and then he applied his stethoscope to the specimen, and bore the negative results philosophically. After about three-quarters of an hour without the least sign of life he disappointedly pronounced the solution inadequate, but determined to make the most of his opportunity and try one change in the formula before disposing of his ghastly prize. We had that afternoon dug a grave in the cellar, and would have to fill it by dawn—for although we had fixed a lock on the house, we wished to shun even the remotest risk of a ghoulish discovery. Besides, the body would not be even approximately fresh the next night. So taking the solitary acetylene lamp into the adjacent laboratory, we left our silent guest on the slab in the dark, and bent every energy to the mixing of a new solution; the weighing and measuring supervised by West with an almost fanatical care.

The awful event was very sudden, and wholly unexpected. I was pouring something from one test-tube to another, and West was busy over the alcohol blast-lamp which had to answer for a Bunsen burner in this gasless edifice, when from the pitch-black room we had left there burst the most appalling and daemoniac succession of cries that either of us had ever heard. Not more unutterable could have been the chaos of hellish sound if the pit itself had opened to release the agony of the damned, for in one inconceivable cacophony was centered all the supernal terror and unnatural despair of animate nature. Human it could not have been—it is not in man to make such sounds—and without a thought of our late employment or its possible discovery, both West and I leaped to the nearest window like stricken animals; overturning tubes, lamp, and retorts, and vaulting madly into the starred abyss of the rural night. I think we screamed ourselves as we stumbled frantically toward the town, though as we reached the outskirts we put on a semblance of restraint—just enough to seem like belated revelers staggering home from a debauch.

We did not separate, but managed to get to West's room, where we whispered with the gas up until dawn. By then we had calmed ourselves a little with rational theories and plans for investigation, so that we could sleep through the day—classes being disregarded. But that evening two items in the paper, wholly unrelated, made it again impossible for us to sleep. The old deserted Chapman house had inexplicably burned to an amorphous heap of ashes; that we could understand because of the upset lamp. Also, an attempt had been made to disturb a new grave in the potter's field, as if by futile and spadeless clawing at the earth. That we could not understand, for we had patted down the mould very carefully.

And for seventeen years after that West would look frequently over his shoulder, and complain of fancied footsteps behind him. Now he has disappeared.

Part II: The Plague-Daemon

I SHALL NEVER forget that hideous summer sixteen years ago, when like a noxious afrite from the halls of Eblis typhoid stalked leeringly through Arkham. It is by that satanic scourge that most recall the year, for truly terror brooded with bat-wings over the piles of coffins in the tombs of Christchurch Cemetery; yet for me there is a greater horror in that time—a horror known to me alone now that Herbert West has disappeared.

West and I were doing post-graduate work in summer classes at the medical school of Miskatonic University, and my friend had attained a wide notoriety because of his experiments leading toward the revivification of the dead. After the scientific slaughter of uncounted small animals the freakish work had ostensibly stopped by order of our sceptical dean, Dr. Allan Halsey; though West had continued to perform certain secret tests in his dingy boarding-house room, and had on one terrible and unforgettable occasion taken a human body from its grave in the potter's field to a deserted farmhouse beyond Meadow Hill.

I was with him on that odious occasion, and saw him inject into the still veins the elixir which he thought would to some extent restore life's chemical and physical processes. It had ended horribly—in a delirium of fear which we gradually came to attribute to our own overwrought nerves—and West had never afterward been able to shake off a maddening sensation of being haunted and hunted. The body had not been quite fresh enough; it is obvious that to restore normal mental attributes a body must be very fresh indeed; and the burning of the old house had prevented us from burying the thing. It would have been better if we could have known it was underground.

After that experience West had dropped his researches for some time; but as the zeal of the born scientist slowly returned, he again became importunate with the college faculty, pleading for the use of the dissecting-room and of fresh human specimens for the work he regarded as so overwhelmingly important. His pleas, however, were wholly in vain; for the decision of Dr. Halsey was inflexible, and the other professors all endorsed the verdict of their leader. In the radical theory of reanimation they saw nothing but the immature vagaries of a youthful enthusiast whose slight form, yellow hair, spectacled blue eyes, and soft voice gave no hint of the supernormal—almost diabolical—power of the cold brain within. I can see him now as he was then—and I shiver. He grew sterner of face, but never elderly. And now Sefton Asylum has had the mishap and West has vanished.

West clashed disagreeably with Dr. Halsey near the end of our last undergraduate term in a wordy dispute that did less credit to him than to the kindly dean in point of courtesy. He felt that he was needlessly and irrationally retarded in a supremely great work; a work which he could of course conduct to suit himself in later years, but which he wished to begin while still possessed of the exceptional facilities of the university. That the tradition-bound elders should ignore his singular results on animals, and persist in their denial of the possibility of reanimation, was inexpressibly disgusting and almost incomprehensible to a youth of West's logical temperament. Only greater maturity could help him understand the chronic mental limitations of the "professor-doctor" type—the product of generations of pathetic Puritanism; kindly, conscientious, and sometimes gentle and amiable, yet always narrow, intolerant, custom-ridden, and lacking in perspective. Age has more charity for these incomplete yet high—souled characters, whose worst real vice is timidity, and who are ultimately punished by general ridicule for their intellectual sins—sins like Ptolemaism, Calvinism, anti-Darwinism, anti-Nietzscheism, and every sort of Sabbatarianism and sumptuary legislation. West, young despite his marvellous scientific acquirements, had scant patience with good Dr. Halsey and his erudite colleagues; and nursed an increasing resentment, coupled with a desire to prove his theories to these obtuse worthies in some striking and dramatic fashion. Like most youths, he indulged in elaborate daydreams of revenge, triumph, and final magnanimous forgiveness.

And then had come the scourge, grinning and lethal, from the nightmare caverns of Tartarus. West and I had graduated about the time of its beginning, but had remained for additional work at the summer school, so that we were in Arkham when it broke with full daemoniac fury upon the town. Though not as yet licenced physicians, we now had our degrees, and were pressed frantically into public service as the numbers of the stricken grew. The situation was almost past management, and deaths ensued too frequently for the local undertakers fully to handle. Burials without embalming were made in rapid succession, and even the Christchurch Cemetery receiving tomb was crammed with coffins of the unembalmed dead. This circumstance was not without effect on West, who thought often of the irony of the situation—so many fresh specimens, yet none for his persecuted researches! We were frightfully overworked, and the terrific mental and nervous strain made my friend brood morbidly.

But West's gentle enemies were no less harassed with prostrating duties. College had all but closed, and every doctor of the medical faculty was helping to fight the typhoid plague. Dr. Halsey in particular had distinguished himself in sacrificing service, applying his extreme skill with whole-hearted energy to cases which many others shunned because of danger or apparent hopelessness. Before a month was over the fearless dean had become a popular hero, though he seemed unconscious of his fame as he struggled to keep from collapsing with physical fatigue and nervous exhaustion. West could not withhold admiration for the fortitude of his foe, but because of this was even more determined to prove to him the truth of his amazing doctrines. Taking advantage of the disorganisation of both college work and municipal health regulations, he managed to get a recently deceased body smuggled into the university dissecting-room one night, and in my presence injected a new modification of his solution. The thing actually opened its eyes, but only stared at the ceiling with a look of soul-petrifying horror before collapsing into an inertness from which nothing could rouse it. West said it was not fresh enough—the hot summer air does not favour corpses. That time we were almost caught before we incinerated the thing, and West doubted the advisability of repeating his daring misuse of the college laboratory.

The peak of the epidemic was reached in August. West and I were almost dead, and Dr. Halsey did die on the 14th. The students all attended the hasty funeral on the 15th, and bought an impressive wreath, though the latter was quite overshadowed by the tributes sent by wealthy Arkham citizens and by the municipality itself. It was almost a public affair, for the dean had surely been a public benefactor. After the entombment we were all somewhat depressed, and spent the afternoon at the bar of the Commercial House; where West, though shaken by the death of his chief opponent, chilled the rest of us with references to his notorious theories. Most of the students went home, or to various duties, as the evening advanced; but West persuaded me to aid him in "making a night of it."West's landlady saw us arrive at his room about two in the morning, with a third man between us; and told her husband that we had all evidently dined and wined rather well.

Apparently this acidulous matron was right; for about 3 a.m. the whole house was aroused by cries coming from West's room, where when they broke down the door, they found the two of us unconscious on the blood-stained carpet, beaten, scratched, and mauled, and with the broken remnants of West's bottles and instruments around us. Only an open window told what had become of our assailant, and many wondered how he himself had fared after the terrific leap from the second story to the lawn which he must have made. There were some strange garments in the room, but West upon regaining consciousness said they did not belong to the stranger, but were specimens collected for bacteriological analysis in the course of investigations on the transmission of germ diseases. He ordered them burnt as soon as possible in the capacious fireplace. To the police we both declared ignorance of our late companion's identity. He was, West nervously said, a congenial stranger whom we had met at some downtown bar of uncertain location. We had all been rather jovial, and West and I did not wish to have our pugnacious companion hunted down.

That same night saw the beginning of the second Arkham horror—the horror that to me eclipsed the plague itself. Christchurch Cemetery was the scene of a terrible killing; a watchman having been clawed to death in a manner not only too hideous for description, but raising a doubt as to the human agency of the deed. The victim had been seen alive considerably after midnight—the dawn revealed the unutterable thing. The manager of a circus at the neighbouring town of Bolton was questioned, but he swore that no beast had at any time escaped from its cage. Those who found the body noted a trail of blood leading to the receiving tomb, where a small pool of red lay on the concrete just outside the gate. A fainter trail led away toward the woods, but it soon gave out.

The next night devils danced on the roofs of Arkham, and unnatural madness howled in the wind. Through the fevered town had crept a curse which some said was greater than the plague, and which some whispered was the embodied daemon-soul of the plague itself. Eight houses were entered by a nameless thing which strewed red death in its wake—in all, seventeen maimed and shapeless remnants of bodies were left behind by the voiceless, sadistic monster that crept abroad. A few persons had half seen it in the dark, and said it was white and like a malformed ape or anthropomorphic fiend. It had not left behind quite all that it had attacked, for sometimes it had been hungry. The number it had killed was fourteen; three of the bodies had been in stricken homes and had not been alive.

On the third night frantic bands of searchers, led by the police, captured it in a house on Crane Street near the Miskatonic campus. They had organised the quest with care, keeping in touch by means of volunteer telephone stations, and when someone in the college district had reported hearing a scratching at a shuttered window, the net was quickly spread. On account of the general alarm and precautions, there were only two more victims, and the capture was effected without major casualties. The thing was finally stopped by a bullet, though not a fatal one, and was rushed to the local hospital amidst universal excitement and loathing.

For it had been a man. This much was clear despite the nauseous eyes, the voiceless simianism, and the daemoniac savagery. They dressed its wound and carted it to the asylum at Sefton, where it beat its head against the walls of a padded cell for sixteen years—until the recent mishap, when it escaped under circumstances that few like to mention. What had most disgusted the searchers of Arkham was the thing they noticed when the monster's face was cleaned—the mocking, unbelievable resemblance to a learned and self-sacrificing martyr who had been entombed but three days before—the late Dr. Allan Halsey, public benefactor and dean of the medical school of Miskatonic University.

To the vanished Herbert West and to me the disgust and horror were supreme. I shudder tonight as I think of it; shudder even more than I did that morning when West muttered through his bandages, "Damn it, it wasn't quite fresh enough!"

Part III: Six Shots by Moonlight

IT IS UNCOMMON to fire all six shots of a revolver with great suddenness when one would probably be sufficient, but many things in the life of Herbert West were uncommon. It is, for instance, not often that a young physician leaving college is obliged to conceal the principles which guide his selection of a home and office, yet that was the case with Herbert West. When he and I obtained our degrees at the medical school of Miskatonic University, and sought to relieve our poverty by setting up as general practitioners, we took great care not to say that we chose our house because it was fairly well isolated, and as near as possible to the potter's field.

Reticence such as this is seldom without a cause, nor indeed was ours; for our requirements were those resulting from a life-work distinctly unpopular. Outwardly we were doctors only, but beneath the surface were aims of far greater and more terrible moment—for the essence of Herbert West's existence was a quest amid black and forbidden realms of the unknown, in which he hoped to uncover the secret of life and restore to perpetual animation the graveyard's cold clay. Such a quest demands strange materials, among them fresh human bodies; and in order to keep supplied with these indispensable things one must live quietly and not far from a place of informal interment.

West and I had met in college, and I had been the only one to sympathise with his hideous experiments. Gradually I had come to be his inseparable assistant, and now that we were out of college we had to keep together. It was not easy to find a good opening for two doctors in company, but finally the influence of the university secured us a practice in Bolton—a factory town near Arkham, the seat of the college. The Bolton Worsted Mills are the largest in the Miskatonic Valley, and their polyglot employees are never popular as patients with the local physicians. We chose our house with the greatest care, seizing at last on a rather run-down cottage near the end of Pond Street; five numbers from the closest neighbour, and separated from the local potter's field by only a stretch of meadow land, bisected by a narrow neck of the rather dense forest which lies to the north. The distance was greater than we wished, but we could get no nearer house without going on the other side of the field, wholly out of the factory district. We were not much displeased, however, since there were no people between us and our sinister source of supplies. The walk was a trifle long, but we could haul our silent specimens undisturbed.

Our practice was surprisingly large from the very first—large enough to please most young doctors, and large enough to prove a bore and a burden to students whose real interest lay elsewhere. The mill-hands were of somewhat turbulent inclinations; and besides their many natural needs, their frequent clashes and stabbing affrays gave us plenty to do. But what actually absorbed our minds was the secret laboratory we had fitted up in the cellar—the laboratory with the long table under the electric lights, where in the small hours of the morning we often injected West's various solutions into the veins of the things we dragged from the potter's field. West was experimenting madly to find something which would start man's vital motions anew after they had been stopped by the thing we call death, but had encountered the most ghastly obstacles. The solution had to be differently compounded for different types—what would serve for guinea-pigs would not serve for human beings, and different human specimens required large modifications.

The bodies had to be exceedingly fresh, or the slight decomposition of brain tissue would render perfect reanimation impossible. Indeed, the greatest problem was to get them fresh enough—West had had horrible experiences during his secret college researches with corpses of doubtful vintage. The results of partial or imperfect animation were much more hideous than were the total failures, and we both held fearsome recollections of such things. Ever since our first daemoniac session in the deserted farmhouse on Meadow Hill in Arkham, we had felt a brooding menace; and West, though a calm, blond, blue-eyed scientific automaton in most respects, often confessed to a shuddering sensation of stealthy pursuit. He half felt that he was followed—a psychological delusion of shaken nerves, enhanced by the undeniably disturbing fact that at least one of our reanimated specimens was still alive—a frightful carnivorous thing in a padded cell at Sefton. Then there was another—our first—whose exact fate we had never learned.

We had fair luck with specimens in Bolton—much better than in Arkham. We had not been settled a week before we got an accident victim on the very night of burial, and made it open its eyes with an amazingly rational expression before the solution failed. It had lost an arm—if it had been a perfect body we might have succeeded better. Between then and the next January we secured three more; one total failure, one case of marked muscular motion, and one rather shivery thing—it rose of itself and uttered a sound. Then came a period when luck was poor; interments fell off, and those that did occur were of specimens either too diseased or too maimed for use. We kept track of all the deaths and their circumstances with systematic care.

One March night, however, we unexpectedly obtained a specimen which did not come from the potter's field. In Bolton the prevailing spirit of Puritanism had outlawed the sport of boxing—with the usual result. Surreptitious and ill-conducted bouts among the mill-workers were common, and occasionally professional talent of low grade was imported. This late winter night there had been such a match; evidently with disastrous results, since two timorous Poles had come to us with incoherently whispered entreaties to attend to a very secret and desperate case. We followed them to an abandoned barn, where the remnants of a crowd of frightened foreigners were watching a silent black form on the floor.

The match had been between Kid O'Brien—a lubberly and now quaking youth with a most un-Hibernian hooked nose—and Buck Robinson, "The Harlem Smoke." The negro had been knocked out, and a moment's examination shewed us that he would permanently remain so. He was a loathsome, gorilla-like thing, with abnormally long arms which I could not help calling fore legs, and a face that conjured up thoughts of unspeakable Congo secrets and tom-tom poundings under an eerie moon. The body must have looked even worse in life—but the world holds many ugly things. Fear was upon the whole pitiful crowd, for they did not know what the law would exact of them if the affair were not hushed up; and they were grateful when West, in spite of my involuntary shudders, offered to get rid of the thing quietly—for a purpose I knew too well.

There was bright moonlight over the snowless landscape, but we dressed the thing and carried it home between us through the deserted streets and meadows, as we had carried a similar thing one horrible night in Arkham. We approached the house from the field in the rear, took the specimen in the back door and down the cellar stairs, and prepared it for the usual experiment. Our fear of the police was absurdly great, though we had timed our trip to avoid the solitary patrolman of that section.

The result was wearily anticlimactic. Ghastly as our prize appeared, it was wholly unresponsive to every solution we injected in its black arm; solutions prepared from experience with white specimens only. So as the hour grew dangerously near to dawn, we did as we had done with the others—dragged the thing across the meadows to the neck of the woods near the potter's field, and buried it there in the best sort of grave the frozen ground would furnish. The grave was not very deep, but fully as good as that of the previous specimen—the thing which had risen of itself and uttered a sound. In the light of our dark lanterns we carefully covered it with leaves and dead vines, fairly certain that the police would never find it in a forest so dim and dense.

The next day I was increasingly apprehensive about the police, for a patient brought rumours of a suspected fight and death. West had still another source of worry, for he had been called in the afternoon to a case which ended very threateningly. An Italian woman had become hysterical over her missing child—a lad of five who had strayed off early in the morning and failed to appear for dinner—and had developed symptoms highly alarming in view of an always weak heart. It was a very foolish hysteria, for the boy had often run away before; but Italian peasants are exceedingly superstitious, and this woman seemed as much harassed by omens as by facts. About seven o'clock in the evening she had died, and her frantic husband had made a frightful scene in his efforts to kill West, whom he wildly blamed for not saving her life. Friends had held him when he drew a stiletto, but West departed amidst his inhuman shrieks, curses and oaths of vengeance. In his latest affliction the fellow seemed to have forgotten his child, who was still missing as the night advanced. There was some talk of searching the woods, but most of the family's friends were busy with the dead woman and the screaming man. Altogether, the nervous strain upon West must have been tremendous. Thoughts of the police and of the mad Italian both weighed heavily.

We retired about eleven, but I did not sleep well. Bolton had a surprisingly good police force for so small a town, and I could not help fearing the mess which would ensue if the affair of the night before were ever tracked down. It might mean the end of all our local work—and perhaps prison for both West and me. I did not like those rumours of a fight which were floating about. After the clock had struck three the moon shone in my eyes, but I turned over without rising to pull down the shade. Then came the steady rattling at the back door.

I lay still and somewhat dazed, but before long heard West's rap on my door. He was clad in dressing-gown and slippers, and had in his hands a revolver and an electric flashlight. From the revolver I knew that he was thinking more of the crazed Italian than of the police.

"We'd better both go," he whispered. "It wouldn't do not to answer it anyway, and it may be a patient—it would be like one of those fools to try the back door."

So we both went down the stairs on tiptoe, with a fear partly justified and partly that which comes only from the soul of the weird small hours. The rattling continued, growing somewhat louder. When we reached the door I cautiously unbolted it and threw it open, and as the moon streamed revealingly down on the form silhouetted there, West did a peculiar thing. Despite the obvious danger of attracting notice and bringing down on our heads the dreaded police investigation—a thing which after all was mercifully averted by the relative isolation of our cottage—my friend suddenly, excitedly, and unnecessarily emptied all six chambers of his revolver into the nocturnal visitor.

For that visitor was neither Italian nor policeman. Looming hideously against the spectral moon was a gigantic misshapen thing not to be imagined save in nightmares—a glassy-eyed, ink-black apparition nearly on all fours, covered with bits of mould, leaves, and vines, foul with caked blood, and having between its glistening teeth a snow—white, terrible, cylindrical object terminating in a tiny hand.

Part IV: The Scream of the Dead

THE SCREAM of a dead man gave to me that acute and added horror of Dr. Herbert West which harassed the latter years of our companionship. It is natural that such a thing as a dead man's scream should give horror, for it is obviously, not a pleasing or ordinary occurrence; but I was used to similar experiences, hence suffered on this occasion only because of a particular circumstance. And, as I have implied, it was not of the dead man himself that I became afraid.

Herbert West, whose associate and assistant I was, possessed scientific interests far beyond the usual routine of a village physician. That was why, when establishing his practice in Bolton, he had chosen an isolated house near the potter's field. Briefly and brutally stated, West's sole absorbing interest was a secret study of the phenomena of life and its cessation, leading toward the reanimation of the dead through injections of an excitant solution. For this ghastly experimenting it was necessary to have a constant supply of very fresh human bodies; very fresh because even the least decay hopelessly damaged the brain structure, and human because we found that the solution had to be compounded differently for different types of organisms. Scores of rabbits and guinea-pigs had been killed and treated, but their trail was a blind one. West had never fully succeeded because he had never been able to secure a corpse sufficiently fresh. What he wanted were bodies from which vitality had only just departed; bodies with every cell intact and capable of receiving again the impulse toward that mode of motion called life. There was hope that this second and artificial life might be made perpetual by repetitions of the injection, but we had learned that an ordinary natural life would not respond to the action. To establish the artificial motion, natural life must be extinct—the specimens must be very fresh, but genuinely dead.

The awesome quest had begun when West and I were students at the Miskatonic University Medical School in Arkham, vividly conscious for the first time of the thoroughly mechanical nature of life. That was seven years before, but West looked scarcely a day older now—he was small, blond, clean-shaven, soft-voiced, and spectacled, with only an occasional flash of a cold blue eye to tell of the hardening and growing fanaticism of his character under the pressure of his terrible investigations. Our experiences had often been hideous in the extreme; the results of defective reanimation, when lumps of graveyard clay had been galvanised into morbid, unnatural, and brainless motion by various modifications of the vital solution.

One thing had uttered a nerve-shattering scream; another had risen violently, beaten us both to unconsciousness, and run amuck in a shocking way before it could be placed behind asylum bars; still another, a loathsome African monstrosity, had clawed out of its shallow grave and done a deed—West had had to shoot that object. We could not get bodies fresh enough to shew any trace of reason when reanimated, so had perforce created nameless horrors. It was disturbing to think that one, perhaps two, of our monsters still lived—that thought haunted us shadowingly, till finally West disappeared under frightful circumstances. But at the time of the scream in the cellar laboratory of the isolated Bolton cottage, our fears were subordinate to our anxiety for extremely fresh specimens. West was more avid than I, so that it almost seemed to me that he looked half-covetously at any very healthy living physique.

It was in July, 1910, that the bad luck regarding specimens began to turn. I had been on a long visit to my parents in Illinois, and upon my return found West in a state of singular elation. He had, he told me excitedly, in all likelihood solved the problem of freshness through an approach from an entirely new angle—that of artificial preservation. I had known that he was working on a new and highly unusual embalming compound, and was not surprised that it had turned out well; but until he explained the details I was rather puzzled as to how such a compound could help in our work, since the objectionable staleness of the specimens was largely due to delay occurring before we secured them. This, I now saw, West had clearly recognised; creating his embalming compound for future rather than immediate use, and trusting to fate to supply again some very recent and unburied corpse, as it had years before when we obtained the negro killed in the Bolton prize-fight. At last fate had been kind, so that on this occasion there lay in the secret cellar laboratory a corpse whose decay could not by any possibility have begun. What would happen on reanimation, and whether we could hope for a revival of mind and reason, West did not venture to predict. The experiment would be a landmark in our studies, and he had saved the new body for my return, so that both might share the spectacle in accustomed fashion.

West told me how he had obtained the specimen. It had been a vigorous man; a well-dressed stranger just off the train on his way to transact some business with the Bolton Worsted Mills. The walk through the town had been long, and by the time the traveller paused at our cottage to ask the way to the factories, his heart had become greatly overtaxed. He had refused a stimulant, and had suddenly dropped dead only a moment later. The body, as might be expected, seemed to West a heaven—sent gift. In his brief conversation the stranger had made it clear that he was unknown in Bolton, and a search of his pockets subsequently revealed him to be one Robert Leavitt of St. Louis, apparently without a family to make instant inquiries about his disappearance. If this man could not be restored to life, no one would know of our experiment. We buried our materials in a dense strip of woods between the house and the potter's field. If, on the other hand, he could be restored, our fame would be brilliantly and perpetually established. So without delay West had injected into the body's wrist the compound which would hold it fresh for use after my arrival. The matter of the presumably weak heart, which to my mind imperilled the success of our experiment, did not appear to trouble West extensively. He hoped at last to obtain what he had never obtained before—a rekindled spark of reason and perhaps a normal, living creature.

So on the night of July 18, 1910, Herbert West and I stood in the cellar laboratory and gazed at a white, silent figure beneath the dazzling arc-light. The embalming compound had worked uncannily well, for as I stared fascinatedly at the sturdy frame which had lain two weeks without stiffening, I was moved to seek West's assurance that the thing was really dead. This assurance he gave readily enough; reminding me that the reanimating solution was never used without careful tests as to life, since it could have no effect if any of the original vitality were present. As West proceeded to take preliminary steps, I was impressed by the vast intricacy of the new experiment; an intricacy so vast that he could trust no hand less delicate than his own. Forbidding me to touch the body, he first injected a drug in the wrist just beside the place his needle had punctured when injecting the embalming compound. This, he said, was to neutralise the compound and release the system to a normal relaxation so that the reanimating solution might freely work when injected. Slightly later, when a change and a gentle tremor seemed to affect the dead limbs; West stuffed a pillow-like object violently over the twitching face, not withdrawing it until the corpse appeared quiet and ready for our attempt at reanimation. The pale enthusiast now applied some last perfunctory tests for absolute lifelessness, withdrew satisfied, and finally injected into the left arm an accurately measured amount of the vital elixir, prepared during the afternoon with a greater care than we had used since college days, when our feats were new and groping. I cannot express the wild, breathless suspense with which we waited for results on this first really fresh specimen—the first we could reasonably expect to open its lips in rational speech, perhaps to tell of what it had seen beyond the unfathomable abyss.

West was a materialist, believing in no soul and attributing all the working of consciousness to bodily phenomena; consequently he looked for no revelation of hideous secrets from gulfs and caverns beyond death's barrier. I did not wholly disagree with him theoretically, yet held vague instinctive remnants of the primitive faith of my forefathers; so that I could not help eyeing the corpse with a certain amount of awe and terrible expectation. Besides—I could not extract from my memory that hideous, inhuman shriek we heard on the night we tried our first experiment in the deserted farmhouse at Arkham.

Very little time had elapsed before I saw the attempt was not to be a total failure. A touch of colour came to cheeks hitherto chalk-white, and spread out under the curiously ample stubble of sandy beard. West, who had his hand on the pulse of the left wrist, suddenly nodded significantly; and almost simultaneously a mist appeared on the mirror inclined above the body's mouth. There followed a few spasmodic muscular motions, and then an audible breathing and visible motion of the chest. I looked at the closed eyelids, and thought I detected a quivering. Then the lids opened, shewing eyes which were grey, calm, and alive, but still unintelligent and not even curious.

In a moment of fantastic whim I whispered questions to the reddening ears; questions of other worlds of which the memory might still be present. Subsequent terror drove them from my mind, but I think the last one, which I repeated, was: "Where have you been?" I do not yet know whether I was answered or not, for no sound came from the well—shaped mouth; but I do know that at that moment I firmly thought the thin lips moved silently, forming syllables which I would have vocalised as "only now" if that phrase had possessed any sense or relevancy. At that moment, as I say, I was elated with the conviction that the one great goal had been attained; and that for the first time a reanimated corpse had uttered distinct words impelled by actual reason. In the next moment there was no doubt about the triumph; no doubt that the solution had truly accomplished, at least temporarily, its full mission of restoring rational and articulate life to the dead. But in that triumph there came to me the greatest of all horrors—not horror of the thing that spoke, but of the deed that I had witnessed and of the man with whom my professional fortunes were joined.

For that very fresh body, at last writhing into full and terrifying consciousness with eyes dilated at the memory of its last scene on earth, threw out its frantic hands in a life and death struggle with the air, and suddenly collapsing into a second and final dissolution from which there could be no return, screamed out the cry that will ring eternally in my aching brain:

"Help! Keep off, you cursed little tow-head fiend—keep that damned needle away from me!"

Part V: The Horror From the Shadows

MANY MEN have related hideous things, not mentioned in print, which happened on the battlefields of the Great War. Some of these things have made me faint, others have convulsed me with devastating nausea, while still others have made me tremble and look behind me in the dark; yet despite the worst of them I believe I can myself relate the most hideous thing of all—the shocking, the unnatural, the unbelievable horror from the shadows.

In 1915 I was a physician with the rank of First Lieutenant in a Canadian regiment in Flanders, one of many Americans to precede the government itself into the gigantic struggle. I had not entered the army on my own initiative, but rather as a natural result of the enlistment of the man whose indispensable assistant I was—the celebrated Boston surgical specialist, Dr. Herbert West. Dr. West had been avid for a chance to serve as surgeon in a great war, and when the chance had come, he carried me with him almost against my will. There were reasons why I could have been glad to let the war separate us; reasons why I found the practice of medicine and the companionship of West more and more irritating; but when he had gone to Ottawa and through a colleague's influence secured a medical commission as Major, I could not resist the imperious persuasion of one determined that I should accompany him in my usual capacity.

When I say that Dr. West was avid to serve in battle, I do not mean to imply that he was either naturally warlike or anxious for the safety of civilisation. Always an ice-cold intellectual machine; slight, blond, blue-eyed, and spectacled; I think he secretly sneered at my occasional martial enthusiasms and censures of supine neutrality. There was, however, something he wanted in embattled Flanders; and in order to secure it had had to assume a military exterior. What he wanted was not a thing which many persons want, but something connected with the peculiar branch of medical science which he had chosen quite clandestinely to follow, and in which he had achieved amazing and occasionally hideous results. It was, in fact, nothing more or less than an abundant supply of freshly killed men in every stage of dismemberment.

Herbert West needed fresh bodies because his life-work was the reanimation of the dead. This work was not known to the fashionable clientele who had so swiftly built up his fame after his arrival in Boston; but was only too well known to me, who had been his closest friend and sole assistant since the old days in Miskatonic University Medical School at Arkham. It was in those college days that he had begun his terrible experiments, first on small animals and then on human bodies shockingly obtained. There was a solution which he injected into the veins of dead things, and if they were fresh enough they responded in strange ways. He had had much trouble in discovering the proper formula, for each type of organism was found to need a stimulus especially adapted to it. Terror stalked him when he reflected on his partial failures; nameless things resulting from imperfect solutions or from bodies insufficiently fresh. A certain number of these failures had remained alive—one was in an asylum while others had vanished—and as he thought of conceivable yet virtually impossible eventualities he often shivered beneath his usual stolidity.

West had soon learned that absolute freshness was the prime requisite for useful specimens, and had accordingly resorted to frightful and unnatural expedients in body-snatching. In college, and during our early practice together in the factory town of Bolton, my attitude toward him had been largely one of fascinated admiration; but as his boldness in methods grew, I began to develop a gnawing fear. I did not like the way he looked at healthy living bodies; and then there came a nightmarish session in the cellar laboratory when I learned that a certain specimen had been a living body when he secured it. That was the first time he had ever been able to revive the quality of rational thought in a corpse; and his success, obtained at such a loathsome cost, had completely hardened him.

Of his methods in the intervening five years I dare not speak. I was held to him by sheer force of fear, and witnessed sights that no human tongue could repeat. Gradually I came to find Herbert West himself more horrible than anything he did—that was when it dawned on me that his once normal scientific zeal for prolonging life had subtly degenerated into a mere morbid and ghoulish curiosity and secret sense of charnel picturesqueness. His interest became a hellish and perverse addiction to the repellently and fiendishly abnormal; he gloated calmly over artificial monstrosities which would make most healthy men drop dead from fright and disgust; he became, behind his pallid intellectuality, a fastidious Baudelaire of physical experiment—a languid Elagabalus of the tombs.

Dangers he met unflinchingly; crimes he committed unmoved. I think the climax came when he had proved his point that rational life can be restored, and had sought new worlds to conquer by experimenting on the reanimation of detached parts of bodies. He had wild and original ideas on the independent vital properties of organic cells and nerve-tissue separated from natural physiological systems; and achieved some hideous preliminary results in the form of never-dying, artificially nourished tissue obtained from the nearly hatched eggs of an indescribable tropical reptile. Two biological points he was exceedingly anxious to settle—first, whether any amount of consciousness and rational action be possible without the brain, proceeding from the spinal cord and various nerve-centres; and second, whether any kind of ethereal, intangible relation distinct from the material cells may exist to link the surgically separated parts of what has previously been a single living organism. All this research work required a prodigious supply of freshly slaughtered human flesh—and that was why Herbert West had entered the Great War.

The phantasmal, unmentionable thing occurred one midnight late in March, 1915, in a field hospital behind the lines of St. Eloi. I wonder even now if it could have been other than a daemoniac dream of delirium. West had a private laboratory in an east room of the barn-like temporary edifice, assigned him on his plea that he was devising new and radical methods for the treatment of hitherto hopeless cases of maiming. There he worked like a butcher in the midst of his gory wares—I could never get used to the levity with which he handled and classified certain things. At times he actually did perform marvels of surgery for the soldiers; but his chief delights were of a less public and philanthropic kind, requiring many explanations of sounds which seemed peculiar even amidst that babel of the damned. Among these sounds were frequent revolver-shots—surely not uncommon on a battlefield, but distinctly uncommon in an hospital. Dr. West's reanimated specimens were not meant for long existence or a large audience. Besides human tissue, West employed much of the reptile embryo tissue which he had cultivated with such singular results. It was better than human material for maintaining life in organless fragments, and that was now my friend's chief activity. In a dark corner of the laboratory, over a queer incubating burner, he kept a large covered vat full of this reptilian cell-matter; which multiplied and grew puffily and hideously.

On the night of which I speak we had a splendid new specimen—a man at once physically powerful and of such high mentality that a sensitive nervous system was assured. It was rather ironic, for he was the officer who had helped West to his commission, and who was now to have been our associate. Moreover, he had in the past secretly studied the theory of reanimation to some extent under West. Major Sir Eric Moreland Clapham-Lee, D.S.O., was the greatest surgeon in our division, and had been hastily assigned to the St. Eloi sector when news of the heavy fighting reached headquarters. He had come in an aeroplane piloted by the intrepid Lieut. Ronald Hill, only to be shot down when directly over his destination. The fall had been spectacular and awful; Hill was unrecognisable afterward, but the wreck yielded up the great surgeon in a nearly decapitated but otherwise intact condition. West had greedily seized the lifeless thing which had once been his friend and fellow-scholar; and I shuddered when he finished severing the head, placed it in his hellish vat of pulpy reptile—tissue to preserve it for future experiments, and proceeded to treat the decapitated body on the operating table. He injected new blood, joined certain veins, arteries, and nerves at the headless neck, and closed the ghastly aperture with engrafted skin from an unidentified specimen which had borne an officer's uniform. I knew what he wanted—to see if this highly organised body could exhibit, without its head, any of the signs of mental life which had distinguished Sir Eric Moreland Clapham-Lee. Once a student of reanimation, this silent trunk was now gruesomely called upon to exemplify it.

I can still see Herbert West under the sinister electric light as he injected his reanimating solution into the arm of the headless body. The scene I cannot describe—I should faint if I tried it, for there is madness in a room full of classified charnel things, with blood and lesser human debris almost ankle-deep on the slimy floor, and with hideous reptilian abnormalities sprouting, bubbling, and baking over a winking bluish-green spectre of dim flame in a far corner of black shadows.

The specimen, as West repeatedly observed, had a splendid nervous system. Much was expected of it; and as a few twitching motions began to appear, I could see the feverish interest on West's face. He was ready, I think, to see proof of his increasingly strong opinion that consciousness, reason, and personality can exist independently of the brain—that man has no central connective spirit, but is merely a machine of nervous matter, each section more or less complete in itself. In one triumphant demonstration West was about to relegate the mystery of life to the category of myth. The body now twitched more vigorously, and beneath our avid eyes commenced to heave in a frightful way. The arms stirred disquietingly, the legs drew up, and various muscles contracted in a repulsive kind of writhing. Then the headless thing threw out its arms in a gesture which was unmistakably one of desperation—an intelligent desperation apparently sufficient to prove every theory of Herbert West. Certainly, the nerves were recalling the man's last act in life; the struggle to get free of the falling aeroplane.

What followed, I shall never positively know. It may have been wholly an hallucination from the shock caused at that instant by the sudden and complete destruction of the building in a cataclysm of German shell-fire—who can gainsay it, since West and I were the only proved survivors? West liked to think that before his recent disappearance, but there were times when he could not; for it was queer that we both had the same hallucination. The hideous occurrence itself was very simple, notable only for what it implied.

The body on the table had risen with a blind and terrible groping, and we had heard a sound. I should not call that sound a voice, for it was too awful. And yet its timbre was not the most awful thing about it. Neither was its message—it had merely screamed, "Jump, Ronald, for God's sake, jump!" The awful thing was its source.

For it had come from the large covered vat in that ghoulish corner of crawling black shadows.

Part VI: The Tomb-Legions

WHEN DR. HERBERT WEST disappeared a year ago, the Boston police questioned me closely. They suspected that I was holding something back, and perhaps suspected graver things; but I could not tell them the truth because they would not have believed it. They knew, indeed, that West had been connected with activities beyond the credence of ordinary men; for his hideous experiments in the reanimation of dead bodies had long been too extensive to admit of perfect secrecy; but the final soul-shattering catastrophe held elements of daemoniac phantasy which make even me doubt the reality of what I saw.

I was West's closest friend and only confidential assistant. We had met years before, in medical school, and from the first I had shared his terrible researches. He had slowly tried to perfect a solution which, injected into the veins of the newly deceased, would restore life; a labour demanding an abundance of fresh corpses and therefore involving the most unnatural actions. Still more shocking were the products of some of the experiments—grisly masses of flesh that had been dead, but that West waked to a blind, brainless, nauseous animation. These were the usual results, for in order to reawaken the mind it was necessary to have specimens so absolutely fresh that no decay could possibly affect the delicate brain-cells.

This need for very fresh corpses had been West's moral undoing. They were hard to get, and one awful day he had secured his specimen while it was still alive and vigorous. A struggle, a needle, and a powerful alkaloid had transformed it to a very fresh corpse, and the experiment had succeeded for a brief and memorable moment; but West had emerged with a soul calloused and seared, and a hardened eye which sometimes glanced with a kind of hideous and calculating appraisal at men of especially sensitive brain and especially vigorous physique. Toward the last I became acutely afraid of West, for he began to look at me that way. People did not seem to notice his glances, but they noticed my fear; and after his disappearance used that as a basis for some absurd suspicions.

West, in reality, was more afraid than I; for his abominable pursuits entailed a life of furtiveness and dread of every shadow. Partly it was the police he feared; but sometimes his nervousness was deeper and more nebulous, touching on certain indescribable things into which he had injected a morbid life, and from which he had not seen that life depart. He usually finished his experiments with a revolver, but a few times he had not been quick enough. There was that first specimen on whose rifled grave marks of clawing were later seen. There was also that Arkham professor's body which had done cannibal things before it had been captured and thrust unidentified into a madhouse cell at Sefton, where it beat the walls for sixteen years. Most of the other possibly surviving results were things less easy to speak of—for in later years West's scientific zeal had degenerated to an unhealthy and fantastic mania, and he had spent his chief skill in vitalising not entire human bodies but isolated parts of bodies, or parts joined to organic matter other than human. It had become fiendishly disgusting by the time he disappeared; many of the experiments could not even be hinted at in print. The Great War, through which both of us served as surgeons, had intensified this side of West.

In saying that West's fear of his specimens was nebulous, I have in mind particularly its complex nature. Part of it came merely from knowing of the existence of such nameless monsters, while another part arose from apprehension of the bodily harm they might under certain circumstances do him. Their disappearance added horror to the situation—of them all, West knew the whereabouts of only one, the pitiful asylum thing. Then there was a more subtle fear—a very fantastic sensation resulting from a curious experiment in the Canadian army in 1915. West, in the midst of a severe battle, had reanimated Major Sir Eric Moreland Clapham-Lee, D.S.O., a fellow-physician who knew about his experiments and could have duplicated them. The head had been removed, so that the possibilities of quasi-intelligent life in the trunk might be investigated. Just as the building was wiped out by a German shell, there had been a success. The trunk had moved intelligently; and, unbelievable to relate, we were both sickeningly sure that articulate sounds had come from the detached head as it lay in a shadowy corner of the laboratory. The shell had been merciful, in a way—but West could never feel as certain as he wished, that we two were the only survivors. He used to make shuddering conjectures about the possible actions of a headless physician with the power of reanimating the dead.

West's last quarters were in a venerable house of much elegance, overlooking one of the oldest burying-grounds in Boston. He had chosen the place for purely symbolic and fantastically aesthetic reasons, since most of the interments were of the colonial period and therefore of little use to a scientist seeking very fresh bodies. The laboratory was in a sub-cellar secretly constructed by imported workmen, and contained a huge incinerator for the quiet and complete disposal of such bodies, or fragments and synthetic mockeries of bodies, as might remain from the morbid experiments and unhallowed amusements of the owner. During the excavation of this cellar the workmen had struck some exceedingly ancient masonry; undoubtedly connected with the old burying-ground, yet far too deep to correspond with any known sepulchre therein. After a number of calculations West decided that it represented some secret chamber beneath the tomb of the Averills, where the last interment had been made in 1768. I was with him when he studied the nitrous, dripping walls laid bare by the spades and mattocks of the men, and was prepared for the gruesome thrill which would attend the uncovering of centuried grave-secrets; but for the first time West's new timidity conquered his natural curiosity, and he betrayed his degenerating fibre by ordering the masonry left intact and plastered over. Thus it remained till that final hellish night; part of the walls of the secret laboratory. I speak of West's decadence, but must add that it was a purely mental and intangible thing. Outwardly he was the same to the last—calm, cold, slight, and yellow-haired, with spectacled blue eyes and a general aspect of youth which years and fears seemed never to change. He seemed calm even when he thought of that clawed grave and looked over his shoulder; even when he thought of the carnivorous thing that gnawed and pawed at Sefton bars.

The end of Herbert West began one evening in our joint study when he was dividing his curious glance between the newspaper and me. A strange headline item had struck at him from the crumpled pages, and a nameless titan claw had seemed to reach down through sixteen years. Something fearsome and incredible had happened at Sefton Asylum fifty miles away, stunning the neighbourhood and baffling the police. In the small hours of the morning a body of silent men had entered the grounds, and their leader had aroused the attendants. He was a menacing military figure who talked without moving his lips and whose voice seemed almost ventriloquially connected with an immense black case he carried. His expressionless face was handsome to the point of radiant beauty, but had shocked the superintendent when the hall light fell on it—for it was a wax face with eyes of painted glass. Some nameless accident had befallen this man. A larger man guided his steps; a repellent hulk whose bluish face seemed half eaten away by some unknown malady. The speaker had asked for the custody of the cannibal monster committed from Arkham sixteen years before; and upon being refused, gave a signal which precipitated a shocking riot. The fiends had beaten, trampled, and bitten every attendant who did not flee; killing four and finally succeeding in the liberation of the monster. Those victims who could recall the event without hysteria swore that the creatures had acted less like men than like unthinkable automata guided by the wax-faced leader. By the time help could be summoned, every trace of the men and of their mad charge had vanished.

From the hour of reading this item until midnight, West sat almost paralysed. At midnight the doorbell rang, startling him fearfully. All the servants were asleep in the attic, so I answered the bell. As I have told the police, there was no wagon in the street, but only a group of strange-looking figures bearing a large square box which they deposited in the hallway after one of them had grunted in a highly unnatural voice, "Express—prepaid. "They filed out of the house with a jerky tread, and as I watched them go I had an odd idea that they were turning toward the ancient cemetery on which the back of the house abutted. When I slammed the door after them West came downstairs and looked at the box. It was about two feet square, and bore West's correct name and present address. It also bore the inscription, "From Eric Moreland Clapham-Lee, St. Eloi, Flanders. "Six years before, in Flanders, a shelled hospital had fallen upon the headless reanimated trunk of Dr. Clapham-Lee, and upon the detached head which—perhaps—had uttered articulate sounds.

West was not even excited now. His condition was more ghastly. Quickly he said, "It's the finish—but let's incinerate—this. "We carried the thing down to the laboratory—listening. I do not remember many particulars—you can imagine my state of mind—but it is a vicious lie to say it was Herbert West's body which I put into the incinerator. We both inserted the whole unopened wooden box, closed the door, and started the electricity. Nor did any sound come from the box, after all.

It was West who first noticed the falling plaster on that part of the wall where the ancient tomb masonry had been covered up. I was going to run, but he stopped me. Then I saw a small black aperture, felt a ghoulish wind of ice, and smelled the charnel bowels of a putrescent earth. There was no sound, but just then the electric lights went out and I saw outlined against some phosphorescence of the nether world a horde of silent toiling things which only insanity—or worse—could create. Their outlines were human, semi-human, fractionally human, and not human at all—the horde was grotesquely heterogeneous. They were removing the stones quietly, one by one, from the centuried wall. And then, as the breach became large enough, they came out into the laboratory in single file; led by a talking thing with a beautiful head made of wax. A sort of mad-eyed monstrosity behind the leader seized on Herbert West. West did not resist or utter a sound. Then they all sprang at him and tore him to pieces before my eyes, bearing the fragments away into that subterranean vault of fabulous abominations. West's head was carried off by the wax-headed leader, who wore a Canadian officer's uniform. As it disappeared I saw that the blue eyes behind the spectacles were hideously blazing with their first touch of frantic, visible emotion.

Servants found me unconscious in the morning. West was gone. The incinerator contained only unidentifiable ashes. Detectives have questioned me, but what can I say? The Sefton tragedy they will not connect with West; not that, nor the men with the box, whose existence they deny. I told them of the vault, and they pointed to the unbroken plaster wall and laughed. So I told them no more. They imply that I am either a madman or a murderer—probably I am mad. But I might not be mad if those accursed tomb-legions had not been so silent.

Jumbee

By Henry S. Whitehead

MR. GRANVILLE LEE, a Virginian of Virginians, coming out of the World War with a lung wasted and scorched by mustard gas, was recommended by his physician to spend a winter in the spice-and-balm climate of the Lesser Antilles—the lower islands o: the West Indian archipelago. He chose one of the American islands, St. Croix, the old Santa Cruz—Island of the Holy Cross—named by Columbus himself on his second voyage; once famous for its rum.

It was to Jaffray Da Silva that Mr. Lee at last turned for definite information about the local magic; information which, after a two months' residence, accompanied with marked improvement in his general health, he had come to regard as imperative, from the whetting glimpses he had received of its persistence on the island.

Contact with local customs, too, had sufficiently blunted his inherited sensibilities, to make him almost comfortable, as he sat with Mr. Da Silva on the cool gallery o' that gentleman's beautiful house, in the shade of forty years' growth of bougainvillea, on a certain afternoon. It was the restful gossipy period between five o'clock and dinnertime.

A glass jug of foaming rum-swizzel stood on the table between them.

"But, tell me, Mr. Da Silva" he urged, as he absorbed his second glass of the cooling, mild drink, "have you ever, actually been confronted with a '*Jumbee*'?—ever really seen one? You say, quite frankly, that you believe in them!"

This was not the first question about *Jumbees* that Mr. Lee had asked. He had consulted planters; he had spoken of the matter of *Jumbees* with courteous, intelligent, coloured storekeepers about the town, and even in Christiansted, St. Croix's other and larger town on the north side of the island. He had even mentioned the matter to one or two coal-black sugar-field labourers; for he had been on the island just long enough to begin to understand—a little—the weird jargon of speech which Lafcadio Hearn, when he visited St. Croix many years before, had not recognised as "English."

There had been marked differences in what he had been told. The planters and storekeepers had smiled, though with varying degrees of intensity, and had replied that the Danes had invented *Jumbees,* to keep their estate-labourers indoors after nightfall, thus ensuring a proper night's sleep for them, and minimising the depredations upon growing crops. The labourers whom he had asked, had rolled their eyes somewhat, but, it being broad daylight at the time of the enquiries, they had broken their impassive gravity with smiles, and sought to impress Mr. Lee with their lofty contempt for the beliefs of their fellow blacks, and with queerly-phrased assurances that *Jumbee* is a figment of the imagination.

Nevertheless, Mr. Lee was not satisfied. There was something here that he seemed to be missing—something extremely interesting, too, it appeared to him; something very different from "Bre'r Rabbit" and similar tales of his own remembered childhood in Virginia.

Once, too, he had been reading a book about Martinique and Guadeloupe, those ancient jewels of France's crown, and he had not read far before he met the word "*Zombi*" After that, he knew, at least, that the Danes had not "invented" the *Jumbee.* He heard, though vaguely, of the labourer's belief that Sven Garik, who had long ago gone back to his home in Sweden, and Garrity, one of the smaller planters now on the island, were "wolves"! Lycanthropy, animal-metamorphosis, it appeared, formed part of this strange texture of local belief.

Mr. Jaffray Da Silva was one-eighth African. He was, therefore, by island usage, "coloured," which is as different from being "black" in the West Indies as anything that can be imagined. Mr. Da Silva had been educated in the continental European manner. In his every word and action, he reflected the faultless courtesy of his European forbears. By every right and custom of West Indian society, Mr. Da Silva was a coloured gentleman, whose social status was as clear-cut and definite as a cameo.

These islands are largely populated by persons like Mr. Da Silva. Despite the difference in their status from what it would be in North America, in the islands it has its advantages— among them that of logic. To the West Indian mind, a man whose heredity is seven-eighths derived from gentry, as like as not with an authentic coat-of-arms, is entitled to be treated accordingly. That is why Mr. Da Silva's many clerks, and everybody else who knew him, treated him with deference, addressed him as "sir," and doffed their hats in continental fashion when meeting; salutes which, of course, Mr. Da Silva invariably returned, even to the humblest, which is one of the marks of a gentleman anywhere.

Jaffray Da Silva shifted one thin leg, draped in spotless white drill, over the other, and lit a fresh cigarette.

"Even my friends smile at me, Mr. Lee," he replied, with a tolerant smile, which lightened for an instant his melancholy, ivory-white, countenance. "They laugh at me more or less because I admit I believe in *Jumbees*. It is possible that everybody with even a small amount of African blood possesses that streak of belief in magic and the like. I seem, though, to have a peculiar aptitude for it! It is a matter of *experience*, with me, sir, and my friends are free to smile at me if they wish. Most of them—well, they do not admit their beliefs as freely as I, perhaps!"

Mr. Lee took another sip of the cold swizzel. He had heard how difficult it was to get Jaffray Da Silva to speak of his "experiences," and he suspected that under his host's even courtesy lay that austere pride which resents anything like ridicule, despite that tolerant smile.

"Please proceed, sir," urged Mr. Lee, and was quite unconscious that he had just used a word which, in his native South, is reserved for gentlemen of pure Caucasian blood.

"When I was a young man," began Mr. Da Silva, "about 1894, there was a friend of mine named Hilmar Iversen, a Dane, who lived here in the town, up near the Moravian Church on what the people call 'Foun'-Out Hill.' Iversen had a position under the government, a clerk's job, and his office was in the Fort. On his way home he used to stop here almost every afternoon for a swizzel and a chat. We were great friends, close friends. He was then a man a little past fifty, a butter tub of a fellow, very stout, and, like many of that build, he suffered from heart attacks.

"One night a boy came here for me. It was eleven o'clock, and I was just arranging the mosquito-net on my bed, ready to turn in. The servants had all gone home, so I went to the door myself, in shirt and trousers, and carrying a lamp, to see what was wanted—or, rather, I knew perfectly well what it was—a messenger to tell me Iversen was dead!"

Mr. Lee suddenly sat bolt-upright.

"How could you know that?" he enquired, his eyes wide.

Mr. Da Silva threw away the remains of his cigarette.

"I sometimes know things like that," he answered, slowly. "In this case, Iversen and I had been close friends for years. He and I had talked about magic and that sort of thing a great deal, occult powers, manifestations—that sort of thing. It is a very general topic here, as you may have seen. You would hear more of it if you continued to live here and settled into the ways of the island. In fact, Mr. Lee, Iversen and I had made a compact together. The one of us who 'went out' first, was to try to warn the other of it. You see, Mr. Lee, I had received Iversen's warning less than an hour before.

"I had been sitting out here on the gallery until ten o'clock or so. I was in that very chair you are occupying. Iversen had been having a heart attack. I had been to see him that afternoon. He looked just as he always did when he was recovering from an attack. In fact he intended to return to his office the following morning. Neither of us, I am sure, had given a thought to the possibility of a sudden sinking spell. We had not even referred to our agreement.

"Well, it was about ten, as I've said, when all of a sudden I heard Iversen coming along through the yard below there toward the house along that gravel path. He had, apparently, come through the gate from the Kongensgade—the King Street, as they call it nowadays— and I could hear his heavy step on the gravel very plainly He had a slight limp. 'Heavy crunch-light-crunch; plod-plod—plod-plod'; old Iversen to the life, there was no mistaking his step. There was no moon that night. The half of a waning moon was due to show itself an hour and a half later, but just then it was virtually pitch-black down there in the garden.

"I got up out of my chair and walked over to the top of the steps. To tell you the truth, Mr. Lee, I rather suspected—I have a kind of aptitude for that sort of thing—that it was not Iversen himself; how shall I express it? I had the idea from somewhere inside me, that it was Iversen trying to keep our agreement. My instinct assured me that he had just died. I can not tell you how I knew it, but such was the case, Mr. Lee.

"So I waited, over there just behind you, at the top of the steps. The footfalls came along steadily. At the foot of the steps, out of the shadow of the hibiscus bushes, it was a trifle less black than farther down the patch. There was a faint illumination, too, from a lamp inside the house. I knew that if it were Iversen, himself, I should be able to see him when the footsteps passed out of the deep shadow of the bushes. I did not speak.

"The footfalls came along toward that point, and passed it. I strained my eyes through the gloom, and I could see nothing. Then I knew, Mr. Lee, that Iversen had died, and that he was keeping his agreement.

"I came back here and sat down in my chair, and waited. The footfalls began to come up the steps. They came along the floor of the gallery, straight toward me. They stopped here, Mr. Lee, just beside me. I could *feel* Iversen standing here, Mr. Lee." Mr. Da Silva pointed to the floor with his slim, rather elegant hand.

"Suddenly, in the dead quiet, I could feel my hair stand up all over my scalp, straight and stiff. The chills started to run down my back, and up again, Mr. Lee. I shook like a man with the ague, sitting here in my chair.

"I said: 'Iversen, I understand! Iversen, I'm afraid!' My teeth were chattering like castanets, Mr. Lee. I said: 'Iversen, please go! You have kept the agreement. I am sorry I am afraid, Iversen. The flesh is weak! I am not afraid of *you*, Iversen, old friend. But you will understand, man! It's not ordinary fear. My intellect is all right, Iversen, but I'm badly panic-stricken, so please go, my friend.'

"There had been silence, Mr. Lee, as I said, before I began to speak to Iversen, for the footsteps had stopped here beside me. But when I said that, and asked my friend to go, I could *feel* that he went at once, and I knew that he had understood how I meant it! It was, suddenly, Mr. Lee, as though there had never been any footsteps, if you see what I mean. It is hard to put into words. I daresay, if I had been one of the labourers, I should have been halfway to Christiansted through the estates, Mr. Lee, but I was not so frightened that I could not stand my ground.

"After I had recovered myself a little, and my scalp had ceased its prickling, and the chills were no longer running up and down my spine, I rose, and I felt extremely weary, Mr. Lee. It had been exhausting. I came into the house and drank a large tot of French brandy, and then I felt better, more like myself. I took my hurricane- lantern and lighted it, and stepped down the path toward the gate leading to the Kongensgade. There was one thing I wished to see down there at the end of the garden. I wanted to see if the gate was fastened, Mr. Lee. It was. That huge iron staple, that you noticed, was in place. It has been used to fasten that old gate since some time in the eighteenth century, I imagine. I had not supposed anyone had opened the gate, Mr. Lee, but now I knew. There were no footprints in the gravel, Mr. Lee. I looked carefully. The marks of the bush-broom where the house-boy had swept the path on his way back from closing the gate were undisturbed, Mr. Lee.

"I was satisfied, and no longer even a little frightened. I came back here and sat down, and thought about my long friendship with old Iversen. I felt very sad to know that I should not see him again alive. He would never stop here again afternoons for a swizzel and a chat. About eleven o'clock I went inside the house and was preparing for bed when the rapping came at the front door. You see, Mr. Lee, I knew at once what it would mean.

"I went to the door, in shirt and trousers and stocking feet, carrying a lamp. We did not have electric light in those days. At the door stood Iversen's house-boy, a young fellow about eighteen. He was half-asleep, and very much upset. He 'cut his eyes' at me, and said nothing.

"'What is it, mon?' I asked the boy.

"'Mistress Iversen send ax yo' sir, please come to de house. Mr. Iversen die, sir.'

"'What time Mr. Iversen die, mon—you hear?'

"'I ain' able to say what o'clock, sir. Mistress Iversen come wake me where I sleep in a room in the yard sir, an' sen' me please call you—I t'ink he die about an hour ago, sir.'

"I put on my shoes again, and the rest of my clothes, and picked up a St. Kitts supplejack— I'll get you one; it's one of those limber, grapevine walking sticks, a handy thing on a dark night—and started with the boy for Iversen's house.

"When we had arrived almost at the Moravian Church, I saw something ahead, near the roadside. It was then about eleven-fifteen, and the streets were deserted. What I saw made me curious to test something. I paused, and told the boy to run on ahead and tell Mrs. Iversen I would be there shortly. The boy started to trot ahead. He was pure black, Mr. Lee, but he went past what I saw without noticing it. He swerved a little away from it, and I think, perhaps, he slightly quickened his pace just at that point, but that was all."

"What did you see?" asked Mr. Lee, interrupting. He spoke a trifle breathlessly. His left lung was, as yet, far from being healed.

"The Hanging *Jumbee*," replied Mr. Da Silva, in his usual tones.

"Yes! There at the side of the road were three *Jumbees*. There's a reference to that in *The History of Stewart McCann*. Perhaps you've run across that, eh?"

Mr. Lee nodded, and Mr. Da Silva quoted:

"'There they hung, though no ladder's rung

"'Supported their dangling feet.'

"And there's another line in *The History*," he continued, smiling, "which describes a typical group of Hanging *Jumbee*:

"'Maiden, man-child, and shrew.'

"Well, there were the usual three *Jumbees*, apparently hanging in the air. It wasn't very light, but I could make out a boy of about twelve, a young girl, and a shriveled old woman—what the author of The *History of Stewart McCann* meant by the word 'shrew.' He told me himself, by the way, Mr. Lee, that he had put feet on his *Jumbees* mostly for the sake of a convenient rhyme—poetic license! The Hanging *Jumbee* have no feet. It is one of their peculiarities. Their legs stop at the ankles. They have abnormally long, thin African legs. They are always black, you know. Their feet—if they have them—are always hidden in a kind of mist that lies along the ground wherever one sees them. They shift and 'weave,' as a full-blooded African does— standing on one foot and resting the other—you've noticed that, of course—or scratching the supporting ankle with the toes of the other foot. They do not swing in the sense that they seem to be swung on a rope—that is not what it means; they do not twirl about. But they do—always—face the oncomer ...

"I walked on, slowly, and passed them; and they kept their faces to me as they always do. I'm used to that ...

"I went up the steps of the house to the front gallery, and found Mrs. Iversen waiting for me. Her sister was with her, too. I remained sitting with them for the best part of an hour. Then two old black women, who had been sent for, into the country, arrived. These were two old women who were accustomed to prepare the dead for burial. Then I persuaded the ladies to retire, and started to come home myself.

"It was a little past midnight, perhaps twelve- fifteen. I picked out my own hat from two or three of poor old Iversen's that were hanging on the rack, took my supplejack, and stepped out of the door onto the little stone gallery at the head of the steps.

"There are about twelve or thirteen steps from the gallery down to the street. As I started down them I noticed a third old black woman sitting, all huddled together, on the bottom step, with her back to me. I thought at once that this must be some old crone who lived with the other two—the preparers of the dead. I imagined that she had been afraid to remain alone in their cabin, and so had accompanied them into the town—they are like children, you know, in some ways—and that, feeling too humble to come into the house, she had sat down to wait on the step and had fallen asleep. You've heard their proverbs, have you not? There's one that exactly fits this situation that I had imagined: 'Cockroach no wear crockin' boot when he creep in fowl-house!' It means: 'Be very reserved when in the presence of your betters!' Quaint, rather! The poor souls!

"I started to walk down the steps toward the old woman. That scant half-moon had come up into the sky while I had been sitting with the ladies, and by its light everything was fairly sharply defined. I could see that old woman as plainly as I can see you now, Mr. Lee. In fact, I was looking directly at the poor creature as I came down the steps, and fumbling in my pocket for a few coppers for her—for tobacco and sugar, as they say! I was wondering, indeed, why she was not by this time on her feet and making one of their queer little bobbing bows—'cockroach bow to fowl,' as they might say! It seemed this old woman must have fallen into a very deep sleep, for she had not moved at all, although ordinarily she would have heard me, for the night was deathly still, and their hearing is extraordinarily acute, like a cat's, or a dog's. I remember that the fragrance from Mrs. Iversen's tuberoses in pots on the gallery railing was pouring out in a stream that night, 'making a greeting for the moon!' It was almost overpowering.

"Just as I was putting my foot on the fifth step, there came a tiny little puff of fresh breeze from somewhere in the hills behind Iversen's house. It rustled the dry fronds of a palm-tree that was growing beside the steps. I turned my head in that direction for an instant.

"Mr. Lee, when I looked back, down the steps, after what must have been a fifth of a second's inattention, that little old black woman who had been huddled up there on the lowest step, apparently sound asleep, was gone. She had vanished utterly—and, Mr. Lee, a little white dog, about the size of a French poodle, was bounding up the steps toward me. With every bound, a step at a leap, the dog increased in size. It seemed to swell out there before my very eyes.

"Then I was really frightened—thoroughly utterly frightened. I knew if that animal so much as touched me, it meant death, Mr. Lee—

absolute, certain death. The little old woman was a 'sheen—*chien*, of course. You know of lycanthropy—wolf-change—of course. Well, this was one of our varieties of it. I do not know what it would be called, I'm sure. 'Canicanthropy,' perhaps. I don't know, but something—something, first-cousin-once-removed from lycanthropy, and on the downward scale, Mr. Lee. The old woman was a were-dog!

"Of course, I had no time to think, only to use my instinct. I swung my supplejack with all my might and brought it down squarely on that beast's head. It was only a step below me then, and I could see the faint moonlight sparkle on the slaver about its mouth. It was then, it seemed to me, about the size of a medium-sized dog— nearly wolf-size, Mr. Lee, and a kind of deathly white. I was desperate, and the force with which I struck caused me to lose my balance. I did not fall, but it required a moment or two for me to regain my equilibrium. When I felt my feet firm under me again, I looked about, frantically, on all sides, for the 'dog.' But it, too, Mr. Lee, like the old woman, had quite disappeared. I looked all about, you may well imagine, after that experience, in the clear, thin moonlight. For yards about the foot of the steps, there was no place— not even a small nook—where either the 'dog' or the old woman could have been concealed. Neither was on the gallery, which was only a few feet square, a mere landing.

"But there came to my ears, sharpened by that night's experiences, from far out among the plantations at the rear of Iversen's house, the pad-pad of naked feet. Someone—something— was running, desperately, off in the direction of the center of the island, back into the hills, into the deep 'bush.'

"Then, behind me, out of the house onto the gallery rushed the two old women who had been preparing Iversen's body for its burial. They were enormously excited, and they shouted at me unintelligibly. I will have to render their words for you.

"O, de Good Gahd protec' you, Marster Jaffray, sir—de Joombie, de Joombie! De "Sheen," Marster Jaffray! He go, sir?'

"I reassured the poor old souls, and went back home." Mr. Da Silva fell abruptly silent. He slowly shifted his position in his chair, and reached for, and lighted, a fresh cigarette. Mr. Lee was absolutely silent. He did not move. Mr. Da Silva resumed, deliberately, after obtaining a light.

"You see, Mr. Lee, the West Indies are different from any other place in the world, I verily believe, sir. I've said so, anyhow, many a time, although I have never been out of the islands except when I was a young man, to Copenhagen. I've told you exactly what happened that particular night."

Mr. Lee heaved a sigh.

"Thank you, Mr. Da Silva, very much indeed, sir," said he, thoughtfully, and made as though to rise. His service wristwatch indicated six o'clock.

"Let us have a fresh swizzel, at least, before you go," suggested Mr. Da Silva. "We have a saying here in the island, that a man can't travel on one leg! Perhaps you've heard it already."

"I have," said Mr. Lee.

"Knud, Knud! You hear, mon? Knud—tell Charlotte to mash up another bal' of ice—you hear? Quickly now," commanded Mr. Da Silva.

The Corpse-Master

By Seabury Quinn

THE ABULANCE-GONG insistence of my night bell brought me up standing from a stupor-like sleep, and as I switched the vestibule light on and unbarred the door, "Are you the doctor?" asked a breathless voice. A disheveled youth half fell through the doorway and clawed my sleeve desperately. "Quick—quick, Doctor! It's my uncle, Colonel Evans. He's dying. I think he tried to kill himself—"

"All right," I agreed, turning to sprint upstairs. "What sort of wound has he?—or was it poison?"

"It's his throat, sir. He tried to cut it. Please, hurry, Doctor!"

I took the last four steps at a bound, snatched some clothes from the bedside chair and charged down again, pulling on my garments like a fireman answering a night alarm. "Now, which way—" I began, but:

"*Tiens*," a querulous voice broke in as Jules de Grandin came downstairs, seeming to miss half treads in his haste. "Let him tell us where to go as we go there, my old one! It is that we should make the haste. A cut throat does not wait patiently."

"This is Dr. de Grandin," I told the young man. "He will be of great assistance—"

"*Mais oui*," the little Frenchman agreed, "and the Trump of Judgment will serve excellently as an alarm clock if we delay our going long enough. Make haste, my friend!"

"Down two blocks and over one," our caller directed as we got under way, "376 Albion Road. My uncle went to bed about ten o'clock, according to the servants, and none of them heard him moving about since. I got home just a few minutes ago, and found him lying in the bathroom when I went to wash my teeth, he lay beside the tub with a razor in his hand, and blood was all over the place. It was awful!"

"Undoubtlessly," de Grandin murmured from his place on the rear seat. "What did you do then, young Monsieur?"

"Snatched a roll of gauze from the medicine cabinet and staunched the wound as well as I could, then called Dockery the gardener to hold it in place white I raced round to see you. I remembered seeing your sign sometime before." We drew up to the Evans house as he concluded his recital, and rushed through the door and up the stairs together. "In there," our companion directed, pointing to a door from which there gushed a stream of light into the darkened hall.

A man in bathrobe and slippers knelt above a recumbent form stretched full-length on the white tiles of the bathroom. One glance at the supine figure and both de Grandin and I turned away, I with a deprecating shake of my head, the Frenchman with a fatalistic shrug.

"He has no need of us, that poor one," he informed the young man. "Ten minutes ago, perhaps yes; now"—another shrug—"the undertaker and the clergyman, perhaps the police—"

"The police? Surely, Doctor, this is suicide—"

"Do you say so?" de Grandin interrupted sharply. "Trowbridge, my friend, consider this, if you please." Deftly he raised the dead man's thin white beard and pointed to the deeply incised slash across the throat. "Does that mean nothing?"

"Why—er—"

"Perfectly, Wipe your pince-nez before you look a second time, and tell me that you see the cut runs diagonally from right to left."

"Why, so it does, but—"

"But Monsieur the deceased was right- handed—look how the razor lies beneath his right hand. Now, if you will raise your hand to your own throat and draw' the index finger across it as if it were a knife, you will note the course is slightly out of horizontal—somewhat diagonal—slanting downward from left to right. It is not so?"

I nodded as I completed the gesture.

"*Très bien*. When one is bent on suicide he screws his courage to the sticking point, then, if he has chosen a cut throat as means of exit, he usually stands before a mirror, cuts deeply and quickly with his knife, and makes a downward- slanting slash. But as he sees the blood and feels the pain his resolution weakens, and the gash becomes more and more shallow. At the end it trails away to little more than a skin-scratch. It is not so in this case; at its end the wound is deeper than at the beginning.

"Again, this poor one would almost certainly have stood before the mirror to do away with himself. Had he done so he would have fallen crosswise of the room, perhaps; more likely not. One with a severed throat does not die quickly, lie thrashes about like a fowl recently decapitated, and writes the story of his struggle plainly on his surroundings. What have we here? Do you—does anyone—think it likely that a man would slit his gullet, then lie down peacefully to bleed his life away, as this one appears to have done? *Non, non;* it is not *en caractère*!

"Consider further"—he pointed with dramatic suddenness to the dead man's bald head—"if we desire further proof, observe him!"

Plainly marked there was a welt of bruised flesh on the hairless scalp, the mark of some blunt instrument.

"He might have struck his head as he fell," I hazarded, and he grinned in derision,

"*Ah bah*, I tell you he was stunned unconscious by some miscreant, then dragged or carried to this room and slaughtered like a pole-axed beef. Without the telltale mark of the butcher's bludgeon there is ground for suspicion in the quietude of his position, in the neat manner the razor lies beneath his hand instead of being firmly grasped or flung away, but with this bruise before us there is but one answer. He has been done to death; he has been butchered; he was murdered."

"WILL YE be seein' Sergeant Costello?" Nora McGinnis appeared like a phantom at the drawing room door as de Grandin and I were having coffee next evening after dinner, "He says—"

"Invite him to come in and say it for himself, *ma petite* "Jules de Grandin answered with a smile of welcome at the big red-headed man who loomed behind the trim figure of my household factotum. "Is it about the Evans killing you would talk with us?" he added as the detective accepted a cigar and demi-tasse.

"There's two of 'em, now, sir," Costello answered gloomily. "Mulligan, who pounds a beat in th' Eighth Ward, just 'phoned in there's a murder dressed up like a suicide at th' Rangers' Club in Fremont Street."

"*Pardieu*, another?" asked de Grandin. "How do you know the latest one is not true suicide?"

"Well, sir, here's' th' pitch. When th' feller from th' club comes runnin' out to say that Mr. Wolkof's shot himself, Mulligan goes in and takes a look around. He finds him layin' on his back with a little hole in his forehead an' th' back blown out o' his head, an', bein' th' wise lad, he adds up two an' two and makes it come out four. He'd used a Colt .45, this Wolkof feller, an' it was layin' halfway in his hand, restin' on his half-closed fingers, ye might say. That didn't look too kosher. A feller who's been shot through the forehead is more likely to freeze tight to th' gun than otherwise. Certain'y he don't just hold it easy-like. Besides, it was an old-fashioned black-powder gun, sir, what they call a low- velocity weapon, and if it had been fired close against the dead man's forehead it should 'a' left a good-sized smudge o' powder-stain. There wasn't any."

"One commends the excellent Mulligan for his reasoning," de Grandin commented. "He found this Monsieur Wolkof lying on his back with a hole drilled through his head, no powder- brand upon his brow where the projectile entered, and the presumably suicidal weapon lying loosely in his hand. One thing more; it may not be conclusive, but it would be helpful to know if there were any powder-stains upon the dead man's pistol-hand."

"As far's I know there weren't, sir," answered Costello. "Mulligan said he took partic'lar notice of his hands, too. But ye're yet to hear th' cream o' th' joke. Th' pistol was in Mr. Wolkof's open right hand, an' all th' club attendants swear he was left-handed—writin', feedin' himself an' shavin' with his left hand exclusively. Novi', I ask ye, Dr. de Grandin, would a man all steamed up to blow his brains out be takin' th' trouble to break a lifetime habit of left-handedness when he's so much more important things to think about? It seems to me that—"

"Ye're wanted on th' phone, Sergeant," announced Nora from the doorway. "Will ye be takin' it in here, or usin' th' hall instrument?"

"Hullo? Costello speakin'," he challenged. "If it's about th' Wolkof case, I'm goin' right over—glory be to God! No! Och, th' murderin' blackguard!

"Gentlemen," he faced us, fury in his ruddy face and blazing blue eyes, "it's another one. A little girl, this time. They've kilt a tiny, wee baby while we sat .here like three damn' fools and -talked! They've took her body to th' morgue—"

"Then, *nom d'un chameau*, why are we remaining here?" de Grandin interrupted. "Come, *mes amis*, it is to hasten. Let us go all quickly!"

WITH MY HORN tooting almost continuously, and Costello waving aside crossing policemen, we rushed to the city mortuary. Parnell, the coroner's physician, fussed over a tray of instruments, Coroner Martin bustled about in a perfect fever of eagerness to begin his official duties; two plainclothes men conferred in muted whispers in the outer office.

Death in the raw is never pretty, as doctors, soldiers and embalmers know only too well. When it is accompanied by violence it wears a still less lovely aspect, and when the victim is a child the sight is almost heart-breaking. Bruised and battered almost beyond human semblance, her baby-fine hair matted with mixed blood and cerebral matter, little Hazel Clark lay before us, the queer, unnatural angle of her right wrist denoting a Colles' fracture; a subclavicular dislocation of the left shoulder was apparent by the projection of the bone beneath the clavicle, and the vault of her small skull had been literally beaten in. She was completely "broken" as ever a medieval malefactor was when bound upon the wheel of torture for the ministrations of the executioner.

For a moment de Grand in bent above the battered little corpse, viewing it intently with the skilled, knowing eye of a pathologist, then, so lightly that they scarcely displaced a hair of her head, his fingers moved quickly over her, pausing now and again to prod gently, then sweeping onward in their investigative course. "*Tiens*, he was a gorilla for strength, that one," he announced, "and a veritable gorilla for savagery, as well. What is there to tell me of the case, *mes amis*?" he called to the plainclothes men.

Such meager data as they had they gave him quickly. She was three and a half years old, the idol of her lately widowed father, and had neither brothers nor sisters. That afternoon her father had given her a quarter as reward for having gone a whole week without meriting a scolding, and shortly after dinner she had set out for the corner drug store to purchase an ice cream cone with part of her righteously acquired wealth. Attendants at the pharmacy remembered she had left the place immediately and set out for home; a neighbor had seen her proceeding up the street, the cone grasped tightly in her hand as she sampled it with ecstatic little licks. Two minutes later, from a spot where the privet hedge of a vacant house shadowed the pavement, residents of the block had heard a scream, but squealing children were no novelty in the neighborhood, and the cry was not repeated. It was not till her father came looking for her that they recalled it.

From the drug store Mr. Clark traced Hazel's homeward course, and was passing the deserted house when he noticed a stain on the sidewalk. A lighted match showed the discoloration was a spot of blood some four inches across, and with panic premonition tearing at his heart he pushed through the hedge to the unmowed lawn of the vacant residence. Match after match he struck while he called "Hazel! Hazel!" but there was no response, and he saw nothing till he was about to return to the street. Then, in a weed-choked rose bed, almost hidden by the foliage, he saw the gleam of her pink pinafore. His cries aroused the neighborhood, and the police were notified.

House-to-house inquiry by detectives finally elicited the information that a "short, stoop-shouldered man" had been seen walking hurriedly away a moment after the child's scream was heard. Further description of the suspect was unavailable.

"*Pardieu*, de Grandin stroked his small mustache thoughtfully as the plainclothes men concluded, "it seems we have to search the haystack for an almost microscopic needle, *n'est-ce pas*? There are considerable numbers of small men with stooping shoulders. The task will be a hard one."

"Hard, hell!" one of the detectives rejoined in disgust. "We got no more chance o' findin' that bird than a pig has o' wearin' vest-pockets."

"Do you say so?" the Frenchman demanded, fixing an uncompromising cat-stare on the speaker. "*Alors*, my friend, prepare to meet a fully tailored porker before "you are greatly older.

Have you forgotten in the excitement that I am in the case?"

"Sergeant, sir," a uniformed patrolman hurried into the mortuary, "they found th' weapon used on th' Clark girl. It's a winder-sash weight. They're testin' it for fingerprints at headquarters now."

"Humph," Costello commented. "Anything on it?"

"Yes, *sir*. The killer must 'a' handled it after he dragged her body into th' bushes, for there's marks o' bloody fingers on it plain as day."

"O.K., I'll be right up," Costello replied. "Take over, Jacobs," he ordered one of the plainclothes men. "I'll call ye if they find out anything, Dr. de Grandin. So long!"

The Sergeant delayed his report, and next morning after dinner the Frenchman suggested, "Would it not be well to interview the girl's father? I should appreciate it if you will accompany and introduce me."

"He's in the drawing room," the maid told us as we knocked gently on the Clark door. "He's been there ever since they brought her home, sir. Just sitting beside her and—" she broke off as her throat filled with sobs. "If you could take his mind off of his trouble it would be a Godsend. If he'd only cry, or sumpin—"

"Grief is a hot, consuming fire, Madame," the little Frenchman whispered, "and only tears can quell it. The dry-eyed mourner is the one most likely to collapse."

Coroner Martin had done his work as a mortician with consummate artistry. Under his deft hands all signs of the brutality that struck the child down had been effaced. Clothed in a short light-pink dress she lay peacefully in her casket, one soft pink cheek against the tufted silken pillow sewn with artificial forget-me-nots, a little bisque doll, dressed in a frock the exact duplicate of her own, resting in the crook of her left elbow. Beside the casket, a smile sadder than any grimace of woe on his thin, ascetic features, sat Mortimer Clark.

As we tiptoed into the darkened room we heard him murmur, "Time for shut-eye town, daughter. Daddy'll tell you a story," For a moment he looked expectantly into the still childish face on the pillow before him, as if waiting for an answer. The little gilt clock on the mantel ticked with a sort of whispering haste; far down the block a neighbor's dog howled dismally; a light breeze bustled through the opened windows, fluttering the white-scrim curtains and setting the orange flames of the tall candles at the casket's head and foot to flickering.

It was weird, this stricken man's vigil beside his dead, it was ghastly to hear him addressing her as if she could hear and reply. As the story of the old woman and her pig progressed I felt a kind of terrified tension about my heart.

. . I he cat began to kill the rat, the rat began to gnaw the rope, the rope began to hang the butcher—"

"*Grand Dieu,*" de Grandin whispered as he plucked me by the elbow, "let us not look at it, Friend Trowbridge. It is a profanation for our eyes to see, our ears to hear what goes on here. *Sang de Saint Pierre,* I, Jules de Grandin, swear that I shall find the one who caused this thing to be, and when I find him, though he take refuge beneath the very throne of God, I'll drag him forth and cast him screaming into hell. God do so to me, and more also, if I do not!" Tears were coursing down his cheeks, and he let them flow unabashed.

"You don't want to talk to him, then?" I whispered as we neared the front door.

"I do not, neither do I wish to tell indecent stories to the priest as he elevates the Host. The one would be no greater sacrilege than the other, but—*ah?*" he broke off, staring at a small framed parchment hanging on the wall. "Tell me, my friend," he demanded, "what is it that you see there?"

"Why, it's a certificate of membership in the Rangers' Club. Clark was in the Army Air Force, and—"

"*Très bien*," he broke in. "Thank you. Our ideas sometimes lead us to see what we wish when in reality it is not there; that is why I sought the testimony of disinterested eyes."

"What in the world has Clark's membership in the Rangers got to do with—"

"*Zut*!" he waved me to silence. "I think, I cogitate, I concentrate, my old one. Monsieur Evens—Monsieur Wolkof, now Monsieur Clark—all are members of that club. *C'est très étrange*. Me, I shall interview the steward of that club, my friend. Perhaps his words may throw more light on these so despicable doings than all the clumsy, well-meant investigations of our friend Costello. Come, let us go away. Tomorrow will do as well as today, for the miscreant who fancies himself secure is in no hurry to decamp, despite the nonsense talked of the guilty who flee when no man pursueth."

WE FOUND Costello waiting for us when we reached home. A very worried-looking Costello he was, too. "We've checked th' finger-prints on th' sash-weight, sir," he announced almost truculently.

"*Bon*," the Frenchman replied carelessly. "Is it that they are of someone you can identify?"

"I'll say they are," the sergeant returned shortly. "They're Gyp Carson's—th' meanest killer th' force ever had to deal with."

"Ah," de Grandin shook off his air of preoccupation with visible effort, "it is for you to find this Monsieur Gyp, my friend. You have perhaps some inkling of his present whereabouts?" The sergeant's laugh was almost an hysterical cackle. "That we have, sir, that we have! They burnt—you know, electrocuted—him last month in Trenton for th' murder of a milk- wagon driver durin' a hold-up. By rights he should be in Mount Olivet Cemetery this minute, an' by th' same token he should 'a' been there when the little Clark girl was kilt last night."

"*A-a-ah*?" de Grandin twisted his wheat- blond mustache furiously. "It seems this case contains the possibilities, my friend. Tomorrow morning, if you please, we shall go to the cemetery and investigate the grave of Monsieur Gyp. Perhaps we shall find something there. If we find nothing we shall have found the most valuable information we can have."

"If we find nothin—" The big Irishman looked at him in bewilderment. "All right, sir. I've seen some funny things since I been runnin' round with you, but if you're tellin' me—"

"*Tenez*, my friend, I tell you nothing; nothing at all. I too seek information. Let us wait until the morning, then see what testimony pick and shovel will give."

A SUPERINTENDENT and two workmen waited for us at the grave when we arrived at the cemetery next morning. The grave lay in the newer, less expensive portion of the burying ground where perpetual care was not so conscientiously maintained as in the better sections. Scrub grass fought for a foothold in the clayey soil, and the mound had already begun to fall in. Incongruously, a monument bearing the effigy of a weeping angel leaned over the grave-head, while a footstone with the inscription OUR DARLING guarded its lower end.

The superintendent glanced over Costello's papers, stowed them in an inner pocket and nodded to the Polish laborers. "Git goin'," he ordered tersely, "an' make it snappy."

The diggers' picks and spades bored deep and deeper in the hard-packed, sun-baked earth. At last the hollow sound of steel on wood warned us their quest was drawing to a close. A pair of strong web straps was let down and made fast to the rough chestnut box in which the casket rested, and the men strained at the thongs to bring their weird freight to the surface. Two pick-handles were laid across the violated grave and on them the box rested. With a wrench the superintendent undid the screws that held the clay-stained lid in place and laid it aside. Within we saw the casket, a cheap, square-ended affair covered with shoddy gray broadcloth, the tinny imitation-silver name plate and crucifix on its lid already showing a dull brown-blue discoloration.

"*Maintenant!*"murmured de Grandin breathlessly as the superintendent began unlatching the fastenings that held the upper portion of the casket lid. Then, as the last catch snapped back and the cover came away:

"Feu noir de l'enfer!"

"Good heavens!" I exclaimed.

"For th' love o' God!" Costello's amazed antiphon sounded at my elbow.

The cheap sateen pillow of the casket showed a depression like the pillow of a bed recently vacated, and the poorly made upholstery of its bottom displayed a wide furrow, as though flattened by some weight imposed on it for a considerable time, but sign or trace of human body there was none. The case was empty as it left the factory.

"Glory be to God!" Costello muttered hoarsely, staring at the empty casket as though loath to believe his own eyes. "An' this is broad daylight," he added in a kind of wondering afterthought.

"*Précisément*," de Grandin's acid answer came back like a whipcrack. "This is diagnostic, my friend. Had we found something here it might have meant one thing or another. Here we find nothing; nothing at all. What does it mean?"

"I know what it means!" The look of superstitious fear on Costello's broad red face gave way to one of furious anger. "It means there's been some monkey-business goin' on—who had this buryin'?" he turned savagely on the superintendent.

"Donally," the other returned, "but don't blame me for it. I just work here."

"Huh, Donally, eh? We'll see what Mr. Donally has to say about this, an' he'd better have plenty to say, too, if he don't want to collect himself from th' comers o' a four-acre lot." Donally's Funeral Parlors were new but by no means prosperous-looking. Situated in a small side street in the poor section of town, their only pretention to elegance was the brightly- gleaming gold sign on their window:

JOSEPH DONALLY
FUNERAL DIRECTOR & EMBALMER
SEXTON ST. ROSE'S R.C. CHURCH

"See here, young feller me lad," Costello began without preliminary as he stamped unceremoniously into the small, dark room that constituted Mr. Donally's office and reception foyer, "come clean, an' come clean in a hurry. Was Gyp Carson dead when you had his funeral?"

"If he wasn't we sure played one awful dirty trick on him," the mortician replied. "What'd ye think would happen to you if they set you in that piece o' furniture down at Trenton an' turned the juice on? What d'ye mean, 'was he dead'?"

"I mean just what I say, wise guy. I've just come from Mount Olivet an' looked into his coffin, an' if there's hide or hair of a corpse in it I'll eat it, so I will!"

"*What's that?* You say th' casket was empty?"

"As your head."

"Well, I'll be—" Mr. Donally began, but Costello forestalled him:

"You sure will, an' all beat up, too, if you don't spill th' low-down. Come clean, now, or do I have to sock ye in th' jaw an' lock ye up in th' bargain?"

"Whatcher tryin' to put over?" Mr. Donally demanded. "Think I faked up a stall funeral? Lookit here, if you don't believe me." From a pigeon hole of his desk he produced a sheaf of papers, thumbed through them, and handed Costello a packet fastened with a rubber band.

Everything was in order. The death certificate, signed by the prison physician, showed the cause of death as cardiac arrest by fibrillary contraction induced by three shocks of an alternating current of electricity of 7½ amperes at a pressure of 2,000 volts.

"I didn't have much time," Donally volunteered. "The prison doctors had made a full post, and his old woman was one o' them old-fashioned folks that don't believe in embalmin', so there was nothin' to do but rush him to th' graveyard an' plant him. Not so bad for me, though, at that. I sold 'em a casket an' burial suit an' twenty-five limousines for th' funeral, an' got a cut on th' monument, too,"'

De Grandin eyed him speculatively. "Have you any reason to believe attempts at resuscitation were made?" he asked.

"Huh? Resuscitate *that*? Didn't I just tell you they'd made a full autopsy on him at the prison? Didn't miss a damn thing either. You might as well try resuscitatin' a lump o' hamburger as bring back a feller which had had that done to him."

"Quite so," de Grandin nodded, "I did but ask. Now—"

"Now we don't know no more than we did an hour ago," the sergeant supplied. "I might 'a' thought this guy was in cahoots with Gyp's folks, but th' prison records show he was dead, an' th' doctors down at Trenton don't certify nobody's dead if there's a flicker o' eyelash left in him. Looks as if we've got to find some gink with a fad for grave-robbin', don't it, Dr. de Grandin?

"But say"—a sudden gleam of inspiration overspread his face—"suppose someone had dug him up an' taken an impression of his fingerprints, then had rubber gloves made with th' prints on th' outside o' th' fingers? Wouldn't it be a horse on th' force for him to go around murderin' people, an' leave his weapons lyin' round promiscuous-like, so's we'd be sure to find what we thought was his prints, only to discover they'd been made by a gunman who'd been burnt a month or more before?"

"*Tiens*, my friend, your supposition has at least the foundation of reason beneath it," de Grandin conceded. "Do you make search for one who might have done the thing you suspect. Me, I have certain searching of my own to do. Anon we shall confer, and together we shall surely lay this so vile miscreant by the heels."

"AH, BUT it has been a lovely day," he assured me with twinkling eyes as he contemplated the glowing end of his cigar that evening after dinner. "Yes, *pardieu*, an exceedingly lovely day! This morning when I went from that Monsieur Donally's shop my head whirled like that of an unaccustomed voyager stricken by seasickness. Only miserable uncertainty confronted me on every side. Now"—he blew a cone of fragrant smoke from his lips and watched it spiral slowly toward the ceiling—"now I know much, and that I do not actually know I damn surmise. I think I see the end of this so tortuous trail, Friend Trowbridge."

"How's that?" I encouraged, watching him from the corners of my eyes.

"How? *Cordieu*, I shall tell you! When Friend Costello told us of the murder of Monsieur Wolkof—that second murder which was made to appear suicide—and mentioned he met death at the Rangers' Club, I suddenly recalled that Colonel Evans, whose death we had so recently deplored, was also a member of that club. It struck me at the time there might be something more than mere coincidence in it; but when that pitiful Monsieur Clark also proved to be a member, *nom d'un asperge*, coincidence ceased to be coincidence and became moral certainty.

"'Now,' I ask me, 'what lies behind this business of the monkey? Is it not strange two members of the Rangers' Club should have been slain so near together, and in such similar circumstances, and a third should have been visited with a calamity worse than death?'

"'You have said it, *mon garçon*,' I tell me. 'It is indubitably as you say. Come, let us interview the steward of that club, and see what he shall say.'

"*Nom d'un pipe*, what did he not tell? From him I learn much more than he said. I learn, by example, that Messieurs Evans, Wolkof and Clark had long been friends; that they had all been members of the club's grievance committee; that they were called on some five years ago to recommend expulsion of a Monsieur Wallagin—*mon Dieu,* what a name!

'"So far, so fine,' I tell me, 'But what of this Monsieur-with-the-Funny-Name? Who and what is he, and what has he done to be flung out of the club?'

"I made careful inquiry and found much. He has been an explorer of considerable note and has written some monographs which showed he understood the use of his eyes. *Hélas,* he knew also how to use wits, as many of his fellow members learned to their sorrow when they played cards with him. Furthermore, he had a most unpleasant stock of stories which he gloried to tell—stories of his doings in the far places which did not recommend him to the company of self- respecting gentlemen. And so he was removed from the club's rolls, and vowed he would get level with Messieurs Evans, Clark and Wolkof if it took him fifty years to do so.

"Five years have passed since then, and Monsieur Wallagin seems to have prospered exceedingly. He has a large house in the suburbs where no one but himself and one servant—always a Chinese—lives, but the neighbors tell strange stories of the parties he holds, parties at which pretty ladies in strange attire appear, and once or twice strange-looking men as well.

"Eh *bien,* why should this rouse my suspicions? I do not know, unless it be that my nose scents the odor of the rodent farther than the average. At any rate, out to the house of Monsieur Wallagin I go, and at its gate I wait like a tramp in the hope of charity.

"My vigil is not unrewarded. But no. Before I have stood there an hour I behold one forcibly ejected from the house by a gross person who reminds me most unpleasantly of a pig. It is a small and elderly Chinese man, and he has suffered greatly in his *amour propre.* I join him in his walk to town, and sympathize with him in his misfortune.

"My friend"—his earnestness seemed out of all proportion to the simple statement—"he had been forcibly dismissed for putting salt in the food which he cooked for Monsieur Wallagin's guests."

"For salting their food?" I asked. "Why—"

"One wonders why, indeed, Friend Trowbridge. Consider, if you please. Monsieur Wallagin has several guests, and feeds them thin gruel made of wheat or barley, and bread in which no salt is used. Nothing more. He personally tastes of it before it is presented to them, that he may make sure it is unsalted."

"Perhaps they're on some sort of special diet," I hazarded as he waited for my comment. "They're not obliged to stay and eat unseasoned food, are they?"

"I do not know," he answered soberly. "I greatly fear they are, but we shall know before so very long. If what I damn suspect is true we shall see devilment beside which the worst produced by ancient Rome was mild. If I am wrong— *alors*, it is that I am wrong. I think I hear the good Costello coming; let us go with him."

Evening had brought little surcease from the heat, and perspiration streamed down Costello's face and mine as we drove toward Morrisdale, but de Grandin seemed in a chili of excitement, his little round blue eyes were alight with dancing elf-fires, his small white teeth fairly chattering with nervous excitation as he leant across the back of the seat, urging me to greater speed.

The house near which we parked was a massive stone affair, standing back from the road in a jungle of greenery, and seemed to me principally remarkable for the fact that it had neither front nor rear porches, but rose sheer-walled as a prison from its foundations.

Led by the Frenchman we made cautious way to the house, creeping.to the only window showing a gleam of light and fastening our eyes to the narrow crack beneath its not-quite-drawn blind.

"Monsieur Wallagin acquired a new cook this afternoon," de Grandin whispered. "I made it my especial business to see him and bribe him heavily to smuggle a tiny bit of beef into the soup he prepares for tonight. If he has been faithful in his treachery we may see something, if not— *pah*, my friends, what is it we have here?"

We looked into a room which must have been several degrees hotter than the stoke-hole of a steamer, for the window was shut tightly and a great log fire blazed on the wide hearth of the fireplace almost opposite our point of vantage. Its walls were smooth-dressed stone, the floor was paved with tile. Lolling on a sort of divan made of heaped-up cushions sat the master of the house, a monstrous bulk of a man with enormous paunch, great fat-upholstered shoulders between which perched a hairless head like an owl's in its feathers, and eyes as cold and gray as twin inlays of burnished agate.

About his shoulders draped a robe of Paisley pattern, belted at the loins but open to the waist, displaying his obese abdomen as he squatted like an evil parody of Mi-lei-Fo, China's Laughing Buddha.

As we fixed our eyes to the gap under the curtain he beat his hands together, and as at a signal the door at the room's farther end swung open to admit a file of women. All three were young and comely, and each a perfect foil for the others. First came a tall and statuesque brunette with flowing unbound black hair, sharp hewn patrician features and a majesty of carriage like a youthful queen's. The second was a petite blonde, fairylike in form and elfin in face, and behind her was a red-haired girl, plumply rounded as a little pullet. Last of all there came an undersized, stoop-shouldered man who bore what seemed an earthen vessel like a New England bean-pot and two short lengths of willow sticks.

"Jeeze!" breathed Costello. "Lookit him, Dr. de Grandin; 'tis Gyp Carson himself!"

"Silence!" the Frenchman whispered fiercely. "Observe, my friends; did I not say we should see something? *Regardez-vous!*"

At a signal from the seated man the women ranged themselves before him, arms uplifted, heads bent submissively, and the undersized man dropped down tailor-fashion in a comer of the room, nursing the clay pot between his crossed knees and poising his sticks over it.

The obese master of the revels struck his hands together again, and at their impact the man on the floor began to beat a rataplan upon his crock.

The women started a slow rigadoon, sliding their bare feet sidewise, stopping to stamp out a grotesque rhythm, then pirouetting languidly and taking up the sliding, sidling step again. Their arms were stretched straight out, as if they had been crucified against the air, and as they danced they shook and twitched their shoulders with a motion reminiscent of the shimmy of the early 1920s. Each wore a shift of silken netlike fabric that covered her from shoulder to instep, sleeveless and unbelted, and as they danced the garments clung in rippling, half-revealing, half- concealing folds about them.

They moved with a peculiar lack of verve, like marionettes actuated by unseen strings, sleep-walkers, or persons in hypnosis; only the drummer seemed to take an interest in his task. His hands shook as he plied his drumsticks, his shoulders jerked and twitched and writhed hysterically, and though his eyes were closed and his face masklike, it seemed instinct with avid longing, with prurient expectancy.

"*Les aisselles*—their axillae, Friend Trowbridge, observe them with care, if you please!" de Grandin breathed in my ear.

Sudden recognition came to me. With the raising of their hands in the performance of the dance the women exposed their armpits, and under each left arm I saw the mark of a deep wound, bloodless despite its depth, and closed with the familiar "baseball stitch."

No surgeon leaves a wound like that; it was the mark of the embalmer's bistoury made in cutting through the superficial tissue to raise the axillary artery for his injection.

"Good God!" I choked. The languidness of their movements ... their pallor ... their closed eyes ... their fixed, unsmiling faces ... now the unmistakable stigmata of embalmment! These were no living women, they were—"

De Grandin's fingers clutched my elbow fiercely. "Observe, my friend," he ordered softly. "Now we shall see if my plan carried or miscarried."

Shuffling into the room, as unconcerned as if he served coffee after a formal meal, came a Chinese bearing a tray on which were four small soup bowls and a plate of dry bread. He set the tray on the floor before the fat man and turned away, paying no attention to the dancing figures and the drummer squatting in the corner.

An indolent motion of the master's hand and the slaves fell on their provender like famished beasts at feeding time, drinking greedily from the coarse china bowls, wolfing the unbuttered bread almost unchewed.

Such a look of dawning realization as spread over the four countenances as they drained the broth I have seen sometimes when half-conscious patients were revived with powerful restoratives. The man was first to show it, surging from his crouching position and turning his closed eyes this way and that, like a caged thing seeking escape from its prison. But before he could do more than wheel drunkenly in his tracks realization seemed to strike the women, too. There was a swirl of fluttering draperies, the soft thud of soft feet on the tiled floor of the room, and all rushed pell-mell to the door.

The sharp clutch of de Grandin's hand roused me. "Quick, Friend Trowbridge," he commanded. "To the cemetery; to the cemetery with all haste! *Nom d'un sale chameau*, we have yet to see the end of this!"

"Which cemetery?" I asked as we stumbled toward my parked car.

"*N'importe*," he returned. "At Shadow Lawn or Mount Olivet we shall see that which will make us call ourselves three shameless liars!" Mount Olivet was nearest of the three municipalities of the dead adjacent to Harrisonville, and toward it we made top speed. The driveway gates had closed at sunset, but the small gates each side the main entrance were still unlatched, and we raced through them and to the humble tomb we had seen violated that morning.

"Say, Dr. de Grandin," panted Costello as he strove to keep pace with the agile tittle Frenchman, "just what's th' big idea? I know ye've some good reason, but—"

"Take cover!" interrupted the other. "Behold, my friends, he comes!"

Shuffling drunkenly, stumbling over mounded tops of sodded graves, a slouching figure came careening toward us, veered off as it neared the Carson grave and dropped to its knees beside it. A moment later it was scrabbling at the clay and gravel which had been disturbed by the grave-diggers that morning, seeking desperately to burrow its way into the sepulcher.

"Me God!" Costello breathed as he rose unsteadily. I could see the tiny globules of fear- sweat standing on his forehead, but his inbred sense of duty overmastered his fright. "Gyp Carson, I arrest you—" he laid a hand on the burrowing creature's shoulder, and it was as if he touched a soap bubble. There was a frightened mouse-like squeak, then a despairing groan, and the figure under his hand collapsed in a crumpled heap. When de Grandin and I reached them the pale, drawn face of a corpse grinned at us sardonically in the beam of Costello's flashlight.

"Dr.—de—Grandin, Dr.—Trowbridge—for th' love o' God give me a drink o' sumpin!" begged the big Irishman, clutching the diminutive Frenchman's shoulder as a frightened child might clutch its mother's skirts.

"Courage, my old one," de Grandin patted the detective's hand, "we have work before us tonight, remember. Tomorrow they will bury this poor one. The law has had its will of him; now let his body rest in peace. Tonight—*sacré nom*, the dead must tend the dead; it is with the living we have business. *En avant*; to Wallagin's, Friend Trowbridge!"

"Your solution of the case was sane," he told Costello as we set out for the house we'd left a little while before, "but there are times when very sanity proves the falseness of a conclusion. That someone had unearthed the body of Gyp Carson to copy his fingerprints seemed most reasonable, but today I obtained information which led me up another road. A most unpleasant road, *parbleu!* I have already told you something of the history of the Wallagin person; how he was dismissed from the Rangers' Club, and how he vowed a horrid vengeance on those voting his expulsion. That was of interest. I sought still further. I found that he resided long in Haiti, and that there he mingled with the *Culte des Morts*. We laugh at such things here, but in Haiti, that dark stepdaughter of mysterious Africa's dark mysteries, they are no laughing matter. No. In Port-au-Prince and in the backlands of the jungle they will tell you of the *zombie*—who is neither ghost nor yet a living person resurrected, but only the spiritless corpse ravished from its grave, endowed with pseudo-life by black magic and made to serve the whim of the magician who has animated it. Sometimes wicked persons steal a corpse to make it commit crime while they stay far from the scene, thus furnishing themselves unbreakable alibis. More often they rob graves to secure slaves who labor ceaselessly for them at no wages at all. Yes, it is so; with my own eyes I have seen it.

"But there are certain limits which no sorcery can transcend. The poor dead *zombie* must be fed, for if he is not he cannot serve his so execrable master. But he must be fed only certain things. If he taste salt or meat, though but the tiniest *soupçon* of either be concealed in a great quantity of food, he at once realizes he is dead, and goes back to his grave, nor can the strongest magic of his owner stay him from returning for one little second. Furthermore, when he goes back he is dead forever after. He cannot be raised from the grave a second time, for Death which has been cheated for so long asserts itself, and the putrefaction which was stayed during the *zombie*'s period of servitude takes place all quickly, so the *zombie* dead six months, if it returns to its grave and so much as touches its hand to the earth, becomes at once like any other six-months-dead corpse—amass of putrescence pleasant neither to the eye nor nose, but preferable to the dead-alive thing it was a moment before.

"Consider then: the steward of the Rangers' Club related dreadful tales this Monsieur Wallagin had told all boastfully—how he had learned to be a *zombie*-maker, a corpse-master, in Haiti; how the mysteries of *Papa Nebo*, *Gouédé Mazacca* and *Gouédé Oussou*, those dread oracles of the dead, were opened books to him.

"'Ah-ha, Monsieur Wallagin,' I say, 'I damn suspect you have been up to business of the monkey here in this so pleasant State of New Jersey. You have, it seems, brought here the mysteries of Haiti, and with them you wreak vengeance on those you hate, *n'est-ce pas*?'

"Thereafter I go to his house, meet the little, discharged Chinese man, and talk with him. For why was he discharged with violence? Because, by blue, *he had put salt in the soup of the guests whom Monsieur Wallagin entertains.*

"'Four guests he has, you say?' I remark. 'I had not heard he had so many.'

"'*Nom d'un nom*, yes,' the excellent *Chinois* tells me. 'There are one man and three so lovely women in that house, and all seem walking in their sleep. At night he has the women dance while the man makes music with the drum. Sometimes he sends the man out, but what to do I do not know. At night, also, he feeds them bread and soup with neither salt nor meat, food not fit for a mangy dog to lap.'

"'Oh, excellent old man of China, oh, paragon of all Celestials,' I reply, 'behold, I give you money. Now, come with me and we shall hire another cook for your late master, and we shall bribe him well to smuggle meat into the soup he makes for those strange guests. Salt the monster might detect when he tastes the soup before it are served, but a little, tiny bit of beef-meat, *non*. Nevertheless, it will serve excellently for my purposes.'

"*Voila*, my friends, there is the explanation of tonight's so dreadful scenes."

"But what are we to do?" I asked. "You can't arrest this Wallagin. No court on earth would try him on such charges as you make."

"Do you believe it, Friend Costello?" de Grandin asked the detective.

"Sure, I do, sir. Ain't I seen it with me own two eyes?"

"And what should be this one's punishment?"

"Och, Dr. de Grandin, are you kiddin'? What would we do if we saw a poison snake on th' sidewalk, an' us with a jolly bit o' blackthorn in our hands?"

"*Précisément*, I think we understand each other perfectly, mon *vieux*." He thrust his slender, womanishly small hand out and lost it in the depths of the detective's great fist.

"Would you be good enough to wait us here, Friend Trowbridge?" he asked as we came to a halt before the house. "There is a trifle of unfinished business to attend to and—the night is fine, the view exquisite. I think that you would greatly enjoy it for a little while, my old and rare."

It might have been a quarter-hour later when they rejoined me. "What—" I began, but the perfectly expressionless expression on de Grandin's face arrested my question.

"*Hélas*, my friend, it was unfortunate," he told me. "The good Costello was about to arrest him, and he turned to flee. Straight up the long, steep stairs he fled, and at the topmost one, *parbleu*, he missed his footing and came tumbling down! I greatly fear—indeed, I know—his neck was broken in the fall. It is not so, *mon sergent*?" he turned to Costello for confirmation. "Did he not fall downstairs?"

"That he did, sir. Twice. Th' first time didn't quite finish him."

Dead Girl Finotte

By H. De Vere Stacpoole

IF, SAID AMAYAT, you have read Mr. Seabrook's book on Haiti, *The Magic Island*, recently published, you must have been struck by the chapter entitled "Dead Men Working in the Cane Fields."

Talking recently on this matter to M. de Travers, the neurologist of Geneva, American born and with a large experience of the West Indies and of the negro mind, he said: "Why not?"

"Because," said I, "it's impossible. It would be easier to make one of Karel Capek's Robots than to take a dead man and put motive power into him and turn him into a slave. You know yourself the post-mortem changes that take place in the tissues of the body; even magic has limits and—"

"A moment," he said. "I mentioned Mr. Seabrook's book as confirmation of the story I had to tell you, and perhaps you will suspend judgment on the whole matter till I have finished.' Then M. Amayat told me de Travers's story, which I give in my own words.

MANY YEARS ago when quite a young man I lived at St. Pierre, Martinique.

St. Pierrc, now a mound of ashes, stood quite alone amongst the towns of the world, there was no other place like it; gay as Paris with a touch of New Orleans; yellow-tinted and palm-topped against the burning blue of the sky, its old French houses looked down upon a bay of sapphire rarely stirred by the great winds and heavy seas that torment the north-eastern side of the island.

I lived in the Rue Victor Hugo, a street that traversed the whole length of the town, and I had only to step on to my balcony to look down on a crowd more astonishing than any dream of the Arabian Nights. Nearly all coloured, of all tints from the octoroon to the chabine, the women gay as tropical birds; idlers, loungers, chatterers, street singers, itinerant sellers of fruit, fish, pastry and heaven knows what, a moving market; a business scene—touched with the charm of the unreal.

I had three rooms all on the same floor, and for personal servant, Baidaux, a young man, a Creole, handsome, dark-eyed, serious and entirely devoted to me; he bought everything and I was never robbed and always sure of the finest mangoes, sapotas and avocats in the market; his coffee was the best in Martinique and he was always there when wanted—except on Sundays. It seems he had a girl, she lived away over beyond Morne Rouge towards Grande Anse, a town on the seaboard to the north-east and twenty miles from St. Pierre; her name was Finotte, and every Sunday he would vanish before dawn, taking his way on foot by the great national road *La Trace*, which, winding like a ribbon over hill and dale by morne and mountain, cocoa plantation and canefield, took him to Finotte.

But always on Monday morning at eight o'clock he would be in my room. pulling up my blind and handing me my morning coffee.

"Bonjou, M'sieur."

"Bonjour, Baidaux—and how is Finotte?"

I dreaded Finotte and the day surely to come when marriage would join them and separate me from Baidaux.

Life has many losses, not the least is the loss of a good servant, but Baidaux was not of the precipitate sort, he was laying by and building his nest as a bird might build, only with francs instead of sticks and feathers. I judged from what he said that it would be at least a year before the happy and unhappy day for me, when Finotte would come to St. Pierre to take her place in that little shop in the Rue du Morne Mirail which he had marked down as their future home.

Ah, well! One Monday morning he did not return; on the Wednesday he returned, but it was not Baidaux, it was a much older man.

"Bonjou, M'sieur."

"Bonjour, Baidaux—and how is Finotte?"

He put up his hands without a word—then I knew she was dead or lost to him.

He made the coffee as usual and put out my clothes.

Yes, she was dead—it all came out gradually; he had arrived to find her dying—she was dead and buried. Of what had she died? He did not know. She was dead. He had seen her buried and had returned. That was all.

He went on with his work. There was nothing else to do except die, and he was not of that sort, and time passed till a month had slipped away, and the carnival came and passed with its rioting and drums, sharply cut off by Lent. Then, it might have been a month later, one evening I found him at the street door talking to an old woman, a *capresse*, very old and wrinkled, her head bound up in a foulard turban. It was Maman Robert, the mother of Finotte.

He told me that, speaking with a look in his eyes I had never seen before, a wild, far-gazing look disturbing as his manner, for he seemed like a person cut off from all reality, and he said that he must go away, leave me for a time, but that he would return soon—perhaps.

He left two days later, and though I did not follow him I knew quite well that his road was the great national road that had led him so often towards Grande Anse and the home of his girl.

Part II

YOU KNOW at St. Pierre everyone knew everyone—the washerwomen by the river Roxalanne—the fruit-sellers in the market by the fort—the old women selling carossoles at the street corners—they were like a big family as far as rumour was concerned; a story started at dawn in the Rue du Morne Mirail would travel down to the Rue Victor Hugo by noon and be on the front by night, and you may be sure that the story of Baidaux wasn't slow in travelling; but no repercussion of it came back to me till one day a *porteuse* in from the hills stopped to speak to my old landlady, Maman Jean, and gave her word of Baidaux.

I must tell you a *porteuse* is—alas!—was—a sort of girl commercial traveller; barefooted and with a great bundle on her head she would take goods from the city all over the island through the country parts, and this girl just in from the north-east had seen Baidaux near Grande Anse. He was looking very wild, living on the plantation of a Creole named Jean Labat, and—it was a pity.

Those were her words.

Yes, it was a pity, a thousand pities when I remembered him as he had been, so bright, intelligent, well-groomed and efficient, and he had been fond of me.

The fondness of a good servant for his master, and conversely, is a thing apart from all other forms of attachment, and those four words of the *porteuse* seemed somehow intended for me, as one might say "Can you do nothing for him?"

I took them to heart and determined to go over to Grande Anse, hunt about, try to find him and if possible bring him back to himself and my service. I started next day, taking with me a bag with a few things and hiring a two-horse trap.

Part III

IT WAS only twenty miles from St. Pierre to Grande Anse —all the same a long journey, for the great national road winds over hill and dale, and it is squealing brakes and labouring horses a good part of the way; but no road in the world is just like that for scenery; the purple mornes and blue distances, the fields of cane and the high woods of balissier and palm and mahogany all lie beneath a blinding light that has got in it something of the mournful nature of darkness.

Here, indeed, to the European mind is a land of things unknown, half known and dimly suspected, for under this riot of colour and light lies the poison of the manchineel apple and the centipede and the fer-de-lance, the poison of plants dealing in death, delirium or madness and old superstitions from the shores of far-off Africa transplanted but growing firmly.

Grande Anse is a little town lying right on the coast; here there are great cliffs hundreds of feet in heights and the beach is of black sand and nearly always alive with a thunderous surf. The cliffs form two promontories, the Pointe du Rochet and the Pointe de Croche Mort. Such is Grande Anse, and I put up at the chief inn of the town, and later that day began to make inquiries about Baidaux.

No one knew of him.

He was interesting to St. Pierre folk because he had been born there, but here he was of no interest. Then I asked about Maman Robert, the mother of Finotte.

Ah, yes, Finotte, she who had died some time ago. Well, she and her mother had lived in the little hamlet of Mirail close to the plantation of Jean Labat. The mother lived there still. Then came silence, and the cause of it was Labat, whose plantation lay near the village. He was both disliked and feared. I could tell that at once by the faces and the shrugs and the drawing back as if from the very name. He grew cocoa and sugar and had a distillery—*rhummerie*—but people did not visit that plantation.

Would anyone lead me to the house of Finotte's mother? No, it was close to the plantation and Jean Labat had dogs.

I might have started out myself despite the dogs and made an attempt to find the place myself, feeling sure that Finotte's mother would be able to put me on the traces of Baidaux—but things turned out differently.

Part IV

IT WAS the second evening of my stay at Grande Anse, and I had gone for a walk on the black sands to watch the waves coming in under the last of the sunset, then, turning at dark, I began to climb the stiff path that leads up from the beach along the side of the great swell of ground that forms the side of the Pointe du Rochet.

The night was moonless, but alight with stars, and it was my idea to reach the top of the bluff, have a look at the starlit world from there and then return to Grande Anse by the track the goats have trodden out in the basalt. The lights had gone out in the little town, where everybody turns in at dark, but I was sure of the inn being open.

More than halfway up I paused. On the skyline just above I saw two men. A man of vast stature and a man of ordinary size, they were walking in single file, and the latter was leading. Then they stopped. I thought they had seen me, but that was not so. They stopped only for a moment, and then the smaller man pointed straight ahead, that is to say, where the bluff ended at the cliff edge and a fall of four hundred feet sheer with nothing but the waves below.

At the pointing the tall man went straight ahead in the direction indicated; but I had never seen a man walk like that before, the way he raised his feet, the way he held himself; why, he seemed a mechanical figure, not a man, a thing wound up to go, not a thing going of its own volition.

He kept on till he reached the cliff edge, but he did not stop, he stepped over, and in an instant there was nothing but the night, the stars and the roar of the sea—and the other man. The other man was Baidaux. I could see that now as he came closer along the skyline. He came to the cliff edge and looked down, then he stood with arms folded looking at the sea.

I had found him—but, heavens, what was all this?

I am a nervous man by nature, but still I have courage if the cause is good or if a certain thing has to be done.

I had to find out about this, and I continued climbing till I reached the top of the bluff just as he was turning from the sea and coming back towards me.

He did not stop on seeing me, he seemed quite indifferent to this new person the night had sprung on him. Close up he recognized me.

"Baidaux," I said, "what is this?"

He stood for a moment without speaking, then he heaved a great sigh as though awakened from sleep. "It is I, Baidaux," said he; "you have seen him. And it is right that you should know about him and about me."

He was no longer a servant or an ex-servant, just a being level in station with me, but with a feeling from the past that it was right that I should know his affairs. He who had told me of his girl and his plans for the future had now to tell me what had happened to him, culminating in the amazing tragedy of a few moments ago.

He led the way down the slope by way of the goat track, and then in the shelter from the wind and by a great clump of tree ferns he sat down on the ground, still warm from the vanished sun, and motioned me to his side.

"In St. Pierre," said he, "you were good to me, and I opened my heart, telling you of my affairs and of my girl; you remember on the Sundays I used to come over here, starting before the light of day and whilst the *Cabri-bois* still filled the woods with sound. Then the day came when I found my girl dying. Maman Robert, her mother, could not say what ailed her, and Maman Fally, who is the doctor for all the workers round these parts, said she had been seized with a fever from the woods. No matter, she died— but you will remember all this; I only say it to keep my mind from travelling astray as one might follow a string in the dark, for the things I have to tell belong indeed to the darkness that is deeper than night.

"I came back to you and life went on. I had no need of it, but I could not cast it away; it is not easy for a man to lose the habit of living even after it has become an evil habit to him.

"I went on as one dead might go on with his work, could he be moved by some spirit of life.

"Then one evening Cyrilla, who was the girl of the landlady where your rooms were, came to me and said:

"'There is one who wishes to speak to you, Baidaux.'

"I went to the door, and there I found the mother of my girl, Maman Robert.

"I said to her, 'What do you want?' and she said, 'I have come to speak to you about Finotte.'

"I said, 'What then about Finotte?' thinking the old woman had come to me for money, as is the way with relatives of those one loves, but I had done her a wrong.

"She answered, 'I have come to you from Finotte—and I would bring you to her,' and as she spoke the flesh crawled on my bones, for I had seen Finotte buried in the place where the people are buried by the palmiste grove near her home—where of a Sunday we used sometimes to go to look on the graves of the dead and say to ourselves, 'Without doubt some day we will be here,' for I never, had the fancy to be buried at St. Pierre.

"I listened to what the old woman said, and I could say nothing to her in reply, till my lips moved and they said, 'Very well—but not now—leave me and I will, come.'

"You remember, I did not leave you at once after that old woman had been. In fact I was afraid. I said to myself, maybe that old woman is not a woman but a Zombie come to betray me and steal my soul. I knew her well—how should one not know the mother of one's girl—but a man's mind is strange and full of fear in the dark and in the unknown.

"Then I put all that by and said to myself, 'I will go.'

"I had always set out on foot on my journeys to Finotte, and before dawn, so as to get there in the early day. I could have taken the stage to Morne Rouge and got a horse from there, but I would go as I had always gone, on foot, so I went past Morne Rouge and the old Galebasse road, past Ajoupa-Bouillon, past the Riviere Falaise, pausing only to rest for a moment by the great gommier that marks where the path to the village of Mirail strikes off from the road.

"Here I stayed an hour, resting in the shade, so that it was past noon when, taking the path, I sought the little house of Maman Robert.

"It lies by the cocoa-fields, and a great wood of balissiers shelters it from the trade wind; you can hear like the voice in the shell the sea on the beach of Grande Anse, and now and then from the wood the call of the siffleur de Montagne.

"Beyond the cocoa-fields lies the *rhummerie*, and beyond that the house of Jean Labat. It is all only two kilometres from here where I sit talking to you now, and the graveyard where the people are buried lies only half a kilometre from the house of Maman Robert.

"I found her in the house, but she would say nothing of the business I had come on—only this, 'I will take you after dark.'

Part V

"And then it happened. The moon had risen, and leading me by the shadows of the trees she crossed a cultivated field to the barren part where the wild canes and sword- grass grow.

"Here she paused, where before us lay a field preparing for cultivation of manioc, and lifting up a finger she said, 'Listen.'

"I heard nothing—nothing but the canes talking to the wind and the voice of the sea very far away.

"Again she said, 'Listen!' yet I heard nothing but the cry of a night bird, far beyond the manioc-field.

"Then the clink of iron, and they came round the bend of the cane clump, breaking the earth with their hoes, followed at a little distance by a boy with a goad as oxen are followed by their driver.

"Four figures in the moonlight. Three men and a girl, walking not as men walk, working as the spindles in the cotton mill, without sense of mind, followed by the boy their driver—and the girl was Finotte, whom I had seen buried, and the tallest of the men was Jaquin, who had died six months before, and I was looking at them and I went not mad.

"For I knew. I, Baidaux, am not an ignorant man, and I knew of the *culte* which is brother to the Culte des Morts. Look you, they give a man a drink that brings the fever, he dies, he is buried; but he is not dead, he only sleeps without breathing; his people mourn him and bury him and leave him in the grave. Then come the wicked ones and dig him up; he breathes again and lives, yet he is not truly alive like you and me, for his mind has left him, for the drug has killed his brain. He can hear and obey but he cannot think, so he can hew wood and draw water and hoe the fields and cut the cane without thought, without word, without pay—except a handful of food.

"Ah! Jean Labat, it was an evil day for you when you took the girl of Baidaux for your slave—but it is finished.

"'Come,' I said to the old woman who was holding to me and pointing, 'our place is not here, lead me to the house of Maman Fally, the woman who deals in herbs and who helped to lay out your daughter who was once my girl.'

"I knew, for my mind had taken the sight of a vulture.

"At the little house where the evil woman lived I knocked and she opened, and with my knife point at her throat she told all.

"'Come,' I said, 'the drug, the drug, I have need of the drug, prepare it or die.' She had it ready prepared and she gave it to me. 'If this fails I will return and kill you,' said. 'It will not fail,' she replied, and I knew she spoke the truth, and I killed her with a thrust of the knife and was caught up in a flame that carried me to the house of Jean Labat, where he lived alone with his wickedness.

"I beat on his door, and he opened it and I drove him with my knife into a room. He was a big man, but I was a legion; he was a coward because he was wicked.

"I made him lie upon the floor. He chose the drug rather than instant death, and he could not return it, for my knife was at his throat. The fever came on before daybreak, and I sat with him to nurse him till the man came who looked after the cooking and house-tending; then I left him, and calling all the hands of the plantation I spoke to them of their wickedness, and they fled, so that there was nothing left but the crowing of cocks and the clapping of doors to the wind and the creeping of the great centipedes that live among the walls of the *rhummerie*, and the three dead men and the girl in the shed where they rested when not at work, and me, me, Baidaux and Labat.

"I had thought to play with him and torment him and make him my slave—but you cannot play with a machine. Tonight I made him drown in the sea. He was no other use."

"And the three dead men and the girl?" I asked.

Baidaux laughed, and rose up and walked away without a word of good-bye, and though he had not replied to my question, I knew that they were no longer working on that plantation.

I watched him away down the goat track, and then passing beyond the trees at the rise of the bluff.

I never saw him again.

Salt Is Not for Slaves

By G. W. Hutter

SEVERAL TIMES before I had noticed the old woman. She always squatted on her low stool as far as possible from the other servants, as if her age did not separate her enough from the young, rollicking blacks. Her years were impossible to reckon. She seemed as old as the island; and a definite, tangible part of it. Haiti's mountains and valleys appeared impressed on her face; and the darkness and mystery of history mirrored in her eyes; eyes which were startling in their strength and intensity; eyes which suggested timelessness more than anything I had ever seen—animate or inanimate. They were incredible in her stooped, bent old body.

She sat immovable save for the quick motions of her long, bony fingers as she sliced pineapples or plucked doves and guineas for the hotel dinner. Her hands worked automatically—she did not need her eyes, which were staring ceaselessly up to the heights of the dark green mountains in the distance.

As I gazed out of my glassless window, waiting for the tropic sun to drop low enough to permit the evening plunge in the concrete 'basin' in the rear garden, I heard a commotion and a violent outburst of Creole. 'Tit Jean, terror-stricken, was scrambling away from the old woman as fast as his little legs could carry him. On the ground by the old woman's stool lay several empty salt cellars, their contents strewn over the grass.

Madame appeared just as the old woman was overtaking the cause of her fury. 'Marie!' she shouted imperatively. The old woman turned, slunk back to her stool, picked it up and resumed her work at the end of the garden.

'Tit Jean was sobbing at the foot of the stairs when I descended in my bathrobe. I asked him the trouble.

"Marie, *pas bonne*," he declared.

When I asked him why Marie was no good, he told me in Creole, broken by sobs, that when he accidentally tripped in passing her stool, she had tried to kill him because a little salt had fallen on her. Yes, that was everything he had done. Her rage was as inexplicable to me as it had been to him, and I gave him the only comfort I knew a five centime piece. This seemed to make his world rosy once more.

He smiled, motioned me to come behind the door and then, in a voice so low that I was forced to bend my head to his level, he whispered, "Voodoo!"

He nodded his head meaningfully towards the garden. When I laughed, terror leaped into his round eyes. I had heard many stories of Voodoo in Haiti, but I could not connect the trivial incident of a small boy accidentally spilling a bit of table salt with any of them. 'Tit Jean, however, was silent. He would say no more. Voodoo was too real and serious a matter with him to be discussed laughingly with a white man.

I walked past the old woman. She looked through me as if I did not exist.

I entered the small boarded enclosure of the "basin", stripped off the bathrobe; and the heat of the day was soon forgotten in the invigorating buoyancy of dear mountain water.

As I walked, dripping wet, by the uplifted eyes, I said, "*Bon soir.*"

"*Bon soir, Monsieur,*" she replied. Even though she hardly glanced at me as she spoke and there was little cordiality in her voice, I felt encouraged. At least she was approachable and I might draw her into conversation.

I was still thinking of her after I had dressed and was seated at dinner. 'Tit Jean was not himself as he served me. He could hardly wait for me to empty the spoon of guava jelly on my guinea; he was in such a hurry to leave the single table I occupied in the corner of the porch. The whites of his eyes showed plainly as I smiled at his uneasiness to be away from me and serve the other guests—they would not ask cynical questions about Voodoo.

As I sipped my after-dinner coffee, I glanced up at the black mountains. I imagined I heard the beat of a tom-tom and I remembered old Marie's gaze directed up to these mountains—seeing all and seeing nothing. 'Tit Jean saw me as I looked at the distant hills, and remained in a corner until I had left the table.

A squawk of a loudspeaker drew me into the large park spreading out before the hotel. A radio concert was being given from the local station and the town had assembled before an enormous receiving set placed in the bandstand. The chatter of Creole was completely stilled by the strains of "Bye, Bye, Blackbird," and the native favourite, "Yes, Sir, That's my Baby."

Standing in a group, their faces beaming with delight, were the servants from the hotel. They were all there, I noticed, except old Marie. Now was a good chance to see the old woman, I thought. Obviously the servants' work was done for the night and I could catch her alone in the garden. I left the spellbound crowd in the park and paused on my way back to the hotel in a cafe to buy a large bag of tobacco.

Marie was sitting on her stool as I had hoped. Casually I strolled around the garden and stopped beside her.

"Would you care for some tobacco?" I asked in French. She reached her bony hand for the bag. "*Oui, Monsieur*. You are very kind."

She began to fill the large calabash pipe which had stuck from her apron pocket. I continued my stroll for a few minutes and then sat down on the outside rim of the 'basin' a few yards from her stool.

She was again staring straight ahead at the mountains.

I lit a cigarette and we both smoked silently. A second cigarette—still another, but not a word from her. She remained motionless—staring.

"You like to look at the hills, Marie?" I began awkwardly.

Without turning she said, "No, *Monsieur* "

"Then why do you stare at them?" I was determined to get some returns from my tobacco.

She took three long puffs before she replied very slowly, "It is because I cannot help but stare at my life. That large mountain is my life. It began at the topmost point and it ends at the bottom. From this seat I can see everything by casting my eyes to the top; and today, *Monsieur*, I have not raised them very high."

"You were born on the mountain?" I prodded her.

"That I do not know"—but many years I spent there as a girl. My master's villa was the only one there. That, also, was many years ago.

"My master was rich and powerful and had many slaves. They say he chose the site for his villa because it was the highest point in all Haiti, and from the door of his home he could look down on his lands extending from Port-au- Prince up to the Cape. His lands were so many that he needed hundreds of slaves to till them and gather in the crops. In some years his coffee alone required a fleet of ships to carry it to France. But he had no mercy for his slaves. He drove them hard, and when they could endure it no more they dropped from exhaustion. Then he sent them up to the slave quarters at the villa just like broken-down horses to be patched up for work again.

"I was always there. I was a house servant. When I grew old-.enough I loved Tresaint. Tresaint was a big, strong, young man, whom his master trusted. He, like me, was there always, and the master made him the overseer of the other slaves. When business called the master away, Tresaint was left in charge of everything. The key to the salt even was left with him."

"The salt?" I asked wonderingly.

"Yes, the salt. Years before—almost the first thing I remember—the master called us before him, the six men and me, and gave his command about the salt. 'Slaves,' he said, 'You are to be under my roof always. There is one order you must not disobey. You shall eat no salt. You will grow strong. You will suffer no sickness; but let one grain of salt pass your lips and you die.' He looked very stern and grim as he said it, and we knew that it was true.

"We did not ask why. The master was to be obeyed, not questioned. We also knew his powers"—powers not in slaves and lands—but other and more mysterious ones he had at his command. That is why we put even the thought of salt from our minds, and grew strong and healthy. Sometimes the quarters were filled with a hundred slaves stricken with the fever of the low rice fields, or with their legs swollen the size of large burros, and all around us were dying like flies; but none of us was sick a day.

"Yes," Marie went on, "all of the men were strong, but Tresaint was the strongest of the six. When he held me in his arms I felt as if he would break every bone in my body, but I loved him for it.

"No slave in the country was as well-off as Tresaint, but he was not happy. Always the misery of the worn-out slaves oppressed him. The harsh words and treatment he dealt out to them seemed to hurt him as well. He must treat them severely when the master was around, but when he was away on one of his trips the others would know at once through Tresaint's kindly manner.

"Strange rumours came to our ears, brought by incoming slaves. They said there was a man in the north of the island around the Cape who was preaching freedom. He taught that the slaves should rise up and throw off the yoke of the French. That they were human beings—not animals—and that they themselves should rule their country. This man was a slave himself. His name was Christophe."

I gasped. Surely that couldn't have been true! Christophe became Emperor Henry of Haiti in 1804. This would make the old woman almost a hundred and fifty years old. It was impossible. Then I looked in Marie's face—a black rock in the moonlight. She seemed centuries older than anything I had ever seen before. She spoke so surely, seemed so certain of what she was saying. I was confused and undecided.

A creaking of shoes at the garden entrance, a babble of Creole and laughter, and the servants were back from the concert. When they saw Marie and me, their talking and laughter stopped. They went quietly to their rooms strewn back of the kitchen along the edge of garden.

The lights in the hotel were flicked out. Everything was quiet. Marie was puffing rhythmically at her pipe.

"And Tresaint—" I urged her on. "Was he interested in these tales of Christophe?"

"Yes, he was interested. He was too interested. That was the cause of everything." Marie spoke earnestly. "Christophe, he said, was the saviour of Haiti. France, herself, had thrown off the yoke of her kings and now Haiti should throw off the yoke of France. The black man should rule his own country. All of this Tresaint would tell me until I became worried for fear that the master would learn of his trusted overseer's burning thoughts.

"Finally there came a time when the master himself was aroused. Christophe had persuaded scores of slaves on the master's lands near the Cape to leave their fields of bondage and flee to him. This news sent the master into a mighty rage. He left the villa at once to sail to the Cape.

"Before the master's carriage had reached Port-au-Prince a great change had come over the villa. Shouts, singing and laughter filled the house. Tresaint, who had always been lenient when the master was away, now became the master himself and treated the slaves as if they were the master's guests. He opened up the wine cellar and invited them in. He did not give them the *tafia* in the tin mugs which was kept for the slaves but he rolled out a keg of the finest rum. Rum that was many years old; and he served it to them in the villa's finest glasses. They skipped and danced about and dropped ashes from the master's cigars on the marble floors.

"I was frightened but Tresaint would not listen to me. He was encouraging them into complete lawlessness. He left the slaves in the main salon. Bare feet which before had known only the feel of rocks and sod plopped delightedly across smooth marble. Soon he appeared, his huge arms hugging bottles and bottles of champagne. With a blow from a sword snatched down from the wail, he cut off the necks—the wine popping and gurgling to the floor. When every slave had a bottle Tresaint mounted the mahogany table in the hall.

"'Friends,' he shouted, 'drink to the health of your new masters—yourselves! We shall be slaves no longer. The day of freedom has come.

Drink!' He drained the upraised jagged bottle with one long draught and dashed it in a thousand pieces on the floor.

"The glass cut my feet as I ran to him.

"'Tresaint! Tresaint! Listen to me,' I begged. 'The master will kill you surely when he returns. Stop this foolish wildness before it is too late.'"

"But the idea of freedom was as strong in his head as the fumes of the liquor. He laughed at my fears and pushed me aside.

"'Women are cowards,' he announced to the cheering crowd, "but I am a man. I am no longer afraid of anybody— not even the master. Lose all fear and you shall be free. The master put fear into us from the start. You five men who have been with me here know what this key means." He held out the smallest key that dangled on the chain around his neck.

"I was terrified. I knew the key. It was to the chest that was filled with salt! What madness was he up to now?

"He saw the terror on my face and called, 'And you too, Marie! You were placed in the master's power at the same time—all by his command about the salt. We shall eat no salt. Why? Because the master forbade it and we are not to question his command. Bah!'

"He threw the key at my feet.

"'We will show the master's power is gone. Marie, fetch some salt. We will cat it and be forever free.'

"I picked up the key and stumbled out of the room, on past the closet that contained the forbidden chest. From the back gallery I dropped the key beside an orange-tree. I hoped this ruse would delay Tresaint in his madness. That in a little while he would come to his senses again when the rum and the wine wore off and would thank me for preventing him carrying out his rash deed.

"I crouched in the corner of the gallery.

"'Marie! Marie!' his voice thundered out from the house but I did not answer.

"In a few minutes he came out to where I was.

"'Where is the key?' he asked.

"I told him I did not know.

"'That doesn't matter. The chest is not so strong that I cannot open it.'

"He put his arm around me.

"'You arc too timid,' he said.

"I returned his embrace with all my strength. I tried to draw him down on a bench while I pleaded and cajoled with him to stay with me.

I pointed out the truth of the master's curse on the salt. I showed him how we had been strong and healthy always just as the master had foretold and that to disobey him would cause our death. If the master's predictions had worked one way they would work the other. But he would not hear me. I called on his love for me but all to no avail. He left me stricken dumb with terror.

"Sounds of blows on wood, a shout of triumph and Tresaint's voice floated out: 'Here, my friends, in one hand you have the salt, in the other the wine to wash the curse away.'

"A moment of silence as I shivered in the heat of midday and then more shouts. They were dancing around in the marble salon, yelling exultantly.

"How long I remained frozen to my seat I do not know, but gradually there beat into my cars a curious sound. The pattering of bare feet was all I heard; the shouts and singing had disappeared.

"Fearfully I crept into the room. Along the sides of the wall were stretched out the slaves from the quarters, stupefied by drink. In the centre were Tresaint and the five others skipping around with waving arms without uttering a sound. The marble floor was covered with jagged pieces of bottles.

"I stood in amazement looking at their bare feet. They seemed unaware of the glass, unaware of everything. Great gashes were in their feet. As he lifted his feet ceaselessly across the floor, two of Tresaint's toes dangled like broken palm leaves. The wounds had a strange unnatural appearance. There was no sign of blood.

"Horrified I looked in Tresaint's face. His eyes did not move, his nostrils and mouth gave no sign of breathing. And as I looked I saw his face set in rigidity, the flesh seemed to drop away leaving nothing but cheek bones and eyes. His ribs stood out through the torn shirt—bare.

"I screamed in horror. He was dead! They were all dead! They were corpses treading a fantastic dance of death.

"My screams awoke the drunken slaves from their stupor. Opening their eyes, without rising from the floor, they saw what I had seen. The truth was plain to them. They cried in terror at the dead dancing bodies. They scrambled to their feet and fled out of the house and down the road. The whole mountainside shook with their yells of horror as they raced away. I was left alone with these prancing shells of men.

"For some reason, I do not know what, unless it was for the love I had borne him, I was impelled to touch him who had been so close to me. I reached for his hand as he passed by in his endless mad dance.

"The fingers closed cold around my hand. The two arms pressed me against the body which stopped still. I could hear and feel my own heartbeat—nothing more. It was as if I was being enfolded by the cool marble of the villa.

"He placed a hand over my heart, then quickly on one of the other forms. He turned his unseeing eyes full from my face to the others. Then those eyes, which had been as glassy and dead as the eyes of a fish two days from the bay, mirrored such horror as the world had never seen. From the dead caverns of the throat came a cry. Half shriek and half groan of such force and terror that my blood froze.

"The others took up the cry. I was mad from horror."

Marie was living again those dead days. Her body was shaking with emotion. Her voice rose and fell reflecting all the horror of her story.

She arose from her stool, stepping fantastically in the moonlight, to show how that macabre measure was trod by the moving dead in the glass covered marble of the salon.

I was too engrossed to interrupt. She talked on:

"Those shrieks of horror meant that they knew they were dead. It was their spirits crying out—crying to be released from their dead bodies.

"My hand was still held by the lifeless fingers—fingers without blood, but with all the strength of iron bands.

"With one accord the forms rushed through the villa, bounding me along with them. Down the road they tore. My feet did not seem to touch thc ground. I felt as if I were being whisked through the air. I screamed at the top of my lungs, but so mighty were their cries that my ears never received a sound coming from my lips.

"Down, down the road we flew. A sight to strike terror into the bravest heart. For miles the screams could be heard and we met nothing on the road but deserted burros. The travellers had heard the fearful noises and the dust that the leaping spirits raised in the afternoon sun had sent them scurrying from the approaching horror, to a safe retreat from the roadside. God, *Monsieur*, it was such a sight that would strike you dead. Six dead men racing and falling down the road, dragging along a woman more gripped by fear and horror than death itself holds. Heads like death; bodies stripped of clothes, the rags fluttering behind them; skeleton ribs showing the dust of the road through their gaunt gaps; the fleshless arms raised, threshing the air; and above all the shrill, deep unearthly yells that came from still throats. On down the road!"

Marie had worked herself up into a fearful pitch of excitement. She arose from her stool.

"Like this they ran!" -And with that she threw open her dress, lifted her arms and began bounding around the garden. Her dress trailed after her as she ran, her arms clutched wildly at the air, and from her throat came a low horrible cry.

There in the moonlight I myself saw that mad race down the mountain. She was no longer an old woman of more than a hundred years, she became a deathless spirit.

I jumped to my feet, throbbing with excitement. She dashed up and caught my hand in a vise-like grip. I had become part of the mad cavalcade.

She ran on, pulling me by her side. I was the living being dragged along by death. I shuddered and wrenched my hand loose from her cold clutch.

She was too wrought up to resume her seat. She continued to move about spasmodically as she spoke:

"On down the road we came—never stopping. On, on, near the city. The other slaves had run down before us and spread the news that dead men were dancing in the master's villa. Crowds filled the roads out from the city. They had heard us coming. They wanted to see with their own eyes. As we bounded around a curve into their midst, they shouted in horror. They had not expected so terrifying a sight. Screaming they turned in their tracks and rushed down the road before us. Like a herd of wild cattle from the hills they stampeded into the city, shoving one another wildly, tripping and falling—all screaming in terror at the oncoming spectacle. Such confusion, fright and horror as no one could picture.

"On in the city we came, heralded by the crazed multitude. Old men throwing away their crutches and running lamely away. Mothers with babies clutched to their breasts, fleeing as if from death itself. The very animals in the town were overcome with terror. Droves of burros charged wildly around the Champ dc Mars; horses, deserted by their drivers, crashed their empty carriages against the palms as the crazed beasts sought to escape the tumult. Goats, dogs and fowls sensed the terror and added their voices to the bedlam of the humans. Still on, on, I was dragged. I was as powerless as a baby in that grip of death. Those long strong bones that had only a few hours before been the hand of my lover jerked me along as if I were one of the rags that fluttered behind the crazed spirits.

"My whole soul had gone out in horror. I thought there was no feeling left in me. Drained by terror as I was, I saw before me a sight that seemed to draw all the horror of the fear-stricken city into my own breast. Directly in front of me were the gates to the cemetery!

"The spirits' screams grew wilder and louder than ever. There seemed a note of triumph to the din as I was whisked through the gate.

"On over the graves we went. My mouth was open wide but no sound came. My eyes felt as if they had fallen on my cheeks; my throat as if it were being clutched by the ghosts of the countless dead as I was yanked from one grave to another.

"With one last effort I tore at the bones around my hand. It was like tearing at the marble tombstones. My eyes could see no more. They closed.

"My body swung through the air and bounded over the ground like this—" The old woman hurtled herself on the grass, turning over several times.

I rushed to her side. It was a violent jolt to an old woman of her years. But she lay there as she fell and continued talking. Spellbound I drank in every word.

"*Oui, Monsieur,* I lay like this. I do not know how long and then I noticed that the cries seemed far away—and different. They were the cries from the frightened city, not the wailing screams of the spirits. I lifted my right hand—it was free. I opened my eyes. There beside me were the bodies, perfectly still, lying peacefully on their backs all in a row. That which had once been Tresaint was nearest me. I reached out fearfully and touched the hand. It was stiff in death.

"I staggered over the graves and out through the cemetery. Some of the braver of the town people did not run when they saw me approaching. They knew that the spirits' shrieks had ceased and that I was alive. They went into the cemetery, on back into the corner where the bodies lay.

"As they lifted up the corpses they discovered a curious looseness to the earth. There were six graves under the covering of sod. Each body had lain evenly over a waiting grave. The spirits had known that, *Monsieur,* and that is why they had rushed down the mountain to set themselves at rest, to release themselves from the dead bodies. That which was Tresaint had tried to drag me to the grave with him, but when he found only the six graves he had flung me aside. There would have been seven graves in the cemetery yonder at the foot of the mountain if I had eaten of the salt.

"Ah! If Tresaint had listened to my warnings my lover would be with me now."

"But the salt, Marie?" I enquired. "By obeying the master—is that what keeps you well and strong?"

"What else could it be?" she answered earnestly. "As surely as the rains come from the sea, if I never tasted salt I should live to be as old as the mountains and as strong."

"Then you will never die?" I asked, struck by the earnestness in the old woman's voice.

"*Monsieur*, have you a match?"

Wonderingly I made a light as she ran her thin fingers over the grass near her head.

"Would you taste this for me?" She dropped a few grains of salt she had pinched between her fingers into my hand.

I made as if I tasted it. "It is salt," I said in a low voice. I was becoming strangely upset—so in sympathy with the old woman's story that I was afraid of a grain of salt.

"Yes," she said, "I thought so. That is why I have told you all this. Everyone who knew my story had died many years ago but now I wanted someone to learn it before I go."

"But you said you would never go unless you tasted—salt." I hesitated on the word. My voice was jumpy. The old woman's strange calm and cryptic remarks after her delirious running around the garden had upset me more than I cared to admit.

"Oh! but I have—this afternoon." Her voice became sharp and venomous. "That little imp of the Black One threw some in my mouth. He said he stumbled and accidentally a few grains hit my tongue—but," her voice became low again, "but what difference does it make how it happened? I have eaten and the curse is upon me. Perhaps a little more will hasten the time."

She licked her hands hungrily, then ran her tongue over the grass.

I shuddered and rose to my feet.

"Good night, Marie," I called weakly as I walked to the hotel door.

"*Adieu, Monsieur*," she answered.

I climbed the stairs to my room. Why did she say farewell instead of good night? I did not want an answer. "Don't be such a fool," I told myself, "as to be worrying over some Voodoo spell of over a hundred years ago."

I undressed and got into bed, but I could not sleep. I arose and poured a stiff drink of rum from a bottle on the washstand. With the drink and a cigarette I felt that I could get to sleep. I reached for my matches. Then I remembered I had left them in the garden. The moon had gone down and the night was inky black, but I thought I could find them by locating the stool and feeling around in the grass.

I slipped on my shoes and bathrobe, and groped my way down the back stairs. As I opened the door, I hoped that old Marie had gone to her room. The dark was thick enough to cut with a knife. I hesitated a moment to get my bearings. I did want a cigarette.

Then out straight in front where I was looking I saw a faint glow. She was still there. The glow brightened and the huge bowl of the calabash pipe took shape before my eyes. And then the face! Plainer than in the moonlight!

Great drops of perspiration rolled down my chilled forehead. I was rooted in horror. My heart pounded the roof of my mouth.

That face! The flesh melted away under my terrified gaze. Nothing was left but the grim bones of the dead.

As I watched, stricken with cold terror, old Marie fell headlong on the cool grass of the garden. I knew she was dead, and I knew how it was she had died.

The Dead Who Walk

By Ray Cummings

Chapter 1: Up from the Grave

THE FIRST of the weird incidents which marked the beginning of the terror occurred at the edge of the Sleepy Valley graveyard. It was a softly moonlit summer evening. The wooded hills, dotted with luxurious country estates, were shining with silver. The somber willow stream that wound beside the big cemetery in the center of the broad valley, glistened pallid. The drooping trees were dark with shadow.

On the shrouded little path between the low cemetery wall and the bank of the stream, a young man and a girl were sitting.

Beside them the undulating spread of tombstones shone like eerie ghosts in the moon-light. From the stream, into the heated air of the summer evening mists rose little glowing spirals which hung poised, like hovering wraiths.

The young man and the girl were engaged to be married. To them, there was nothing here which was frightening or gruesome. They were talking of themselves, their future.

"But it seems too long, Ruth," he was saying. "Waiting until September."

"Nonsense, Alan dear. How can you expect a girl to get ready for her wedding all in a—"

The words dried on her smiling lips as she sucked in her breath with a sudden gasp. Her face was suddenly drawn in the lines of stark fear. She was staring out into the pallid graveyard.

"What the matter, Ruth?" he demanded.

"That—that grave over there. Look!" Her voice was hollow, hardly audible.

The man stared. To young Alan Grant, for a second or two, it was only a stare of puzzled surprise. A startled wonderment.

And then an amazed horror flooded him so that he jumped to his feet, drawing the slender brown-haired Ruth Thompson up with him. Transfixed, they peered. The girl clung to him now with terror-stricken fingers.

It was a grave quite near them, a mound of new earth on which the funeral flowers still lay in a little withered heap. The new marble headstone gleamed silvery-white in the moonlight. Grant knew who was buried here. It was a middle-aged farmer from down the valley, a fellow named Peters.

It had been a tragic thing, some three months ago. The stalwart Peters, with his crops gone bad for the two past summers, failing to finance himself for this year's harvests, had brooded. Then suddenly he had lost his reason, killed his wife and infant child. And had run wildly to report it to the police. He had cut his throat before their horrified eyes.

The insane Peters was buried here. And as Grant and the girl now stared, they saw that the mound of earth was moving!

For that stricken moment they could only stand and stare. The soft, loose dirt of the three months old grave was moving, as though some gigantic worm underground were struggling up! A crack opened. A little heave of dirt rose up and fell aside with a ghastly rattle and thump in the silence of the moonlight night. A heaving, breaking grave mound! Like a hatched egg, with shell breaking from the struggles of its emerging occupant! The insane Peters, dead three months with slashed throat, emerging now from his grave! Clods of earth were falling aside. A crevasse yawned.

Horror so numbed them that they stood transfixed, shuddering, chilled, so that the Weird unearthly scene blurred before their gaze. How could the dead man struggle up now from this grave which had entombed him for three months? Yet, he was doing it! The clods of earth were being shoved aside. The little mound was breaking upward!

How long they stood there, breathless, Alan Grant and Ruth Thompson never knew. Then, suddenly, she sagged against him, fainting from terror. Quickly, he seized her, lifted her slim body into his arms and ran swiftly back along the path.

"I'm all right, Alan," she murmured presently. "You can—put me down."

He set her on her feet tenderly. With his arm around her, they ran on. Then, from a little distance where the path wound up an ascent to overlook the river and the undulating graveyard, they stopped, panting, turned and stared again. The grave of the insane Peters was still in sight down there by the river. Its head-stone was a tiny white blob.

The ghastly incredible thing hadn't been some wild trick of their imagination. A hole yawned there now, at Peters' grave. A hole from which clods of earth rhythmically were rising, earth and stones coming up and falling aside with a clatter of grisly little thuds which were audible even at this distance.

A dead thing emerging! Was the coffin down there broken now from the heaving struggles of its dead occupant? Grant's horrified imagination pictured the upward heaving lid, lifting and scattering that soft stony earth.

"Ruth, are we crazy?" he gasped. "Do you see what I think I'm seeing? A dead man coming out ..."

They stared, holding themselves against the numb instinct to run, held by the fascination of horror.

The weird struggle of the emerging thing went on. And then, suddenly, from the black rectangle which was the yawning grave, an arm came up. Then a head and shoulders reared, thick wide shoulders, a head of straggling gray-black hair.

The dead, mad Peters! From the grave his body came struggling up until in a moment he was standing on the ground, sagging against his tombstone, exhausted by his struggle. One of his arms was around the marble headstone to steady himself.

Unearthly figure! At this distance, Grant could only imagine the slashed throat. But the head dangled sidewise horribly, unsupported by the muscles that had been cut. The undertaker's white surgical bandage over the gaping wound was dimly apparent.

"God in Heaven!" Grant murmured.

The ghastly thing was staggering away from its grave now. Its knees were buckling as it walked with exhausted, dragging step. It was threading its way uncertainly among the tombstones! It was coming up the hill!

Again Grant fled with the girl. Was this ghastly roaming thing really an insane man who had killed his wife and child?

Had he come out of his grave now seeking some new victims? The horror within Grant was even more ghastly as he realized that it was true. Fearfully he shot a glance behind him. Far down in the graveyard the staggering dead thing was still visible. It had stopped again as though gathering strength, steadying itself against the side of a tombstone.

They had turned at the upper corner of the cemetery. A small cottage was here, with a big workshop where headstones were engraved close beside it. Now, at eleven o'clock this Sunday evening, both buildings were dark and silent.

"Old man Dillon should be here," Ruth said, her voice trembling.

"Asleep, probably. We'll rout him out, and call the sheriff."

Big Jake Dillon, engraver of headstones, was groundkeeper of the cemetery. He lived here alone in the small, two-story cottage.

Furiously, they pounded on its big knocker. There was only silence. From here, the ground out in the cemetery rose over a slight hillock. The staggering dead thing was in a hollow behind it. Grant was tense, shuddering. Did he dare hesitate here with Ruth? The damnable thing might come over the hillock at any moment.

It was half a mile to the home of Grant s family, one of the luxurious summer residences on the southern, inner slope of the valley. Ruth's home, where she lived with her step-uncle, Eben Thompson, was just beyond it. Too far to go! The sheriff should be notified at once!

It was a swift rush of incoherent thoughts that poured through his head as Grant pounded on the gate-house door. Then suddenly as he rattled the knob, he realized that the door was unlocked. It yielded abruptly to their pressing bodies and they staggered forward into a dark hallway.

"Dillon! Oh, Dillon. Wake up!" Grant's peremptory call echoed eerily through the silence of the dark house.

Ruth quickly drew the outer door closed after them. Grant reached out and shot the bolt. At least that would bar the ghastly roaming thing if it came here! The door closed out the moonlight. The little hall here was black.

"Dillon! For God s sake aren't you here? Where's your telephone?"

No answer! Nothing but a heavy brooding silence.

"I think I remember a telephone here in the reception room," Ruth whispered.

Chapter 2: The Dead Die Again

IN A DIM, wicker-furnished reception room they found a telephone on the wall. Grant seized it, called Sheriff John Stark in the Village of Sleepy Valley two miles away.

"You're drunk," the sheriff growled, when he had listened to Grant's half coherent rush of words.

"Am I? Well, you come and see. Miss Thompson and I are in the gatehouse. Dillon doesn't seem to be here."

"Alan—Oh my God—Look!" Ruth suddenly gasped. She had gone to the moonlit window. "Alan! It's out here now!"

Grant gasped it to the Sheriff.

"Holy Mother of God!" the sheriff's voice sputtered. "I'll be right out there."

Grant hung up, joined Ruth at the window. Out among the tombstones, some fifty feet away, the ghastly figure of the dead Peters stood wavering.

The knees of the corpse were almost buckling, but with demoniac strength it held itself erect. Grant's gorge rose at the ghastly sight, black burial clothes shrouding the gaunt figure. The head was bobbling as it rolled sidewise on its gaping neck. Then the unearthly thing took a forward staggering step, and the moon-light fell upon the face.

The sight was horrible! A noisome countenance, pallid, pinched and bloodless, the rotted horror of a man's face three months dead! The dead eyes were staring wildly with their weird look of insanity.

"Oh Alan, what shall we do?" Ruth's voice was a whimper of terror. "He—it—the damned thing can't get in here. Look, it's moving away." The grisly walking corpse, as though confused, demoniac, had turned and was staggering diagonally off. In a moment it was lost behind a big gleaming mausoleum. In the dim little reception room, a new rush of horrified thoughts swept Grant. Where was Dillon? If he was here, why hadn't he answered? Was he upstairs now?

Under any normal circumstances, the husky young Grant was afraid of nothing. He strode back into the hall. At the steeply ascending little stairs he pushed Ruth away.

"Stay here just a minute," he admonished. "I'll go up. That thing outside can't get in

"Through a window, maybe, Alan? Oh my God, don't leave me!"

"I won't be half a minute."

He went up swiftly. There were two bedrooms upstairs. He dashed into them. No one, nothing, here. The room which Dillon used was in order. The bed was unrumpled.

"Alan! Alan!"

From down in the lower hall, Ruth's terrified voice floated up. He took the steps three at a time to dash to her side.

"I heard something!" she whispered, shivering. "Back by the kitchen! Oh Alan, something is here in the house with us. It's gotten in the house."

He kept her behind him as he advanced slowly into the dim narrow back hallway. The dark kitchen door-way yawned before them. There was no sound—save the pounding of his heart against his ribs and the tremulous breathing of the girl. Then he heard a whimper, a rustle and a vague scraping thump. Something was here in the dark kitchen! Something—down on the floor in the corner. It moved! And then he saw it vaguely.

With a pounce, Grant was down on the floor. The figure squealed as he seized it, jerked it erect. A voice gasped shrilly

"Oh my God! Oh, don't kill me!" Suddenly Grant laughed hoarsely. The straggling moonlight through the kitchen window revealed the cowering captive—a big, overgrown boy, with an overlarge head that wobbled on a spindly neck.

"Good Heavens, it's only Willie Green!" Grant exclaimed, immense relief in his voice. "Willie, what in hell are you doing here?"

It was the son of the housekeeper at Ruth's home, the half-witted houseboy. He was chattering with terror. In infancy he had lost one eye. The empty, red-rimmed socket was squinted now with his fright. The other eve stared wildly at Grant.

"Was goin' home from the movies," he chattered. "There's a dead man walkin' out there in the graveyard.

"I seen him—"

"So did we," Grant agreed. He eyed the boy grimly. Willie's mind, childlike, was incongruous with his powerful, nearly six-foot gangling frame. "Where's Jake Dillon?" Grant demanded.

"I dunno. I came in here to tell him what I seen—then I got scared worse. I heard you come in here. I thought it was the dead thing so I hid here in the kitchen."

He checked himself, sucked in his breath with new terror.

Grant stiffened, and flung a protecting arm around the girl's trembling body. Outside the house, footsteps were audible. The tread of heavy footsteps on the gravel path. Willie squealed.

"Shut up!" Grant admonished.

For a moment the three of them stood in stricken silence, enveloped by the dimness of the kitchen. Was it the dead man walking outside? The tread sounded firm, heavy. Someone approaching the front door. Then the knob rattled. A low muttered voice sounded, with words that were faintly audible in the silence

"What in Hell!"

Grant shoved the big half-witted youth back into the kitchen. With Ruth close beside him, he strode for-ward through the hall. The knob of the front door was being impatiently rattled.

"Who are you?" Grant said suddenly.

"An' sure, who the hell are you in my house?" the outside voice retorted.

"Jake Dillon," Ruth said.

Grant threw the bolt of the door. A switch was here in the hall beside him. The place flooded with light as Jake Dillon strode in.

"Well, Mr. Grant—Miss Thompson -"

Dillon was astonished, trying to be deferential to these wealthy young summer residents of the Sleepy Valley summer colony. Then he gaped as the chattering, white-faced Willie came shambling forward.

"Say, what the devil, if you don't mind my askin'!" Dillon gasped. He was a big, beetle-browed fellow, thickset, powerful, with long dangling arms. He stood gaping with incredulity as Grant swiftly told what had happened.

"That suicide Peters came out of his grave?" Dillon growled. "Is that what yer tellin' me, Mr. Grant? Sure you're joshin'

"He ain't! I seen it too!" Willie Green chattered. "A walkin', insane dead man. I seen him comin' up the hill through the graveyard. He's out here now, somewhere."

"You didn't see him?" Grant demanded.

"My God no! I just come from the village. Been there all evenin'."

"Well, it's out there just below the brow of the hill," Grant said. "It was up here within fifty feet of the door a few minutes ago. Ruth, you stay here with Willie. Come on, Dillon, I'll show you."

The cemetery keeper's ham-like fists had doubled. But they relaxed, and at the door he suddenly hung back.

"I dunno," he mumbled. "Glory be—I ain't afraid of nothin' alive. But how can you kill a dead man? He's already dead."

How indeed? The terror of things gruesome, unnatural, not to be understood, is like no other terror.

"I phoned for the sheriff," Grant said. "He ought to be here any minute."

The sound of the sheriffs arriving car mingled with Grant's weird thoughts. The car came dashing up the nearby road. Then it stopped, and the stalwart sheriff and three other men tumbled out of it.

"Oh, here you are, Mr. Grant," the sheriff greeted. "Look here, if this is some practical joke or something—dragging us all the way out here."

"It isn't," Grant said fiercely. "The cursed thing is out there in the cemetery. Or if it's gone, you'll see its open grave. Miss Thompson and I saw it. So did Willie Green here. It heaved itself up out of its grave, and—"

"Oh my God, here it is!" one of the men suddenly gasped, his voice broke. At the brink of the nearby hill the ghastly figure had appeared. Straggling clouds momentarily obscured the moon. But the Weird staggering corpse was closer now than before. And this time, with its limp dragging step, it was advancing upon the house!

"It is Peters!" the sheriff murmured. The automatic in his hand leveled before him. But his arm shook.

His voice quivered with awed terror. "Peters—a dead man -"

The gruesome corpse, limp as a drunken man about to fall, came wavering forward. One of its arms seemed gesturing, as though it was trying to disperse this little group of frightened, living people. Then the sheriff's gun spat its flame and leaden slug. His trembling hand sent the shot wild. But he fired again. The staggering corpse flung up its arms, fell face down.

Grant with the other men, in a moment ran forward. It was the corpse of Peters beyond question, the noisesome rotting body of the insane farmer who had killed his loved ones and slashed his own throat three months ago. The stench of the grave rose from it now as it lay motionless, with the sheriff's bullet in its rot-ting brain!

Chapter 3: Ghosts Walk Too

THOSE WERE the first of the weird incidents which came to engulf the quiet neighborhood of Sleepy Valley with terror. A dead man, rising from his grave, staggering away, to do God knows what, then brought down, rendered inert by a sheriffs bullet. The thing was so incredible that the outside world, hearing of it by radio and newspaper, gave it little credence.

But Sleepy Valley could not smile or scoff it away. The rotting corpse of the insane farmer Peters was carefully examined. There was nothing about it that seemed abnormal. It was a rotting thing which had been dead for three months, with the Sheriffs bullet embedded in its brain. Its grave too, was examined. A yawning hole of upheaved earth, with the broken coffin at the bottom.

Even then Sleepy Valley might have treated the thing as a ghastly passing incident, never to be explained. But the next night another grave yawned! Another dead man was seen roaming!

This one was not caught. The first night, only one, nearby farmer saw it. Then the next night hysterical reports said that it had been glimpsed staggering through the woods, far down the valley from the graveyard.

A wave of hysteria swept the somnolent little village, the wealthy estates, the broad farming areas back from the valley. And then, a young girl claimed that a dead man had awakened her by knocking on her bed-room window ...

"But that's all nonsense," Ruth's uncle exclaimed a few evenings later. He was in his home where a few of his friends among the summer residents had gathered. "This sort of wild tale must stop. These ignorant farmers will plunge us all into panic. Why, good God, a dozen families here on the south slope quit their homes today! Went back to New York. This is madness!"

He was a big, distinguished looking man of forty-odd, this Eben Thompson, Ruth's uncle. He stared gravely at his guests, with apprehensive, blood-shot eyes. But he was obviously not so scoffing as he wished to appear. He tried to smile, but his gaze kept straying to the shadowed room corners. His fingers ruffled his iron-gray hair with a nervous gesture.

"Corpses stalking around our graveyard," young Grant's father muttered. "Every time I say that, it sounds wilder. Yet it's true! There was one that did, undoubtedly. My son saw it—my son and Ruth—others."

Intelligent men, faced with the impossible, which suddenly had become an indisputable fact! They could only reiterate futilely the same incredible phrases.

Terror was here, even in this quiet living room of the luxurious Thompson bungalow where none but intelligent, educated people were assembled. Young Alan Grant could feel the terror now as he sat quietly in a shadowed corner beside Ruth—feel it within himself, and sense it from the others. The moonlit rectangles of the living room windows were things of horror, as though any moment, here, within half a mile of the big graveyard, a dead man might appear at one of the windows—dead eyes staring in, malevolent with hatred for the living.

Mayor Allen of Sleepy Valley, rotund, cherubic, was here at Thompson s this evening. His face was any-thing but cherubic now, with its habitual smile faded into a grayish grimness. He mopped his bald-spot.

"Jake Dillon is watching the graveyard all night every night," the mayor said. "But if any more of those dead things come out ..."

"Oh quit it," Eben Thompson rejoined querulously. "Don't let's sit here chewing over this like hysterical women. Who would like to play some bridge?"

"Dillon has asked the town council to furnish him a permanent guard," the mayor persisted. "Why, good Lord, of course we will. Sheriff Parker and his posse are scouring the woods for that corpse they say was roaming there -"

"Trying to capture a dead man!" young Grant's father said with a lugubrious laugh. "We've come to that! How can you blame Parker's nerves for being shattered, his posse for being so nervous that they're afraid to scour the Woods at night? My Heavens, we don't want our community ruined. People selling their homes for next to nothing and moving out. They're beginning to do just that already."

Outside the Thompson living room the sound of an arriving car was audible. At the portiered doorway of the living room, unnoticed, the gangling figure of Willie Green was standing. He was listening, awed, apparently frightened as his single eye stared weirdly from one to the other of the speakers.

"Sleepy Valley!" Mayor Allen was exclaiming. "How we've all fought to keep the noisy highway from coming through to disturb our romantic quiet! He laughed ironically. "And now, if this damned weird thing keeps up, all the world will be tramping here to our door. Sleepy Valley, overrun with newsreel cameras, newspaper men, broadcasters."

"Publicity that Won't do us any good," Grant's father assented. "If people are afraid to live here ..."

The front doorbell rang harshly. A visitor arrived, a tall, stoop-shouldered man named John Stark. He was a road construction engineer, chief prospective bidder for the projected road. Young Alan Grant saw him stop and pat Willie's shoulder, murmuring something to the halfwit as they passed at the door.

Stark was grave and grim as he greeted the half dozen people here. "They told me I'd probably find you here, your Honor," he said to the rotund little Mayor Allen. "Look here, I don't Want to add any fuel to this weird thing. I haven't told anyone He stared around the room.

"Told anyone, what?" the big, distinguished-looking Eben Thompson demanded.

"Why I—I saw another one of the damned things!" Stark said. "A woman, this time. My God, she must have been dead for years. Horribly rotted, with grey hair streaming down, shrouding a body with clothes and flesh rotting away from it. I saw her face—not much more than a skull with noisome pits of flesh. But she was walking, staggering!"

Ruth, the only woman in the room, gave a little cry of horror.

"Easy, Stark," Eben Thompson warned. "When was this?"

"I'm sorry, Miss Thompson—Why, it was just after sundown tonight. She was walking by the river. Then she fell in—sank."

In the awed horrified silence, a maid's voice sounded from the doorway. "There's a telephone call for Mr.

Alan Grant."

"Who is it?" young Grant demanded as he jumped up.

He was tense. It seemed suddenly as though now, tonight, the unearthly thing must be breaking in with some new horror.

"A man," the maid said, as he drew her out into the dim hallway. "A man. He wouldn't give his name. But it sounded like—like Mr. Dillon over at the cemetery. Oh Mr. Grant, is this terrible thing ..."

Grant brushed past her toward the telephone at the other end of the long hall. And suddenly from a shadowed recess, Willie Green jumped forward.

"Say Mr. Grant, listen! I got somethin'" to tell you." The half-wit's single eye glowed with his excitement. His voice was low, furtive.

Momentarily Grant paused, the big loutish figure of the boy barring him from the telephone. "What is it, Willie?" he demanded.

Willie's voice dropped lower.

"I seen that walkin' dead woman Mr. Stark was talkin' about. Only he lied. I seen him watchin' her as she walked along the river path. She didn't fall in no river. She went off from the path an' went into the cliff."

Was that what Jake Dillon now was calling about?

"Thanks, Willie," Grant said. He tried to shove the boy aside, but the half-wit clung to him.

"Wait Mr. Grant, listen! I got somethin' else to tell you. That walkin' dead woman—I was so scared I stood by a tree an' she passed pretty close to me. She was in the moonlight, an'—Listen, Mr. Grant, the ghost of her was there too. I seen it, I sure did."

"All right, Willie ..."

"No, listen. It had eyes, I'm tellin' you. They glared at me. Two floatin' eyes! But her corpse didn't have no eyes, because her face was too rotted—"

Grant shoved him away and seized the telephone.

"Hello," he said. "This is Alan Grant."

"I'm Jake Dillon," the cemetery keeper's low hurried voice answered. "I got something I want to tell you, Mr. Grant."

Almost Willie's exact words! "What is it?" Grant demanded. "Not over the phone. There was a woman came out of her grave tonight. I saw the grave—old lady Johnson who died more than five years ago. My God, I guess she's around here somewhere."

"I heard about her," Grant said. "Phone the sheriff, Dillon."

"I did. He said there was a Mr. Stark who notified him. He said him an' some men were lookin', but they couldn't find any corpse. They were here a while ago. Somethin' I want to tell you private. Come over here, will you?"

The telephone clicked as though it had been disconnected. Grant rattled the receiver.

"Hello, hello, Jake Dillon?"

"Yes, I'm here. Listen, come over, Mr. Grant. It's damned important I can't dare tell you over the phone."

"You're at the cemetery gatehouse?"

"Yes. Come to the back door. Come by the road. Sure, if I was you, I wouldn't go down through the cemetery."

Dillon hung up. For a moment Grant stood beside the little telephone taboret, pondering. The big half-witted Willie Green had shambled away. Then Grant thought he saw him at the other end of the dim hallway, where a small side door led into the shadowed outer garden. The door seemed to open. Someone or something darted out. Grant ran down the hallway, out into the yard. Nothing was visible outside but the dim outlines of shrubs and trees, faint in the starlight. Overhead, the moon was shrouded by a low, swiftly passing cloud.

It was only a scant half mile to the cemetery gatehouse. Grant walked quickly. Dillon's voice had been urgent. Was this something more than the gruesome mystery of corpses breaking out of their graves?

Grant thought so, of course. Something rational back of all this horror, this terror which for days now had been throwing little Sleepy Valley into hysteria. Why had John Stark, the construction engineer, lied about having seen the ghastly corpse of the old woman throwing itself into the river and sinking? Or had Willie Green been mistaken, or lying about that?

The ghost of the walking corpse, a ghost with glowing eyes! Could a ghost animate the body which in life it had inhabited? Absurd! Behind all this, something rational must be lurking—something murderous?

The big undulating, pallid reaches of the graveyard were beside Grant now. Winding paths between eerie white blobs of the tombstones, and the occasional rectangles of the larger, marble and granite mausoleums.

No staggering corpse was visible, but the brow of the hill here hid most of the cemetery in the lower hollow. The front of the little cottage gatehouse of Dillon was dark and silent, and as Grant approached it, a sudden Wariness was on him.

Had Dillon lured him here? That seemed unreasonable, but Grant was unarmed. For a moment he hesitated. He was close beside the cottage now, and presently he advanced, walking on the grass beside the gravel path, so that his footsteps were soundless. The side reception room windows were dark. At the rear of the house, one of the side kitchen windows showed a little light.

Soundlessly Grant crept to it. The shade was almost down, but stooping, he could see through the crack under it. At the kitchen table, big Jake Dillon was sitting. A shotgun was lying on the table at his elbow. He was partly facing Grant, examining a big chunk of something black in his hands. It glistened in the light, a jagged irregular black lump as big as a man's fist, with the light shining from its myriad facets.

In a moment Grant was at the back door. His knock at once brought Dillon.

"Who is it?" the gatekeeper's voice demanded through the door.

"It's I, Alan Grant."

The door bolt shot. The door opened, disclosing Dillon's bulky figure. Grant's swift look past him showed that Dillon had left the shotgun on the table. Grant stepped in. Dillon shoved the door closed behind him and shot the bolt. The gleaming black chunk was in the cemetery keeper's hand. He turned from the door, tense, excited.

"Did you see any walkin' corpse as you came along?" he demanded. Grant shook his head.

"What's that you've got there?"

"I found it. I want to ask your advice."

The big kitchen center light was not lighted. There was only a single hooded globe over a cabinet against the inner wall. Dillon drew Grant there.

"Let me show you under the light. I found this tonight, Mr. Grant. Down by the river."

"You had something to tell me? About this?"

"Yes. This, an' that corpse of the old woman -" Dillon shuddered. But in his tense voice and his gleaming eyes, it seemed to Grant that there was something more like cupidity. "I saw her when she came out of her grave, but I guess maybe she didn't see me."

Amazing that anyone could talk so calmly about a dead woman! But Grant accepted it. How else could one talk, these weird days? Silently, Grant listened to the cemetery keeper's low, swift explanation.

Just at dusk tonight, he had seen the staggering figure of the rotted corpse of old Mrs. Johnson. Then he had lost sight of it—and in searching around he had stumbled upon a small cave-mouth, in the honeycombed cliff, at the north slope by the river.

"She wasn't in there," Dillon was saying. "I never did see her again. But in the cave I found this. A whole pile of it's in there, with burlap bags thrown over it."

He displayed the glittering black rock.

"What is it?" Grant demanded.

"Black marble. Listen, Mr. Grant, I know somethin'- about marble. I ought to! I work with it a lot here with the headstones. But this isn't ordinary marble. It's statuary marble. It's as fine-grained, as pure as Carrara marble. And Carrara marble's only white. This in the cave is all pure black."

A rush of wild conjectures leaped into Grant's enraged and startled mind.

"I didn't know who to tell," Dillon was adding with swift, vehement earnestness. "But I can trust you. I want to know what to do about this. If maybe there's deposits of that around here—under the graveyard maybe, so deep that it's never been found before—it might come out in these caves or the lowlands down by the river. Millions maybe, for any of us who owned—"

A loud sound in the kitchen checked him, a slow scraping, a little scratching creak.

Grant and Dillon whirled.

To Grant it was a chaos of numbed startled horror. The kitchen was empty, save for them. A window behind the table was open, with moonlight streaming in now mingling with the kitchen light. Through the window, Grant had a glimpse of the empty side yard.

"Holy God!" Dillon suddenly gasped.

He staggered sideways, stood staring across the kitchen with his heavy jaw sagging, his eyes fairly popping. And Grant stared for that stricken instant, frozen with horror.

The shotgun on the table was moving! Grant gulped, unbelieving, his eyes wide with terror. Slowly it moved at first, with the low scraping sound which had attracted their attention. Then, abruptly, it moved rapidly sidewise, reared itself up into the air, suspended by levitation as its barrel swung with muzzle pointing bluntly toward Dillon.

And then it spat—a roar of flame, smoke and leaden shot hurtling across the big kitchen. The electric light bulb splintered and was extinguished. But the moonlight still showed the suspended gun as it floated in mid-air. Then the other barrel roared.

Grant closed his eyes involuntarily at the sight. The big body of Dillon, face torn away by the concentrated buckshot charge crashed to the floor. For just a second longer the gun, floating in mid-air, hung poised. Then, as though suddenly the weird force which had animated the swinging shotgun were expended, it dropped, hit the floor with a rattling thump and lay motionless!

Chapter 4: The Phantom Killer

IN THE smoke-filled kitchen, Grant crouched, his senses reeling. The roar of the gun seeming still to echo through his horrified brain. The dead bleeding body of Dillon lay beside him with the moonlight on it. Face blown away, a mass of gory pulp.

He groped his way frantically for the door. The gun lay here on the floor, inert now as he staggered over it. The back kitchen door wouldn't yield to his frenzied jerks. Then he recalled that Dillon had locked it. He fumbled, slid the bolt, staggered out into the pallid moonlit night. The air cleared his gasping lungs, reeling head.

Nothing was visible here in the upper reaches of the cemetery. For a moment he stood peering around him, his flesh creeping in grisly anticipation of new terrors. Then he realized that his right eye hurt. He recalled that with the first blasting shot which had crashed over his head and extinguished the light, he had thrown himself sidewise and down. His face had struck a corner of the kitchen cabinet. The blow was puffing his eye. The bruised flesh around the socket was swelling it shut.

With his head cleared, he started back for the gatehouse. He must phone for the sheriff, and for Eben Thompson to notify his father. At the back door, he stopped momentarily to gaze into the cemetery*, then tensed. Far down to the right, where the reaches of the cemetery sloped off to the river, something was moving! A walking corpse? A weird unearthly-looking man's figure was walking with staggering tread.

Grant was hardly conscious that he had run from the little gatehouse and was dashing down the hill. For just a moment he saw the staggering distant thing more clearly. A dead man! One of its arms waved limply.

It staggered with dragging tread, as though its legs were almost paralyzed. Then it fell. It rose again. Horror filled Grant as he ran. But there were other things on his mind now. The gruesome horror of the super-natural was mingled with the grim determination to probe this mystery.

The staggering dead thing had vanished when Grant reached the foot of the hill. Had it wandered toward the river? He turned that way, came to the river path. It was darker here. Moonlight glistened on the sullen, slow-moving water. The willows drooped, heavy, hardly moving in the breathless night air. To one side, four or five hundred feet up the stream, a small footbridge crossed it. Was there something crouching behind the rail, midway on the bridge?

For a moment Grant thought so. He started that way, turned a bend of the stream where a jagged rocky cliff face stood almost at the river's edge.

For an instant, as Grant passed beyond the end of the cemetery, he swept a glance in at the pallid tomb-stones. He stopped, shocked with a new rush of startled horror.

Half a dozen graves yawned here! Ragged holes out of which, quite evidently, the ghastly dead occupants had emerged! Was the big cemetery about to spew out all its dead? Dead people, noisome, stenching things, revolting now at their entombment, struggling out to attack the living!

Grant flung away the wild crazy thoughts. Of course they were wild! This must be something different from that, the work of a scheming, rational, murderous living villain. A countryside terrorized. People moving away from a cemetery which seemingly could not hold its dead. Black marble, perhaps in a vast deposit somewhere here, a deposit of pure black statuary marble perhaps of incalculable value. Jake Dillon, killed by that ghastly gun so that he could not tell what he suspected.

The rush of half coherent thoughts surged through Grant's mind as he turned back toward the river. And suddenly, again, he saw a moving figure. An upright blob, on this side of the river, past the end of the little footbridge. Shadows at the bottom of the ragged cliff engulfed it. Then he saw it again. A staggering corpse? It did not quite seem so, this time!

Quietly Grant stalked forward until the figure was no more than fifty feet ahead of him. He saw that it was a man prowling, poking at the ragged, rocky face of the little cliff. A small flashlight was suddenly illumined, its little spot of light slowly moving along the face of the rocks as the man shifted forward. He came presently into a patch of moonlight.

John Stark! The construction engineer! He was prowling here, searching the geological formation of the cliff-face down here in the hollow, lower than most of the cemetery level. He was probably searching to determine the location or the extent of the rare deposits. Grant could not doubt it.

And other things now came leaping into his memory. That click of the telephone when he was talking to Dillon. Had that been Stark listening at some telephone extension in Eben Thompson's home to overhear what Dillon was saying? That figure darting from the Thompson hall, out the side door—had that been Stark too?

Grant's fists clenched, his jaw hardened with determination.

The prowling man did not hear Grant approaching. Grant crept silently, catlike, his fists doubled. Suddenly he sprang.

Stark's little hand torch clattered to the ground as he whirled swiftly. He met Grant's rush with a blow in the chest. Their bodies collided. Grant's fist smashed into Stark's face and he went down, Grant on top of him.

"You damned murderer," Grant panted. "Got you now -"

In the background of his consciousness he was ironically aware that he had assaulted the construction engineer with very little evidence that the fellow was the murderous villain. But the look of sheer fury* and fear on the fellows face convinced Grant that he had made no mistake. Stark ripped out an oath, and with incredible agility twisted loose, heaved Grant away and jumped to his feet.

Grant was up almost as quickly. He saw that his adversary* had turned to run. Already Stark was ten feet away. Then he checked himself, whirled again to face Grant. A big huntsman's knife hung in a holster at his belt. He had had no time to draw it during Grant's first onslaught. But in the moonlight now, as Grant gathered himself to leap, he saw Stark's hand go for the knife.

Then with a gasp, Grant drew back. He stood staring, shaken despite all the weird things of incredible horror that he had witnessed. Now he could only stand limp, frozen into silence.

Stark's hand was reaching for the knife—but it never got there. From the holster the knife came slithering, floating mysteriously in the air. The moonlight glittered on its steel blade as for a split second its point poised in front of Stark s wildly staring eyes. Then, almost too quick to be seen, it plunged itself point first into his chest!

Stark s scream of terror turned to a choked rattle of the blood in his throat as he fell, the knife buried to its hilt.

How long Grant stood there numb, he never knew. Then he ran forward, bent down. Stark was dying. With even* gasping breath, blood gushed in a crimson stream from his mouth. His white shirt was a welter of crimson around the buried knife. His glazing eyes stared upward, trying to focus on Grant.

"Got me!" he groaned. "Come closer—I'll tell -"

The blood in his throat choked him. Grant bent low, his lips close to Stark s ear.

"Black marble goes under the cemetery," Grant hissed. "You were hoping to buy it, to make it useless as a burying place."

"Yes, that's true. And to have the motor road come through here for transportation. There would have been millions for me. We probably couldn't patent the—this way was best—everything going fine. But he—"

"He?" Grant bent lower. The dying man's breath gurgled horribly in his throat. "I could have—gotten the road through," Stark gasped. "And the way we've been terrorizing—all this property would be easy to buy. But he—he wouldn't share equally. Damn him, I knew I couldn't trust him when he figured he didn't need me anymore. Now he's killed me—like he'll kill you."

A torrent of blood choked the faint Words. For a moment Stark's body twitched with a feeble paroxysm. Then he was motionless, dead glazed eyes staring blankly up at Grant, the light of the living gone from them.

For an instant Grant stayed there on his knees. Then a chilling burst of laughter from the moonlight nearby brought him shuddering to his feet.

"The ghost of a walking dead man killed him! I seen it! I seen the ghost stab him! I can see ghosts in the moonlight! Other people can't see 'em but I can! I seen this one kill him!"

Out midway on the little footbridge, the half-wit Willie Green stood gibbering with insane laughter. Grant rushed for him, but he fled across the narrow bridge. On the opposite bank, Grant caught him.

"Willie! Damn you, stop laughing." Horror, excitement, seemed to have thrust the half-witted boy into hysteria. He laughed wildly.

"Don't kill me, Mr. Grant! I didn't kill nobody. I jus' been watchin' what's goin' on these nights. I told you I saw the ghost of that dead old woman. Sometimes they're right beside the walkin' corpse—but sometimes I seen 'em loose."

"You saw a ghost here just now?"

"Sure I did."

He burst again into his chilling, eerie laughter. Grant shook him roughly by the shoulders.

"Stop that, Willie! Tell me quietly now, a ghost was here, it stabbed that man with that knife?"

"Sure it did. I seen it!"

"Then which way did it go?"

Willie gestured.

"Over there, other side of the river."

"You mean over along the bottom of the cliff?"

'Yeh. There's a cave-mouth there. All the walkin' corpses go into it when they get through roamin'. An' they come out of it, too. That's where the corpse of old Mrs. Johnson went. I guess they all live there when they ain't walkin' out through the graveyard,"

The cave which Jake Dillon had described, when he had found the bags of black marble! Grant shoved the hysterical half-wit away and strode for the bridge.

"Where you goin', Mr. Grant? You goin' to that cave? Ah my God, not with me!"

"You go home, Willie. You keep your mouth shut, hear me?"

The half-wit turned and fled. Grant crossed the bridge. At the weltering body of Stark he stopped, drew out the knife, wiped its bloody blade on his jacket and put it in his pocket.

The cave-mouth yawned black and silent. More tense, more cautious than he had ever been before in his life, Grant moved through the little ten-foot winding passage. In the solid blackness he stood a moment, listening, waiting tensely for his eyes to adjust themselves to the greater darkness.

A little glimmer of yellow glow was faintly apparent. The tunnel turned an angle, opened into the fetid cave. Grant stared. Nothing here. Over by one wall he saw the pile of black marble chunks. They were in burlap bags now.

The glow was coming from a distant recess. Cautiously, Grant went there, saw a huge flat slab of rock that seemed to have been moved aside.

Faint, flickering yellow light streamed out. Knife in hand, again Grant advanced into another little tunnel. It was only ten feet long, a steeply rising rock floor with a little brink ahead where it opened to the inner grotto, from which the yellow glow was streaming. Slowly Grant went up the ascent. At the brink he crouched, the hair crawling upright on the back of his neck as he stared breathlessly at a scene of incredible, ghastly horror.

Chapter 5: Conclave of the Dead

IT WAS a large grotto, of mouldy earthen floor and glistening rocky walls from which moisture was soddenly dripping. On large stones, to one side, a big candle stood. Its faint eerie glow dimly illuminated the underground apartment, casting crouching monstrous shadows on the rocks. Peering, Grant sucked in his breath, with his first swift glance of horror. In a little group, where the candlelight fell full upon them, the ghastly occupants of the hidden grotto were gathered.

Conclave of the dead!

Nearly a dozen corpses were here—men and women, ghastly things spewed from the grave. Some were tying stretched on the ground as though asleep. Others sat propped against the rocks, mutely staring at each other with rotting eyes. It was a ghastly conclave, so ghastly that here, at close range, Grant was sickened.

The candlelight painted the horrible dead faces, the pinched, gray-white rotted countenances. Some, dead for years, sat with moldering garments barely clinging to the festering horror of their dead flesh. Faces pitted, leprous with crawling maggots.

Mute, silent company of the dead! One of them began moving from behind the main group, a ghastly decaying figure of an old woman struggled to her feet, staggering forward with limp, dragging leg. Old Mrs. Johnson, her face bones visible behind the moist festering flesh. Her eye-sockets, pits of horror, seemed to stare around at her dead companions. Her rotted mouth yawned with a ghastly grimace as she regarded them.

Slowly she dragged herself forward as though about to administer to the others who sat so horribly, silently staring at her. Then suddenly it seemed as though her strength gave out. She slumped to the floor, her back braced against the wall. On her rotted neck, her head still was bobbling. After a moment it settled to one side, grotesquely dangling.

Then suddenly, the weird animating force transferred itself to the candle. The flame flickered. Then the candle rose waveringly up from the rock, poised in mid-air, crossed the cave and settled itself down again.

The first sweep of horror had left Grant. Tense, alert now, he was peering with appraising eye, freed at last from the confusion of terror of the supernatural. Vaguely he was aware that his right eye was throbbing with pain. The blow from the corner of the kitchen cabinet when he had thrown himself down as Dillon was shot, had puffed the flesh. His right eye was closed now. With his left eye he stared intently. One-eyed, like the one-eyed half-wit, Willie Green.

"I seen the ghost that stabbed Mr. Stark!"—Willie's words echoed in Grant's mind.

And Grant was noticing things now, little things that no one would ever notice in the horrible moonlight of the graveyard. The corpse of old Mrs. Johnson, as she had come forward here, had had an arm missing—a blank area which was restored when she slumped inert. The bottom end of the candle as it swayed through the air was gone.

Was it an almost invisible black ghost here, doing these things? In those few seconds, as he stared, Grant was aware that, down on the ground he could dimly see a moving patch of blackness, a small irregular area where the ground was blotted out. And above it, very vaguely now he could discern a moving outline—an upright black shape of emptiness. The background of the candlelit cave was visible, as though it mingled or was visible through the blob of blank, blurred emptiness.

And then Grant saw the eyes. As though the silent shadow of nothingness had suddenly turned to face him, two round holes, side by side, were apparently nearly six feet above the ground. More clear than the blank shadow itself, they were weird tiny holes, like eyes staring. And then, the candlelight seemed to glint on them. Tiny panes of glass!

Grant had moved now over the brink, into a rock shadow where he stood flattened against the wall with his knife clutched in his hand. The vague blob of emptiness was fairly near him. His legs tensed as it came closer. Then he leaped.

The almost invisible thing must have heard him. Grant was aware of the eyes turning in his direction. He hurtled against a solid body. An arm went around him. A gloved hand gripped his wrist as he tried to stab with his knife.

At the contact, Grant felt his hands tingling with an electric shock. There was a hiss of discharged current as he and his adversary swayed, locked together, grimly struggling—a little sizzling hiss. Then the hiss was gone. Suddenly, in the eerie candlelight, Grant found himself clutching a black-robed, hooded man. He wore a visor pane of tiny eye-holes, covered with queer-looking glass that glowed luminously.

The knife had fallen to the floor. For a moment they swayed, struggling fiercely. Then, abruptly Grant tripped, staggering over one of the corpses. He fell, the bulk of the robed man on top of him. Strangling fingers gripped at his throat, shutting off his breath. The weird little eye-panes stared down at him. He could see now where it seemed that a metal brace held them at the bridge of the man's nose. A pince-nez brace that would mark the nose bridge.

Grant's mind in that split second swept back to the scene in Eben Thompson's living room, where half a dozen men had been gathered. These glasses, operating under strange optical conditions of polarized light perhaps, to see out through the area of electric invisibility which this murderous villain had flung around himself—that strain would easily make a man's eyes go bloodshot.

He remembered seeing those bloodshot eyes! And now he recalled what before he had barely noticed—that same man, who never ordinarily wore glasses, had had a red mark at the bridge of his nose!

"Why," Grant gasped. "By God, I know you, Eben Thompson!"

Ruth's step-uncle! It was Eben Thompson who had joined with Stark in this daring scheme—and then had murdered Stark, to keep all the huge stake for himself!

"By God, I'm onto you at last!" Grant's words, hissing with all the force of his cold hatred for this beast, startled Thompson. Momentarily his grip on Grant relaxed.

And as Grant heaved and struggled against his powerful adversary, the hooded mask over Thompson's face was torn askew. The candlelight showed his red-rimmed, watery eyes, his sweating features, contorted with a murderous lust.

"You, Grant,'*' he panted. "Should have done for you long ago. I thought—what you were seeing would add to the terror. My best witness

He was chuckling. He thought that his weight was holding Grant pinned. But with a frenzied desperation, Grant tore loose, lunged away, and plunged back.

The impact knocked the older man off balance. Thompson's head went back against a jagged point of the rocky cave-wall. Then, with the chaos of his own wild frenzy, Grant tore him from the ground, hurled his head down, pounded until Thompson's skull cracked, until the body went limp, dead.

The eerie candlelit cave was suddenly silent. The mute dead things, sitting as though in ghastly conclave, stared at Grant horribly as he staggered past them through the fetid caves, out into the freshness of the moonlit summer night.

The huge deposits of amazingly pure black statuary marble have enriched little Sleepy Valley. The details of the electric invisibility which Stark and Thompson so gruesomely used are fairly well known now. They are not given much publicity, being a thing too dangerous in the hands of skillful criminals.

Obviously, it was Stark who developed the apparatus. Much of it was found hidden in his home and secret laboratory in New York. In principle, its working was simple. A fabric treated with special black dyes, electrified so that, in effect, it was totally incapable of reflecting light. There was a complete color absorption, except for the two small areas of insulated glass, the eyeholes through which the wearer was enabled to see outward through the dead-black area surrounding him.

There was a faint reflection here, the eyes of the ghost which Willie Green saw upon several occasions. The clutch of Thompson's hands upon the corpses, the gun, the candle, created areas of blankness, unnoticeable in moonlight.

The limp, dragging legs of the corpses, supported by the invisible Thompson, added only horror. But in the cave, at closer view and calmer, more appraising gaze, Alan Grant saw quite clearly the blank space that was the clutch of Thompson's hand upon the candle.

The total absorption of light would not, of itself, have created the complete illusion of invisibility—merely a hole of blankness behind which the background was blotted out. A sort of black, ghostly shadow. But in the working of the Stark-Thompson apparatus it was found that around the body so enveloped, a natural magnetic field was created.

As Einstein demonstrated many years ago, light-rays, passing from a background around an obstructing object, are bent to follow the natural curve of the magnetic field.

Thus the normally reflected light-rays from the background behind Thompson, instead of being blocked by his body, were in a large measure bent around it, reaching the observer in front so that he saw the back-ground apparently unobstructed. The observer's attention thus was focused away from the black shadow.

Curiously, our two eyes are a material aid in this portion of the optical phenomena. With two eyes, viewing an object from different points, we are always enabled partially to see around any obstructing object.

With two eyes we see some of the background which, with one eye, is not visible. A two-eyed man thus, had less chance of seeing the slight abnormality of the weird scenes, while to a one-eyed man the illusion of in-visibility was partially destroyed. Ironic, that Grant, with one eye injured and closed, and the one-eyed Willie Green, were best equipped to see the murderous Thompson!

Grant and Ruth are married now. They have moved from Sleepy Valley. The graveyard there brings too many ghastly memories.

The House in the Magnolias

By August Derleth and Mark Schorer

IF YOU had seen the magnolias, you would understand without further explanation from me why I went back to the house. My friends in New Orleans realized that it was just such a place as an artist like myself would light upon for his subject. Their objections to my going there were not based on notions that the house and its surroundings were not fit subjects for really excellent landscape paintings. No, they agreed with me there. Where they disagreed ... But I had better fill in the background for you before I get too far ahead in my story.

I had been in New Orleans a month, and still had found no subject in that old city that really satisfied me. But, motoring one day out into the country with Sherman Jordan, a young poet with whom I was living during my stay in the city, we found ourselves about four miles out of New Orleans, driving along a little-used road over which the willows leaned low. The road broadened unexpectedly, and the willows gave way to a row of sycamores, and then, in the evening dusk, I saw the house in the magnolias for the first time.

It was not far from the road, and yet not too close. A great veranda with tall pillars stretched its length in front. The house itself was of white wood, built in the typical rambling Southern plantation style. Vines covered great portions of its sides, and the whole building was literally buried in magnolias—magnolias such as I have never seen before, in every shade and hue. They were fully opened, and even from the road I could see the heavy waxen artificiality of those nearest.

"There's my picture!" I exclaimed eagerly "Stop the car, old man."

But Sherman Jordan showed no inclination to stop. He glanced quickly at his watch and said by way of explanation: "It's almost six; we've got to get back for our dinner engagement." He drove on without a second glance at the house.

I was disappointed. "It would have taken only a minute," I reproached him.

I must have looked glum, for just as we were driving into New Orleans, he turned and said: "I'm sorry; I didn't think it was so important." I felt suddenly, inexplicably, that he was not sorry, that he had gone past the house deliberately.

I said: "Oh, it doesn't make any difference. I can come out tomorrow."

He was silent for a moment. Then he said:

"Do you really think it would be such a good picture?"

"I do," I said, and at the same instant I thought that he didn't want me to paint that house. "Will you drive me out tomorrow morning?" I added.

"I can't," he said shortly. "I've promised Stan Leslie I'd go boating with him. But you can have the car, if you really insist on painting that house."

I said nothing.

As we left the car he turned and said almost sharply: "Still, I think you might find better subjects if you tried."

A cutting reply about my wasted month in New Orleans was on the tip of my tongue, but I held it back. I could not understand my friend's utter lack of enthusiasm. I could not chalk it up to an inartistic eye, for I knew Sherman Jordan could be depended on for good taste. As I went upstairs to dress, there remained in my mind the picture of that lovely old house, surrounded by rich magnolias, marked off by the swaying sycamore trees.

My eagerness had not abated when I stepped from Jordan's car next morning, opened the gate, and went up the path under the sycamores to the house in the magnolias. As I mounted the steps, walked across the veranda, and lifted the knocker on the closed door, I thought of painting a close-up of magnolias. I was turning this idea over in my mind when the door opened suddenly, noiselessly. And old woman stood there, apparently a Negress, dressed plainly in starched white. Her face held me. It was peculiarly ashy—really gray—unhealthy. I thought: "The woman is ill." Her eyes stared at me; they were like deep black pools, bottomless, inscrutable, and yet at the same time oddly dull. I felt momentarily uncomfortable.

"Is the master in?" I asked.

The woman did not answer, though she continued to stare at me. For a moment I thought that perhaps she was deaf. I spoke loudly, and very distinctly, repeating: "Is your master in? May I see your master?"

A faint shadow fell across the floor of the hall behind the servant, and in an instant, a second woman appeared. "What is it?" she asked sharply, in a deep, velvety voice. The woman was so astonishingly attractive that for a moment I could not speak for admiration. She was almost as tall as I was, and very shapely. Her hair was black and drawn back loosely from her face. Her complexion was swarthy, almost olive, with a high color in cheeks and lips. In her ears were golden rings. Her eyes, which were black, shone from dark surrounding shadows. She wore a purple dress that fell almost to the floor. Her face as she looked at me was imperious; behind her dark eyes were smoldering fires.

She waved the servant aside and turned to me, repeating her question: "What is it, please?"

With my eyes on her face, I said: "I am John Stuard. I paint. Yesterday, driving past your place here, I was so attracted by the house that I felt I must come and ask your permission to use it as a subject for a landscape."

"Will you come in?" she asked, less sharply.

She stepped to one side. I muttered my thanks and went past her into the hall. Behind me I could feel the woman's alert eyes boring into me. I turned, and she gestured for me to precede her into the drawing room leading off the hall. I went ahead. In the drawing room we sat down.

"You are from New Orleans?" she asked. She leaned a little forward, her somber eyes taking in my face. She was sitting in shadow, and I directly in the light from the half-opened window.

"No," I replied. "I live in Chicago. I am only visiting in New Orleans."

She looked at me a moment before replying. "Perhaps it can be arranged for you to paint the house. It will not take long? How many days, please?"

"A week, perhaps ten days. It is quite difficult."

She appeared suddenly annoyed. She was just about to say something when some distant sound caught her ear, and she jerked her head up, looking intently into a corner of the ceiling, as if listening. I heard nothing. Presently she turned again. "I thought it might be for only a day or two," she said, biting her lower lip.

I began to explain when I heard the old servant shuffle toward the door that led out to the veranda. The woman before me looked up quickly. Then she called out in a low persuasive voice: "Go back to the kitchen, Matilda."

Looking through the open drawing room doors, I saw the servant stop in her tracks, turn automatically, and shuffle past the door down the hall, walking listlessly, stiffly.

"Is the woman ill?" I asked solicitously.

"*Non, non,*" she said quickly. Then she said abruptly: "You do not know my name; I am Rosamunda Marsina."

Belatedly I said: "I am glad to know you. You live here alone?"

There was a pause before she answered me. "The servant," she said, smiling lightly. She looked a little troubled. I felt that I should not have asked.

To cover my embarrassment, I said: "You have a nice plantation."

She shook her head quickly. "It is not mine. It belongs to Miss Abby, my aunt Abby. She is a Haitian."

"Oh, I see," I said, smiling; "She lives in Haiti?"

"No, she does not live in Haiti. She did live there. She came from there some years ago."

I nodded, but I did not quite understand. Looking about me, I could see that everything was scrupulously clean and well taken care of, and this was certainly a large house for a single servant to keep so well. I had seen from a glance at Miss Marsina's hands that she had no share in the labors of the household.

Miss Marsina bent forward again. "Tell me, say, I give you permission to paint the house—you would stay—in the city?"

My eyes dropped confusedly before hers, and at her question my face fell, for my disappointment was evident to her. I had hoped she would ask me to live in the house for the time that I painted it. Once more I started an explanation to Rosamunda Marsina, suggesting that I might find some place in the neighborhood where I could get a room for the time, but throughout my explanation, I openly shamelessly hinted at an invitation from her to stay here.

My speech seemed to have its effect. "Perhaps I could give you a room for that time," she said reluctantly

I accepted her invitation at once. She fidgeted a little nervously, and asked: "When do you wish to begin painting?"

"I should like to start sketching tomorrow. The painting I shall have to do mostly late in the afternoon. I want to get the half-light in which I first saw the house—"

She interrupted me abruptly. "There will be some conditions to staying here—a request I must make of you, perhaps two." I nodded. "I am not a very sociable creature," she went on. "I do not like many people about. I must ask you not to bring any friends out with you, even for short visits. And I would rather, too, that you didn't mention your work out here unless necessary—it might reach the ears of Aunt Abby; perhaps she would not like it."

I saw nothing strange in her request, nothing strange in this mysteriously beautiful woman. "I shouldn't think of bringing anyone, Miss Marsina," I said. "I feel I am presuming as it is."

She stopped me with a quick, abrupt "*Non,*" and a slightly upraised hand. Then she smiled. "I shall expect you tomorrow then."

Both of us got up and walked to the door. I said, "Good-by" almost automatically. Then I started walking down the path, away from the house, feeling Rosamunda Marsina's eyes on me. Suddenly I heard running footsteps, light footsteps, and turned to meet Miss Marsina.

"One thing more, Mr. Stuard," she said hurriedly, talking in a low voice as if afraid of being overheard. "Tomorrow—is it necessary for you to bring your car? Cars disturb me." She looked pathetically at me.

"I shall not bring the car," I said.

She nodded, quickly, shortly, and ran back into the house without pausing. Looking back from the road, I saw her standing at the open window of the drawing room, watching me.

I found Rosamunda Marsina waiting for me next morning. She seemed a little agitated; I wondered whether anything had gone wrong.

"Shall I bring in the equipment and my easel?" I asked.

"Matilda can bring it to your room," she said. "Come with me. I am going to put you on the ground floor."

She turned and led the way into the house and down the hall. Opening a door not far beyond the drawing room she stretched out her arm and indicated the charming old chamber which I was to occupy, a room with great heavy mahogany bureau and four-poster, with a desk, and windows opening directly on the garden at the side of the house.

"It's lovely," I murmured.

She looked at me with her dark eyes, not as sharp today as they had been the day before. They were limpid and soft, tender, I thought. Then abruptly I caught a flash of something I was not meant to see; it was present only for a moment, and her eyes veiled it again—unmistakable fear!

She could not have known that I had seen, for she said: "You must not venture off the grounds, and not behind the house. And you will not go to any of the other floors?"

I said: "No, certainly not."

Matilda shuffled into the room, and without a word or a glance at us, put the equipment down near the bed. She departed with the same dragging footsteps.

"A curious woman," I said.

Rosamunda Marsina laughed a little uncertainly. "Yes; she is very old. She came here with my aunt."

"Oh," I said. "Your aunt is *here*, then?"

She looked at me, shot a quick startled glance at me. "Didn't I tell you?" she asked. "I thought I told you yesterday—yes, she is here. That is why I have made so many requests of you; it is because I don't want her to know you are here." Her voice betrayed her agitation, though her face remained immobile.

"She can hardly help seeing me some time, I'm afraid."

"*Non, non*—not if you do as I say." Once again fear crept into her eyes. She spoke quickly in a low voice. "She is a near-invalid. She has a club foot, and never leaves the back rooms of the second floor because it is so difficult for her to move." Rosamunda Marsina's hand was trembling. I took it in my own.

"If she would object to my being here, perhaps I had better go to one of your neighbors," I volunteered.

She closed her eyes for a moment; then flashed them open and looked at me calmly, saying impetuously: "I want you to stay. My aunt must not matter—even though she does. You must stay now; I want you to stay. She is not really my aunt, I don't think. She brought me from Haiti when I was just a little girl. I cannot remember anything. She is much darker than I am; she is not a Creole."

Again I had an uncomfortable feeling that something was wrong in the house, and for a moment I had the impression that Rosamunda Marsina was begging me to stay. "Thank you," I said; "I'll stay."

She smiled at me with her lovely dark lips and left the room, closing the door softly behind her.

That night the first strange thing happened. Rosamunda Marsina's suggestive attitude, the vague fear that haunted her eyes, the sudden inexplicable agitation of her voice—these things had prepared me. Perhaps if I had gone to sleep at once, I would have known nothing. As I lay there, half asleep, I heard a distinct sound of someone walking on the floor above me, in some room farther back than my own. I thought of Miss Marsina's aunt Abby at once, but recollected that the woman was a cripple and a near-invalid, and would not be likely to be up and about, especially not at this hour. Yet the footsteps were slow and dragging, and were accompanied by the sound of a cane tapping slowly at regular intervals against the floor. I sat up in bed to listen. Listening, I could tell that it was only one foot that dragged. Abruptly, the footsteps stopped. Miss Abby had gotten out of her bed somehow, and had walked perhaps to the wall of the room from the bed. I heard guttural sounds suddenly, and then the dragging footsteps retreating. The woman talking to herself, I thought.

Then, above the dragging footsteps, I heard a disturbing shuffling which seemed to come from somewhere below, followed by sounds as of doors closing somewhere. In a moment, all was quiet again; but only for a moment—for suddenly there came a thin, reed-like wail of terror, followed at once by a shrill scream. I sat up abruptly. A window went up with a bang, and a harsh, guttural voice sounded from above. The voice from above had a magic effect, for silence, broken only by the sudden shuffling of feet, fell immediately.

I had got out of bed, and made my way to the door leading into the hall. I had seen on my first visit that the house lacked artificial light, and had brought an electric candle along. This I took up as I went toward the door. I had it in my hand as I opened the door. The first thing its light found was the white face of Rosamunda Marsina.

"Someone called ... I thought," I stammered.

She was agitated; even the comparatively dim illumination from the electric candle revealed her emotion. "*Non, non*—there was nothing," she said quickly. "You are mistaken, Mr. Stuard." Then, noticing the amazement which must have shown on-my face, she added, uncertainly: "Perhaps the servants called out—but it is nothing; nothing is wrong."

As she said this, she gestured with her hands. She was wearing a long black gown with wide sleeves. As she raised her hands, the sleeves fell back along her arms. I think I must have started at what I saw there—at any rate, Rosamunda Marsina dropped her arms at once, shot a sharp glance at me through half-closed eyes, and walked swiftly away, saying, "Good night, Mr. Stuard." For on the white of her arms, I saw the distinct impressions of two large hands—hands which must have grasped her most cruelly, and only a short while before. Then, so suddenly as to leave me gasping, it came to me that Rosamunda Marsina had been waiting for me in the hall, waiting to see what I would do—and, I felt sure, sending me back into my room against her will!

I slept comparatively little that night.

In the morning I wanted to say something to my hostess, but I had hardly come from my room before she herself spoke. She came to me at the breakfast table, and said: "You must have had a powerful dream last night, Mr. Stuard. There was nothing wrong as you thought—nor did the servants call out!"

At once I understood that she was not talking for me. Her face was white and strained, her voice unnaturally loud. As quickly, I answered in an equal raised voice. "I'm sorry. I should have warned you that I am often troubled by bad dreams."

Miss Marsina lost her tensity at once. She shot me a grateful glance, and left the room immediately. But I sat in silence, waiting for a sound I felt must come. I had not long to wait— a few moments passed—then, from upstairs, came the soft sound of a door closing. Someone had been listening, waiting to hear what Rosamunda Marsina would say to me, what I would answer!

From that moment I knew that I would get no more painting done until I knew what mystery surrounded the house and Miss Marsina.

I sketched my landscape that morning, and my hostess stood watching me. I liked her lovely dark face peering over my shoulder as I worked, but both of us were a little uneasy, and I could not do my best work. There was about her an air of restraint which interposed itself mysteriously the moment she tried to enjoy herself. She seemed a little frightened, too, and more than once I caught her eyes straying furtively to the second-floor windows.

The second night in the house was a hot, sultry night; a storm was brooding low on the horizon when I went to bed, but it must have passed over, for when I woke up somewhere between one and two in the morning, the moon was shining. I could not rest, and got out of bed. For a few moments I stood at the window, drinking in the sweet smell of the magnolias. Then, acting on a sudden impulse, I bent and crawled through the open window. I dropped to the ground silently and began to walk toward the rear of the house unconsciously, forgetting my promise to Miss Marsina. I remembered it suddenly, and stopped. Then I heard a slight sound above me. I stepped quickly into the shadow of a bush, just at the corner of the house, where I could see both the side and rear of the house.

Then I looked up. There at the window of the corner room I saw a bloodless face pressed against the glass; it was a dark, ugly face, and the moonlight struck it full.

It was withdrawn as I looked, but not before I had got an impression of malefic power. Could it have been the face of Aunt Abby? According to what Rosamunda Marsina had said, that would be her room. And what was she looking at? Over the bushes behind the house, beyond the trees— it would be something in the fields. I turned. Should I risk trying to see, risk her spotting me as I went along the lane?

Keeping to the shadows, I moved along under the low-hanging trees, looking toward the fields. Then suddenly I saw what Miss Abby must have seen. There were men in the fields, a number of them. I pressed myself against the trunk of a giant sycamore and watched them. They were Negroes, and they were working in the fields. Moreover, they were probably under orders, Miss Abby's orders. I understood abruptly that her watching them was to see that they did their work. But Negroes that worked at night!

Back in my room once more, I was still more thoroughly mystified. Did they work every night? It was true that I had seen no workers anywhere on the plantation during the day- just passed, but then, I had not left the front of the house, and from there little of the plantation could be seen. I thought that next day surely I would mention this to Rosamunda Marsina, and the incidents of the night before, too.

Then I thought of something else. All the while that I had stood watching the Negroes, no word had passed among them. That was surely the height of the unusual.

But on the second day, I found that I had to go into New Orleans for some painting materials I had not supposed I would need, and for some clothes, also, and thus lost the opportunity to speak to Rosamunda Marsina before evening.

In the city, I went immediately to Sherman Jordan's apartment. Despite the fact that I had promised Rosamunda Marsina that I would say as little about my stay with her as possible, I told my friend of my whereabouts.

"I knew pretty well you were out there," he said. His voice, was not particularly cordial. I said nothing. "I daresay you are completely entranced by the beautiful Creole who lives there?"

"How did you know?" I asked.

He shrugged his shoulders, giving me a queer look. "There are stories about," he said.

"About Miss Marsina?" I felt suddenly angry.

"Not especially. Just stories about that place. Nothing definite. If you haven't noticed anything, perhaps it's just idle gossip." But Jordan's attitude showed that he did not believe the stories about the house in the magnolias to be just "idle gossip."

And I *had* noticed something, but instantly I resolved to say nothing to Jordan. "What stories?" I asked.

He did not appear to have heard my question. "They're from Haiti, aren't they?"

I nodded. "Yes. The old woman is a Haitian. The girl is not." Was he getting at something?

"Haiti—a strange, fascinating place." He stood looking out of the window. He turned suddenly. "I'd like to beg you to drop that work out there, John, but I know it wouldn't be of much use asking that, now you've started. There's something not right about that place, because strange stories don't grow out of thin air."

"If there's anything wrong out there, I'm going to find out."

He shrugged his shoulders. His smile was not convincing. "Of course," he said. Then: "You know, there's an old proverb in Creole patois—'*Quand to mange avec diab' tenin to cuillere longue.*'"

"I don't understand Creole patois," I said, somewhat irritated.

"Literally, it is: 'When you sup with the devil, be sure you have a long spoon.'"

"I don't follow you," I said.

He smiled again. "Oh, it's just another warning."

I had no desire to listen longer to anything so indefinite and vague; so I changed the subject. I don't think anything he could have told me would have influenced me; I would have gone back to that house and Rosamunda Marsina no matter what was lurking there. But I expected nothing so strange, so horrible, as that which I did discover.

I returned to the house that evening, and again put off saying anything to Rosamunda. But she herself afforded me an unlooked for opening before I went to bed that night. She had come down from upstairs, and I could see at once that there was something she wanted to tell me.

"I think it's only fair to tell you," she said, "that your door will be locked tonight, after you have gone to bed."

"Why?" I asked, trying not to betray my astonishment.

"It is because it is not desirable that you walk around at night."

This hurt me a little, suggesting as it did that perhaps I might make use of the darkness to spy out the house. I said: "Rosamunda, there are stories about this house, aren't there?"

I was sorry at once, for she looked suddenly very frightened. "What do you mean?" she asked.

"I have heard things in New Orleans," I said slowly.

She mastered herself a little, asking: "What?"

"Oh, nothing definite," I replied. "Some people think that there is something wrong out here."

"Something wrong? What?"

"I don't know."'

"Have you seen anything wrong?"

"No ..." I hesitated, and she caught my dubious tone.

"Do you suspect anything?" she asked.

"I don't know," I said.

She looked at me a little coldly. Already I was beginning to repent my having spoken to her about the house. Also, she had suspected at once that I had broken my promise to her and had talked about the house. I had not foreseen that, and cursed myself for a fool. I had succeeded only in creating an atmosphere of tension.

That night I was awakened by a sharp cry of terror, which was cut off abruptly even before I was fully awake. I was out of bed instantly standing in the middle of the room, listening. Once I fancied I heard the sound of Rosamunda's voice, a low, earnest sound, as if she were pleading with someone. Then, silence. How long I waited, I do not know. At last I took up my electric candle and made for the door. Then I remembered that it would be locked—as Rosamunda had told me. Yet I reached out and turned the knob, and the door was not locked!

I looked cautiously out into the hall. But I had time to see only one thing: a bloodless face, convulsed with hatred, staring into mine—the same face I had seen against the window of the second floor—and above it, a heavy cane upraised. Then the cane descended, catching me a glancing blow on the side of the head. I went down like a log.

How long I lay there I do not know; it could not have been long, for it was still dark when I came to—and found Rosamunda's frightened eyes watching my face anxiously, felt her delicate fingers on my forehead. I struggled to sit up, but she held me quiet.

"Be still," she murmured. Then she asked quickly: "You are not badly hurt?"

"No," I whispered. "It was just enough to put me out."

"Oh, it was my fault. If I had locked the door it would not have happened."

"Nonsense," I said quickly. "If I hadn't been so curious ... if I hadn't heard your voice ..."

"I am glad you thought of me, John." It was the first time she had used my Christian name, and I felt more pleasure than I cared to admit. But before I could express my sentiment, she said swiftly: "In the morning you must go."

"What? Go away—and not come back?"

She nodded. "If you do not go away, both of us will suffer. I should not have let you come, let you stay."

Boldly I said: "I'm not going until I can take you with me."

She looked closely at me; then bent quickly and kissed me. For a moment I held her in my arms; then she pushed me gently away. "Listen," she said. "In the morning you must go with your baggage. Go anywhere—back to New Orleans. But at sundown, come back to me. You must not be seen by Aunt Abby. I will wait for you in the magnolias just below the veranda."

I stood up, steadying myself against the doorframe. "I'll come back, Rosamunda," I said.

She nodded and fled down the hall. I went back into my room and packed my things.

In the morning I departed ostentatiously, making it certain that the older woman, Abby, had seen me go. But in the evening I was back. I never left the vicinity, and was within sight of the house all day. How could I leave there—when Rosamunda might be in danger? I approached the house that evening effectively screened by low trees and the magnolias.

Rosamunda was standing before the veranda, almost hidden in the bushes. She was agitated, standing there twisting her handkerchief in her hands. She ran forward a little as I came up. "Now I must tell you," she breathed. "I must tell someone—you. You must help me." She was obviously distraught.

I said: "I'll do anything I can for you, Rosamunda."

She began to talk now, rapidly. "We came from Haiti, John. That is a strange island, an island of weird, curious things. Sometimes it is called the magic island. And it is. Do you believe in magic things?"

I did have a knowledge of magic beliefs, some old legends I had picked up in the Indian country, and quite a collection of tales I had heard from levee Negroes. I nodded, saying: "I know very little of it, but I think it can be."

"You have never been to Haiti?"

"No," I replied.

She paused, turned and looked a little fearfully at the house; then spoke again. "There are many strange beliefs in Haiti," she said, talking slowly, yet betraying an eagerness to finish. Then she looked deep into my eyes and asked: "Do you know what a *zombi* is?"

I had heard weird half-hinted stories of animated cadavers seen in Haiti, whispered tales of age-old Negro magic used to raise the dead of the black island. Vaguely, I knew what she meant. Yet I said: "No."

"It is a dead man," she went on hurriedly, "a dead man who has been brought out of his grave and made to live again and to work!"

"But such a thing cannot be," I protested, suddenly horrified at an idea that began to form in my mind, a terrible suggestion which I sought to banish quickly. It would not go. I listened for Rosamunda's hushed and tense voice.

"Believe me, John Stuard—they do exist!"

"No, no," I said.

She stopped me abruptly. "You are making it hard for me."

"I'm sorry," I said. "I will believe you." But inwardly I protested; surely such a thing could not be! Yet I could not banish from my mind the memory of strangely silent figures working the fields at night.

Rosamunda spoke swiftly, her words coming in an agonized rush. "That woman—Abby— she knew how to raise these people from their graves. When we came to New Orleans, we came alone. Just the two of us. She was in a hurry to get out of Haiti; I now think she was wanted in Port au Prince. I do not know. I was only a little girl, but I can remember these things. Every year they come more and more distinctly to me. Soon after we were here, the slaves came."

I cut in: "What slaves?"

"They are in the cellars—many of them. All Negroes. We keep them in the cellars all day; only at night Abby sends them out to work. I have been so afraid you might find them, for you heard them screaming—and you might have seen them in the fields at night."

"But surely you don't mean—you can't mean ..."

"I do. *They are dead!*"

"But, Rosamunda ...!"

"Please, let me tell you what I know." I nodded, and she went on. "I was quite old when Matilda came. She was the last of them. All along up to her, the slaves came, one after the other. I never saw them come. One day they were just here; that is all. But many nights Abby was gone—and soon after, slaves would come. Abby always took care of them herself, making sweet bread and water for them. They ate nothing more. After Matilda came, something happened. Aunt Abby hurt herself, and couldn't leave the house. She wouldn't have a doctor, and since then she could leave her room only with great difficulty. She had a speaking tube put into her rooms; it ran down into the cellars, so that she could direct the men—those poor dead men—into the fields. They were taught to come back as soon as light showed in the eastern sky. Only Abby could direct them, but I could tell Matilda what to do. Over Matilda Abby had no power—it often happens that way.

"After she came, there were no more slaves. I was quite grown then, and I came on a newspaper one day that told of a series of grave robbings that had been climaxed by the recent snatching of the body of a colored woman, Matilda Martin. That was right after Matilda came. Since then, I have known. At first it was horrible for me to live here, but there was no place for me to go. I have been living with these dead men and Abby, John, and I cannot go on—and I cannot leave these poor dead ones behind me. I want to go away with you, but they must be sent back to the graves from which she took them."

Looking at her frightened yet determined face, I knew that she would go away with me. I did not want the house, nor the magnolias; I wanted Rosamunda Marsina. "There is a way, then, to send them back?" I asked, still only half believing her shocking story.

She nodded eagerly. "They must be given salt—any food with salt—and they will know they are dead, and will find their way back to their graves."

"And Miss Abby?" I said.

She looked at me. "She is too strong; we can do nothing if she knows."

"What shall we do?" I asked.

Rosamunda's eyes went suddenly cold. She said: "Matilda can be directed to Abby. Only I can direct her. Matilda hates Abby as I do. Abby is a fiend—she has robbed these dead of their peace. If I go from here, she must not be able to follow—else she will hound us until we are dead, and after that ... I don't want to think what might happen then."

An idea came to me, and at first I wanted to brush it aside. But it was persistent—and it was a way out. "Rosamunda," I said, "send Matilda up to Abby."

Rosamunda looked at me. She nodded. "I was thinking that way," she said. "But it must be before she has the salt, because once she has tasted salt there is nothing left for her but to find her grave."

Then she shot a frightened glance at the windows of the second floor. She clutched my arm. "Quick," she murmured. "They will be coming from the cellars soon. We must be ready for them. They never refuse food, never. I have made some little pistachio candies, with salt. We must give the candies to them."

She led the way, almost running into the house. I came silently after her. Below me I could hear the shuffling of many feet, and above, the dragging footsteps of Miss Abby, moving away from her speaking tube. Rosamunda snatched up the little plate of candy and preceded me to the back door.

Then suddenly the cellar doors opened, and a file of staring men shuffled slowly out, looking neither to right nor to left, seeing us, yet not seeing us. Rosamunda stepped boldly forward, holding out the plate. The foremost of them took a piece of the salted candy, and went on, munching it. Their black faces were expressionless. When the Negroes had all taken of the candy, Rosamunda turned to reenter the house. "Come quickly," she said. "Soon they will know." I hesitated, and saw—and my doubts were swept away, leaving my mind in chaos.

The little group had stopped abruptly, huddled together. Then, one by one, they began to wail terribly into the night, and even as I watched, they began to move off, hurriedly now, running across the fields toward their distant graves, a line of terrible, tragic figures against the sky.

I felt Rosamunda shuddering against me, and slipped my arm gently around her. "Listen!" she said, her voice trembling. Above us I could hear suddenly the angry snarling voice of Miss Abby. At the same time the sound of wood beating wood came to us: Abby was pounding the walls with her cane.

Matilda stood in the kitchen, and Rosamunda went up to her at once, addressing her in a soft, persuasive voice. "Above there is Abby, Matilda. Long ago she took you away from where you were—took you to be her slave. You have not liked her, Matilda, you have hated her. Go up to her now. She is yours. When you come down, there will be candy on the table for you."

Matilda nodded slowly; then she turned and began to shuffle heavily into the hall toward the stairs. Upstairs, silence had fallen.

Both of us ran from the kitchen, snatching up two small carpet-bags which Rosamunda had put into the corridor, and which she pointed out to me as we went. We jumped from the veranda and ran down the path. Behind us rose suddenly into the night the shrill screaming of a woman in deadly terror. It was shut off abruptly, horribly. Rosamunda was shuddering. We turned to run. We had gone only a little way down the deserted road when we heard the nearby sound of a woman wailing. That was Matilda. Rosamunda hesitated, I with her, pressed close in the shadow of an overhanging sycamore. We looked back. A shadowy figure was running across the fields; in the house a lamp was burning low in the kitchen. And yet, was it a lamp? The light suddenly flared up. I turned Rosamunda about before she had time to see what I had seen. Matilda had turned over the lamp. The house was burning.

Rosamunda was whimpering a little, the strain beginning to tell. "We'll have to go away. When they find Abby dead, they'll want me."

I said, "Yes, Rosamunda," but I knew we would not have to go away, unless that fire did not burn. We hurried on to New Orleans, and went to Jordan's apartment.

Next day it was discovered that the house in the magnolias had burned to the ground, Miss Abby with it. The Creole woman, Rosamunda Marsina, had spent the night with her fiancé in the apartment of Sherman Jordan—so said the papers. Jordan had seen to that. Rosamunda and I were married soon after and went out to rebuild that house.

Since then, I have tried often to dismiss the events of that horrible night as a chaotic dream, a thing half imagined, half real. But certain things forbade any such interpretation, no matter how much I longed to believe that both Rosamunda and I had been deceived by too vivid belief in Haitian legends.

There were especially those other things in the papers that day—the day the burning of the house was chronicled—things I kept carefully from Rosamunda's eyes. They were isolated stories of new graveyard outrages—that is what the papers called them, but I know better—*the finding of putrefied remains in half-opened graves of Negroes whose bodies had been stolen long years ago – and the curious detail that the graves had been half dug by bare fingers, as if dead hands were seeking the empty coffins below.*

The Empire of the Necromancers

By Clark Ashton Smith

THE LEGEND of Mmatmuor and Sodosma shall arise only in the latter cycles of Earth, when the glad legends of the prime have been forgotten. Before the time of its telling, many epochs shall have passed away, and the seas shall have fallen in their beds, and new continents shall have come to birth. Perhaps, in that day, it will serve to beguile for a little the black weariness of a dying race, grown hopeless of all but oblivion. I tell the tale as men shall tell it in Zothique, the last continent, beneath a dim sun and sad heavens where the stars come out in terrible brightness before eventide.

Part I

MMATMUOR and Sodosma were necromancers who came from the dark isle of Naat, to practise their baleful arts in Tinarath, beyond the shrunken seas. But they did not prosper in Tinarath: for death was deemed a holy thing by the people of that gray country; and the nothingness of the tomb was not lightly to be desecrated; and the raising up of the dead by necromancy was held in abomination.

So, after a short interval, Mmatmuor and Sodosma were driven forth by the anger of the inhabitants, and were compelled to flee toward Cincor, a desert of the south, which was peopled only by the bones and mummies of a race that the pestilence had slain in former time.

The land into which they went lay drear and leprous and ashen below the huge, ember-colored sun. Its crumbling rocks and deathly solitudes of sand would have struck terror to the hearts of common men; and, since they had been thrust out in that barren place without food or sustenance, the plight of the sorcerers might well have seemed a desperate one. But, smiling secretly, with the air of conquerors who tread the approaches of a long-coveted realm, Sodosma and Mmatmuor walked steadily on into Cincor

Unbroken before them, through fields devoid of trees and grass, and across the channels of dried-up rivers, there ran the great highway by which travelers had gone formerly between Cincor and Tinarath. Here they met no living thing; but soon they came to the skeletons of a horse and its rider, lying full in the road, and wearing still the sumptuous harness and raiment which they had worn in the flesh. And Mmatmuor and Sodosma paused before the piteous bones, on which no shred of corruption remained; and they smiled evilly at each other.

'The steed shall be yours,' said Mmatmuor, 'since you are a little the elder of us two, and are thus entitled to precedence; and the rider shall serve us both and be the first to acknowledge fealty to us in Cincor.'

Then, in the ashy sand by the wayside, they drew a threefold circle; and standing together at its center, they performed the abominable rites that compel the dead to arise from tranquil nothingness and obey henceforward, in all things, the dark will of the necromancer. Afterward they sprinkled a pinch of magic powder on the nostril-holes of the man and the horse; and the white bones, creaking mournfully, rose up from where they had lain and stood in readiness to serve their masters.

So, as had been agreed between them, Sodosma mounted the skeleton steed and took up the jeweled reins, and rode in an evil mockery of Death on his pale horse; while Mmatmuor trudged on beside him, leaning lightly on an ebon staff; and the skeleton of the man, with its rich raiment flapping loosely, followed behind the two like a servitor.

After a while, in the gray waste, they found the remnant of another horse and rider, which the jackals had spared and the sun had dried to the leanness of old mummies. These also they raised up from death; and Mmatmuor bestrode the withered charger; and the two magicians rode on in state, like errant emperors, with a lich and a skeleton to attend them. Other bones and charnel remnants of men and beasts, to which they came anon, were duly resurrected in like fashion; so that they gathered to themselves an ever-swelling train in their progress through Cincor.

Along the way, as they neared Yethlyreom, which had been the capital, they found numerous tombs and necropoli, inviolate still after many ages, and containing swathed mummies that had scarcely withered in death. All these they raised up and called from sepulchral night to do their bidding. Some they commanded to sow and till the desert fields and hoist water from the sunken wells; others they left at diverse tasks, such as the mummies had performed in life. The century-long silence was broken by the noise and tumult of myriad activities; and the lank liches of weavers toiled at their shuttles; and the corpses of plowmen followed their furrows behind carrion oxen.

Weary with their strange journey and their oft-repeated incantations, Mmatmuor and Sodosma saw before them at last, from a desert hill, the lofty spires and fair, unbroken domes of Yethlyreom, steeped in the darkening stagnant blood of ominous sunset.

'It is a goodly land,' said Mmatmuor, 'and you and I will share it between us, and hold dominion over all its dead, and be crowned as emperors on the morrow in Yethlyreom.'

'Aye,' replied Sodosma, 'for there is none living to dispute us here; and those that we have summoned from the tomb shall move and breathe only at our dictation, and may not rebel against us.'

So, in the blood-red twilight that thickened with purple, they entered Yethlyreom and rode on among the lofty, lampless mansions, and installed themselves with their grisly retinue in that stately and abandoned palace, where the dynasty of Nimboth emperors had reigned for two thousand years with dominion over Cincor.

In the dusty golden halls, they lit the empty lamps of onyx by means of their cunning sorcery, and supped on royal viands, provided from past years, which they evoked in like manner. Ancient and imperial wines were poured for them in moonstone cups by the fleshless hands of their servitors; and they drank and feasted and reveled in fantasmagoric pomp, deferring till the morrow the resurrection of those who lay dead in Yethlyreom.

They rose betimes, in the dark crimson dawn, from the opulent palace-beds in which they had slept; for much remained to be done. Everywhere in that forgotten city, they went busily to and fro, working their spells on the people that had died in the last year of the pest and had lain unburied. And having accomplished this, they passed beyond Yethlyreom into that other city of high tombs and mighty mausoleums, in which lay the Nimboth emperors and the more consequential citizens and nobles of Cincor.

Here they bade their skeleton slaves to break in the sealed doors with hammers; and then, with their sinful, tyrannous incantations, they called forth the imperial mummies, even to the eldest of the dynasty, all of whom came walking stiffly, with lightless eyes, in rich swathings sewn with flame-bright jewels. And also, later, they brought forth to a semblance of life many generations of courtiers and dignitaries.

Moving in solemn pageant, with dark and haughty and hollow faces, the dead emperors and empresses of Cincor made obeisance to Mmatmuor and Sodosma, and attended them like a train of captives through all the streets of Yethlyreom. Afterward, in the immense throne-room of the palace, the necromancers mounted the high double throne, where the rightful rulers had sat with their consorts. Amid the assembled emperors, in gorgeous and funereal state, they were invested with sovereignty by the sere hands of the mummy of Hestaiyon, earliest of the Nimboth line, who had ruled in half-mythic years. Then all the descendants of Hestaiyon, crowding the room in a great throng, acclaimed with toneless, echo-like voices the dominion of Mmatmuor and Sodosma.

Thus did the outcast necromancers find for themselves an empire and a subject people in the desolate, barren land where the men of Tinarath had driven them forth to perish. Reigning supreme over all the dead of Cincor, by virtue of their malign magic, they exercised a baleful despotism. Tribute was borne to them by fleshless porters from outlying realms; and plague-eaten corpses, and tall mummies scented with mortuary balsams, went to and fro upon their errands in Yethlyreom, or heaped before their greedy eyes, from inexhaustible vaults, the cobweb-blackened gold and dusty gems of antique time.

Dead laborers made their palace-gardens to bloom with long-perished flowers; liches and skeletons toiled for them in the mines, or reared superb, fantastic towers to the dying sun. Chamberlains and princes of old time were their cupbearers, and stringed instruments were plucked for their delight by the slim hands of empresses with golden hair that had come forth untarnished from the night of the tomb. Those that were fairest, whom the plague and the worm had not ravaged overmuch, they took for their lemans and made to serve their necrophilic lust.

Part II

IN ALL things, the people of Cincor performed the actions of life at the will of Mmatmuor and Sodosma. They spoke, they moved, they ate and drank as in life. They heard and saw and felt with a similitude of the senses that had been theirs before death; but their brains were enthralled by a dreadful necromancy. They recalled but dimly their former existence; and the state to which they had been summoned was empty and troublous and shadow-like. Their blood ran chill and sluggish, mingled with water of Lethe; and the vapors of Lethe clouded their eyes.

Dumbly they obeyed the dictates of their tyrannous lords, without rebellion or protest, but filled with a vague, illimitable weariness such as the dead must know, when having drunk of eternal sleep, they are called back once more to the bitterness of mortal being. They knew no passion or desire or delight, only the black languor of their awakening from Lethe, and a gray, ceaseless longing to return to that interrupted slumber.

Youngest and last of the Nimboth emperors was Illeiro, who had died in the first month of the plague and had lain in his high-built mausoleum for two hundred years before the coming of the necromancers.

Raised up with his people and his fathers to attend the tyrants, Illeiro had resumed the emptiness of existence without question and had felt no surprise. He had accepted his own resurrection and that of his ancestors as one accepts the indignities and marvels of a dream. He knew that he had come back to a faded sun, to a hollow and spectral world, to an order of things in which his place was merely that of an obedient shadow. But at first he was troubled only, like the others, by a dim weariness and pale hunger for the lost oblivion.

Drugged by the magic of his overlords, weak from the age-long nullity of death, he beheld like a somnambulist the enormities to which his fathers were subjected. Yet, somehow, after many days, a feeble spark awoke in the sodden twilight of his mind.

Like something lost and irretrievable, beyond prodigious gulfs, he recalled the pomp of his reign in Yethlyreom, and the golden pride and exultation that had been his in youth. And recalling it, he felt a vague stirring of revolt, a ghostly resentment against the magicians who had haled him forth to this calamitous mockery of life. Darkly he began to grieve for his fallen state, and the mournful plight of his ancestors and his people.

Day by day, as a cup-bearer in the halls where he had ruled aforetime, Illeiro saw the doings of Mmatmuor and Sodosma. He saw their caprices of cruelty and lust, their growing drunkenness and gluttony. He watched them wallow in their necromantic luxury, and become lax with indolence, gross with indulgence. They neglected the study of their art, they forgot many of their spells. But still they ruled, mighty and formidable; and, lolling on couches of purple and rose, they planned to lead an army of the dead against Tinarath.

Dreaming of conquest, and of vaster necromancies, they grew fat and slothful as worms that have installed themselves in a charnel rich with corruption. And pace by pace with their laxness and tyranny, the fire of rebellion mounted in the shadowy heart of Illeiro, like a flame that struggles with Lethean damps. And slowly, with the waxing of his wrath, there returned to him something of the strength and firmness that had been his in life. Seeing the turpitude of the oppressors, and knowing the wrong that had been done to the helpless dead, he heard in his brain the clamor of stifled voices demanding vengeance.

Among his fathers, through the palace-halls of Yethlyreom, Illeiro moved silently at the bidding of the masters, or stood awaiting their command. He poured in their cups of onyx the amber vintages, brought by wizardry from hills beneath a younger sun; he submitted to their contumelies and insults. And night by night he watched them nod in their drunkenness, till they fell asleep, flushed and gross, amid their arrogated splendor.

There was little speech among the living dead; and son and father, daughter and mother, lover and beloved, went to and fro without sign of recognition, making no comment on their evil lot. But at last, one midnight, when the tyrants lay in slumber, and the flames wavered in the necromantic lamps, Illeiro took counsel with Hestaiyon, his eldest ancestor, who had been famed as a great wizard in fable and was reputed to have known the secret lore of antiquity.

Hestaiyon stood apart from the others, in a corner of the shadowy hall. He was brown and withered in his crumbling mummy-cloths; and his lightless obsidian eyes appeared to gaze still upon nothingness. He seemed not to have heard the questions of Illeiro; but at length, in a dry, rustling whisper, he responded:

'I am old, and the night of the sepulcher was long, and I have forgotten much. Yet, groping backward across the void of death, it may be that I shall retrieve something of my former wisdom; and between us we shall devise a mode of deliverance.'

And Hestaiyon searched among the shreds of memory, as one who reaches into a place where the worm has been and the hidden archives of old time have rotted in their covers; till at last he remembered, and said:

'I recall that I was once a mighty wizard; and among other things, I knew the spells of necromancy; but employed them not, deeming their use and the raising up of the dead an abhorrent act. Also, I possessed other knowledge; and perhaps, among the remnants of that ancient lore, there is something which may serve to guide us now. For I recall a dim, dubitable prophecy, made in the primal years, at the founding of Yethlyreom and the empire of Cincor. The prophecy was, that an evil greater than death would befall the emperors and the people of Cincor in future times; and that the first and the last of the Nimboth dynasty, conferring together, would effect a mode of release and the lifting of the doom. The evil was not named in the prophecy: but it was said that the two emperors would learn the solution of their problem by the breaking of an ancient clay image that guards the nethermost vault below the imperial palace in Yethlyreom.'

Then, having heard this prophecy from the faded lips of his forefather, Illeiro mused a while, and said:

'I remember now an afternoon in early youth, when searching idly through the unused vaults of our palace, as a boy might do, I came to the last vault and found therein a dusty, uncouth image of clay, whose form and countenance were strange to me. And, knowing not the prophecy, I turned away in disappointment, and went back as idly as I had come, to seek the moted sunlight.'

Then, stealing away from their heedless kinfolk, and carrying jeweled lamps they had taken from the hall, Hestaiyon and Illeiro went downward by subterranean stairs beneath the palace; and, threading like implacable furtive shadows the maze of nighted corridors, they came at last to the lowest crypt.

Here, in the black dust and clotted cobwebs of an immemorial past, they found, as had been decreed, the clay image, whose rude features were those of a forgotten earthly god. And Illeiro shattered the image with a fragment of stone; and he and Hestaiyon took from its hollow center a great sword of unrusted steel, and a heavy key of untarnished bronze, and tablets of bright brass on which were inscribed the various things to be done, so that Cincor should be rid of the dark reign of the necromancers and the people should win back to oblivious death.

So, with the key of untarnished bronze, Illeiro unlocked, as the tablets had instructed him to do, a low and narrow door at the end of the nethermost vault, beyond the broken image; and he and Hestaiyon saw, as had been prophesied, the coiling steps of somber stone that led downward to an undiscovered abyss, where the sunken fires of earth still burned. And leaving Illeiro to ward the open door, Hestaiyon took up the sword of unrusted steel in his thin hand, and went back to the hall where the necromancers slept, lying a-sprawl on their couches of rose and purple, with the wan, bloodless dead about them in patient ranks.

Upheld by the ancient prophecy and the lore of the bright tablets, Hestaiyon lifted the great sword and struck off the head of Mmatmuor and the head of Sodosma, each with a single blow. Then, as had been directed, he quartered the remains with mighty strokes. And the necromancers gave up their unclean lives, and lay supine, without movement, adding a deeper red to the rose and a brighter hue to the sad purple of their couches.

Then, to his kin, who stood silent and listless, hardly knowing their liberation, the venerable mummy of Hestaiyon spoke in sere murmurs, but authoritatively, as a king who issues commands to his children. The dead emperors and empresses stirred, like autumn leaves in a sudden wind, and a whisper passed among them and went forth from the palace, to be communicated at length, by devious ways, to all the dead of Cincor.

All that night, and during the blood-dark day that followed, by wavering torches or the light of the failing sun, an endless army of plague-eaten liches, of tattered skeletons, poured in a ghastly torrent through the streets of Yethlyreom and along the palace-hall where Hestaiyon stood guard above the slain necromancers. Unpausing, with vague, fixed eyes, they went on like driven shadows, to seek the subterranean vaults below the palace, to pass through the open door where Illeiro waited in the last vault, and then to wend downward by a thousand thousand steps to the verge of that gulf in which boiled the ebbing fires of earth. There, from the verge, they flung themselves to a second death and the clean annihilation of the bottomless flames.

But, after all had gone to their release, Hestaiyon still remained, alone in the fading sunset, beside the cloven corpses of Mmatmuor and Sodosma. There, as the tablets had directed him to do, he made trial of those spells of elder necromancy which he had known in his former wisdom, and cursed the dismembered bodies with that perpetual life-in-death which Mmatmuor and Sodosma had sought to inflict upon the people of Cincor. And maledictions came from the pale lips, and the heads rolled horribly with glaring eyes, and the limbs and torsos writhed on their imperial couches amid clotted blood. Then, with no backward look, knowing that all was done as had been ordained and predicted from the first, the mummy of Hestaiyon left the necromancers to their doom, and went wearily through the nighted labyrinth of vaults to rejoin Illeiro.

So, in tranquil silence, with no further need of words, Illeiro and Hestaiyon passed through the open door of the nether vault, and Illeiro locked the door behind them with its key of untarnished bronze. And thence, by the coiling stairs, they wended their way to the verge of the sunken flames and were one with their kinfolk and their people in the last, ultimate nothingness.

But of Mmatmuor and Sodosma, men say that their quartered bodies crawl to and fro to this day in Yethlyreom, finding no peace or respite from their doom of life-in-death. and seeking vainly through the black maze of nether vaults the door that was locked by Illeiro.

The Devil's Dowry

By Ben Judson

SOMETHING knotted hard and tight in my throat. A feeling of eerie loneliness swept over me, though I was not alone in the room. The doctor fumbled with the sheet a moment, pulling it up over the sallow face on the bed. A low feminine sob convulsed from the bent, gray head of the woman slumped on the opposite bedside; a sigh rattled dustily in the old parson's throat.

Dr. Peleg's yellow, parchment-like visage gazed at the three of us. There seemed to be almost a leer of triumph in the cruel lines about his mouth and I hated the man without knowing why. His impenetrable eyes glimmered with a strange, unholy light as they rested on the form beneath the sheet, and they seemed covetous and sinister.

They left me finally, Dr. Peleg with his shaking, knotted fingers; Julie's father, spare and grim as an old Puritan in his black cloth; and her mother, Lucy Anthony, stooped and stunned with grief.

I sat gently on the edge of the bed, and reverently uncovered the still, beautiful face. Julie Anthony slept peacefully in the misty twilight of the room. Why was it I refused to believe her dead? Was it because, even when death had scooped gray shallows in her youthful cheeks, those things we had shared in common kept her life alive *in me?* Because, only a few days ago, we had been joyously planning the details of our marriage?

I stooped to kiss the unfaded lips—crimson like a gash in her livid skin—half expecting to feel their warm response to my caress. But they were cold and motionless, and ever after their contact lingered on my mouth, cold, empty.

Standing up then, I replaced the sheet, and marched dumbly from the gray room.

The shadows gathered thickly on the stairway as I descended. In the circle of light at the foot a thin, dark-skinned man was standing, talking in a low tone with David Anthony. There was an angry frown on the preacher's dry, taut face. But it was the aspect of the Negro that caught my interest and suspended my descent on the steps.

There was something repulsively evil about the thick lips, the glaring, shadowed eyes. I had seen that sinister face before; I searched my memory quickly.

Presently the Negro bowed himself out deftly before the threatening advance Julie's father made. There was a sneer pregnant with evil on those grotesque lips. I rushed down as the door closed firmly.

"Who was that?" I demanded.

"Simone, the faith-healer," Mr. Anthony replied, and turned into the parlor where his wife sat huddled in an old, butterfly chair.

I stood by the rail-post, mouth half open. I remembered, then. A couple of weeks ago, my boss, the editor of the *Evening Mercury*, had sent me into the tenement district for a story about a Negro sorcerer who claimed he could raise the dead. But I came away with only a bruised shin when my foot crashed through a rotted stair tread. But I had seen the face, and recognized the man again as Simone.

What had the old Negro wanted? Did he think he could bring life into Julie's mute body with his witchcraft? My mouth settled grimly. There had been ugly, vague whisperings about black Simone's operations. I stuck my head into the parlor and motioned to David Anthony. He followed me back into the hall shortly.

"What did Simone say, exactly?" I asked.

The parson's long face gazed at me sternly. "You're not thinking, George—?" he queried.

"No—no," I replied hastily. "He's a fake, I know. But there are stories. Ugly stories."

"Of what sort?"

"That the people he has brought back have never been—natural—afterward. I have seen some of them. Negroes, mostly."

"He wanted money. Five hundred dollars. He said he would return it if he failed!"

We stood mute for several minutes. The feeling of emptiness descended heavily upon me. Finally I stirred. "I'm going—for a walk," I whispered, my voice husky.

I WALKED dumbly, for what seemed hours, not noticing the direction I took. I went as if in a dream—as if all that had happened before had been a horrible nightmare.

It was with a shock that I realized I was passing through Dwight Street. Dwight Street is in the downtown area, hemmed in by blackened tenements, littered with filth and the offspring of the dregs of the city. It was in one of these tenements that Simone lived and brewed his jungle magic.

I tried to analyze what I had been doing, and the revelation was startling. Searching, searching for some hope that Julie could not be dead, not dead forever! And the search had led me unconsciously to Simone's doorstep!

As I passed a blackened doorway, a finger beckoned to me. I hesitated, peering into the darkness of the opening. A voice hissed evilly. "Simone want to see you!"

I determined to go on again, then paused a second time. Finally I stepped into the hallway, searching vainly with my eyes for the origin of the voice. The air was dank and heavy with the odor of unclean bodies, and I shrank away from it, as if to compress myself into as little space as possible.

The darkness thinned out a little as my eyes became accustomed to the lightlessness. A small dark shape moved ahead of me, up the stairway.

"Come!" the voice demanded.

I followed, avoiding mechanically the hole in the staircase into which my foot had slipped previously. Three flights my guide and I ascended, passing rotted doors from which black, hostile faces peered out at me.

Simone waited for me in a dingy backroom. The Negro youngster hesitated on the doorsill, urging me inward. His eyes shown round and dead white; an unreasoning terror seemed to grip his features in an agony of indecision and shake his small frame with aspen-like convulsions. As I entered, he scuttled back down the narrow, tottering stairway.

Simone greeted me with a silent nod. He indicated a lone chair, and squatted himself on a disheveled cot. The place reeked with the mingled odors of decay, human sweat and strange herbs. A single, blackened oil-lamp flickered on the floor; its unsteady light, vaulting upwards, cast distorted shadows on the crumbling walls, and brought out the Negro's face in grotesque relief.

"I knew you would come," the thick lips muttered, "but have you faith in my powers?"

I stared through the gloom at black Simone. In the darkness his snug-fitting, American clothes seemed to fall away, and I saw there a half-naked savage, a voodoo high priest, mumbling his weird incantations.

A strange fit of trembling seized me, and I tried to shake off the hallucination. The sickening realization came to me that I might almost believe in the powers he claimed!

Simone bolted up suddenly. There was a wild, barbaric gleam in his eyes. "You shall have proof of my ability," he promised. "Wait!"

I clung to my chair while the Negro vanished into another part of the tenement, for I was tempted to spring from my seat and rush madly from the room, down the treacherous stairs, and into the purer freedom of the street. But I waited.

Presently there were shuffling sounds outside the door. An old, wild-eyed Negro slouched in before Simone's prodding. He stared crazily about the room, fixed his bulging eyes on me momentarily, and then slunk like a whipped animal into a corner.

Simone gazed at me with a melancholy expression in his eyes. "A moon ago," his voice rumbled, "Old Lazar lay cold in death. But *he* had faith, his people had faith. Again he walks among the living!"

My eyes shifted to old Lazar, who gibbered incoherently in his corner. A shudder racked my frame. One could well believe Lazar had died! He seemed still dead! A black ghost, doomed to the shadowy vale between life and death, belonging to neither. Rather Julie dead than to exist in this state of unnatural obliteration!

I sat up with a start. My God, I was believing!

"But Lazar is mad!" The words vomited forth from my throat with jerky haste.

"Death is not a pleasant experience," Simone said gravely. "But Lazar will get over it. There is much to forget."

A maelstrom of fantastic thoughts swirled in my brain. What if Simone were a voodoo *hougan*, a votarist of black art? If he could call Julie back to my arms, was not that all that mattered? Could there not be something outside the ken of matter-of-fact understanding, whose cosmic, dark powers we could not realize, because we refused to believe in them?

I got up shakily. "I'll speak to Julie's father," I said, and my voice sounded unreal and hollow.

Simone bowed me out of the room, and I descended, clinging to the railing, the darkness swirling dizzily about me. In the dingy room it had seemed very natural that I should go to David Anthony and convince him that Simone's witchcraft was rational and moral. But now, relieved somewhat from that macabre atmosphere which seemed to emanate from Simone and Lazar, my courage to profess a belief in the Negro sorcerer's cult began to ebb.

At the foot of the rickety flights of stairs I paused abruptly. A figure which seemed oddly familiar to me blackened the doorway to the street.

The figure hesitated momentarily as I advanced into the light cast in from the street, started, and scuttled down the unlit hallway. I saw the face as it streaked through the blob of yellow light, and it was a face filled with the fear of discovery.

It was Doctor Peleg!

A hoarse cry of astonishment choked in my throat. I trembled by the doorway, not knowing whether to run from the insanity that I felt was pressing upon me, or to pursue the doctor and demand an explanation of his strange action.

I crept back into the hall, but nothing except blackness and closed doors reached my senses. Shortly I turned, walked into the street.

Maybe, I thought, Doctor Peleg had come, as I had, seeking the aid of the witch-doctor, his own powers having failed. The thought comforted me a little, but the evil, terrified glimmer I had seen on his face provoked sinister doublings in my mind.

With quick, but uncertain, steps I strode back to the Anthony house.

DAVID ANTHONY gazed at me with grave concern. "Don't you think you had better get some sleep?" he inquired.

I tried as much as possible to erase the look of hysteria from my eyes. "I would like to talk to you—seriously—for a while," I asked, "if it won't disturb you and Mrs. Anthony."

"Mrs. Anthony has retired," the preacher informed me.

We sat in the dully lit parlor and I attempted to put an easy inflection in my voice, but the nervous gestures of my face and hands betrayed my lack of calm. David waited with a quiet resignation.

"How did you come to know Doctor Peleg?" I asked. "He wasn't your family physician."

"I saw him in church one Sunday about two weeks ago. He was new to the congregation, and asked me if he might talk to me some time. He came to the house Monday evening, and we discussed our different religious beliefs. He called quite often after that.

"WHEN JULIE was taken ill, our regular physician confessed his inadequacy to handle her case. It was a disease he had never heard of, he said. A kind of sleeping sickness, but with unusual complications.

"Doctor Peleg seemed to show some knowledge of the disease, and suggested a possible cure. So Julie was put under his care."

The preacher slumped into his chair. His face stared vaguely at me, drawn, white and motionless. Then he demanded, "Why do you ask?"

"I saw Peleg at the tenement where Simone lives," I replied.

David started forward, his jaw unhinging. "What?"

I shrank into my chair. I had confessed more than I had intended.

"You were there?" David Anthony's voice was sharp.

MR. ANTHONY was frowning meditatively by the time he had wormed from me the full details of my excursion to the witch-doctor's flat. "What possible connection could Peleg and Simone's acquaintance—if that is really so—have with Julie's death?"

"I don't know," I acknowledged. "But our first step is to find out *just what that acquaintance means*!"

I was silent a moment. A suggestion hovered on the tip of my tongue in cowardly embarrassment. Finally, hardening my jaw muscles, I blurted forth:

"Why not let Simone try his faith-healing? It might offer a clue!"

David gazed at me sternly. "That minister of the devil! A man of true faith would not demand payment for his healing."

"I will scrape together the five hundred." There was a desperate tremor in my voice, and I clutched the arms of my chair in a vise-like grip.

"No!" Mr. Anthony was adamant. "If God willed Julie be returned to this life, he would grant me as much power as a—pagan!"

I WANDERED the streets listlessly, much as I had earlier in the evening. Late pedestrians glanced at me askance, some pityingly. In their faces I read: drunkard, madman. To a young girl who whispered concernedly to her escort I shouted suddenly: "I am not drunk!" They gaped at me in surprise, and I reeled off in confusion.

I could feel it urging me forward madly, that relentlessness and exasperation born of despair and inactivity. I must do *something*, if only to hunt out Dr. Peleg and twist a confession from his seamy, hateful throat. Otherwise, my reason would wither in a chaos of insanity.

Tomorrow they would bury Julie. Then she would be gone, forever. Was she not lost to me now? I could not seem to realize that. She still existed for me in flesh and blood, though she lay cold and motionless. Till tomorrow, then, I could have hope, though it were born of insanity.

I had a few hundred dollars in the bank. The rest I could borrow from the paper. The office would make me an advance. I had been there a long time. It would have to.

My pace quickened. Street corners slid by in a blur. The breath came short and excited in my windpipe. Simone would take my promise; I would write him a note. Tonight, while I engaged David Anthony in conversation, Simone would perform his miracle! How surprised the old preacher would be! I rushed on ...

Simone greeted me distrustfully. I pushed the door in, and strode into the room. The place seemed to light up with the infectious delirium that raged in my eyes. I clung to the old Negro's hand, and my words tumbled forward in staccato confusion.

"I have the money!" I shouted. "Tomorrow—it's in the bank—I'll write a note. Come with me. I believe—I believe!"

Simone gazed at me, frowning. Then, shaking his head, he said to me in a low sepulchral voice, "It is too late!"

My hands dropped to my sides. My mouth slumped open. The world crashed suddenly about me, dinning in my ears with a horrible, threatening roar.

"But surely," I stuttered. "She has been dead only a few hours!"

"I cannot do it."

"I have faith in you."

The wicked eyes stared at me piercingly. "You are mad!"

I mumbled to myself. "Mad!" The black man seemed to hear me, and leered maliciously. Then something snapped in my head, as if a joint had sprung back into place. The air began to clear of the mist and headiness.

"Why," I demanded coolly, "did Doctor Peleg come to see you?"

Simone drew back into himself. He seemed to move away from me, though he made no step. "I do not know Doctor Peleg," he replied.

Shortly I descended from the tenement and made my way home.

JULIE was buried late the next afternoon.

The winches that lowered the casket into the grave ceased their humming. I turned, with Mr. and Mrs. Anthony, back to the car that had brought us to the cemetery. Another large chapter in my life had ended, I thought.

I returned to work the next day. Towards evening, the editor called me to his desk. "There's been a throat-slitting on Dwight Street," he informed me. "I want you to cover it, George. It's in the tenement where the witch-doctor hangs out. An old black fellow got mixed up with a razor."

Not waiting to ask questions, I raced to the street and grabbed a cab. The hackie dropped me in front of the wooden building. It seemed to lean crazily over the sidewalk, threatening to crush us. There was a cop standing guard by the entrance.

"*Evening Mercury.*" I flashed my card and leaped up the tottering stairs. On the fourth landing, outside Simone's doorway, two rookies were lifting the corpse into the wicker basket. A large pool of blood crept slowly over the uneven floor towards the stairwell. The dead Negro's head swung grotesquely from the shoulders by the cords in the back of the neck.

I peered intently in the basket at the distorted face. "Swing your light over here, Burke?" I asked a sergeant who was watching the work. Eyes, glazed and insane, stared at me from the police coffin.

It was Lazar, Simone's crazy patient!

"This was one of the witch-doctor's 'dead men,'" I whistled.

"That's one zombie won't walk again!" the sergeant remarked dryly.

"Get any suspects—any witnesses?" I demanded.

"Not a thing!" Burke snorted. "All these boogies can do is gape and roll their eyes!"

"What about the witch-doctor?"

"Not a smell of him."

"Looking for him?"

"Yeah, in a way. Got nothing on him, though."

"Listen," I confided in him. "I've got a hunch Simone knows plenty about this. But if you hang around for him, I'll bet you anything he doesn't show up."

"So?" Burke gazed at me skeptically.

"So," I continued, "you and the rookies beat it. Keep the cop away from the Street entrance, too. I'll wait in Simone's room, and grab him if he comes in."

Sergeant Burke pondered a moment. Finally he shrugged. "Suits me," he said.

I crept as unobtrusively as possible into the witch-doctor's room while the rookies bore the body outside. Presently I heard the police car drive off, and the darkness of night closed in about me completely. I waited, hunched forward on the cot, straining my ears for sounds.

Muted whisperings filtered in through the cracked walls. But no evidence of the black sorcerer. The minutes tramped heavily by, drawing themselves into hours. Presently I found myself nodding; a leaden apathy seized my eyelids, and my head slumped forward into my lap.

I DO not know how long I rested in that state of semi-consciousness. I was not entirely asleep, for I seemed to have some perception of the blackness and strange, hidden movements about me, betrayed by squeaking boards and ghostly rustlings. Slowly, a vague uneasiness pricked through my drowsiness, beating on the muffled alarm of some instinctive sixth sense.

Though the rousing seemed to take an age of effort, the final awakening came with a rapidity that jerked my remaining senses into a trembling awareness. My breathing came heavily, as if I had been running a great distance, my eyes strained through the thick blackness, and the beating of my heart thumped warningly against my ribs. Out of some subterranean depths, a low, muffled *boom – boom – boom* reverberated ominously against my eardrums!

Raising myself quickly from the cot, I struck a match. The light flickered momentarily on the bare, crumbling walls of the cubicle, then dropped to oblivion onto the floor. Creeping to the door, I drew it open a few inches, and listened intently.

Except for the dull, muted thumping from below, the building slept in tomblike stillness. The booming sounded weirdly savage and unholy, like the drumming of some heathen blood-rite. Under its awful threat, all my city-bred sophistication seemed to fall from me like rotted garments, and I stood naked and afraid, like a superstitious pagan in the black, spectre-haunted forest.

Squaring my shoulders, I slunk to the stairwell and descended, clinging to the railing, avoiding the shadowy doorways. Three banks of unlighted, creaking stairways can seem infinitely long when fear forces one to tread lightly and with unsteady feet. Thus sinners must descend into hell.

The thought never entered my head to escape into the street. The drums pulled me on and down with their relentless, hypnotic spell. I crept into the Stygian blackness of the rear hall, the booming growing louder and louder, more articulately savage.

Underneath the stair casing, a rectangular line of light discovered a flimsy door to me. I pulled it open cautiously, peered into the inferno of pagan rhythm and dancing lights below. The odor of sweating, straining bodies rushed up to sting my nostrils, and beneath the even booming, I heard the incessant thumping of naked feet.

I pushed unwilling feet down the stone steps. On my right was a solid brick wall, which right-angled to the left beyond the landing at the foot. As I drew myself downwards, a sea of bobbing, black heads came into view. These formed a rough, thick circle about a small clearing, within which a smaller circle of naked savages danced, swaying and writhing in demoniac ecstasy. At the far edge of the clearing, three

Negroes bent over long, slender drums, beating with the heels of their fists on the rawhide surface. A wild, possessed gleaming shown in the eyes of the votaries, and they all swayed involuntarily to the heavy voodoo music.

But it was the object within the ring of dancers that started my mouth open, drew rigid every muscle in my body, and sucked in a gasp of fear and wonder in my throat.

Over a low, crude altar bent the thin, taunt face of the witch-doctor. A black robe covered his skeleton-like body, and in his extended hand he held a long slender needle like a hypodermic. His protruding lips drew back in a fit of ugly, devilish passion, and his nostrils swelled and deflated under the force of his convulsive breathing.

Slowly the hand descended. Under the advancing needle lay the exposed breast of a girl—a nude white girl, still as death!

It was Julie!

My crouched legs straightened under me, and a shriek of insane fury retched from my lungs. As I sprang forward, every head started around, the booming of the drums ceased, the dancers stiffened in their mad careers, and Simone's hand paused in its downward thrust.

I crashed to the hard, earthen floor; hundreds of milling bodies pressed about me; a titanic fist smashed against my cheek, and the chaos of light and noise faded from my senses.

A SOFT, grey light gradually flooded my senses. My eyes opened, and I gazed upwards. Over me tottered the unpainted front of the tenement building. The twilight of dawn slowly filled the sky. An intense aching gripped my body and head, and the sharp edge of a stone pressed against one shoulder. I was sprawled in the gutter of Dwight Street!

I got up shakily, attempting to brush the filth from my rumpled clothes with my hand. It was with pain that I hobbled onto the sidewalk.

How had I come here? What horrible nightmare evoked strange, fearful memories in my brain? I gazed into the ever-open doorway of the tenement. I had seen Julie in that weird jungle sprouted like a fungi in a modern city!

Or had I? I remembered clearly the order from my boss, the editor; the murdered body of Lazar; the long waiting in Simone's flat. But after that point, reality faded into the grotesqueness of an insane dream. Had it all been a dream, provoked by the murky, unlovely atmosphere of the tenement? Had Simone found me napping in his room, and tossed me unceremoniously into the gutter?

There was one way to find out—to reenter the place and search for the subterranean mystery house where the witch-doctor performed his devilish rites. If I found nothing, I had but dreamed. If I found the altar—I prayed I would not—I had *not* dreamed!

I hesitated at the entrance. I hated to think of exploring the place alone. What could I do against a hundred frenzied blacks, the restraint of civilization forgotten in the orgy of savage mysticism?

The steady, irregular clack of a policeman's boot reached my ears. I waited, and shortly a blue-coated rookie approached.

The cop eyed me suspiciously. I showed him my press card, and explained I had been tossed out of the tenement for attempting to investigate old Lazar's murder. He agreed, a little reluctantly, to accompany me within, after a good deal of persuasion.

"How do I know you haven't been off on a drunk?" he grinned at me.

I assured him I hadn't and we merged into the blackness of the tenement hall. The rookie's searchlight revealed the door that opened into the cellar. He threw the yellow beam into the depths below, and we descended the stone stairway.

The cellar was there, just as I had seen it—brick walls, earthen floor, wide, low ceiling. But there were no blacks, no sacrificial altar, no dusky priest. Yet, clinging to the atmosphere, I could still detect a faint, acid stench of reeking contorted bodies.

"I guess I was wrong," I muttered.

The rookie snorted sardonically, and we proceeded up the steps and onto the street again. I left the cop at the doorway to resume his beat, and turned towards home. Half an hour later, I phoned into the office that the murder of Lazar was unsolved, and tumbled into bed, having left a note for the landlady to call me at eight-thirty.

IT WAS shortly after nine the next morning that I stumbled into the Anthony's parlor. He seated himself, and I swung into action immediately.

"I saw Julie last night—her body, at least."

"What?"

"In the basement of the tenement on Dwight Street where Simone, the witch-doctor, lives."

David Anthony eyed me narrowly. "You were there last night?"

"Of course!" There was an exasperated rasp in my throat. "I saw her, I tell you!"

"She was buried two days ago!" There was that look of cautious inquiry in his eyes, which seemed to question my sanity.

"But she is not in her grave now!" I shouted the last, and watched for the effect it would have on him. He cowered back in his chair, wide-eyed and frightened.

Then I launched into the detail of what had happened last night. David stared at me unblinking, terrified lest I could make him believe. But I hammered home my one point. "I had never seen the basement before last night. Yet when I entered it with the cop, it was exactly the same as I had seen it during the ritual! The same—even the smell was there—except the Negros were gone; the altar, Simone, and Julie were gone!"

He sat thinking a moment. In a weak voice, then, as if uttering his last feeble defense against my argument, he quavered, "How do you know it was Julie? Might it not have been some other woman?"

I gazed at him sternly. "Is there anyone, except you and your wife, who would know her better?"

"No ..." his head shook infirmly. "But can you prove it?"

"Yes!"

David searched my face. "How?"

"Open Julie's grave!"

WE GROUPED anxiously about the slowly yawning hole, David Anthony; Carl Doran, the medical examiner; the caretakers; and myself. Finally the winches were let down, and the gray box rose slowly.

Doran raised the lid. David had turned his eyes away, not daring to look. It was with difficulty that I forced my own eyes into the—*empty box*!

The breaths of the caretakers and the medical examiner sucked in. David swung his head around, and his features were ghastly pale and taunt.

"God in Heaven!" I heard the old preacher murmur under his breath. He turned his pitiful countenance to me. "God, God, I prayed you were insane!" he whimpered.

"Come!" I yelped, swinging to the waiting car in the road.

"What's next?" barked the examiner.

"We drop Mr. Anthony, pick up a couple of dicks at headquarters, and lump it down to Dwight Street before dark."

But I noted with uneasiness the sun dip slowly into the horizon as I raced into the city. "We'll have to leave you at the station, Mr. Anthony," I shouted.

Sergeant Burke and Conway, plain-clothesmen, slid into the rear seat of the car after I had helped David out. The preacher was pale and fluttering in a sort of dream, as if reality had suddenly vanished for him in the weird, chaotic sub-world he had just glimpsed. I felt sorry for the old man.

But the visible minutes were slipping by. I jammed the shift into second, and we grated forward at a leap. Burke slid an automatic into my jacket-pocket.

Parking the car just off Dwight Street, we walked swiftly and unobtrusively to the entrance of the tenement. The shadows had already gathered thickly.

Light, invisible feet scurried up the stairways as we filed in the door from the street. We tramped up the shaking steps, lighting the ascent with torches. Caution was useless. Notice of our coming had spread as if we had entered with a brass band.

Simone's room was empty. We shoved our way into adjoining flats, but the occupants only stared at us with stolid, ill-concealed hatred, their heavy lips clamped shut. We gave up, finally, and trooped to the cellar. But the search of that fetid-aired cavern yielded no more than the motionless lips of the tenants.

Burke threw up his hands. "You're not finding anything *here!*" he exclaimed.

"Let's find Doc Peleg," I suggested.

"Who's he?"

"The guy that buried Julie Anthony. I caught him snooping around here the night after her death."

"Let's go!" Burke started up the steps.

"Wait—!" I called. The sergeant paused. "I'm going to stick here, in case Simone comes in. The rest of you leave with plenty of racket, so the boogies upstairs will think we've all gone. Nab Peleg, if you can, and pump him for all you can get. Ought to be able to hold him for a material witness. David Anthony might know his address."

They nodded assent, and clomped up the steps. Their feet resounded like thunder in the low cellar as they progressed over the hall. Squatting on the upper step, I waited in the dark near the hall door, my ear pressed to the flimsy panel.

I sat there, my hand on the revolver in my pocket, for perhaps half an hour. No unusual sound, no movements.

Suddenly the wind rushed away from my back. I started half around, jumping to my feet. The door had been thrust open without warning. A heavy pain shot into the top of my skull I tottered down into an incredibly brilliant void of light, and felt myself bumping over the hard steps. The brilliance swiftly receded, and blackness swam over me.

A LONGITUDINAL seam of terrific pain shot across my pate, as if my head had been split open. My eyelids fluttered weakly, and dim light flickered in my brain. My body lay extended on a hard even surface, and my joints ached as if they had been wrenched suddenly out of their natural position. Somewheres to my right I could hear a regular thudding, repeated at short intervals, as of a pick-axe striking into hard earth.

I remembered waiting behind the hall door, the surprise attack from behind, and the vicious crack on the head that sent me toppling down the hard steps into oblivion. But where was I now?

A damp, earthy smell filled my nostrils. I opened my eyes cautiously. Above, heavy, cobwebbed rafters supported a rough wooden ceiling. Could I still be in the basement of the tenement?

I turned my head to the right, towards the sound. In a narrow, oblong pit, already several feet deep, a burly, sweating Negro, bared to the waist, was methodically chopping out the stony earth. At one end of the pit, which was assuming much the shape of a grave, stood Simone, his back toward me. A grave! For whom? Me? I shuddered. Simone then must have cracked me over the head, and thought he had killed me!

I inspected, with as little movement as possible, the object on which I lay. Three heavy planks, athwart a couple of saw-horses, formed a crude sort of table. My limbs were unbound, I noted thankfully.

Suddenly a voice—Peleg's voice—rasped on my left! My eyes snapped across the small, ill-lit room. The altar I had seen the night before—or had more time elapsed?—rested several feet away. It was a low, wooden affair, and on it stretched a body, wrapped in coarse sheeting, except for the head. But I could not discern the features distinctly, because of the dim light and because Peleg stood partly in the way.

"She's coming around!" the voice sounded exultantly.

She—could she be Julie? God, what monsters were these, giving and destroying life at will? Had Simone really succeeded in raising the dead?

Simone grunted, but did not stir from his post by the grave. Silence, marked off by the thud of the axe ...

"Ain' she deep enough fo' de body yit?" a puffing voice whined. No answer.

I knew I would have to act, and act quickly, if I intended to get out alive—and get *her* out ... *Alive,* I said mentally, and then wondered. Could Julie be *alive* now? Would, I asked myself, I want Julie alive now—would she want to be alive—alive like the gibbering Lazar? A low moan came from the body on the altar. Now—now I must strike! I doubled my legs under me, whirled towards Simone, and leaped forward. The witch-doctor half-turned; the pick-axe suspended in the air. Surprise and fear shot across the Negroes' faces. My body shocked against Simone, and he tumbled into the pit, sprawling on the Negro workman. Both of them lay in a heap at the base of the hole.

The burly, half-naked Negro disentangled himself from the sorcerer and started up, cold, frenzied fear on his countenance. Simone lay inert. The falling pick-axe had cloven his skull. But the workman advanced upon me, despite his fear!

I whirled, seized one of the plankings of the rude bench upon which my supposed corpse had lain, and flung its further end at the Negro's head. He ducked, but his move was too late. His body thudded into the pit, and lay still.

"Reach for the ceiling!" Peleg's voice rasped behind me. I whirled and found myself staring into the muzzle of an automatic—my automatic, probably.

Peleg laughed, a short, horrid cackle. "That hole was made for you," he chortled, "and you're going to be put into it!"

THE doctor leaned back against the altar, watching with vicious pleasure for the effect this would have on me. The gun advanced in his hand, slowly, slowly. When his arm was fully extended, his already flexing finger would—An icy sweat broke over my body. Had I succeeded thus far to be mowed down by a bullet from my own gun?

The grin on Peleg's face became more cruel, more sardonic, more insane. In a few seconds that muzzle would bark once, twice, and I would fall backwards, writhing into the pit with the others.

The white form behind Peleg raised slowly. Wide eyes sprung to meet mine, snapped back to the doctor, and to the automatic. It was Julie! I lowered my gaze to the gun again, before its direction might discover her awakening to Peleg.

I heard the soft flurry of cloth whipping through the air; the gun spat: leaden pellet spewed dirt at my feet. I sprang forward. Julie had flung herself upon the doctor's arm, breaking his aim.

The gun cracked again as Peleg jerked himself around, but I ducked it on the run, bursting through the remaining wood-bench. We crashed together, and sprawled on the hard earth, the automatic flying through the air from the doctor's hand.

The struggle didn't last long. The doctor was old and not too strong, and despite my injuries, was soft game for my frenzied, hammering fists. He soon lay quiet bloody-faced and mute.

I felt Julie's body press against me as I raised myself. I took her into my arms, and gazed into her eyes. They smiled back at me, though uncomprehending and frightened. There was no insanity there, as I had seen in Lazar's eyes.

WE WENT over to the police hospital the next day, Burke, the D. A. and myself. The nurse had mopped most of the blood from Peleg's face, and he lay scowling at us from his cot.

Burke took the matter in hand in his characteristically rough manner. He drew a chair close to the bedside and glared at the doctor. "You gonna talk or no?"

Peleg flinched back. "What have you got on me?"

"Plenty! Simone told us practically everything. And every time you leave something out, we're going to punch that nasty face of yours when we get you back to headquarters!"

Peleg didn't know Simone was dead.

"F'r instance," Burke said, "you might start with the white slave ring you been running!" That aspect of Peleg's activities had been turned up by the police just a few days previously.

Peleg's watery eyes roved over our faces, panic-stricken.

"Come on!" Burke growled.

PELEG talked. Simone's "dead people" had not really died. They had been induced to a coma approximating death by a drug Simone had brought to the United States from his native Haiti. In cases like Julie's, Peleg had administered the drug, first making himself acquainted with his victim and the victim's family. The victims were brought back to life by a powerful counteractant injected with a hypodermic, and restored to the family for a sizable fee, or, if the victim were a young and pretty girl, Peleg sold them into slavery on the Barbary coast. Lazar, who had been a maniac before his alleged "raising," had gotten to talking wildly, so Simone stopped his vague accusations with a razor.

JULIE recovered quickly. I took her—with the ring on the correct finger—to a retreat in the pines of north Vermont the day after Peleg's trial. We kept the newspapers from her, in the little northern jungle now our paradise.

She is sane, perfectly. But every once in a while a vague, troubled expression comes into her eyes, as if to ask, "Where was I, those three days?" and I wonder just how much of a sorcerer Simone was …?

The Walking Dead

By E. Hoffmann Price

WHEN WALT Connell heard the diffident tapping at the back door, he assumed an expression of judicial sternness. Plato Jones, who spaded Connell's garden, must be returning with a fantastic story to account for a week's absence and the six dollars which Connell had given him to buy some orange wine. But it was Plato's wife who tapped at the door, a plump, comely black woman with a small parcel under her arm.

"Evenin', Mr. Walt." she began. "My man Plato ain't come back yet."

Tears were streaming down her face. Connell was saddled with a problem. Taking on a servant entailed responsibilities. He'd have to help her somehow.

"That no-good man of yours probably drank my orange wine and now is afraid to come back." Connell said.

"No sir, no sir!" Amelia protested. "Plato don't drink nuthin!"

"Well, maybe I can help." Connell temporized.

"Yes, sir, Mr. Walt!" Amelia beamed through her tears. "I knew you'd take care of me."

She thrust into his hands a paper-wrapped parcel.

"I baked y'all a chocolate cake for lunch when you go to get that no-good man! And I fixed up some salted cashew nuts, too."

Her guile had caught him totally off guard. He had accepted the present. Nothing to do but resign himself to a sixty-mile drive down the Mississippi Delta where the *Cajuns* convert undersized oranges into fragrant, blasting wine: a no-man's land where a century or more ago. Lafitte's pirates found refuge.

THE NEXT morning Connell thrust Amelia's gift of chocolate cake and cashew nuts into the parcel compartment and headed down the west bank. He spent the forenoon searching small town jails as he worked his way down the Delta, but no news of Plato. His last chance was Venice, at the end of the highway.

Venice was half a dozen shacks plus a general store not much larger than a piano box. The girl behind the counter was uncommonly attractive—one of those substantial *Cajun* women, with luxurious curves, and plump, firm breasts as inviting as her amiable smile. Connell, however, managed to shift his glance to her dark eyes and began his oft repeated query concerning Plato and his red flivver.

Marie shook her head. Ker eyes suddenly became somber as she said. "You're too late."

"What do you mean?" Connell, catching her by the wrist felt her tremble.

"I didn't have any orange wine." she began, lowering her voice almost to a whisper. "So he went back."

Something was distinctly salty.

"You'd better tell me," he said in a quiet voice that impelled her attention.

Marie was wavering, but she was afraid. Finally she compromised, "We can talk better in back here."

Connell followed her to the rear of the tiny store. The crude, primitive room contained an oil stove, a small wooden table. In the further comer was a bed.

"You won't never see your man again," began Marie, drawing up a chair for Connell. "Not with walking dead men like they got at Ducoin's plantation."

"Walking dead men!" he echoed, leaping to his feet. "Who's Ducoin? What—"

But Connell's query was cut short. The Cajun girl's hand closed about his arm, drawing him to her side.

"I'll tell you later," she whispered. Her dark, smouldering eyes were still haunted, but her lips suggested reasons for delay.

Under other circumstances. Connell would have welcomed the hint, but something about her furtive glance and unnatural eagerness combined with her sinister remarks to repel him. But Connell made little progress. As he drew away, her arm slipped about his neck and her ripe, voluptuous curves pressed him closely as she pleaded, "Don't go ... I'm terribly scared ..."

She was. But Connell wasn't. And that warm, plump body was as inflaming as orange wine. He drew her to him, stroked her black hair, caressed turn flesh that trembled at his touch, and tried to entice her further remarks about walking dead men.

However, it did not work as he intended. His presence did reassure her, but the contact made his pulse pound like a riveting hammer, and the sudden rise and fall of her breasts showed that it was becoming mutual....

Marie's dark eyes were no longer haunted by anything but a desire to get closer. Presently she forgot to brush away an exploring hand; and yielded her eager lips.

And then Connell learned that the Delta offers more than orange wine....

IT WAS close to sunset before he remembered Plato and renewed his inquiries.

"Honest, I couldn't help it." Marie protested. "I didn't have any wine left and just as that man was going to leave, in comes Ducoin with a load. And he tells Plato to come along, he'd fix him up. And I didn't dare warn him."

"Wait till I get at Ducoin!"

"Don't!" implored Marie. "He'll know I told you. And you can't do nothing. Plato's a walking corpse by now—and I'll be one, too, if Ducoin finds out—"

She tried to detain Connell, but he broke clear before her full-blown fascinations could conspire with her sinister hints. She had merely delayed the quest; and Connell headed up the river, toward that mysterious plantation.

Ducoin's house loomed up above the surrounding orange groves, nearly a quarter of a mile from the highway. Its remnants of white paint made it resemble a gaunt, ancient tomb. As Connell pulled up, he saw a Model T parked in a clump of shrubbery. Plato's decrepit red Lizzie!

And then Connell received a shock. A file of blacks emerged from the orange groves. Their black faces were vacant. They shambled toward the left wing of the house with the grotesque gait of animated dummies.

The sodden, lifeless *clump, clump, clump* of their feet sounded like clods of earth dropping on a coffin. Their arms dangled limp as rags.

Connell shuddered. No wonder that the ignorant *Cajuns* considered them walking dead men.

Clump, clump, clump. The most poverty stricken and oppressed black laborers jest and chatter at the end of a day's work; but these black men stalked in silence broken only by the shuffling crunch of their flat feet.

Following the file came a white man who wore boots and riding breeches. His heartless, handsome face was tanned and deeply lined. Intelligent but relentless. His dark eyes were as cryptic as his smile as he confronted Connell.

"Looking for someone?"

"Yes. A man named Plato." said Connell. "Are you Pierre Ducoin?"

"That's the name." admitted the taskmaster. "But there are no strangers on this plantation."

The more Connell saw of Ducoin, the less he liked him. There was something uncanny about the man.

As Connell hesitated, something compelled him to glance towards the veranda that ran the fall length of the house, some ten feet above the ground level. Framed by a French window was a girl whose dark eyes and lovely, delicate features for an instant made him forget that she was clad only in a chiffon robe which, half parted, revealed enticing glimpses of silken legs, and a body to which clung the caressing haze of sheer fabric that betrayed slender, olive-tinted curves ... the amorous inward sweep of her waist ... pert breasts that any hand larger than her own could conceal....

Her lips were silently moving, and she was gesturing for him to leave at once. But she had overlooked her own loveliness. Connell was staying.

"I'm Walt Connell, and I think you're mistaken," was the retort. "Let me talk to your men. One of them might know about him."

That play was better than making a liar of Ducoin by mentioning Plato's flivver, half concealed in the shadows.

For a moment Ducoin's eyes flared with a light that Connell was certain could not be the reddish sunset glow; his aquiline features tightened, then suddenly he smiled and amiably agreed.

"Do that in the morning. Too late now. This plantation reaches all the way out to the bay, and most of my crew is quartered at the further end. Take us an hour or more to go out, and it's getting dark. Make yourself at home—there is plenty of room here, and you can look in the morning."

A grim-faced black woman served dinner in a vast, high-ceiled room facing the west. Fried chicken, Creole gumbo, rice, and corn bread. All tastily seasoned, except for an utter lack of salt. Connell, reaching for the only shaker on the table, then noticed it contained only pepper.

"Sorry," apologized Ducoin, "but we've run all out of salt. It's rather primitive down here on the Delta. We shop only once a week."

Dinner, despite Ducoin's easy cordiality, was a decided strain. Connell was wondering at the absence of the lovely girl who had warned him.

"Working many men?" he asked.

"A dozen or two," Ducoin carelessly answered. "Haitians, mostly—sullen, stolid brutes, but good workers."

He changed the subject. Connell was relieved when the woman served them night-black, chicory-tinctured coffee, and a pony of excellent brandy.

Ducoin remarked, "We turn in early here. Plantation hours begin before sunrise. Aunt Célie will show you your room. In the morning, you can make the rounds with me."

Connell followed the grim-faced woman down the hallway. Her morose, stolid demeanor confirmed Ducoin's comment on the temperament of his workers; yet Connell was distinctly perturbed. And as the door closed behind Aunt Célie, he received a distinct shock.

The moon was rising, casting a shimmering, silvery glow over the black expanse of open fields. Men were at work, digging and hoeing. Utterly unheard of, a night shift on a plantation. Connell heard the thudding blows of their implements, but not a murmur, not a spoken word.

There wasn't an overseer, yet they toiled on, methodically, as though motor driven, never pausing to lean on their hoes for a breathing spell. They advanced in an unwavering line, grotesquely combining the precision of military drill with the uncouth, ungainly movements of dummies.

Connell shivered and shook his head. Questioning such unnatural creatures would be futile. One glimpse of them and Plato would have taken to his heels. He wondered if his servant might not have abandoned his flivver, frightened out of all reason by the uncanny spectacle of Africans working without song and chatter.

A soft, furtive stirring in the hall just outside of his room made him start violently. Something softly slinking down the hall had paused at his door. By the moon glow that penetrated the shadows, he saw the scarcely perceptible motion of the knob. Something was stealthily seeking him. A silent bound brought Connell to the fireplace, and out of the moonglow. His trembling fingers closed on a pair of massive tongs.

He watched the door soundlessly swing inward. A nebulous spindle of whiteness cleared the edge of the jamb: a spectral, shimmering whiteness that for an instant froze Connell's blood. Then he saw the intruder was the girl who had warned him.

She paused to close the door, and as she turned from the threshold Connell for the first time realized how lovely she was. Her tiny feet were bare, and her shapely legs, gleaming like ivory exclamation marks through the sheer, gauzy fabric of her nightgown, blossomed into seductive curves that fascinated Connell.

The vagrant breeze shifted drawing the misty fabric closer, revealing her perfections as though she were clad in no more than bare loveliness. The filmy silk clung to the inward curve of her waist, and caressed the firm, delicious roundness of her breast. She was a lovely unreality in the vague light that made her face a sweet, pallid mask, and her black hair a succession of gleaming highlights.

She advanced a pace before she saw Connell.

"Leave at once." As she spoke, she caught his arm. She was trembling violently.

"What's wrong?"

"It's not too late." she whispered as Connell seated himself, and drew her to the arm of his chair. "My uncle is out putting the night shift to work. "I'm Madeline Ducoin."

"I came here to get a man named Plato." insisted Connell.

"He's one of them now." said Madeline, shuddering. "A walking corpse."

'That's absolute rot! How can a dead man walk?"

"You saw them, didn't you?" Madeline countered sighing and shaking her head.

As she leaned toward the window and gestured at the macabre figures that toiled in the moonlight, her dark hair caressed Connell's cheek, and he felt the supple flex of her slender body. Madeline at least was real in the moon- haunted glamour. His arms closed about her. and drew her to his knee. She was still trembling, but at his touch; she snuggled up like a contented kitten.

Pillowing her head on his shoulder, she looked up and repeated "Please leave, before it's too late."

Connell laughed softly and said. "Never had a better reason for staying."

For a moment they crossed glances in the moonlight. His arms tightened about her, and she did not draw away. And then as though by common impulse, their lips met, and Connell felt the ecstatic shiver that rippled down her silk clad body. She tried to catch his wrist, brush aside the hand that caressed the gleaming curves of her thigh.

Her inarticulate murmur of protest, breathed in Connell's ear, further inflamed his blood; and his possessive caresses for the moment brushed aside the hovering presence of mystery and horror. Each seemed to feel that the other was a haven of reality in the devil-haunted plantation.

The lacy hem of her gown was creeping clear of her knees. Connell's kisses were stifling her murmured protests. Madeline's breath came in ever quickening gasps. She was clinging to him, the pressure of her firm young breasts telling him that she really did not want him to desist.

If Ducoin was making the rounds of his spectral plantation where black automatons tilled the fields by moonlight, there was no hurry. Connelly's ardent caresses were calling to the surface all the fire and passion of Madeline's Latin blood. She was lonely and frightened, and his purposeful persistence thrilled and assured her. Her final protest ended in a sigh and a murmur and a silky embrace that became as possessive as Connell's enfolding arms.

"We'll soon leave, darling." As he emerged from his chair; she still clung to him.

"Aunt Célie is asleep." Her whisper was an invitation." And Uncle Pierre won't be back for quite a while ..."

She caught his hand.

"You'll take me with you, won't you?" Madeline murmured, flinging back her disarrayed dark hair; and extending alluring arms. "When we leave ..."

"I'll take you away from here, forever and always," he promised.

For a long time their murmurings mocked the horrors that marched blindly across the spreading fields of the moon flooded Delta. Finally Madeline slipped from Connell's arms; and gestured toward the moon blot on the floor.

"It's getting late, sweetheart," she whispered. "We'll go to New Orleans as soon as I can pack up."

Connell followed her, and watched her hastily bundle together odds and ends selected from her wardrobe. A strange, mad night. Going in search of a man and finding this incredible armful of loveliness. It was all fantasy, but Connell's lips still tingled from the fire of her kisses. Let Pierre Ducoin keep the secret of the uncanny walking dead men. Plato would eventually appear with some wild story accounting for his absence. It was utterly incredible that he would have lingered long enough to have left any clues. Amelia's African guile had fairly bludgeoned Connell into this mad search.

He watched Madeline dressing in the moon glamour. Once he reached New Orleans with that delicious loveliness, he would pension Plato for life.

They stole through the shadows of the orange grove to Connell's *coupé*. He took Madeline's suitcase and raised the turtle back. Something was stirring in the baggage compartment.

"*Mon Dieu!*" gasped Madeline.

"Is that you, Mr. Walt?" whispered a familiar woman's voice. Amelia Jones emerged. "Did you get Plato?"

Then she saw Madeline, and her voice trailed into reproachful indefiniteness. Connell was betraying his colored folks.

"What the devil are you doing here?" he demanded.

"I just followed," said Amelia. "In case that no good man didn't want to come home."

Her plump, comely face was agleam with perspiration. It was a wonder she had not suffocated in the stuffy baggage compartment during that long search down the Delta. Connell helplessly glanced at

Madeline who was nervously fingering his arm. Amelia painfully clambered out of the turtle back.

"Get back in there. Amelia," Connell abruptly ordered. "I'll fix the top."

But the woman shook her head.

"No, sir, Mr. Walt. I'm goin' to find him myself. I knows you're too busy, and I'm much obliged for the ride." Her glance shifted, and she saw the familiar model T. "That's Plato's Ford. I'll get him. Don't you wait here no longer, Mr. Walt."

Amelia's contradictory blend of stubbornness and humility got under Connell's skin. He couldn't sell his niggers down the river that way; neither could he leave Madeline another night in that fiend-haunted plantation house. But his indecision was costly.

Dark forms slipping from the shadows closed in on them. Ducoin's black laborers! Their eyes were not blind but staring, unfocused and unseeing.

Their faces were utterly devoid of expression. Walking dead men, moving with the slow, horrible motion of animated corpses.

"Get back, you devils!" snarled Connell, thrusting aside a clutching hand and driving home with his fist; but it was like hammering the trunk of a tree. Not a gasp, not a grunt, not a change of expression. Madeline screamed as other hands clutched her.

Though Connell's fists crunched against bony faces, and chunked wrist deep into leathery stomachs, he made no more impression than on tackling dummies. Kicking, slugging, and gouging as the tangle of voiceless black men overwhelmed him, Connell's brain became a vortex of honor. He knew now why the *Cajuns* called them walking corpses.

They could not be alive. There was no resentment or wrath at his frantic, savage blows. Somewhere he heard a terrified wailing and a scurrying. Amelia was taking cover. The walking corpses seemed unaware of her presence.

Madeline's outcries were throttled. As Connell vainly battled, he caught glimpses of her silk clad legs flailing in the moonlight, heard the ripping of cloth as her ensemble was tom to ribbons by her captors. Then he was smothered by the irresistible rush. A sickening, musty, charnel stench stifled him. Iron muscles, leathery bodies, exhaling the odor of incipient decay, yet more powerful than any living thing, crushed him to the border of unconsciousness. They seized him and Madeline as though they were logs, and hauled them up the veranda stairs and into Madeline's room.

Connell heard Pierre Ducoin's familiar voice.

"Too bad," he ironically commented as the blacks dropped their burdens, and pinned Connell to the floor with their bony knees. "Aunt Célie told me something was going on."

Then he turned to the corpse men, and spoke in a purring, primitive language, more rudimentary than any Haitian patois: the old savage dialect of Guinea.

They bound Connell's hands and feet to a chair, and flung Madeline carelessly across her bed. Though half conscious, she was stirring and moaning, and instinctively trying to draw her tattered ensemble down about her hips. And then Aunt Célie appeared, black, sombre and malignant. The sinister black woman knelt beside the hearth and struck light. In a moment she had a fire kindled and was heaping it with charcoal.

The walking corpses lined themselves against the wall awaiting orders. It was only then that Connell fully realized what had mauled and pounded him and Madeline.

They were breathing; but their lack of expression reminded him of a dog he had once seen in a vivisection laboratory. The greater portion of the animal's brain had been removed; it lived, but it was a living log. And those black men had only enough brain left to let their reflexes function.

"How do you like my crew of *zombies*?" murmured Ducoin as the woman set a kettle of water over the glowing coals.

Zombies! That one word rounded out Council's rising horror. They were corpses stolen from unguarded graves and had been reanimated by a primal necromancy to serve as farm cattle! *Zombies*, toiling as no dumb beast could. Rich profits, farming a plantation with hands like those. He wondered why Aunt Célie knelt swaying and muttering before the kettle into which she tossed dried herbs, and bits of bark and roots and pebbles.

"Pretty nice, eh?" was Ducoin's satirical comment. "I learned the trick at Haiti, and I'm going to add you to my string of zombies. Once Aunt Célie mixes you a drink you won't be so interested in women."

Wrath blazed in Ducoin's eyes as his glance shifted to his disheveled niece.

"I don't know what you two were doing." he murmured, "but I can fairly well guess. Or else she wouldn't have been so willing to go away

with you. Just another no-good wench. She'll be a very good zombie herself—"

"You damn' dirty rat!" snarled Connell. "Do you mean—"

"Certainly," answered Ducoin. "After fooling around with you, she's no niece of mine. In this day and age I can't give her what she deserves, but making her a zombie is different. Nobody will inquire out here on the Delta. And she'll not be playing around with strangers anymore."

Another guttural command. The corpse men marched over to Madeline's bed as returning consciousness stirred her. Connell, struggling against his bonds, saw them stripping her dress to tatters as they throttled her into submission. Shuddering with horror at the grisly contact. Madeline finally surrendered, and the zombies methodically lashed her to another chair. Her dress was a pitiful rag. Her clawed breasts were half exposed; and her bruised legs peeped through the remnants of her hosiery.

Ducoin chuckled at Connell's frenzied struggles.

"That won't do you any good. I'll leave a guard here to watch you while Aunt Célie and I finish the brew that'll make both of you zombies'''

At Ducoin's command all but one of the zombies filed out of the room. Before he and Aunt Célie followed the Creole paused to remark. "You were looking for Plato. All right, I'm sending Plato in to help watch you. Now see how you like the white man's burden!"

They left. But presently, as the fumes from the kettle stifled and dizzied Connell, he heard approaching footsteps *clump-clump-clumping* down the hall.

The black apparition which stood framed in the doorway froze his blood. Plato had returned a loose-jointed shambling, lifeless hulk that moved in response to the zombie master's command.

"Good God in heaven!" he groaned.

'That's why I warned you." whispered Madeline. "I saw Plato before and after."

"If I'd only left—"

"I'm still glad you didn't. Walt. It was such a ghastly, lonely life. Becoming a living corpse is better than never having lived."

A wave of nausea racked Connell. He and Madeline would presently be the companions of that horrible hulk.

"Hitch your chair over, bit by bit." Madeline continued. "Maybe I can get you loose."

Connell's cramped efforts moved the chair a scant fraction of an inch. At the rasp of wood the heads of the zombies shifted. They had their orders. Not a chance.

"Plato." said Connell. "Loosen my hands. Plato, don't you remember me?"

Over and over, he repeated the name. The blank, sightless face seemed to change for an instant.

"Maybe he's not been this way long enough to forget everything," whispered Madeline. "Try again— "

The oft-repeated name got unexpected results, but not from the zombie. Plato's wife, Amelia, came slinking from the hallway. Her black plump face became slate grey as she stared into the ruddy glow.

"Where's my Plato? Mr. Walt, was you talkin' to him?"

Then she saw the hulk that had been Connell's servant.

"Plato! Don't you hear me talkin' to you?"

Not a sign of life. That blasted brain could not absorb a new impression.

"Plato, honey, can't you hear me?"

Finally, grey and trembling, the woman turned to Connell.

"Mr. Walt. I can't do nuthin'. Plato's dead."

Connell realized that Amelia's persuasion had made less impression than his own authoritative voice.

"Untie us. Amelia," he said.

She had scarcely reached the chair when Plato's ponderous hand lashed out, flinging her into a corner.

"Mr. Walt," said the woman, as she struggled to her feet. "I'm goin' to the village to get help. That devil don't know I'm here, and I'll get some friends."

She stepped into the hall. Connell renewed his struggles. Once or twice Madeline contrived to jerk her chair a fraction of an inch toward him, but a zombie leaped forward, bodily picked her up; and set her in a comer. They did nothing to thwart Connell's struggles against his bonds. The orders had not covered that.

Finally Connell contrived to spread the knotted strands of clothesline.

"Hang on; darling." he panted. "I'll be clear in a second."

"But what good will it do?" moaned Madeline. "They'll block you before—"

"Maybe I can toss you out the window, chair and all."

He knew that he had no chance against his grisly captors, but anything was better than waiting for that deadly brew to receive the missing ingredients that would make them living corpses. Connell heard footsteps and relaxed his desperate efforts. His blood froze, and a stifled oath choked him.

It was Amelia. She had a small parcel wrapped in paper. Damn her, why hadn't she run to the village like she'd said she would?

"Plato, honey." she pleaded "I brought you somethin' good."

"For God's sake, go to the village!" shouted Connell.

"That would be wasted effort." said a sardonic voice.

Ducoin crossed the threshold accompanied by Aunt Célie and several zombies. His sinister presence, and the living dead, seemed to freeze Amelia with horror. She had lost her chance to make a break.

"I guess we'll have a number three zombie," murmured Ducoin.

The living dead now blocked the doorway. Aunt Célie lifted the lid of the kettle, and added a pinch of powder from a small packet. She stirred the villainous potion, and drew off a cupful and held it to Connell's lips.

"You might as well drink it." said Ducoin. "If you don't—" His gaze shifted to Madeline's trembling bare body and he resumed, "These zombies will do anything I tell them. How would you like to see one of them—"

His words trailed to a whisper, but Connell knew what would happen to Madeline, before his eyes.

And then the last remnant of cord that bound his wrist yielded. His freed hand flashed out, striking the steaming beverage from Ducoin's hand. As the Creole recoiled, Connell's other hand jerked loose, gripping him by the throat. The sudden move caught Ducoin off guard. Since the master was present, the zombies did not interfere; and Ducoin, throttled by Connell's savage grasp, could not articulate an order.

Sock! Connell's fist hammered home, driving Ducoin crashing into a comer, dazed and numb. Connell struggled with the bonds at his ankles, but only for a moment. Aunt Célie seized his elbows from the rear.

Once Ducoin recovered his voice—!

Amelia was free. But instead of running, she approached Plato.

"Jes' yo' taste one, honey." she crooned, placing a salted cashew nut in the bluish, sagging mouth of her dead husband.

There was a mumbling and a drooling, a sudden flash of perception as the salty tidbit mingled with the saliva; then an inarticulate, bestial howl.

Ducoin and Aunt Célie flung themselves forward.

"Stop her!" yelled Ducoin. *"She's giving them salt!"*

Too late. Burly, powerful Plato had become a raging maniac. Amelia thrust cashew nuts into the mouth of the other zombie. Another incredible transformation. Another slavering, howling brute.

A pistol cracked, but only once. Ducoin's weapon clattered into a corner. Plato and his companion closed in.

The room became a red hell of slaughter. The insensate hulks were pounding and trampling and flinging Ducoin and Aunt Célie about like bean bags.

They hungrily licked splashed blood from their hands, and renewed the assault. Other zombies came from the fields, tasted a salted nut, and joined the butchery. And presently there was only a shapeless, gory pulp that they were trampling and beating into the floor ...

The zombies desisted for lack of fragments left to dismember. Then they clambered to their feet, utterly ignoring Amelia and the two prisoners. They shattered the window, cleared the sill, and dashed across the field. Against the moonglow, Connell saw them burrowing into the ground like dogs.

Amelia, sobbing and laughing, was releasing him and Madeline.

"Mr. Walt," the woman explained "when I saw my Plato. I remembered somethin' my ole grandmammy told me years ago, about them zombies cuttin' up that way when they ate salt. Then I remembered the cashew nuts I gave you. Now, praise de Lord, Plato is plumb dead, and all the other zombies are goin' to their graves like Christians. They always do that, when they get salt. But first they messes up the man what made them zombies."

"But how did he do it?" wondered Connell as he helped Madeline into the car.

"I don't know anything about it, except that according to the law in Haiti, it's a capital offense to administer any drug that produces a coma. And I think that's the real reason Uncle Piene decided to finish me—he found me reading an old book of Haitian statutes, not long ago, and was afraid of my suspicions."

"Mr. Walt," interrupted a voice from the rumble seat, "you're goin' to need a maid for the new missus, ain't you?"

"Absolutely," assured Connell, "but you'd better take a vacation for a couple of weeks before you come to work ..."

The Graveyard Rats

By Henry Kuttner

OLD MASSON, the caretaker of one of Salem's oldest and most-neglected cemeteries, had a feud with the rats. Generations ago they had come up from the wharves and settled in the graveyard, a colony of abnormally large rats, and when Masson had taken charge after the inexplicable disappearance of the former caretaker, he decided that they must go. At first he set traps for them and put poisoned food by their burrows, and later he tried to shoot them, but it did no good. The rats stayed, multiplying and overrunning the graveyard with their ravenous hordes.

They were large, even for the *Mus decumanus,* which sometimes measures fifteen inches in length, exclusive of the naked pink and gray tail. Masson had caught glimpses of some as large as good-size cats, and when, once or twice, the grave diggers had uncovered their burrows, the malodorous tunnels were large enough to enable a man to crawl into them on his hands and knees. The ships that had come generations ago from distant ports to the rotting Salem wharves had brought strange cargoes.

Masson wondered sometimes at the extraordinary size of these burrows. He recalled certain vaguely disturbing legends he had heard since coming to ancient, witch-haunted Salem—tales of a moribund, inhuman life that was said to exist in forgotten burrows in the earth. The old days, when Cotton Mather had hunted down the evil cults that worshiped Hecate and the dark Magna Mater in frightful orgies, had passed; but dark, gabled houses still leaned perilously toward each other over narrow cobbled streets, and blasphemous secrets and mysteries were said to be hidden in subterranean cellars and caverns, where forgotten pagan rites were still celebrated in defiance of law and sanity. Wagging their gray heads wisely, the elders declared that there were worse things than rats and maggots crawling in the unhallowed earth of the ancient Salem cemeteries.

And then, too, there was this curious dread of the rats. Masson disliked and respected the ferocious little rodents, for he knew the danger that lurked in their flashing, needle-sharp fangs; but he could not understand the inexplicable horror that the oldsters held for deserted, rat-infested houses. He had heard vague rumors of ghoulish beings that dwelt far underground, and that had the power of commanding the rats, marshaling them like horrible armies. The rats, the old men whispered, were messengers between this world and the grim and ancient caverns far below Salem. Bodies had been stolen from graves for nocturnal subterranean feasts, they said. The myth of the Pied Piper is a fable that hides a blasphemous horror, and the black pits of Avernus have brought forth hell-spawned monstrosities that never venture into the light of day.

Masson paid little attention to these tales. He did not fraternize with his neighbors, and, in fact, did all he could to hide the existence of the rats from intruders. Investigation, he realized, would undoubtedly mean the opening of many graves. And while some of the gnawed, empty coffins could be attributed to the activities of the rats, Masson might find it difficult to explain the mutilated bodies that lay in some of the coffins.

The purest gold is used in filling teeth, and this gold is not removed when a man is buried. Clothing, of course, is another matter; for usually the undertaker provides a plain broadcloth suit that is cheap and easily recognizable. Sometimes, too, there were medical students and less reputable doctors who were in need of cadavers, and not overscrupulous as to where these were obtained.

So far Masson had successfully managed to discourage investigation. He had fiercely denied the existence of the rats, even though they sometimes robbed him of his prey. Masson did not care what happened to the bodies after he had performed his gruesome thefts, but the rats inevitably dragged away the whole cadaver through the hole they gnawed in the coffin.

The size of these burrows occasionally worried Masson. Then, too, there was the curious circumstance of the coffins always being gnawed open at the end, never at the side or top. It was almost as though the rats were working under the direction of some impossibly intelligent leader.

Now he stood in an open grave and threw a last sprinkling of wet earth on the heap beside the pit. It was raining a slow, cold drizzle that for weeks had been descending from soggy black clouds. The graveyard was a slough of yellow, sucking mud from which the rain-washed tombstones stood up in irregular battalions. The rats had retreated to their burrows, and Masson had not seen one for days. But his gaunt, unshaven face was set in frowning lines; the coffin on which he was standing was a wooden one.

The body had been buried several days earlier, but Masson had not dared to disinter it before. A relative of the dead man had been coming to the grave at intervals, even in the drenching rain. But he would hardly come at this late hour, no matter how much grief he might be suffering, Masson thought, grinning wryly. He straightened and laid the shovel aside.

From the hill on which the ancient graveyard lay he could see the lights of Salem flickering dimly through the downpour. He drew a flashlight from his pocket. He would need light now. Taking up the spade, he bent and examined the fastenings of the coffin.

Abruptly he stiffened. Beneath his feet he sensed an unquiet stirring and scratching, as though something were moving within the coffin. For a moment a pang of superstitious fear shot through Masson, and then rage replaced it as he realized the significance of the sound. The rats had forestalled him again!

In a paroxysm of anger, Masson wrenched at the fastenings of the coffin. He got the sharp edge of the shovel under the lid and pried it up until he could finish the job with his hands. Then he sent the flashlight's cold beam darting down into the coffin.

Rain spattered against the white satin lining; the coffin was empty. Masson saw a flicker of movement at the head of the case and darted the light in that direction.

The end of the sarcophagus had been gnawed through, and a gaping hole led into darkness. A black shoe, limp and dragging, was disappearing as Masson watched, and abruptly he realized that the rats had forestalled him by only a few minutes. He fell on his hands and knees and made a hasty clutch at the shoe, and the flashlight inconveniently fell into the coffin and went out. The shoe was tugged from his grasp, he heard a sharp, excited squealing, and then he had the flashlight again and was darting its light into the burrow.

It was a large one. It had to be, or the corpse could not have been dragged along it. Masson wondered at the size of the rats that could carry away a man's body, but the thought of the loaded revolver in his pocket fortified him. Probably if the corpse had been an ordinary one, Masson would have left the rats with their spoils rather than venture into the narrow burrow, but he remembered an especially fine set of cuff links he had observed, as well as a stickpin that was undoubtedly a genuine pearl. With scarcely a pause he clipped the flashlight to his belt and crept into the burrow.

It was a tight fit, but he managed to squeeze himself along. Ahead of him in the flashlight's glow he could see the shoes dragging along the wet earth of the bottom of the tunnel. He crept along the burrow as rapidly as he could, occasionally barely able to squeeze his lean body through the narrow walls.

The air was overpowering with its musty stench of carrion. If he could not reach the corpse in a minute, Masson decided, he would turn back. Belated fears were beginning to crawl, maggot-like, within his mind, but greed urged him on. He crawled forward, several times passing the mouths of adjoining tunnels. The walls of the burrow were damp and slimy, and twice lumps of dirt dropped behind him. The second time he paused and screwed his head around to look back. He could see nothing, of course, until he had unhooked the flashlight from his belt and reversed it.

Several clods lay on the ground behind him, and the danger of his position suddenly became real and terrifying. With thoughts of a cave-in making his pulse race, he decided to aba don the pursuit, even though he had now almost overtaken the corpse and the invisible things that pulled it. But he had overlooked one thing: The burrow was too narrow to allow him to turn.

Panic touched him briefly, but he remembered a side tunnel he had just passed and backed awkwardly along the tunnel until he came to it. He thrust his legs into it, backing until he found himself able to turn. Then he hurriedly began to retrace his way, although his knees were bruised and painful.

Agonizing pain shot through his leg. He felt sharp teeth sink into his flesh and kicked out frantically. There was a shrill squealing and the scurry of many feet. Flashing the light behind him, Masson caught his breath in a sob of fear as he saw a dozen great rats watching him intently, their slitted eyes glittering in the light. They were great misshapen things, as large as cats, and behind them he caught a glimpse of a dark shape that stirred and moved swiftly aside into the shadow; and he shuddered at the unbelievable size of the thing.

The light had held them for a moment, but they were edging closer, their teeth dull orange in pale light. Masson tugged at his pistol, managed to extricate it from his pocket, and aimed carefully. It was an awkward position, and he tried to press his feet into the soggy sides of the burrow so that he should not inadvertently send a bullet into one of them.

The rolling thunder of the shot deafened him, for a time, and the clouds of smoke set him coughing. When he could hear again and the smoke had cleared, he saw that the rats were gone. He put the pistol back and began to creep swiftly along the tunnel, and then with a scurry and a rush they were upon him again.

They swarmed over his legs, biting and squealing insanely, and Masson shrieked horribly as he snatched for his gun. He fired without aiming, and only luck saved him from blowing off a foot. This time the rats did not retreat so far, but Masson was crawling as swiftly as he could along the burrow, ready to fire again at the first sound of another attack.

There was a patter of feet, and he sent the light stabbing in back of him. A great gray rat paused and watched him. Its long ragged whiskers twitched, and its scabrous, naked tail was moving slowly from side to side. Masson shouted, and the rat retreated.

He crawled on, pausing briefly, the black gap of a side tunnel at his elbow, as he made out a shapeless huddle on the damp clay a few yards ahead. For a second he thought it was a mass of earth that had been dislodged from the roof, and then he recognized it as a human body.

It was a brown and shriveled mummy, and with a dreadful unbelieving shock Masson realized that it was moving.

It was crawling toward him, and in the pale glow of the flashlight the man saw a frightful gargoyle face thrust into his own. It was the passionless, death's-head skull of a long-dead corpse, instinct with hellish life; and the glazed eyes swollen and bulbous betrayed the thing's blindness. It made a faint groaning sound as it crawled toward Masson, stretching its ragged and granulated lips in a grin of dreadful hunger. And Masson was frozen with abysmal fear and loathing.

Just before the Horror touched him, Masson flung himself frantically into the burrow at his side. He heard a scrambling noise at his heels, and the thing groaned dully as it came after him. Masson, glancing over his shoulder, screamed and propelled himself desperately through the narrow burrow. He crawled along awkwardly, sharp stones cutting his hands and knees. Dirt showered into his eyes, but he dared not pause even for a moment. He scrambled on, gasping, cursing, and praying hysterically.

Squealing triumphantly, the rats came at him, horrible hunger in their eyes. Masson almost succumbed to their vicious teeth before he succeeded in beating them off. The passage was narrowing, and in a frenzy of terror he kicked and screamed and fired until the hammer clicked on an empty shell. But he had driven them off.

He found himself crawling under a great stone, embedded in the roof that dug cruelly into his back. It moved a little as his weight struck it, and an idea flashed into Masson's fright-crazed mind. If he could bring down the stone so that it blocked the tunnel!

The earth was wet and soggy from the rains, and he hunched himself half upright and dug away at the dirt around the stone. The rats were coming closer. He saw their eyes glowing in the reflection of the flashlight's beam. Still he clawed frantically at the earth. The stone was giving. He tugged at it, and it rocked in its foundation.

A rat was approaching—the monster he had already glimpsed. Gray and leprous and hideous it crept forward with its orange teeth bared, and in its wake came the blind dead thing, groaning as it crawled. Masson gave a last frantic tug at the stone. He felt it slide downward, and then he went scrambling along the tunnel.

Behind him the stone crashed down, and he heard a sudden frightful shriek of agony. Clods showered upon his legs. A heavy weight fell on his feet, and he dragged them free with difficulty. The entire tunnel was collapsing!

Gasping with fear, Masson threw himself forward as the soggy earth collapsed at his heels. The tunnel narrowed until he could barely use his hands and legs to propel himself; he wriggled forward like an eel and suddenly felt satin tearing beneath his clawing fingers, and then his head crashed against something that barred his path. He moved his legs, discovering that they were pinned under the collapsed earth. He was lying flat on his stomach, and when he tried to raise himself, he found that the roof was only a few inches from his back. Panic shot through him.

When the blind horror had blocked his path, he had flung himself desperately into a side tunnel, a tunnel that had no outlet. He was in a coffin, an empty coffin into which he had crept through the hole the rats had gnawed in its end!

He tried to turn on his back and found that he could not. The lid of the coffin pinned him down inexorably. Then he braced himself and strained at the coffin lid. It was immovable, and even if he could escape from the sarcophagus, how could he claw his way up through five feet of hard-packed earth?

He found himself gasping. It was dreadfully fetid, unbearably hot. In a paroxysm of terror, he ripped and clawed at the satin until it was shredded. He made a futile attempt to dig with his feet at the earth from the collapsed burrow that blocked his retreat. If he were only able to reverse his position he might be able to claw his way through to air … air …

White-hot agony lanced through his breast, throbbed in his eyeballs. His head seemed to be swelling, growing larger and larger; and suddenly he heard the exultant squealing of the rats. He began to scream insanely but could not drown them out. For a moment he thrashed about hysterically within his narrow prison, and then he was quiet, gasping for air. His eyelids closed, his blackened tongue protruded, and he sank down into the blackness of death with the mad squealing of the rats dinning in his ears.

The Grave Gives Up

By Jack D'Arcy

Chapter 1: A Voice from the Dead

IT WAS a melancholy night. Dampness impregnated the sultry autumn air. The light of the moon filtered faintly through a huge black cloud that hung over the face of the heavens. Somewhere from the great swamp near the graveyard a whippoorwill sobbed; and the throbbing sound echoed the anguish in the heart of Gordon Lane.

He sat alone in his small bachelor apartment in the eastern end of the town. A fire crackled on the hearth, and a book lay upon his lap. Yet he could not see the type for the tears that dimmed his vision.

For two weeks now he had seen none of his friends. Mechanically, he had gone about his daily duties with that numbing pain in his heart that pumped a deadly emotional opiate to his brain.

Once he had sworn that he could not live without Janice and she had laughed at him. Now he knew that his words were not mere lover's rhetoric. Since that awful day a fortnight ago, something within him had died. When Janice had been killed in the automobile accident, the soul of Gordon Lane had been slain with her.

The overwhelming love that he had borne her had evolved into a great sorrow which gnawed like the Spartan fox at his heart. Despite the heat of the fire, he shuddered as he thought of Janice's slim white body lying in the coldness of the dank earth.

Within his breast he could feel that coldness as surely as if he had been lying in the grave with her. Within his brain was a deadness, a lifelessness, as if his body, too, was interred in a mossy stone crypt on the other side of town.

And if Death himself had entered the room at that moment, he would have been a welcome visitor to Gordon Lane.

For the first time in a week, the phone bell jangled. Lane did not stir at its metallic summons. Again and again it shrilled until it finally hammered into his consciousness.

He turned slowly to the table at his side and lifted up the instrument. In a dull listless voice, he said, "Hello."

A sound came over the wire as if from a great distance. It was tired and dispirited as a weary breeze that stirred sere autumn leaves. Yet the words it uttered crashed into Lane's ear like a thunder clap.

"Gordon? Is that you, Gordon?"

Lane's pulse leaped, and for the first time since the funeral his heart pumped surging vibrant life through his veins. But what slew his lethargy was the stimulating toxin of stark terror.

Like a fluttering kite it rose in his pulses; like the wings of a black bat it beat against his brain. For the rustling voice that had come to him over the wire was the voice of Janice!

Lane's hand was hot as he clutched the phone to his breast. His face was white and there was a tremor in his tone as he answered.

"Yes, this is Gordon. Janice! Janice, where are you? Where—"

Again Lane heard the voice of the woman he had loved more than life itself; and it seemed to come from a great distance as if it had been projected from the borderland of the netherworld from which no man has ever returned.

"Gordon—Gordon—" For an instant the dreariness left her tone and her words came pantingly like a hot wind over hell. "Gordon! Come to me—I need you! I need you. I—"

THE NEXT SYLLABLE was an inarticulate, strangled fragment in her throat. From somewhere in the realm of infinity Lane heard a stifled scream—a scream that caused the black bat in his brain to beat its dark wings more furiously. Then there was silence.

"Janice!" Lane rasped her name into the mouthpiece. "Janice!"

But there was no answer. If that voice had come from the grave, it had returned to its awful prison once more. If, for a fleeting moment, the other world had opened its locked doors, they were sealed again now. The complete silence of the receiver seemed to mock him.

Lane dropped the telephone upon the table and fell into his chair. Diamonds of sweat were on his brow.

His face, far whiter than the glacial snows, was painted a ghastly hellish red by the licking flames of the fire. He resembled a phantom before the gates of hell.

Two facts seared themselves into his throbbing brain. He had heard *her* voice; and she was dead. For a long time he stared into the fire as if in those flickering yellow tongues he would read the awful mystery which confronted him.

Was it madness that assailed him? Had the burden of grief he had borne for the past two weeks, caused a delicate hairline between sanity and madness to break? Was the phone call an illusion which existed only in his own tortured mind?

Two distinct fears met and clashed within him—fear for his own sanity and fear that he had for a moment communicated with that unknown uncharted world beyond the grave.

Slowly his mind began to function logically through the maelstrom in his head. Slowly his thoughts became translated to action. He moved toward the telephone; picked it up with trembling fingers. A moment later the operator's voice was in his ear.

"Operator." He made a desperate effort to make his tone casual. "This is Gordon Lane of the County Attorney's office. I believe my phone rang a few minutes ago. Have you a record of the call?"

There was a moment's silence.

"Yes, sir. You were called at nine-sixteen. We have the record here."

Lane could feel his heart pound up against his breast like a pendulum weighted with ice.

"And can you tell me where the call originated?"

Again there was a short silence; a heavy ominous silence in which shadowy phantoms bred in Lane's mind. Then the operator's voice rasped on the wires again.

"Why yes, Mr. Lane. That call was made from one-eighty-one Lenora Street."

Lane's hand gripped the phone with all its strength. It was as if he had to cling to something material, to anchor himself against the terrifying nebulae of his thoughts.

"One-eighty-one Lenora," he said and his voice was dry as a cactus stalk. "That's the Gaunt Hill cemetery."

"That's right."

There was a dull click at the other end of the wire as the operator broke the connection. But Gordon Lane did not replace the phone immediately. His hot, perspiring hand held the receiver clutched hard against his breast as if it was an aegis against the incredible thing which he must now believe.

Janice had called him. It had been her voice. And the call had come from Gaunt Hill on the other side of town. Gaunt Hill, where Janice's lovely tender body lay buried in a cold marble crypt!

TWENTY MINUTES LATER, Lane's coupe slithered to a halt before a rectangular two-story building. His nervous finger jerked against a bell in the doorway. An immaculate butler opened the door.

"Dr. Ramos," said Lane pantingly. "Is he in?"

"Hello, Lane," a voice greeted him from the foyer. The doctor, wearing his hat and coat had spoken. "I was just going out. What can I do for you?"

Lane crossed the threshold. His eyes were brilliant with a shining fever. His hair was rumpled and his face was a dirty, ashen grey. As he spoke his voice was hoarse and thick with feeling.

"I've got to see you a moment," he said. "At once. Privately."

Ramos regarded him with a professional eye. Then quietly he replaced his hat on the hall tree.

"All right. Come on into the office."

He led the way to a book-lined sanctuary, and took a seat beside his desk. Lane threw himself in a huge overstuffed chair and stared with his glassy eyes at the doctor.

Already he felt somewhat better. For the doctor symbolized everything that was reasonable. Ruddy-faced and solid, he held the respect of the ancient town. He was firmly opposed to all that might even be suspected of mysticism.

He was a complete atheist, a crass materialist, fond of good food and better wines. If anyone in town could explain away the mad thing that had happened to Lane that night, the man was Dr. Ramos.

Lane's white knuckles gripped the sides of the chair.

"Listen, Doctor," he said slowly. "It's about Janice."

Ramos raised his eyebrows.

"Janice," he said. "Now listen, Lane. You've got to steady yourself on that score. Death comes to us all. You've got to get hold of yourself. I—"

"Wait a minute, Doctor. It's not that. It's—Well, you signed her death certificate, didn't you?"

Ramos' eyes narrowed. A peculiar expression was on his face as he nodded at the younger man.

"Well," went on Lane and there was a terrible tenseness in his tone, "was she dead? Are you sure that she was really dead? Are you sure?"

He had risen from his chair and now he pounded excitedly on the smooth top of the desk. Ramos made no reply until Lane's outburst had exhausted itself in a fit of words.

"My boy," he said at last, in a grave sympathetic voice, "I know what suffering must have gone on in your heart. But you must fight it with your reason. You must. Janice is dead. I saw her dead. You saw her interred. There can be no doubt about it."

"Then," said Lane, and his voice was the voice of a man who fears the words he speaks, "how did she speak to me tonight? Where did her voice come from if she is dead? Is my ear so attuned that I can hear a voice from Beyond?"

A shadow, almost imperceptible, flickered into the doctor's eyes. The ruddiness of his face grew a shade lighter. He leaned forward slightly in his chair.

"What's that you say?" he breathed. "You heard her voice?"

"From the grave, I heard it. She telephoned me. Said she needed me. And the call came from Gaunt Hill cemetery."

RAMOS' FACE WAS dark for a fleeting instant. Then it became normal again. He rose and crossed the room. He flung a fraternal arm about Lane's shoulder.

"My boy," he said, "there's a simple explanation. You would have thought of it yourself if you hadn't been so overwrought. It's a joke. A cruel practical joke, played by some unfeeling fool who is trying to frighten you. Janice died here in my sanitarium. Of that I can assure you. Here, I'll give you a sedative. Take it and go to bed."

Gordon Lane came to his feet. It seemed that in that single instant, the cobwebs of fear had been brushed from his brain. There was something within him that was stronger than the terror that had held him in its icy thrall. Something stronger than any other emotion he had ever experienced.

Now the thing was clear at last. Now he knew where his duty lay. Now he knew what he must do.

"No," he said and his voice was resolute, "I want no sedative. No matter what hideous thing is behind that call tonight, I *know* that it was the voice of Janice. I know further that she needs me. I shall go to her. She spoke to me from Gaunt Hill. That is all I know. So it is to Gaunt Hill that I must go. She needs me."

He turned on his heel and strode toward the door. Ramos' voice, pitched oddly, came to him on the threshold.

"Wait a minute, Lane. Now don't be a fool. Janice is dead, I tell you. Don't go to Gaunt Hill tonight."

As Lane turned to face the doctor, it seemed to him that there was a cloud of apprehension in Ramos' eyes.

"I'm going," he said simply. "Now."

Ramos crossed the room and stood in the doorway facing Lane. He put his hands on the younger man's shoulders and gazed squarely into his eyes. An odd sensation came over Lane in that moment. He could feel the blood mount to his face, feel its swift rhythmic beat in his temples.

"Don't go to Gaunt Hill tonight," said Ramos, speaking each word in a measured spondee beat. "Don't go."

Again Lane was aware of that odd lulling throb in his temples, but the knowledge of Janice's need was a strong impelling force in his breast. Roughly he took the doctor's hands from his shoulders.

"I must go," he said quietly.

He strode past the other, through the hall and out of the sanitarium. A moment later his coupe raced, a shadowy phantom through the deserted streets; it sped, a ghostly vehicle through the town, toward the marshy swamp on whose sloping bank reposed that city of the dead—the Gaunt Hill cemetery.

Chapter 2: The Dead Alive

THE TOMBSTONES were white, motionless specters in the night. Overhead the stark leafless branches of the trees waved in the breeze like the naked arms of some black Lorelei beckoning to disaster. The lethal silence which hung over the graveyard was not the silence which occurs through mere lack of sound. Rather it was a positive thing, a throbbing silence which as-sailed the senses as surely as the beat of savage drums.

On the right, near the entrance, a squat building loomed against the faint, clouded moonlight. That, Lane knew, was the caretaker's lodge. No light shone in its windows. Lane walked past the place on quiet feet. He had no wish to disturb the men at this hour.

He realized the explanation for his presence here would sound ridiculous in another's ears. As he moved noiselessly through the steles, it seemed as if the directing portion of his brain was a detached part of him. Quite clearly he knew what he must do.

He walked directly toward the Lansing mausoleum where Janice was buried. Dead or not dead, whether she were in the crypt, whether she were in Hell or Heaven, she had said she needed him. And he had come.

Yet despite his grim resolve, despite his firm purpose, he was not entirely unafraid. That uncanny telephone call had pricked his delicate nervous system with the pin of fear. And now in this ancient graveyard that had spread its earthy cloak over decayed corpses since the days of the Spaniards, there was an eerie electric atmosphere.

What it was he did not know. Normally he had not the weak man's fear of death and dead things. But here tonight he felt that some intangible horror stalked him; that some invisible monster strode at his side.

He started for a moment as he saw a black rectangular shape rise from a tombstone, flap black wings and fly off in the face of the moon. An involuntary shudder ran through his body, for at that moment it seemed as if the bat presaged some dire happening; as if it were a forerunner of the evil thing that was destined to happen.

On his left, some forty feet this side of the Lansing tomb, stood a square marble edifice. Lane recognized it as the burying place of the Cervantes family, the old clan of the town who could trace their ancestry back to the brave days of Balboa.

Then, abruptly, he halted. A sound had broken that deathly silence. A faint creaking noise had reached his eardrum. And it had come from the tomb of the Cervantes!

For a long moment Gordon Lane stood motionless. But inside him there was no stillness. Fear swirled like a misty cloud within his heart. The vague apprehension that had been with him suddenly crystallized into a definite horror that the unknown thing which he had feared was at last imminent.

Again he heard the creaking sound. Long drawn-out and undulating it crawled into his hearing. Then it ended, punctuated by a lower note like the grunt of a wallowing swine.

GORDON LANE'S will held him where he was, held him firmly from obeying all his screaming instincts to run from this place of evil. His face was white and in his eyes shone a mighty resolve as he deliberately turned his face toward the tomb.

His hand reached out and touched the handle on the crypt door, and his fingers were colder than the metal which they clasped.

He turned the handle and pushed his weight against the massive oaken door. Slowly it swung inward. The darkness that poured into his eyes was almost a material thing. Dank air seeped into his nostrils. The frightful odor of decaying flesh filtered into his lungs.

His cold fingers groped in his vest pocket, and found a package of matches. Then as he was about to strike the match, he heard a sigh—a human sigh!

It was a weary, discouraged exhalation like the last whisper of a damned soul. With effort Lane held his fingers steady as he struck the match.

The tiny light flared eerily in the chamber. Ghostly flickering shadows danced on the damp stone walls as the little flame burned unevenly. Lane's eyeballs pained him as he stared strainingly into the gloom. The walls were lined with coffins of ancient wood. A rat scurried across the floor at his feet.

The match burned low and seared his fingers. Hastily he lit another. Then as he stood there, holding that tiny inadequate light in his hand, he felt a cold snake of terror crawl along his spine. Wings of panic beat in his brain.

His eyes stared straight ahead of him, and in their depth was a glazed expression of fearful doubt as if he trembled to believe the thing he saw.

For directly opposite him the lid of a coffin was rising. The rotted, dust-covered wood made an odd creaking sound as it moved, a sound like the off-key note struck on a ghostly violin.

Then as it lifted higher, Lane saw the hand that was moving it. It was a grey and bony hand with long prehensile fingers. Tightly they grasped the edge of the coffin lid and thrust it upward.

Then an arm appeared—a tenuous, naked arm like the ashen tentacle of some fiendish octopus. Lane's eyes dropped from the ghastly sight for a moment and focused upon the tarnished silver nameplate of the coffin. Then as the words engraved there registered on his mind, a white madness froze his nerves.

For the man who was rising from the tomb had been dead for over a hundred years!

The creaking noise increased. Wildly, Lane glanced about him. On all sides the lids were moving. Thin, emaciated arms appeared pushing, pushing up the covers which sealed the corpses in their tombs. Verily, the grave was yielding up its dead.

It was no longer the human concept of fear that coursed through Lane's arteries. It was now an overwhelming dread; that awful paralyzing force which deluges man when he witnesses the violation of all natural law; of all the things that he has been taught to believe.

THE DEAD WERE rising up around him! The dead who never returned were rising from their coffins, coming back to an earthly sphere. They were bursting the inviolate bonds of the grave, shattering all natural law in one unholy manifestation.

Gordon Lane's heart cried, "Flee!" His brain reeled dazedly before the incredible sight he witnessed, but his muscles were beyond his control. Some unseen vise held his sinews in mighty thrall. His legs were rooted to the spot where he stood.

Again the match burned his finger. His shaking hands essayed to light another. For darkness redoubled the terror of the tomb. Again the match flickered to jerky light.

Glassy eyes stared at Lane. The lifeless gaze of the dead stared at the intruder who had blasphemed their tomb with his presence. Their faces were horrible things over which the white hand of death had passed, leaving its indelible mark.

They were blank, expressionless faces, devoid of all intelligence, sans all life and animation. Gaunt, bony chests thrust themselves from filthy, ragged shreds which hung about their unearthly shoulders. But their eyes held the most awful thing of all.

They were the eyes of men who have gazed upon the unholy mysteries of the netherworld; eyes which have traveled across the Styx itself and witnessed the iniquitous evil of the banks of Hell.

And behind all this lay an insufferable pain, an agony of the soul which even Death's great power had been unable to release.

Lane never knew how long he stood there, exchanging scrutiny with these Things that had climbed back from the abyss. It seemed that infinity ticked past and the muscles of his body remained completely beyond his control.

Then came the thing that broke the paralysis. A scream ripped through the air; a scream pregnant with terror and agony. And despite its unnaturally high-pitched tone, Gordon Lane recognized the voice.

Janice!

That single fact smashed into his numbed consciousness with a force that precluded all else. The blood surged through his arteries once more.

He flung the burning match to the floor. He spun around on his heel and raced like one possessed from the dank interior of this frenzied vault of death.

The cool fresh air of the night hit his face like a wave of cold water. As he ran he once again heard that awful scream hammer with dreadful force through the fetid atmosphere of the graveyard.

He changed his direction slightly. Now he knew whence that scream came. It had emanated from the Lansing crypt. There was no doubt of that.

Despite the terrific strain under which he was laboring, relief pumped into his heart. If that voice was Janice's—and he knew it was—she was alive! Alive! She had returned from the tomb to him!

He crashed up against the door of the mausoleum. His trembling fingers found the handle and turned it. He raced into the tomb.

"Janice!" he cried. "Janice!"

There was no reply save the mocking reverberations of his own voice hurled back at him by the stone walls of the vault. Once again he groped for his matches, struck one and stared about him.

There was no sign of life here. Death was indicated by the solid line of coffins which flanked the wall.

SWIFTLY, LANE WALKED about the cavernous chamber. Swiftly his eyes glanced at the silver nameplates on the coffins. Then at last he came to a halt at the rear end of the room. Reposing on a marble slab lay a bier, and on the gleaming argent at its base was written the name of the woman that Gordon Lane had loved above life itself.

He fell to his knees beside the coffin, murmuring her name. Then as his hands gripped the coffin lid to wrench it off, his match went out. Feverishly he struck another. He held it, flickering and dancing in his left hand, while he jerked the lid up with his right.

With a hollow thud the cover fell back. Lane leaned forward, lowering his match. A vague relief had temporarily banished the dread he had felt. Janice had needed him; even in death she had needed him. And now he was here.

He bent lower over the bier, staring into the little pool of light cast by the match. Slowly his eyes dilated, slowly the old fear seeped back into his veins. Slowly he became conscious once again of the gnawing horror inside him.

For the coffin was empty!

Chapter 3: Zombies

GORDON LANE let the match go out. He stood there in the thick darkness. Was this madness that assailed him? Had he taken leave of his normal physical world and through some unholy device been transported to a realm of evil paradox?

Janice was not there. Janice had broken her tomb, had slashed through the fetters of death even as had those ghastly things in the crypt of the Cervantes.

What unearthly things were happening here? Was this a case for the blue uniformed officer of the police, or the black robed servant of the church?

Then he moved. He strode swiftly toward the still open door of the vault. If a few moments ago he had taken care to avoid the keeper of the cemetery, he was seeking him now. Perhaps the caretaker could clear up the ghastly mysteries of the night.

He raced from the tomb and headed toward the distant gate of the graveyard.

With his fists he hammered on the wooden door of the lodge. After a while he heard a creaking footstep within the building. Then the door opened, and an old man in pajamas stood upon the threshold.

A pair of grey, rheumy eyes stared at Lane. A twisted, distorted mouth snarled at him.

"Why do you wake me at this hour? Are you a ghoul? Are you—?"

"No, no!" cried Lane. "But there's hell abroad in this cemetery. Dead men are walking. Dead men are rising from their tombs. And a girl is missing. Gone from the Lansing crypt."

Something flickered in the old man's eyes. Something evil and calculating. A frown corrugated his brow. Then he stepped aside.

"Come in," he said, and his voice was soft, slimy. "Come in. Perhaps we should telephone the police."

He stepped aside and Lane entered the house. A telephone stood on a table near the window. The old man indicated it.

"Go on," he said. "Call. If there is evil here we two cannot cope with it. Call the police."

LANE NODDED. This, of course, was the sane thing to do. Supernatural or human, the pair of them could not cope with the terrifying forces which had been unleashed this night. He picked up the receiver.

He did not see the expression of sadistic triumph which had crawled into the old man's eyes. He did not see the contorted grey, feral lips as the caretaker took a step toward him. He did not see the solid metal object that the old man held firmly in his right hand.

True, he heard the faint hissing sound as the blackjack hurtled down through the air toward his temple. But then it was too late. The club smashed hard against his skull. A streak of dancing light flashed across his vision.

Then blackness seeped in—total blackness that was even darker than the sable atmosphere of the tomb where he had seen the grave give up its dead.

Gordon Lane had no way of knowing how much later he opened his eyes. Directly above him a grotesque shadow danced on a rocky ceiling. His head throbbed achingly. With an effort he raised his head and looked about him. He blinked dully as he stared at the uncanny scene which met his eyes. His first thought was that he had been struck down by the Reaper's scythe and that now he lay in some dank tomb of the underworld.

The rocky chamber was illuminated by a score of candles, which cast their unsteady light dispiritedly in the room. Far over to the left a half-dozen creatures worked with pick and shovel.

They moved in their task like robots. Their thin arms swung mechanically through the air as they dug. No expression was on their drawn faces.

And as Lane stared at them, he inhaled sibilantly as he realized what they were. They were the Things he had seen resurrected from the Cervantes tomb!

Zombies! Snatched by some unholy hand from their surcease of the grave to slave for some iniquitous force. Lane felt the skin on the back of his neck tighten. Then he was aware of an ugly chuckle behind him.

Slowly he turned his aching head. There, standing directly over him, was the caretaker of the cemetery. His face was a twisted, ugly thing and in his hand the naked blade of a knife gleamed eerily in the flickering light of the candles.

Lane looked at him and beyond him. Needles seemed to prick his eyeballs. His throat was suddenly dry. His heart stood still. For there, at the other end of the cavern, clad in a single diaphanous garment, was Janice Lansing!

Unsteadily Lane got to his feet.

"Janice," he cried and his voice was like a hollow echo in the rocky room. "Janice!"

But she did not look at him. Her usually vivacious, lovely face was drab and blank. Her eyes were turned toward a dark-garbed figure who sat some little distance from her.

Her full red lips were drawn thin and taut across her teeth, and in her eyes was a gleam of ineffable anguish. Shocked by her appearance, Lane cried out again.

"Janice! Janice! It's Gordon. Janice, can't you hear me?"

FOR A LONG moment there was a tense silence, broken only by the metallic clang of pick and shovel against the shale-filled earth. Then through the chamber there sounded a voice—a voice which was vaguely familiar to Gordon Lane's ears. Yet which somehow seemed to hold a malignant threat.

"No, you fool, she cannot see you. She can see only what I will her to see. But you, you shall see death before another dawn. You were warned not to come here tonight."

Lane lifted his eyes. He stared through the murkiness of the chamber. Slowly the figure was limned before him. Then as recognition dawned he uttered a gasp of utter astonishment.

For the speaker was Dr. Ramos!

Yet it was not the Ramos that Lane had once known. The bluff ruddiness of the man's face now seemed to be the crimson stain of blood. The hearty, solid voice had lost its affable tone and it now held an awful note of doom.

The doctor's casual atheism which the village had tolerated suddenly became a fearful thing to Gordon Lane. It was a black unholiness—a defiance to the very God who had created him.

From the other side of the room, Lane noticed that the sounds of shoveling had ceased. He was aware of a low, animal-like rumble of voices. He turned his head to see the six emaciated Things that had once been men, standing stock still, their tools in their hands.

Their eyes were fixed on the dark figure of Dr. Ramos and in the depths of their gaze was the most appalling menace of evil that Lane had ever seen.

Ramos' flashing dark eyes turned to them. He fixed them with a satanic gaze.

"Work, you dogs," he snarled. "You, Cataran!"

The caretaker stepped forward. He thrust his knife in his belt and snatched up a crimson-stained whip which lay on the rocky bottom of the cavern. The doctor's eyes were still fixed, glittering obsidian marbles, upon the creatures that had crawled from their tombs.

Cataran lifted the whip. Its rawhide sang a bitter *ziraleet* in the air. The lash bit deep into flesh. Blood, black and terrible, streaked down the cadaver's body and ran onto the fresh earth.

The man opened his ashen lips and his vocal cords vibrated in a terrible cry of affliction. Yet, Lane noted, the Thing made no move to attack its torturer. The others seized their tools and resumed their arduous labor.

The flicker of life which had registered on their faces a moment ago was gone now. They had returned to the lifeless life which seemed to hold them in its awful thrall.

Gordon Lane was frozen with horror. Janice, too, must be held fast in this overwhelming power of Ramos. She had not even glanced at him, Gordon. Her eyes were fastened to the dark figure of the doctor who sat upon a shelf of rock, for all the world like some wicked monarch surveying his wretched subjects.

"That'll do, Cataran," said Ramos. "Let them work. There is much to be done tonight. This shall be our night of nights. The treasure we've recovered thus far will be as nothing if we can find the Grail. It must be here. We've searched everywhere else that I can think of."

LANE TURNED to Ramos. No longer could he control the potent wrath that welled within him as he gazed at Janice. He rushed toward the doctor.

"You swine!" he roared and the echoes of his anger filled the catacomb. "What have you done? What evil thing have you wrought? Curse you, lift your evil spell off Janice or I'll tear you to pieces with my own hands!"

Ramos smiled evilly as he looked down at him. Even as he finished the sentence Lane was aware of the cold steel of Cataran's blade pressed against the flesh of his neck.

"You are a fool," said the doctor. "You have blundered in here. You shall never blunder out. You know too much. Your girl knew too much. That is why she is here. That is why my spell is upon her."

He indicated the laboring creatures with a wave of his hand. "Those," he said contemptuously," shall die, too, when I am done with them. They mean little. I needed bodies for my work and I took them. But Janice pried into my affairs. She shall never do so again. When I am finished with her, when her beauty tires me, she, too, shall join those creatures in the grave once more."

Despite the threat of the knife at his jugular, Gordon Lane hammered against the rock with impotent fists.

"In God's name, man—" he began.

Ramos rose from his seat, and it was as if the devil himself had etched the expression on his face.

"God!" he said. In the single syllable was all the hate, all the contempt and loathing that a voice can muster, and in his eyes there had crawled a look that had been born in the eyes of Lucifer on the day he had damned his Master.

"God," said Ramos again. Then he spoke rapidly and terribly. A torrent of horrible blasphemy poured from his bitter lips. Words evil and ugly as a Black Mass poured in Lane's shocked ears.

"God," said Ramos again. "What has your God done for me? On my distaff side my people were Indians, Incas. The men of the Christian God slew them, slaughtered them, robbed them. I curse your God, and from Him I take back what is rightfully mine—the treasures He has taken from me."

Panting he resumed his seat. His eyes fell upon the graven image of lifeless beauty at his side. Then a smile crept across his mouth, a ghastly, ugly smile.

"You shall die, Lane," he said more quietly. "And it is fitting that you die by Janice's hand. Because of her love for you, I have been unable to control her will completely. There is some deep emotion for you within her that thwarts me. But in time I shall shatter it and she shall be mine, all mine. When you are dead the power within her that withstands me shall crumble. I shall have your girl, Lane. And she shall slay you with her own hands. She shall drive a knife through your heart."

He turned to the girl and thrust a dirk into her slim hand. "Janice," he said.

Chapter 4: A Diseased Brain

A WAVE of jealous loathing rippled through Gordon Lane's body as he saw how completely submissive the girl was to the beast in whose thrall she was inexorably held. Yet a flicker of hope went through him. She still loved him! And that love had kept her from submitting entirely to the mad doctor. The depth of that love had resisted his black arts.

"Janice," said Ramos again, and the quiet menace in his tone was more threatening than his roaring demands of a moment ago. "You will take that dirk. You will plunge it into the heart of that man there." He pointed a finger at Lane and for the first time since he had come to this chamber, Janice looked at him. "You will slay him," said Ramos again. "Because you hate him. You loathe him. You shall kill him. Cataran, stand back."

The caretaker's voice rose in protest.

"He will overpower her," he said in a cracked, hysterical tone. "I shall slash with my knife, too."

"Stand back, you fool! It is not her strength she is using. Stand back."

Cataran stood back. His knife's blade no longer touched the flesh of Lane's neck. And now Janice advanced upon him.

At that moment, Gordon Lane knew that he would rather have gazed into the heart of Hell itself than behold the sight which he confronted then.

The woman he had loved beyond all else had metamorphosed into a snarling, savage beast. Her beauty had evolved into a satanic evil thing. Hate and loathing were in her face as she approached to slay the man she had once pledged to love until death.

Until death! The phrase struck Lane's mind ironically. Perhaps she had obeyed that vow literally. Perhaps she was now beyond death, and had come from the grave to slay, to kill.

Slowly she came toward him. Lane took a step forward and stretched out his arms.

"Janice," he said, a suppliant appeal in his tone. "Janice, it's Gordon. You must know me!"

For a moment it seemed to him that Janice wavered in her death-dealing march. But then

Ramos' voice cracked like an icy whip through the room.

"Slay him! Slay the thing you hate!"

Lane essayed to catch the girl's eye. Yet even when their gazes met no sign of recognition shone in her face. Closer and closer she came, like a crazed tigress stalking her prey. Then, in an instant she was upon him.

Lane had no desire to harm her. It seemed a simple matter to take the weapon away from this fragile girl. Why Ramos had permitted this farce to begin he did not understand. He reached out his hand to take the dirk from her slim hand as easily as possible.

And then a moment later he was fighting with all his strength for his life.

The thing that grappled with him was not Janice Lansing. It was possessed of the strength of a terrible fiend. Lane seized her right wrist in his hand. Her left clawed like a beast's talon at his face and blood streaked in rivulets down his chin.

NEVER HAD woman been born who possessed such terrible strength. And then as Lane glanced over her shoulder he saw the countenance of the doctor. It was taut and dripping with sweat as if the man was undergoing some awful strain.

Then in an instant the significance of Ramos' words came to him. "It is not her strength she is using!" Dear God! It was not her own strength. It was Ramos'!

In a blazing flash Lane understood part of the enigma. Janice was held fast in the invisible tentacles of Ramos' mind. Lane had heard of the doctor's proficiency at hypnotism. Janice was at the complete mercy of Ramos' brain. And somehow, through some devilish refinement of mesmerism, he was pouring his own strength into her body.

Desperately Lane grappled with the girl. The power of an Amazon was in her arms. He could feel her hot breath on his face, could see the bared teeth as she snarled at him, and all the while, her terrible might was bringing her arm down—bringing that gleaming blade closer to his heart.

Sweat, cold and glistening as drops of ice, stood on Gordon Lane's brow. The demoniac power which the girl derived from the evil force in Ramos' head drove the knife down closer and closer to his body.

Lane leaned his face over toward the girl, and spoke to her softly.

"Janice—Janice—This is Gordon. Gordon, who loves you. Janice, you must remember."

There was a pleading agony in his tone. Their eyes met. It seemed to him that for an infinitesimal fraction of a second the driving force of her arm abated. For a fleeting moment he thought he saw a glimmer of intelligence, of recognition in her eyes.

And it was then that he made his move. Beyond her the veins were standing out on the doctor's forehead. He seemed under a great strain.

Lane's hand tightened on the girl's wrist, wrenched it hard. He brought up his right and seized the hilt of the dirk. Then he snatched it from her.

He thrust her away from him and took a step backward. Cataran's cry of alarm echoed staccato through the catacomb. In an instant, Ramos rose to his feet. His hand dropped to his coat pocket.

The flickering candlelight danced crazily on the blue steel barrel of the revolver he jerked from his coat. It came up to aim at Lane's heart.

But Gordon Lane did not hesitate. With a serpent-like movement he drew back his arm, then he hurled it forward with all his strength. The dirk hurtled through the air.

Even as Ramos' revolver spoke the blade ate its way avidly into his shoulder. The doctor uttered a cry of pain, and stumbled forward. His foot slipped and he fell with a crash.

Janice Lansing fell forward into Lane's arms. Then Lane heard a slithering footfall at his side. Grinning evilly, Cataran approached with his own blade, prepared to slay. Lane sidestepped, swinging the girl around. Then his right lashed out. It cracked with a sickening sound on the point of the other's jaw. Cataran dropped to the floor.

TIGHTLY GORDON HELD the girl in his arms. Now she looked up at him, wonder and bewilderment in her face.

"Gordon," she whispered. "Gordon. I knew you'd come. How did you find me? What had he done? Don't let him take me again, Gordon! Don't!"

"He won't," said Lane grimly. "Nor will he ever take *them* ... Look!"

He indicated the six workmen. Since Ramos had fallen it seemed that the spell which held them had been broken, too. Exhausted they had fallen to the fresh earth they had dug. They stared at each other with wondering, bewildered eyes.

"For God's sake," cried Lane, "why did he do this to you?"

A shudder ran through the girl's slim body. "For two reasons," said Janice. "First, he made violent love to me and I refused him. Second, I learned his awful secret."

Lane indicated the prostrate emaciated Things which lay on their backs at the rear of the cavern.

"You mean the secret of that?"

She nodded. "It was when I was convalescing. He permitted no one to see me, telling people I was much worse than I was. That was when he was making love to me. Then one day I came upon him and Reeves, the undertaker, talking to Cataran. I didn't mean to eavesdrop. But after hearing the first few words, I had to listen to the rest.

"They—" She shivered as she glanced toward the exhausted creatures behind her. "They were patients of his over a period of time—

who had no immediate relatives or friends. Or at least whose people didn't care much what happened to them. He used to advertise in weekly country papers offering to take care of indigent relatives. He treated them with a preparation of *Cannabis Indica*. That stupefied them, rendered their wills supine to his devilish hypnotism."

Lane shook his head. "He must be mad."

"I think he is. He boasted of all this to me when he warned me what he would do if I refused him. Reeves, the undertaker, would bury his 'dead' live men. Ramos would sign the death certificate and with his reputation in the town there was no suspicion."

"But," said Lane. "What if these distant relatives had wanted to see the body laid out? What if I had not been out of town when you were supposed to have been at the undertaker's? If I had learned of your supposed death early enough to have viewed your body as well as have attended the funeral?"

"He had that worked out, too," said Janice. "You see, it was arranged that when Reeves laid out a corpse, he was to arrange the coffin so that the body was completely covered. The head seen through thick glass was the only thing visible."

"THE DRUG reduced respiration. The thick glass would also screen the almost imperceptible movement of slow breathing. Of course, I was buried in the family vault. But the others took the places of the dead Cervantes whose bodies Ramos burned. When he put them into the coffin in the mornings, he would order them in their hypnotic spell to arise at a certain hour. They were so obedient to his will that they awoke and reported to the catacombs ready for labor on the stroke of midnight."

Lane nodded. "And with Cataran in his pay that would explain why the Cervantes tomb was unlocked. So that the 'dead' men could get out. But, darling, why? For God's sake, why? Is the man merely mad that he did these incredibly evil things?"

"I'm certain he's mad," she said slowly. "Yet there was one completely sane motive for what he did. Ramos had always hated the Church. Far back he was descended from the persecuted Incas. He hated Christianity. One day when cleaning out the Cervantes tomb, Cataran found an old map that revealed the whereabouts of buried Church treasures that the Spaniards had taken from the Indians five hundred years ago.

"Ramos wanted them. Apparently they were worth a great deal of money and they were buried in the catacombs of the graveyard. He dared not let anyone know. For then they would have become the property of the Church. Neither his blasphemous views nor his cupidity would permit that.

"Those poor creatures were his laboring slaves. They dug at night for the treasure. During the day they returned to their coffins, held there by Ramos' drug and by hypnosis. He did the same thing to me, fighting to dominate me completely."

"But tonight," said Lane. "The phone call."

"I suddenly awoke in my coffin. For a short while I was in complete possession of my faculties. He had always had more trouble keeping the spell on me than he did with the others."

Lane's arm tightened about her shoulder. "And I know why," he said.

"Anyway, I ran from the crypt. Ran to Cataran's house and phoned you. Cataran found me and dragged me away."

She lifted her eyes, glanced across the room and uttered a little moan.

"Look! He moved. He's not dead."

"No," said Lane. "But after this he'll be where he can do no harm."

She clung to him.

"Oh, Gordon, I'm afraid. I shall always be afraid while he's alive. To know that someone can have such power over me."

FOR A LONG moment they held each other. Then Gordon Lane knew what he must do.

"Darling," he said, "go to Cataran's cottage. Phone the police. Bring them here at once. I'll wait here and keep guard. Hurry, darling."

She smiled at him bravely and ran out of the dank catacomb.

Lane glanced around the room. The six emaciated Things lay almost unconscious on the ground. Perhaps they would live; perhaps they would pay with their lives for the ghastly thing that Ramos had done to them.

Cataran lay motionless on the floor. Ramos stirred uneasily. Lane crossed the room and picked up the revolver that the doctor had dropped. In his head there burned Janice's words. "I shall always be afraid while he lives!" He bent down over the prostrate figure of the fiend and leveled the gun. There was no compunction in his heart as he sent two bullets crashing into Ramos' diseased brain.

Zombie

By Carl Moore

ALCIDE cringed away from the savage kick, cowered back, his thick lips trembling, his eyes rolling whitely, grotesquely, in his black face. Twin worms o£ blood trickled from lacerated lips where the white man's boot had struck.

"It's true, sar, it is true," he gibbered. "I swear it!"

Jim Herriott glared at the colored boy, took a deep drink from the square-faced bottle and wiped his mouth on his sleeve.

"Damn you, Alcide! You're lying! Why should Ti Poum hate me? Why should she go to the sorceress?"

The Negro's face was ashen. "Because your white woman comes tomorrow, sar! Ti Poum has sworn that she will never give you up in life or in death!"

Herriott snorted, glared about. Heat was hazy in the air beyond the screened veranda. The scent of flowering bougainvillea, wisteria, and honeysuckle came to him mixed with the odors of blood muck, burning smudge and musk. The odor of Haiti!

"She and Maman Celie will put the *wanga-morts* on you, sar! You will sicken and die! You will—"

"Get out, you *sal macaque*, you dirty black ape! Do you think I'm afraid of all the devils and voodoo in Haiti! Get out!"

Alcide, still cringing, fled into the rambling house, his bare feet scuffling noiselessly.

Herriott drank again, sat down uneasily in a reed rocker. Suddenly he laughed. Was he afraid? Why had he been so angry with Alcide for bringing him the warning? Because he was afraid ? Or because Ti Poum hated him so?

THIRTY minutes later he glared at himself in his shaving mirror. Two sunken bloodshot eyes stared back. Unshaven jowls, weakly twisted lips. He paced the floor, his heels banging solidly. Suddenly he threw back his head and laughed.

"So it's got you, Jim Herriott, got you at last! Three years! Three years of heat, hell, and loneliness! And just with the goal in sight you crack up! The tropics have got you Herriott, the tropics! And you'll never be the same!"

Again he sank down in a chair, his head in his hands. Two women held his thoughts. Ti Poum, she of the bronze skin, the demanding, alluring body with its full, tantalizing breasts, small waist, flaring hips, and tapering thighs. Youth incarnate in flesh, ageless, century wise in spirit. Ti Poum who had come to mean so much to him during the last year of loneliness.

In his mind he contrasted her with the woman that would be his on the morrow. Marie Terrill, even now approaching Port au Prince and Hinche to wed her betrothed. Three years ago he had told her goodbye and she promised to wait until he could send for her. Three years it had taken, three years of throbbing hell in tropic heat, and now that the time was at hand Jim Herriott knew in his heart that it was too late.

Black Haiti had him, the tropics were part of him, burned and blistered into his brain, into his very soul.

Inwardly he sickened at the things he had done during the last year, the depths of depravity to which he had sunk. Again the cool white vision of Marie danced before his eyes.

"No! By God Himself, I'm not beaten!" From a peg on the wall he took a holstered gun, strapped it about his waist. "Afraid, afraid, am I?" he snorted.

Another pull at the rum bottle. He hurled it into a corner where it smashed into a thousand pieces, snatched a helmet from a chair and made for the door.

The sudden glare of the sunshine made him blink painfully. Perspiration began to pour from every pore before he had crossed the clearing. A high, hot wind whistled about his ears with a sinister note. He muttered over and over to himself, "No, no! Not yet! Not yet!"

FROM the shaded doorway of the white painted house a pair of black eyes watched, black eyes set in a black face. Before Herriott's swaying body disappeared into the brush, Alcide slipped out of the house like a shadow and trotted after him. In his hand he bore a polished *cocomacaque*, a fearful bludgeon all of three feet in length.

Still mumbling to himself Herriott tore his way through the brush. He was oblivious of thorned limbs that tore at his clothing, stinging fronds that slapped his perspiring face. Damn Ti Poum! Damn Ti Poum! Ti Poum who made him what he was, unfit, soiled, a victim of the tropics! And now Ti Poum, cast aside, dared to go to Maman Celie to put the death curse on him!

An open glade. Herriott paused craftily. Guinea grass, bleached by the sun, matted by the wind, tossed in brakes and swales, spotted with scarlet poinsettias like flecked blood in a madman's beard. A hard-packed trickle of trail leading across it to a banana grove, and peeping grotesquely through the green trees the mouldering, straw thatched roof of Maman Celie's *caille*. Maman Celie the Sorceress, the voodoo priestess!

Back in the brush, well hidden, Alcide also paused. He too heard the steady *thump, thump, thump* coming from the dilapidated hut He too trembled as a deep throated, elemental scream issued from it to fill and reverberate in the weird glade.

"Papa Guede! Moin Papa Guede! Moin fai lavie! Moin fai lamor!"

Herriott stepped into the clearing, started on a lope for the hut. His face was pasty beneath the tropical tan. He knew what those words meant, knew the significance of that ululating implication. The voodoo priestess within was imploring *Papa Guede*, the god of death, to come to her assistance. Ti Poum was inside also. Together the two were constructing the *wanga-morts*, the voodoo charm that would bring death to Jim Herriott! Death! When a new life, a fife with the woman he loved and wanted was to be his on the morrow!

At the open door of the hut he stopped, peered wildly inside. The interior of the smelly hovel was filled with smoke. A steady *thump, thump, thump* beat about dirty walls. His eyes grew used to the gloom. Between grotesque streamers of smoke he saw an open bed of gleaming coals. To one side crouched a withered crone, a battered man's hat on her head, a pipe clinched between her teeth. Between her withered knees she held a leering skull, in her talon-like hand a human thighbone. The thighbone beat a rhythmic tattoo on the skull. *Thump, thump, thump!*

HERRIOTT breathed hard through his nose, peered closer. Suddenly a scream and he saw the slender figure of Ti Poum leap into vision, whirling and vibrating. Her eyes were frenzied, her lips contorted as she leaped, turned, twisted before the red glowing fire. Wild hands tore at her clothing, cast it aside. Her whole body seemed inspired diabolically. Loins quivered, breasts heaved, voluptuous flesh swayed. To Herriott, watching, she was sensuality incarnate.

Thunderstruck, unable to move, he watched the bronze body of the maddened girl gyrate and whirl, weave and wave. Suddenly she swooped, plunged both hand6 into the glowing coals and shrieked in ecstasy as she straightened, her palms full, running over. The old hag, Maman Celie, joined her voice to the shrieks of Ti Poum, then suddenly all was silence as the bronze figure collapsed, prostrated itself before the fire. Only the quivering breasts, the trembling plateau of her waist, proved the presence of life.

"Damn you! Damn you!" grated Herriott. *This was the woman who had made him unfit!* This was the woman who would put the death curse on him, would keep him from Marie, would ruin his chances for manhood and happiness. He yanked at the revolver, stepped into the hut.

That forward step saved Jim Herriott's life. On catlike feet Alcide had crept closer and closer. The polished *cocomacaque* made a gleaming arc through the air. The white man moved forward, the bludgeon hit the upper rim of the hut door, twisted in the black man's hand, lost force yet slapped savagely against Herriott's head.

Stunned, Herriott staggered forward, stumbled and sprawled over the nude bronze body of Ti Poum. It twisted and writhed against him. He turned, glared upward into the maddened eyes of Alcide. He saw the descending dub then suddenly all was bleak, merciful blackness.

HIS eyes opened slowly. For a moment he lay quiet, staring straight upward into the emerald greenness of a mango tree. Slowly it all came back to him. Ti Poum, the *Papa Guede* rite, the sudden appearance of Alcide. Perhaps he was dead. Perhaps the voodoo *wanga-morts* had worked already.

To the right came a sound—*pat—pat—pat*. He turned his head slowly. A jungle of congo grass and ironwood shrub cut off his vision. Persistently the *pat—pat—pat*. He struggled to his feet, made toward the sound.

In the midst of a small clearing he came on Ti Poum. The torn garment was wrapped heedlessly about her shoulders. Split and tom it revealed long inches of bronze skin, a section of flaring hip, a quivering breast beneath a rounded arm that held a shovel. *Ti Poum was pounding down earth on a fresh mound, some six feet in length.* Even at his horror at her action, he found his blood pounding dangerously in his veins.

At the sound of his coming she turned. Her eyes flashed fire. White teeth parted.

She said, "Do not fear, beloved. No one will know."

Pat—pat—pat—the shovel on the mound.

"No one—" Horror smote him. "What do you mean, Ti Poum?"

Pat—pat—pat.

"I mean, beloved, Maman Celie and I can be trusted. We will not tell that you killed Alcide."

He leaped forward, seized her by the shoulders, whirled her to him, glared at her. Unafraid she gazed back, eyes black, lips parted. Bronze breasts touched his own, stirring him to new excitement.

"I killed him?" he gasped. "How could I kill him when I was unconscious? How—"

"He swung the dub, beloved, but you caught it on the barrel of your gun. Then you shot him."

Dumbfounded he looked at the gun. One shot was gone from the chamber. He thrust it back in the holster and looked on dumbly as she finished patting earth on the lonely grave.

She went back to the house with him, back through the brush, following him closely. Once he heard her singing, looked back and saw that she had plucked a scarlet flower and placed it behind her ear. It looked like a blood dot on a field of ebon. She smiled and he hurried on. The drums had already started in the dark hills behind them.

Later he sat on the screened veranda the bottle at his elbow. She came to tell him that his meal was ready. As he ate, she hovered behind him. He sensed her, smelled her, felt her presence. Once she touched his shoulder and he whirled, knocked dishes from the table. She stood smiling, neither dodging nor fleeing.

"Damn you," his voice was hoarse, "don't think for a minute that this helps you. Marie will be here tomorrow and when I go to meet her, I tell the *gendarmerie* the whole story. If I killed Alcide, I killed him in self-defense. This gives you no hold on me. I told you it was all over between us, and I mean it!"

Her voice was low, amused. "Do not be angry, beloved. Of course you may report murder if you like. And when they question me, I will tell them Alcide and you fought—*over me!* That woman of yours will like that."

Herriott stared at her for a moment, then went to the veranda, the bottle neck clasped tightly in his hand. As he gazed into the moonlight of the clearing, he could hear the muffled chatter of the field hands in their group of *cailles* a few hundred yards away. Once he heard singing and shuddered. Once he heard laughter but could not be sure whether it came from the house or from somewhere else,

HOURS later he went to his bedroom. His head was a blazing torment. Slowly he disrobed, leaving his garments where they fell. Sweat stained, weary, aching in every limb he crawled into the bed. How long he lay there before sleep overtook him he never knew. His fitful dreams were those of a man half sleeping, wild, tumultuous. He groaned at the muffled sound of the faraway drums, groaned at the soft singing coming from the field quarters.

Suddenly a vision of Marie danced before his eyes. He saw her hair, saw her white loveliness, her cool skin. And he saw himself as he was. Again he groaned. It seemed as though Marie stood beside the bed in all her white glory, her breasts small and high, rising and falling, her eyes glowing with love, her arms extended.

He turned to her, and suddenly she was with him. She forgave him! The booming of the drums seemed to fade to nothingness. There was no night, no heat, no moonlight—only Marie. He gathered her into his arms, moaned aloud as fevered lips sought and found soft flesh. He felt her strain toward him.

When he awakened the next morning he was alone in the wide bed. On the crumpled pillow beside him lay a single red flower.

IN spite of her youth Marie Terrill was wise. Three years she had waited for Jim Herriott and she expected change, but not as great a change as she perceived in the tall gaunt skeleton with the burning eyes that met her at Port au Prince. There was something strange and unreal about him, utterly different from the lover she had yearned for so long. His kiss was hardly a kiss. There was no response in his lean frame when she pressed her white loveliness so hotly against him and enfolded him in her hungry arms.

Nevertheless she married him that very evening and, when he did not come to her that night, she wondered why he sat stern and silent at a window all during the black hours. It took most of the next day driving in his Ford to reach the Hinche plantation. Once when the car hit a tremendous bump in the mountain trail, she jolted with it and brushed close against him. She laughed, but the laughter stopped when she saw his eyes.

Her skirt had flared up at the bump, the hem was now in her lap, exposing rounded, silken knees topped by inches of white flesh. His eyes were fixed hungrily on that sleek whiteness. He seemed about to reach for her, to gather her into his arms, but caught himself with an oath and drove on. The rough trip was completed in silence.

At the house she met the few servants, who kowtowed respectfully at Jim's rough tones. Desiré, the new houseboy, Chiquita the fat cook. "And this," said Jim bluntly, "is Ti Poum."

He made no explanation of her presence, simply turned and stalked away leaving the two women facing each other. Marie sensed enmity from the start but she smiled and murmured something. The bronze girl answered, not respectfully, but as to an equal.

In her room Marie disrobed. For long moments she stood before a speckled mirror, her breasts unfettered, her hips covered by a wisp of thin chiffon. This was her body, meant for the man she loved, yet he did not want it! Her hands stroked velvety skin, her eyes probed. Suddenly she sensed other eyes and whirled, her hands covering her high breasts protectively.

At the doorway Ti Poum swept the white slenderness with scornful gaze. Her words were spat from a curled crimson mouth. "And he married *you!*"

Before Marie could answer, the bronze woman was gone.

That night the field hands gave a dance in celebration of their master's wife. Jim Herriott and Marie sat in the shadows and watched the orgy grow madder and madder. The three *tambours, papa, maman,* and *boula* throbbed their mad music. The conch shells shrilled and the gourds rattled. The perspiring blacks drank from open bowls of *tapia* and the dancing grew wilder and wilder. Marie was shocked, repulsed. At her side Jim Herriott sat entranced, his eyes glazed, fixed on the grotesque figures.

Suddenly the circle cleared. Someone threw a handful of green herbs on the fire. A great swirling smoke, aromatic and eye-burning arose and into the smoke whirled a mad bronze figure. Clad only in loin cloth Ti Poum whirled and gyrated in an age-old dance. Her flesh was oiled, gleaming in the red glow of the fire. Lithe muscles played beneath gleaming skin. Soft flesh vibrated and challenged.

THE drums thudded, the conches wailed, a hundred bare feet beat the packed earth. Closer and closer she whirled to the Herriotts. Marie felt the muscles of her husband's arm tense beneath her fingers, saw his eyes protrude, his lips part as he licked at them feverishly.

For a moment the dancer paused before him. Her eyes were coals of black fire. Her lips were mockery. Something thudded lightly to the earth in front of Jim Herriott and the dancer convoluted into the smoke again.

Jim Herriott snatched at the thing the dancer had dropped. His eyes grew even wider as he thrust it into his shirt. Abruptly he jerked his wife to her feet, muttered, and headed back to the house. She followed meekly.

Once in the front room he drew the object from his shirt and gazed at it with blanched face. She peered over his shoulder. It was a doll, some six or seven inches in height.

"Jim," she gasped, "what does it mean? It looks like you!"

"It means nothing," he replied angrily and tossed it to the mantel. Still ashen beneath his bronze he went onto the veranda a bottle in his hand.

Hours later Marie clad herself in her most seductive negligee. It revealed the alluring shadow between high breasts, accented the small waist, the enticing flare of her hips. As she sank down on the arm of his chair, one long white leg was plainly revealed. Her fingers sought his hair.

"Jim," softly, "it's time for sleep."

Somehow he got to his feet, somehow he held her at arm's length and gazed into her passionate eyes. His voice was hoarse. "Marie, you've got to understand, you've got to help me. Trust me, dear, and know I love you. But I can't have you for a while yet. There's something I must overcome, something I must beat."

The drums still throbbed and boomed, seemed to echo from the surrounding mountains. For a moment she flamed to anger—no woman likes to be repulsed—then, as she saw the tortured despair in his bloodshot eyes, she turned and went back into the house.

That night she slept alone in her own bed. Far into the night she heard Jim Herriott groaning and cursing in the next room.

When she went to breakfast the next morning, she peered at her husband's empty bed. On one crumpled pillow was a red hibiscus flower.

THREE days passed in like manner. Jim Herriott drank more and more. Marie felt like an outsider as she watched the bronze woman, Ti Poum, take charge of the house. But she kept her silence. She remembered the tortured look in her husband's eyes.

On the fourth night she was awakened by her husband's frantic voice. He was half screaming, half wailing. "No! No! I tell you, no! Go away! You're dead!"

She ran to him, found him crouched at his screened window peering wild-eyed at the moonlit glade. At the farther edge of the clearing she saw a shambling figure. A black man whose flesh seemed somehow to irradiate a ghastliness, who walked with downcast eyes and shuffling footsteps. Somehow the odor of the grave seemed to fill the clearing, to fill the very room.

"No ! No!" screamed Herriott, "you're dead, damn you, dead!" His fingers clawed madly at the strong scream.

Marie tried to console him, tried to calm him, but she too was badly frightened. What did it all mean?

The figure came on like an automaton. It shuffled toward them, head drooping, shoulders stooped. Up the cobbled pathway, onto the wood of the steps, through the screen door. Wildly Marie listened for the sound of footsteps but the walking man made no sound. Closer and closer to the very window where the man and woman cowered.

It raised its head. Marie's scream joined those of her husband for the eyes that peered in at them held no light. Not like those of a blind man, but staring, unfocused, unseeing—*like those of a dead man! The face was vacant, empty, not only expressionless but seemingly incapable of expression. Only the lips were drooling.*

Marie fainted beside the collapsed body of her husband.

IT was the bronze woman, Ti Poum, and the man, Desiré, who found them, brought them back to consciousness. Jim Herriott slept like one

drugged but Marie could only shudder. Ti Poum laughed.

"It was a dream," she said scornfully, maliciously. But as Desiré turned away, his black face ashen, Marie heard him murmur fearfully, "A *zombie!* The dead that walk! Voodoo!"

Herriott was gone when Marie awakened. All day she stayed at the house trying to puzzle the thing out. Once she asked Desiré but he shuffled his feet and evaded her questions. Jim came in from the fields for dinner but he was morose and silent, drinking even more than usual. He had no word for her, hardly a look.

The creaking of his floor awakened her that night. She heard him go onto the porch, watched through her window until his figure appeared in the moonlit clearing. He bore a shovel across one shoulder. Sudden-

ly a bronze shadow flicked out of the bush and stood before Jim Herriott.

She heard the sound of their voices, hoarse and high. She heard the woman's shrill laughter, saw her husband drop the spade and leap at her. There came the ripping of cloth. Ti Poum stood naked in the moonlight before Jim Herriott. From where she watched Marie could see the deep rise and fall of peaked breasts. She heard her husband curse, sickened as she saw snaky arms slide about his neck. Would he make love to this woman before her very eyes?

The sound of a blow, vicious, thudding, and the bronze figure sprawled on the ground at Jim Herriott's feet. He leaned over her, hands crooked like talons, and the watching woman was glad, glad. She thrilled and hoped he would kill the cowering woman at his feet. For a moment he bent so above her, and wheeled and shambled into the reed jungle. Presently Ti Poum arose and staggered away into the shadows.

Marie arose, hurried into a dress, and slipped across the clearing in the direction her husband had taken. The thorns tore at her, rent her thin dress to tatters, scratched her breasts, her thighs, her calves, cruelly. On she went, following the trail.

PRESENTLY she knew she was lost. How long she groped blindly, beat about fruitlessly in the almost impenetrable brush she did not know. Once she sank down sobbing in the bloody muck of the trail. Something soft and slimy slid across her bare arm and she leaped to her feet to race on and on. Suddenly she paused. The sound of laughter—mad laughter! Jim Herriott's laughter!

She fought her way into a moonlit glade. There in the exact center crouched her husband on hands and knees like a great beast. A mound of fresh earth was to his right. He was peering down into a black pit laughing, laughing like a demented man. She hurried to him, touched his shoulder.

He whirled, his lips bared in a snarl, his eyes mad. Suddenly he again broke into laughter and collapsed at her feet. Somehow she brought him around, got him started on the back trail. To all her questions he responded wearily, "You wouldn't understand, you wouldn't understand!"

Another glade. As they stepped into it, words froze on her lips. Coming directly toward them was the shuffling Negro who had peered in their window. His head was bent, his shoulders sagging, drooping. This time Jim Herriott did not scream. He stepped aside, pulled Marie with him. The thing came on, looking neither to right nor left. As it passed, eyes always on the trail, feet noiseless in their hopeless shuffle, it emanated a mustiness, a dankness. *The odor of the grave!*

The two, man and wife, made their way home in silence. Jim went directly for a drink. Marie stood before him.

"Whatever it is, you've got to tell me, Jim! Something dreadful has happened, is happening. I'm your wife, Jim, please let me help you!"

He told her there in the patch of moonlight that swarmed through the screened window. He told her of three years of loneliness, three years of incessant sun, tropical, burning hell. He told her of the drums in the hills night after night, how they eat their way into a man's very heart. With compressed lips she listened and he did not spare himself.

When he had finished, she said, "Jim, you didn't kill that man! No corpse could live and walk like that! The woman Ti Poum has done this thing to you, to frighten you, to make you send me away!"

Off in the hills the drums throbbed and boomed. The huge *Aradas* roared in the distance like the enraged howlings of a gorilla who beats his chest in the rutting season.

"A *zombie!* A *zombie!*" muttered Jim. "The dead that walk. No, no, Marie, I killed him! Ti Poum brought him from the grave to do her bidding, to haunt me. You saw him! He's dead!"

"Then it's an illusion," she persisted. "Voodoo! Superstition, that's all. Well go home, Jim, get away from it all."

"No illusion," his voice was dull. "*The grave was empty.*"

Silence. Her body seemed to turn to ice as the blood chilled and congealed in her veins. Then she took his downcast head in her hands, looked him in. the eyes, and said gently, "Together, Jim, together we'll face it." For suddenly she had seen the solution. "It doesn't matter what you've done. That's over. Together we'll see it through."

He leaned his head against her shoulder and wept like a child. Gently she led him to the bed. Presently they both forgotten the throbbing drums and all that they signified.

IN the morning the bronze woman, Ti Poum, was gone. The only evidence of her leaving was the little voodoo doll that still lay on the mantelpiece. A steel pin pierced its forehead through and through, pinning it to the wooden shelf.

When Herriott went to bed raving with a brain storm, they summoned a doctor from the city who treated him for sunstroke. But in her heart Marie knew better. Never did he regain consciousness, never did he recognize her. He died cursing Haiti, cursing Ti Poum, cursing the drums that throbbed so incessantly.

The few whites in the district as well as all the natives tapped their heads significantly when they spoke of Jim Herriott's widow. For she had a coffin brought all the way from Port au Prince and buried her husband in the clearing before the house. She scarcely cried as they lowered his body into a crude grave and covered it with the soil he hated—or loved.

For Marie Herriott believed in an eye for an eye. The woman, Ti Poum, was responsible for her husband's death and she wanted vengeance. Something within told her that sooner or later Ti Poum would return to loot the grave of the man she desired.

NIGHT after night Marie sat at the window her husband's revolver in her lap. She listened to the thousand night noises, listened to the distant wailings, heard and saw strange things in the moonlight. But nothing happened. On the fourth night her body was unable to bear the strain. Shortly after midnight she nodded desperately and soon she slept. The sun in her face awakened her.

Wide-eyed with fear she ran into the clearing. The grave was untouched.

Again that vigil night after night with the booming of the drums keeping time to the beat of her heart. She cursed. She prayed that Ti Poum would appear. But nothing happened. Half dead with fatigue, for her days were also sleepless, she gazed across the clearing.

Suddenly the gun clattered to the floor. From the brush and reeds emerged a figure. It walked with downcast eyes, with drooping shoulders, with shuffling footsteps, radiating a strange, pulsing light. She stifled a scream and waited, rigid and cold with horror. Straight up the flagstones, up the steps, onto the veranda his feet making no sound. At her window it raised its head and she peered into the dead expressionless eyes of Jim Herriott, her husband.

Somehow she managed to get onto the veranda. He did not turn but continued to peer into the room.

"Jim, Jim," she sobbed, tore at his arm, turned him half around. The vacuity, the nothingness of his expression! Horror! Terror! She pressed close to him, tried to put his muscleless arms about her. His hands were cold, pulseless. She pressed her lips against his mouth, started back at the dank flabbiness of his lips. Even as she cowered away, she heard the voice coming from the opposite side of the clearing.

"Beloved! Come! Come!"

Dutifully Herriott turned, plodded toward that summoning voice. She watched him go helplessly. As he crossed the clearing, she saw the figure of abronze woman step into the clearing and beckon imperiously. The zombie shuffled on, neither hurrying nor lagging.

With dull, dead eyes Marie Herriott watched her husband disappear. From the jungle came the shrill sound of mocking laugher. The drums in the hills seemed to magnify it, to enhance its taunting wickedness. Marie, arose and walked dully into the clearing toward her husband's grave.

AFTER her sickness a brother came to take her home. On shipboard and even after she arrived in the states, she had nothing to say. Hour after hour she would sit alone, head bent as if listening, listening. Only once did she tell the story and then to Dr. Sanders, famed psychologist. He listened in silence, then patted her hand. His voice was gentle.

"Mrs. Herriott, you must rid yourself of such illusions. You are no child, you are a grown, normal woman. Can't you see it was the sun, the heat, the monotony? Jim Herriott is no *zombie,* as you call them. That is impossible! He has not risen from the dead at the hands of a voodoo priestess. It is illusion, illusion!"

She shook her head and smiled. Her head was bent as if listening to something far away. "No. It is not illusion. I opened his grave, pried the lid off the casket with my own hands. And it was empty. Listen! Listen!"

The doctor listened, but he could hear nothing. He did not know that she was still listening to the far off drums of black Haiti.

Revels for the Lusting Dead

By Arthur Leo Zagat

Chapter 1: Delegation from the Tomb

LINDA LORAY tried not to show her disappointment and growing uneasiness as she asked the hotel clerk whether he knew Holt Carst—the man she had come to Torburg to wed.

"Yes," he replied, eyes narrowing in his young but strangely grey-hued, brooding countenance. "Everybody in Torburg knows Holt Carst." His glance flickered over Linda's face with a curious intentness, dropped to the brass-framed card, flat on the counter, that bore the words:

ON DUTY: Dan Thilton

"Mr. Carst wired me to come by the late train," Linda explained, "but he wasn't at the station and there was no message for me." She was poignantly conscious of the dusty hush of the lobby, of its somehow desolate emptiness. "How can I reach him?"

"Hard to say." The girl had a queer impression that Thilton was holding something back deliberately, perhaps maliciously. "There are no more trains till morning. Best thing for you is take a room here and wait for Carst to get in touch with you." He shoved the register at her; thrust a pen into her hesitant fingers.

The ancient, musty inn was vaguely repulsive to her, but there was nothing else for her to do but sign: Linda Loray, Boston.

Thilton turned and took a key from a rack whose hooks were completely filled. He came out from behind the counter, moving slowly, not from weariness but as though trammeled by some odd reluctance. His tall frame was a little stooped, a little awkward with the earthbound clumsiness peculiar to men born in the hills.

"This way," he murmured, picking up Linda's bag and motioning across rutted floor tiles toward a staircase at the other end of the dim foyer. Linda reached the worn steps, started to mount them. "Lije," Thilton called, behind her. "Oh, Lije!"

A big door slid open in the lobby wall at right angles to the staircase, and the cloying, sick-sweet odor of funeral flowers was all about the girl. She turned, startled, and looked through the doorway.

The flowers were piled around a makeshift bier in what must be the dining room of the old hotel. They formed a bank of blood-red roses, of lilies wax-white as death itself, and on that bank a dull ebony coffin rested. Two huge candles were burning on either side of it.

There was no lid to the coffin, so that from her slight eminence Linda looked right down into it. She saw a black frock coat clothing a man's body—a coat unnaturally stiff as are only the garments of the dead.

The dead man's hands were decorously folded on the rigid chest, but even lifeless they were pallid, rapacious claws; their bony fingers half-curled as if still eager to tear some helpless, quivering flesh.

The head was completely bald. The face was lashless, wax-white as the lilies. It resembled the visage of an albino vulture. Beneath the closed, blue eyelids the skin sagged in the pendulous dark pouches of dissipation, and the way the livid lips were thinly puckered branded those moribund features with lascivious cruelty.

"I'm going upstairs, Lije," Thilton said, "to show this lady to her room. Watch things, will you?"

"Sure," a toneless, heavy voice responded. "Sure, Dan."

Linda looked at the man who had opened the door from within. The watcher of the dead was as tall as Thilton, as spare-framed and gangling, but much older. His hair was iron-grey, his cheeks deeply seamed, weather-beaten. And in his hands there was—a shotgun! Its black barrel slanted across his torso and one calloused forefinger rested on the trigger. Watcher of the dead indeed! The man called Lije was a guard of the dead. An armed guard!

Against what impossible menace was he armed? Against what ghouls who would violate a coffined corpse?

Thilton, in motion again, forced Linda to recommence her climb, lest he collide with her. He unlocked the door of a room at the head of the stairs, shifted the key to the inside, put her bag down and departed without a word.

Despite the questions hammering within Linda's skull, questions she oddly dared not voice. Despite her perturbation over Holt Carst's failure to meet her, the exhaustion of her long journey welled up drug-like in her, numbed her. She was already half-asleep as she undressed, and when she crept into the creaking bed, it was as though she crept into immediate, tangible oblivion …

THOUGH she had slept long enough to warm the harsh cotton sheets, Linda Loray's slim body seemed molded within ice when she awoke—as frigid and as utterly incapable of motion! Fear, naked and terrible, was a presence in the room, a livid crawl in her veins.

The sound that had startled her to the quick came again—a thin cry shrilling out of the night. This time the incredible words were clear and terrifying.

"They're coming! The dead are coming!"

Running footfalls thudded toward the hotel. "The dead—they're alive again!" The shout was right under Linda's window, and the pound of frightened feet was first dull on the hard-dirt path from Torburg's single street, then hollow on the inn's porch planks. "They're com—" A door slammed, cutting off the cry.

"Lije!" a muffled voice shouted from below. Now the sounds of trampling feet were within the house, the sounds of voices husky with apprehension but too low for Linda to distinguish the words …

She was dreaming, she tried to tell herself, and then her fear-frozen brain was demanding, can one dream noises alone, seeing nothing, feeling nothing except the pressure of one's lids against aching eyeballs, the pressure of lids one fights un-availingly to open?

It must be a dream. In no waking moment did one hear a voice crying that the dead were alive. Only in a nightmare did one's muscles refuse the bidding of a brain squeezed between the jaws of terror's dreadful vise. Only in a nightmare were one's nostrils so stuffed with the odor of funeral flowers that one could hardly breathe.

Of course! The smell of the flowers from that improvised morgue below, seeping up through the moldering walls and warped floors of the crumbling structure, had inspired a dream of horror. If she could only get her eyes open, if she could only come fully awake ...

It was no dream! Linda was staring at the cold, hueless glow of moonlight that crept into the musty chamber. She was awake now, without possibility of question, and she still heard those ominous sounds.

Hushed voices quivered with some dreadful urgency. Something scraped ponderously, as though a heavy piece of furniture was being moved across the lobby floor to barricade the entrance.

On the faded quilt that weighed Linda down, the lunar luminance lay, shaped in a sharp-edged rectangle by the frame of the window through which it seeped. The oblong was deeply notched by a triangular black shadow. The girl focused her attention on that strange silhouette, trying by pondering the puzzle its odd shape presented to take her mind from the more fearful puzzle of the weird warning she had overheard, of the threat against which the preparations below were being made.

The sky had been dark when she had toiled up the deserted street from the railroad station. The moon must be now just rising. It was the shadow of a building, then, that lay on the coverlet. Linda recalled seeing a church, across the wide Main Street from the inn. Inevitable landmark of a New England village, its steeple had pointed a slender finger to the heavens. The moon was behind it now and this somber triangle was the shadow of the steeple's tip.

There had been an iron-fenced graveyard beside the church...

Thud! That dull sound was outside the inn. It was the thump of stone on soft earth. Thud! Ridiculous to think—that they were made by tombstones falling, one by one, on the soft loam of the graves they marked, that the sounds came from the graveyard...

Rusty hinges screamed protest against being disturbed! There had been an iron gate in that iron fence. It was opening! Who, what, was opening it?

Casting the quilt and sheets off her body, Linda sat there for a moment in a daze. Then suddenly her bare feet struck the floor, and she came erect.

The sheer silk of her nightgown was no armor against the sharp chill of the upland night. Gooseflesh prickled her nubile breasts. Muscles tautened across her flat abdomen, shrinking from the frigid sting. The cold struck through to the very marrow of her bones, but the girl did not hesitate. The imperative need to know what was going on was impelling her to the open window through which the moonlight—and the scrape of dragging feet on flagstones—came.

She reached it, peered through it. The tiny burial place was plain in a pale weird light that lay on it like a transparent shroud.

Linda saw the black oblong of an open grave. It was for the dead man, of course, who was laid out in the dining room below. But there was another, and another; and on the grass behind them their headstones lay, askew as if just now they'd toppled to the ground.

The earth from those empty graves was not neatly piled but had erupted from the black holes, as though it had been thrust up from beneath.

The shadow of the church was black along the front of the graveyard, along the tall fence that a century ago had been wrought by patient sledges to wall the graveyard in, so that Linda's staring gaze could not make out what it was that moved there. But something moved there, many things, in fact, and from within the shadow came the faint scrapings that had seemed to her the sound of bony feet on the flagstones that paved the churchyard paths...

Whatever was there moved toward the curb, moved across the curb and out into the street. The darkness not so intense there, Linda made out the form of a man; other forms followed him. The leader came nearer still, came into a patch of pale moonlight.

A scream formed in Linda Loray's throat, was held there by the swelling of her larynx that cut off all her breath but a wheezing gasp.

Moldering garments fluttered about that scrawny shape, and through the rents in them grey-whiteness flashed that could be only skeleton ribs. Its head was grotesquely askew on twisted shoulders, and its face ...

It had no face!

It had only a serrated, grinning gap where its mouth ought to be, two great stygian pits for eyes. That macabre countenance was earth-smeared, and something flapped against a grey-white cheek-hollow, like an ear that had rotted loose.

An ear that flapped with the grisly, limping gait of the thing as it crept along. The thing passed into shadow again. But the shape that followed it was no less gruesome, nor was the one that followed next ...

They went across that patch of revealing luminance, and darkness hid them from Linda once more. But the shadow could not shut from her ears the scrape, scrape which told her that the spectral procession paraded straight up the path to the inn, that it mounted the steps to the hotel porch.

It could not keep her from hearing the rat-a-tat of bony knuckles on the door below her window, and the sepulchral voice that boomed a summons.

"Open!" it called. "Open for the League of Lazarus."

Chapter 2: The Dead Attack

LINDA LORAY'S trembling fingers bit into the window sill. It wasn't—it couldn't be true. She had not seen living corpses marching from their violated graves. They were not clustered beneath her, hidden from her by the porch roof, demanding admittance to the very house that sheltered her.

Such things could not happen. Yet—

"Open!" the dead leader of the dead boomed once more. "We have come for our brother and his bride."

His bride! The bride of the dead? There had been only one coffin down there. There had been no keys missing from the rack in the lobby—no other room was occupied …

It could not be she whom they meant. How could it? In the morning she would be a bride, but not of a dead man. Of Holt Carst, who was vibrantly, heart-stirringly alive.

"Not this time," a voice shouted. "We ain't going to let you in." It wasn't Dan Thilton's voice. "This Lazarus business is going to stop right now." It was the voice of Lije, the man who had watched a corpse with a shotgun in his hands. "Henry Fulton's going to be buried proper, and he's going to stay buried."

Where was Holt? Why had he not met her at the station? What business could he have so important as to keep him from her? Saying goodbye he had murmured, "It's only for a few weeks, sweetheart, but it's going to seem like years. I dread the thought of our being separated."

Linda had smiled through her tears. "You don't really mean that, Holt. You've only known me for a month, surely you couldn't have gotten as used to having me around as all that."

"I've known you forever, Linda—in my dreams." She felt that way about him, too. She seemed always to have known his lithe, straight figure, his dark eyes that could be so gay, that could glow with such tenderness. "Known, and loved you forever." From the first time she had met him; his every little gesture had been utterly familiar, as when he tossed his head to fling back his shock of ebon hair from his high, white brow. "I'll send for you as soon as I can."

Then the trainman had called, "All aboard! All ab-o-oard!" And Holt's arms had crushed her to him, his lips hot on hers.

"Take me with you," Linda had gasped against his lips. "Now." But he had thrust her from him and sprinted through the train gate …

The great city had been lonelier than ever, after that, for the orphaned girl. She had had no friends, few acquaintances, before Holt Carst had come into her life. She had been content with her job and her books. But there had been no contentment in the time of waiting after he had returned to Torburg. It had been almost agony, relieved only by the thought that it would soon be over …

Now, there was a tentative rattle of the door latch below, and then an ominous moment of silence.

It was ended by a piercing whistle. Then another whistle answered it.

Central in the graveyard, a moss-stained family tomb glimmered palely in the moonlight. Peering to make out whence that second whistle had come, Linda saw the great bronze door of that tomb swing open; saw one, two, a half-dozen more of the spectral figures issue from it. They clustered about a shaft standing just within the graveyard gate, a "broken pillar" of archaic funeral design.

The grisly shadows gathered about that symbol of grief. They swayed, and the pillar swayed with it. It toppled, fell!

The shadows lifted the monument from where it had fallen, shuffled off with it. They shuffled out through the gate. They were carrying the cylindrical gravestone horizontally between them and the way they carried it made their purpose plain.

The stone that had been intended to stand forever as a memorial to someone's loved one—was to be a battering ram!

She must warn those below! Linda shoved herself away from the window, got moving across the room. The dimness was like some invisible, viscous flood, clinging to her limbs, clogging her progress. It required infinite effort to get her to the door, but she reached it at last, fumbled at the key till it clicked over. She reached the outer hall, leaned over the rail at the stairhead.

"Watch out," she called, managing only a husky whisper. "They're bringing something to break the door in."

"Let them," Lije grunted. His head didn't turn. He was standing in the center of the lobby, facing the place where Linda knew the entrance door was, though she could not see it. Another man was beside him, shorter, stockier. Both had guns to their shoulders, the barrels pointing at the door. They were straddle-legged, indomitable, but Linda saw that their hair and the backs of their heads were wet with perspiration.

It was deathly cold in that hotel lobby. The sweat that dampened the skin of those two men was the sweat of fear...

The clerk, Thilton, was nowhere in sight. A stir came into the lobby from beyond the unseen entrance, the thump of burdened feet on the porch planks.

"Don't try any tricks," Lije shouted, "or we'll shoot."

A laugh answered him, hollow and horrible. The crash of stone against wood obliterated it.

"Jehoshaphat!" the other man whimpered. "They're doin' it. They're breakin' in."

"Can't stop them," Lije grunted. "But we can give them a taste of lead when they get the door knocked down. Hold your fire till you can see them, Jed."

The battering ram thundered again. Wood splintered. Bolts, riven from their ancient fastenings, shrieked shrilly.

"Lead!" Jed exclaimed. "What good's lead against ?em? You can't kill the dead!" His voice pitched upward to a squeal. "You can't kill ..."

Crash!

"That's what I'm going to find out. No use running now, there ain't no place to run to."

Linda wanted to get back into her room, to lock her door and cower behind it. But she couldn't. She couldn't move—she could only lean over the rail and stair ...

Crash!

The whole structure shook with that thunderous impact, but apparently the door still held. The old inn was built like a fortress. It had been built as a fortress, decades ago. It must date back to the War of 1812, perhaps to the Revolution.

Light wavered on the steps. Linda had a sensation of eyes upon her, of malign eyes watching her. She looked around... The dining room door was open. She could see through it. She could see the flower-banked coffin, the body—

The dead man's lids were open! Some shortening of their muscles, drying, must have pulled them open. A dark fire glittered in those eyes that should have been glazed and sightless!

CRASH!

A scream tore out through Linda's throat, but whatever its volume it was drowned by the final appalling detonation as the battered door gave way; by the deafening explosion of the two shotguns in the confined space.

Orange-red flares streaked from the gun muzzles. Frantic fingers pumped reloading bolts. A skull-countenanced figure leaped toward the defenders, leaping downward as though from piled shards of the shattered portal. Lije's gun poured its charge pointblank into the attacker.

As though that lethal burst had been the harmless spurting of a child's cap pistol the apparition came on, laughed mockingly.

Others leaped behind it, a ghastly pack. Jed's shotgun blasted again ... Then Jed's shriek was a scarlet thread of agonized sound. The two defenders went down under that macabre rush. A pile of green-scummed shrouds, of tossing skeleton limbs, hid the men from Linda. But a carmine stream dribbled out from under the seething mass, across the rutted tiles.

A single figure, that of the grim leader, extricated itself from that heaving, awful mound. Linda's eyes followed him, her limbs once more rigid in the grip of a nightmare paralysis. The animate skeleton came inexorably toward the stairs. He was coming for her, coming to take her ...

No! At the last moment he veered, went into the room where the dead man lay. He was sitting up! Henry Fulton, dead, mourned for dead, was sitting up in his coffin!

"Welcome, brother," the spectral captain of the spectral troop intoned, "welcome to our company of the dead."

Fulton, the body of Fulton, lifted his dead arms. But it was not to the living corpse that his hands extended. It was not to the apparition in the doorway that his face was turned. It was the almost nude form of the staring girl to whom the orbs of black fire were lifted. It was Linda towards whom those pallid hands thrust, their grisly fingers curved like rapacious claws.

"All in good time," the other answered that look and that gesture. "You shall have your bride to warm your earthen bed for you—as have all your brothers of the League of Lazarus. But first ..."

Icy fingers clutched Linda's arm! She wheeled, flailing out a small fist in reflex of terror. Lent strength, virulence, by her terror, that fist spattered against flesh, broke her captor's grip. She glimpsed a man staggering back against the corridor wall behind her—Thilton! She leaped for the open door of her room, slammed it closed—locked it in the same motion. Leaned against it gasping, alternating waves of frigid cold and torrid heat chasing each other through her body, a long shudder shaking it.

Chapter 3: Saved—For What?

DEEP in Linda Loray's throat there was a whimper of animal fear. She knew now why Thilton had induced her to stay here the night, why he had not been down there in the lobby with its defenders, who were now shredded flesh, dismembered bones ...

He was one of them, an accomplice of the incredible creatures who called themselves the League of Lazarus. He had snared their bride for them, their bride for the dead.

"Miss Loray." His whisper came through the thin panel. "Let me in. I can get you away. I can save you."

The corners of Linda's lips twitched, distorting her mouth to a humorless smile.

"For God's sake, Miss Loray! Let me in quick, before they see me."

"No." Linda was surprised to find her voice steady, was surprised that she had a voice at all. "You can't fool me."

"I'm not trying to fool you. I'm trying to help you. I'm your friend."

"Then prove it. Find Holt Carst. Get him for me—"

"Good Lord! Carst's—"

The whisper cut off, was replaced by the padding of stealthy feet on the worn hall carpeting. Then there was other feet, coming up the stairs. They stumbled, those feet, uncertainly, as if they were numbed by sleep—or by death.

They thumped on the landing outside. The doorknob turned against Linda's back and the door pressed against the bolt she had shot.

"It's locked," the voice of the corpse's leader said. Something answered him.

It wasn't a voice. It was a thick, tongue-less mumble that had the inflection of words, though it was utterly unintelligible. It was fuzzed by the throaty vibration that is called the death rattle, but it was not made by a man dying. It was made by a man coming alive after being dead.

"Open!" the first voice demanded. "Open for your groom."

Linda cowered away from the door, went wheeling across the room, blind panic driving her as far away from those voices of the dead as she could get. Flesh-less knuckles gartered against the flimsy portal, and the panel shook.

The wall stopped Linda, and she cowered against it, her dilated pupils on the thin barrier that was all that was between her and—nameless doom. There was the sound of splitting wood. The door must give …

The girl felt every blow on that door as though it was delivered on her own cringing flesh. There was no hope for her—no escape.

Escape? Hysteric laughter twisted her larynx. She was at the window, the open window... She heaved herself up to the sill, squirmed through to the slanting porch roof outside. Abruptly she could think again …

She reached in, pulled the window shade down, then the window itself. That would gain her precious moments, moments that would mean the difference between safety and disaster. They would look for her within the room first, beneath the bed, in the closet. Meantime she could run along the porch roof, let herself down at the end of the house, where she wouldn't be seen by those who were still below.

She heard the door crash in, the sound distinct through the glass pane. She twisted to start the flight she had planned—and froze!

A footfall on the path below had pulled her eyes downward. She saw Holt. Her lover. He was running up the path, his stride, the jaunty pose of his head, unmistakable. He was running straight toward that smashed entrance, straight into the clutches of the terrible things who were making saturnalia below!

Behind Linda the shade rattled as someone brushed against it. She still had a chance, but if she called to Holt, to warn him, she would betray herself.

"Holt!" she cried. "Don't go in there, Holt. Stop. Stop!"

He halted. Shade fabric ripped and the sash thumped up, behind Linda. She heard the rattling mumble of the dead-alive. Beneath her Holt was looking about him, startled, uncertain whence her cry had come.

"Run, Holt!" the girl screamed, leaning far over the edge. "Run!"

Something touched her back, snatching at it, something clammy-cold. She flinched from it, lost her balance, went hurtling over the porch roof, went hurtling down to the darkness below …

Sight flashed to Linda in the whirling eye-blink of time that she fell—a vision of Holt's gaping, startled countenance; of the animate corpses pouring down from the porch and swarming over him. Agony burned into her that her sacrifice had been futile. Then she crashed into the branches of a bush that whipped her face, lashed her almost nude body. Breath, all but the faintest trace of consciousness itself, was jarred from her as her body pounded those branches to the ground. She was catapulted sidewise, hurled into dank, earthy darkness that enveloped her brain.

HER wounds netting her with a garment of pain, Linda Loray weltered slowly back to realization of the miracle that she was still alive.

Stygian darkness weighed heavily upon her, darkness so complete that she could be sure her eyes were open only by the feeling of lids stretched wide to stare. Clotted silence brooded about her. Then she began to make out small sounds.

There was a pit, pit, pit, regular as a clock tick, not far away. Pit, pit, pit. It might be water dripping, drop by drop, from a tiny pipe leak.

There was, every now and then, a rustling crackle. Linda had some time, somewhere, heard a sound like that before. It vaguely disturbed her that she could not identify it... Then it came again, a little louder, and she remembered. It was the sound the timbers of an old house make, drying out, settling, never quiet still, never silent.

There was another sound, faint but continuous, a soughing overtone to the others. It seemed to come from over her head where, she realized, the blackness was not quite so absolute. A soft, chill breeze seemed to brush down on her from above, bringing that vague whisper with it.

A breeze. The sound of a breeze. The sound of a breeze flowing through damp grass, yet above her ... Then she knew.

She was in the cellar of the old inn! She had not fallen directly upon that bush, but upon the lateral branches of it, on the side towards the house. The strong branches had acted like springs, had thrown her light form under the porch, into the hotel's basement. So swiftly had it happened, with no one's eyes upon her, that it must have seemed as though she had vanished magically, leaving no trace.

Her heart pounded against her aching ribs. She was saved. A miracle had saved her!

And then, inwardly, she groaned. She was saved, but in her stead the ghastly things that had risen from the grave, the spectral beings who called themselves the League of Lazarus, had seized Holt Carst, her lover. What had they done to him? Had they served him as they had served Lije and Jed? Was he lying out there on the lawn, torn?

The thought she dared not word even in her own mind lifted Linda to her feet. She twisted to the wall beside her, groped for the place whence came the wind. She found it—a narrow opening between short stone pillars that supported the foundation beams of the hotel. By pulling herself up to the very tips of her toes she could bring her eyes level with it.

She peered out, fearful of what she might see, yet knowing that she must look for it. At first, the dim glow that met her gaze blinded her, so complete had been the darkness here. But after a moment, she saw that she was looking out between the under-planking of the porch and the debris-strewn ground beneath it. Beyond, where spread the luminance of a moon now high in the heavens, she discerned the base of the bush that had saved her, the shaggy lawn, even the path where Holt Carst had been when she had spied him.

The grass was trampled, the path rough with footmarks. But no blood stained them, no fragments of a body strewed them.

There was no sign of Holt Carst there, no sign that he had been killed. What then? They could not have let him go. They must have taken him off with them, to the inferno whence they came. They must have carried him off to Satan alone knew what hellish fate!

Linda's figure tightened on the jagged edge to which she clung. Holt! A voice within her groaned. What have they done to you?

And then terror struck at her once more. There was a rasp behind her, a stealthy scrape of wood on wood …

She swung about, trembling hand to quivering breast, dry lips twisting. There was light in the cellar now; a vertical sheet of yellow light slicing down from a yellow slit in the black roof to be cut off in a narrow, zig-zag line by ladder-like stairs at the other end of the basement.

The slit in the roof widened, slowly. Its rim was scalloped by a set of knuckles. A shadow blotched the opening, a man's shadow that grew upon the stairs, grotesquely deformed, grimly ominous. The trapdoor came fully open, and Linda saw Dan Thilton crouched over it, peering down.

She had not been thrown into this basement quite unobserved. He had seen her, and now he was coming for her!

Furtively, as though he believed her unconscious of his advent and feared to alarm her before he could get her in his clutches, he lowered first one, then another cautious foot to the top of the ladder. He came down, slow and silent, the inexorable messenger of the dead.

Linda crouched, darted along the wall, her unshod feet noiseless on the earthen floor; fiercely glad that her almost naked body was unhampered by garments that might rustle.

Thilton reached the base of the ladder, started straight across for the spot where Linda had lain. No doubt, now, that it was she for whom he searched—that he knew exactly where she should be.

The girl's outstretched fingers touched stone, warned her that she had reached the basement's corner. She twisted, crouched motionless, her eyes on the prowler, a daring plan budding behind her aching brow.

When Thilton got to the outer wall she would dart straight across the cellar to the ladder. She could be up and out, the trapdoor closed, before he was aware of her. There must be some way to fasten it down, some way to imprison him, long enough at least for her to escape from the inn, for her to rouse the village to Holt's rescue.

She waited. Out of the path of light from above, Thilton was only a moving bulk, hardly discernible, blacker against blackness. He reached the foundation wall, grunted beneath his breath. Now was her chance. Now!

She launched into a run, swift and silent as a bat's flight. She was yards from the corner, she was halfway to the ladder. She was …

Her toe stubbed against something, and she went down. Rocks bruised her. Rocks rattled down about her. Not rocks but coal. She had run into a pile of coal in the blackness and it avalanched down upon her in thunderous betrayal.

Chapter 4: Prisoner of Doom

LINDA LORAY heard the sharp intake of Thilton's breath. She heard his feet scrape as he whirled, heard him cry out, sharply, as he plunged toward her.

"Miss Loray!" Even then there was something stealthy in the sound of his footfalls, something furtive. "Thank God you're alive! I thought …"

He reached her, bent to her, the round shape of his head silhouetted against the trapdoor's light. Linda's hand flailed for it, holding a chunk of coal she had grasped as she fell. The impromptu missile landed square on the man's temple, the thud it made sending a sick shudder through the girl despite her desperation.

He collapsed heavily upon her, quivered, and was still. Hysteria wrenched at Linda's larynx. She throttled the scream, fought from under the man's dead weight. Bits of the coal showered from her as she gained her feet, and she lunged for the ladder.

She slipped as she reached it, barked her shin against the sharp edge of the lowermost rung. Excruciating pain shot up her leg. She clutched with frantic hands at the splintery wood, pulled herself erect. She was up the ladder and out on the lobby floor; she was tugging at the heavy trap door.

Its weight came up, swung over, tore itself from her bleeding fingers with a ponderous crash. The hole in the floor was closed, but there was no bolt, no lock, nothing to hold it shut. Linda looked frantically about her, for the moment oblivious of the shambles that made of the tiled floor a slaughter-house horror. A deep-seated club chair was only a few feet away, its stalwart frame promising weight enough for her purpose. She leaped to it, grasped its arms and tugged at it.

It moved easily, sliding too easily on the carmine fluid which lay in pools along the floor, but something caught a leg of the chair before it was wholly on the trapdoor and Linda darted around behind it to push it the rest of the way.

She halted—and dropped to her knees beside a bound, recumbent form the chair had hidden from her.

"Holt," she gasped. "Oh, Holt!"

It was her lover, his ankles, his wrists lashed, a gag forced between his jaws! It was Holt, his clothes half torn from him, a livid bruise on his cheek, but alive. Alive and not a prisoner of the revenants.

Linda's flying fingers untied the knot that held the gag in his mouth, pulled the rag from it. Then they flew to the lashings on his wrists.

"What happened?" she demanded. "What happened to you, my dear?"

"Got away—from—those things," he mumbled. "Came back here … look for you. Thilton jumped me from the stairs … conked me … But you, Linda, why did you stay here? Why …?"

"He told me to." Holt's hands were free and he was helping Linda loosen the lashings that bound his legs. "Thilton. He said you were busy, couldn't be reached till morning."

"The dog!" Their fingers touched and the old electric tingle ran through the girl. "I was busy—trying to get the villagers together to fight that damned League of Lazarus. Trying to convince the townsmen that there's nothing supernatural about the League. Your train had already left when Fulton died, and there was no way of stopping you. But I left word with Thilton to send Lije up to my house with you when you came. You would have been safe there. Dan's in cahoots with them. I always suspected him."

He was free now. They were both on their feet, and Linda was in her lover's arms. "You poor dear," he murmured. "You must have gone through hell. But everything's all right now. I'll take you home and then I'm going after them." He was shrugging out of his coat, was putting it around her. "I'll lick them alone if there's no other way."

"What are they?" Linda cried, snuggling into the warmth of her sweetheart's fur-lined coat, doubly comforting because it was his, because it was redolent with the spicy tang of his tobacco, of his masculinity. "What are they?"

Carst's eyes went bleak, his lips tight. "I don't know. Nobody knows. They first showed up when old Winthrop died, while I was in Boston. His body vanished and a girl vanished, too. That's happened three times since, and they've got all Torburg terrorized, so nobody sticks his nose out of doors when any man lies unburied, anywhere in town. This time I made up my mind to stop the damn business. I sent Lije Carberry here to guard Hen Fulton's body, and Jed Storm to watch the graveyard while I tried to get the town aroused. But it wasn't any use."

"No. It was no use." Linda's eyes widened, as Holt's words reminded her of what had happened here and the sight of that which was strewn through the lobby—struck sickness through her as it had not when she was so frantic. "Take me out of here, Holt. Take me away from here."

"Yes dear," said Holt; he looked down at her tattered nightgown, added, "As soon as you get some clothes on. Where are they?"

"Upstairs. But I'm not going up there again." She shuddered. "I'm going just as I am. Come on."

"You can't run naked through the streets. Your feet will be all cut up. You'll freeze to death ... Wait—I'll run up and get something for you to put on."

"No! Holt—" But he was already across the lobby, was already halfway up the stairs, taking them two at a time.

Horrible as was the thought of going up to that room again, the thought of remaining alone here was still worse. Linda ran after him, across the slippery tiles. She reached the staircase, started up.

Carst yelled something, up there. His voice cut off. A black shadow whirled into being at the head of the stairs. It swooped down on Linda, enveloped her with its darkness. It swirled about her, was drawn tight, pinning her arms to her sides, pinning her legs together. Sightless, helpless in those swathing folds, Linda suddenly felt something jammed against her face, smelled a pungent, heady sweetness.

Hands gripped her, lifted her. She tried not to breathe, but her laboring chest broke the seal she put on her windpipe. The fumes gusted into her lungs, swirled up into her skull. She was slipping, slipping down into vertiginous dark.

Just as her senses left her she heard the tongueless mumble of the revived corpse to whom she had been promised as a bride. But her last thought was of her lover.

Had they killed Holt, up there? Or …

A thing mewled, close by. And although Linda Loray could not see what it was, because she had not yet summoned up courage to open her eyes, she knew by the sound it made that it was blind and mindless and without hope that death would ever come to release it from its agony …

Linda was sick with nausea. The stone upon which she lay on her side was damp and cold against her lacerated skin, and the odor of death was in her nostrils, the stench of corruption.

There were other living things about her. Vague noises told her so; a sighing breath, sluggish movement, the rub of two surfaces one upon the other. There was a hollow, reverberant quality to the sounds that told her she was in a more than ordinarily large space, and that the exit to it was closed. But it was the mewling that bothered, the half-human, half-animal cry that seemed a prophecy of what she was to become.

Something touched her thigh, something cold and slimy. It started to crawl across her quivering skin. Linda snatched at it, flung the squirming, noisome thing away from her, trembling with revulsion. And suddenly she summoned up enough courage to open her eyes.

A green and spectral light pulsed against those throbbing, pupil-dilated eyes. It came from flames that danced out of a trephined skull supported on a tripod of human thigh bones at one end of the space about which she stared. The skull's eye-sockets were filled with the green flame. It glared through the jagged triangle of its nose-pit, gleamed iridescent from its lipless, grinning mouth.

The ghastly luminance played across a wide floor of damp-blackened stone. It stroked the pillars of massive arches that curved overhead to form an interlaced roof, from which dripped serrated stalactites like tears frozen to stony icicles. It probed the shadows between the ranged pillars, thrust flickering fingers through a wide-meshed lattice-work of rusted strap iron and showed Linda what it was that moved—what it was that mewled ...

They were humans who were caged there! Naked women! Young girls, or rather girls who once had been young, and now were ageless from suffering.

Linda could see three of them. The one who mewled lay on her side, her knees drawn up and pressed into her belly, her head and shoulders curled over so that her blue-veined breasts lay against those knees. Even in that emerald light the wealth of hair that cascaded over the huddled form gleamed with warm red tints. Once the girl must have been very beautiful. Once—before whatever frightful experience she had passed through had ravaged her, had left her a face a mouthing mask of horror and her body a bundle of agonized flesh ...

The others, on either side of the girl on the floor, were erect and clinging to their cage-bars with fingers that writhed worm-like against the rust-red straps. Their heads were pressed against the bars, the curls of one golden as the sun, the luxuriant crown of the other raven black.

The faces of these two, turned as if they were trying to see one another, were contorted with a strange animal ferocity, with a mindless hate. Their red lips pulled away from their white teeth in silent snarls, their long-lashed eyes were orbs of lurid wrath. But, and this was most horrible of all, they made no sound and somehow Linda knew that they could make no sound, that somehow speech was lost to them forever.

Abruptly the ghastly illumination flared into brightness! Linda twisted to the source of the new light, saw that another skull, on its thigh-bone tripod, had blazed into being at the other end of the crypt.

This macabre flambeau was at the focal point of a tiered amphitheatre rising behind it. The seats on that stepped and curving rise were gravestones, so ancient that the stone flaked from them, that their inscriptions were indecipherable beneath a coating of green mould. Between them and the flaming skull three coffins stood erect, the central one taller and more ornate, and lidless, though the others were closed.

In the moment Linda saw all this an unseen bell filled the chamber with a melancholy tolling. Like a death-knell...

A scream rang out. The terror-filled sound pulled Linda's eyes back to the cages across from her. The red-haired girl had sprung to her feet! She clawed at the barrier that penned her in, and the rattling of the decrepit iron mingled with her screams, with the fading notes of the bell that had tolled.

The cacophony aroused Linda to action at last. She thrust frantic hands against the floor beneath her, to shove herself to her feet. She lifted herself. Something tightened across her hips, her ankles.

Linda clawed at the wide canvas straps. They had been loose enough not to impress her until this moment, but they held her inescapably. She writhed around, discovered she was free to sit up, to bend and tear at the strange lashings.

"Don't be in such a hurry, dearie," a laugh cackled in her ear. "You must first be properly dressed for your wedding."

The girl could not see whence the hag had come, but she was bending over her, thrusting a sharp chin into Linda's face; her eyes gleaming like black beads out of rheumy sockets, her great nose hooked and vulpine, her skin yellow, wrinkled parchment, her teeth yellow fangs in a drooling mouth.

Linda's own scream added itself to the turmoil. She struck at the witch …

Fleshless fingers caught her wrist. They tightened, and with amazing strength they held Linda stiff, motionless. The tiny, evil eyes fastened on hers. The red rims expanded, the black orbs within them were great dark pools into which Linda slid.

The girl went limp. "What must I do?" she asked, her voice lacking expression.

"Obey Ninita," the hag cackled triumphantly. "Obey Ninita, and Ninita will give you a groom such as many a girl might envy. But first, here is your wedding dress."

She released Linda, bent and lifted from the ground a bundle of white fabric. "See, is it not pretty?" she asked, shaking it out.

It hung from her taloned hands, long and white and shapeless. It was such a gown as no bride had ever before been proffered. It was such a garment as long ago was used to clothe the dead. It was a shroud!

Chapter 5: Hell's Bridal Sport

LINDA LORAY plucked at the hooks that fastened the canvas straps to rings in the floor. Her fingers were clumsy, her eyes slitted and dreamy, her face utterly expressionless.

She got herself free, came slowly to her feet, stood there docilely. Ninita tore from her the few remaining shreds of her night gown, and slipped the shroud over her head.

Even when the harsh skin of Ninita's fingers rasped her bruised breast and sent fierce pain darting through her, Linda did not move. Even when the hag's long nails tore a new wound among the many on her lacerated abdomen she did not wince.

But when Ninita stepped back to admire her handiwork, and indicated with a gesture that she might turn, the muscles in Linda's thighs tensed for the quick leap she planned, the flight from the hag toward a door she remembered having glimpsed to one side of the banked gravestones. Her quick yielding to the witch's hypnosis had been altogether simulated, had enabled her to avoid a real surrender.

Linda wheeled—but she did not make that intended leap toward escape possible.

She had delayed too long, and the way of possible escape she had spotted was now impossible. The curved rows of seats were now thronged by the dead-alive who had earlier raided the inn. They sat on the monuments that should have weighed them down in the long sleep, the sleep from which by some inconceivable necromancy they had been evoked, and every eyeless socket of that grinning, serried host was turned upon her.

There was no hope now, utterly no hope, of getting past them. They would surely intercept her.

Even if by some miracle she should avoid their clutching, skeleton fingers, whose awful power she had witnessed when Jed and Lije had gone down beneath their ravening rush, the door was blocked to her.

If they had shaken her with revulsion, thc being that strode in through that darksome entrance was horrible beyond conception.

Words brushed Linda's tortured mind, words from a Book even the mere memory of which, was sacrilege in this cloistered theatre of hell:

"And when He thus had spoken, He cried with a loud voice, 'Lazarus, come forth!' And he that was dead came forth, bound hand and foot with grave clothes; and his face was bound about with a napkin."

He who came through that doorway—which Linda saw now was shaped like the door of a tomb—and glided rather than walked, was "bound hand and foot with grave clothes; and his face was bound about with a napkin." The napkin covered his face, so that Linda could not see it, and if in that moment she could be glad of anything, she was glad that this was so.

For as he reached the center coffin of the three that stood behind the green-flaming skull and took his place within it, the deep-toned bell tolled once more and the rustling, expressionless voices of the dead ranked above it dully chanted his name.

"Lazarus! Hail Lazarus!"

Lazarus bowed that white-bound, faceless head, and they were silent. His white-swathed arm gestured to his right.

The lid that covered the coffin to which he motioned slid down, seemingly into the very rock beneath it. In that place of fluttering, earth-rotted rags, of white grave clothes, no contrast could have been more ghastly than the meticulously frock-coated figure revealed within that upended casket; no long-dead skull more horrible than the staring, waxy, sex-ridden face of Henry Fulton.

Lazarus gestured to the left.

The lid of the coffin on that side slid down. Linda's eyes widened, watching it wondering what weird figure it would reveal.

There was none, none at all. The coffin was empty.

"The bride!" Lazarus' voice boomed out and echoed into the hollow resonance of the crypt. "Let the bride come forth!"

The unseen bell tolled again. But now it was not a single peal that filled the great vault. The muted strokes of the bell came again and again, and its tone changed, so that it formed a welling threnody. Higher in pitch, the sound of another, smaller bell joined it, merged with it.

The measured melody of the mellower bell was the melody of the Wedding March from Lohengrin. Beneath it, deep and hollow, shaking Linda to the very core of her being, the greater gong beat out the slow, measured notes of Chopin's Funeral March.

"Go, dearie," Ninita whispered behind her. "Go to your place."

Linda was marching toward that empty coffin, her quivering limbs keeping time to those strangely intermingled processionals that beat about her and carried her onward on the bosom of their palpitant flood. She went steadily toward the casket that awaited her.

What else was there for her to do? What else save carry out her pretense of conquest by the hag's hypnosis, hoping against hope that something might occur to save her from that to which she seemed doomed?

There was still within her, deep within her, the utterly mad, utterly unwarranted thought that perhaps Holt was still alive, that somehow he had once more escaped the minions of Lazarus and would somehow rescue her before it was too late.

She reached that waiting corpse-box, entered it. The bells moaned to silence.

"Dearly beloved," Lazarus intoned, in sepulchral mockery of the words with which so many a devoted minister had commenced his discourse on the inscrutable ways of his God, ways that were here denied. "Dearly beloved, tonight we welcome among us a new brother to our unholy company. Tried and tested in the ways of evil is he, so that he has been accounted fit to be one of us. We have with us too the bride he has selected to warm him in the cold companionship of the grave to which he is destined. Living, she shall feed her dead spouse with the life that is in her, so that the chains of death shall not bind him, the earth not hold him. So that, in the long years, he shall join with us in our nightly revels.

"Such is our custom. But, as is also our custom, before the grisly rites of their nuptials are consummated, we shall indulge him who was known among the living as Henry Fulton, and her who, still living for a space, bears the name of Linda Loray, with a foretaste of those orgies we of the League of Lazarus have preserved for the centuries since first they were presented in the arenas of Imperial Rome. Is this your will?"

"Aye," the spectral congregation cried from their high banked gravestones. "Aye. It is our will."

"So be it. And now our faithful Ninita, what have you conceived for our pleasure?"

The hag hobbled to the center of the open space and ducked in an almost ludicrous curtsey. "Something you'll like," she cackled, "I'm sure. Something to which I've trained my pretty ones with much trouble."

"Proceed."

The old witch curtsied again, limped toward the cages. There was a key suddenly in her hand. She unlocked the cage against whose bars the golden-haired girl pressed.

"Come, Naomi. Come my sweet."

The girl darted past her, the green luminance stroking her unclothed limbs, flashing on her curves, on the secret charms of her sleek body. She crouched, knuckles to the ground, lips drawn back snarling from her gaping mouth, her eyes not human eyes but the lurid orbs of a maddened beast.

"And Jane. You've been impatient for this time, I know."

The key creaked in the rusty lock; the dark-haired maiden was whining as once Linda had heard a dog whine, eager to be at another's throat. The iron door clanged open.

Jane leaped from the enclosure. She stopped for a moment, gazed about her, evidently dazed. Linda was conscious of the impulse to veil her eyes from that gleaming nakedness, a nakedness not only of body but of murdered soul. Some horrible fascination prevented her, kept her staring at those nude girls out there, those girls who were circling now, heads thrown back, faces virulent with hatred and contorted with a fierce animal ferocity, arms crooked before them, palled fingers curved to hooked claws.

"Go get her!" Ninita screamed. "Jane! Get her, Naomi."

They sprang at each other. They were clawing at each other. They were tumbling on the stone, snarling, biting, gouging. And the grisly spectators were not silent, but howling with delight.

Their screams blasted down on Linda, beating against the coffin within which she stood—cries of encouragement, cries of lewd pleasure evoked by the naked limbs flashing in that throbbing green light. With each shrewd blow, with each handful of hair torn from a bleeding scalp, with each gory rake of tearing nails across palpitant flesh, a shriek of sadistic ecstasy shrilled from the yelling watchers.

Blood smeared the stony floor now, blood bathed the unclad flesh of the maniac girls who fought for the delectation of the dead-alive in a gladiatorial fray more awful than ever had been staged in ancient Rome.

Linda managed to drag her staring eyes from the dreadful sight—only to see the frock-coated man who should be dead leaning out of his casket; his eyes, that should be glazed, aflame with the dark light of frenzied ecstasy, and spittle drooling from the corners of his writhing lips—that should be frozen and still forever …

"That's the way, my little one!" Ninita's cry dragged Linda's eyes back to the arena. "Finish her, Naomi."

The dark girl lay flat on the stone, quivering feebly. The other kneeled on her, a scarlet-smeared, monstrous shape. Naomi's torn hands were clenched on the other's throat, were tightening, and in a sudden, brittle silence Linda heard the grate of collapsing gristle.

Jane, the terrible shape that had been Jane, writhed once, and was still. The victor lifted her head to receive the plaudits of the mob.

There were no longer eyes in that contorted, carmine mask!

Chapter 6: Dreadful Dilemna

THEY had been taken away, the dead body of Jane, and Naomi who less mercifully was still alive.

The green light wavered under the labyrinth of weeping arches, between the thick dark pillars of that demoniac cloister. Sick with horror, Linda Loray shrank within the casket from which she dared not move;

listened to the voice of the cerement-clothed being who had been acclaimed as Lazarus.

"Well done, my Ninita," he was saying. "You have pleased us. And what other little entertainment have you devised for us?"

"One that I think you'll like even better," the hag responded, the seams of her saffron visage twisting in what she must have meant to be a smile. "An improvement on a device of Nero's of which you have told me."

"On with it then. Our bridegroom grows impatient."

"For this I must call help," the woman replied. She hobbled to the opposite end of the crypt, passing the further flambeau. Linda saw her reach the end-wall beyond it; saw for the first time that it was broken by a door.

Ninita opened that door, and came limping back. A shadowy form moved through the opening, came into the light.

Even in the full illumination the newcomer was still a shadow. He was all black; his lithe body, his legs, his arms, his hands and even his head covered by a skin-tight, dull black garment. He faced Lazarus and lifted a long, coiling black whip in salute.

Ninita's key rattled in the lock of the middle cage, the one where the auburn-haired girl was.

What had happened to those other two had been horrible, but at least they had been wholly mad and in all likelihood had no conception of what they were doing, perhaps had not even felt pain. She had seen this other suffer in anticipation, had heard her scream at the sound of the bell that had announced the gathering of the league. She would know exactly what was occurring, would suffer trebly because she was not—insane.

The cage door opened. "Come, Lillian," Ninita said. "It's your turn now."

There was no sound in response, no voice, no movement.

"Lillian!" the hag exclaimed sharply. "Quickly!"

A murmur ran through the assemblage. Then Ninita was coming out into the open again, and she was trembling with fright.

"Master!" she quavered. "It—she—Lillian is dead. Dead from fright. And I have no other to substitute for her. We shall have to dispense with what I had prepared for her."

"Thank God!" Linda breathed. "Oh thank God."

"You should have taken better care of her," Lazarus rebuked the scrawny old panderess of sensation. "You may take her place."

"No!" the woman screamed. "No!" Terror convulsed her countenance. She went down to her knees, her arms flung out in entreaty. "I have served you well. I do not deserve payment such as that."

"It is by your negligence that the brotherhood is cheated of its pleasure."

"Pleasure?" the witch squalled. "What pleasure will you have watching this old flesh lashed, these old bones broken! Look!" In an agony of desperation she tore at her clothing, ripping it from her in rags. In seconds she was naked as her victims, her sere and scrawny flesh exposed, her thighs yellow pipe-stems, her torso a bag of bones against which her wrinkled breasts lay flat and hideous. "But you need not be deprived of your game. There," she leaped erect, "there is one well-formed and beautiful. There is the one who should be here in the arena for your delight."

She pointed—straight at Linda!

"Yes!" the fleshless voices of the dead-alive roared. "Yes! Give her to us. Lazarus, give her to us!"

"Silence," their lord thundered. "Silence. It is for me to decide."

They were still, ghastly still... Linda stood motionless as the napkined head turned toward her. She could not see the eyes behind it, but she could feel them upon her.

A sound broke that stillness, a sound more horrible than the chorused voices of those living corpses. It was a mumble, the tongueless mumble of the one who was too newly dead to have relearned speech, protesting the loss of the bride that had been destined to him.

"No," Lazarus intoned. "It is not for me to choose. I have promised her to our novice brother. I cannot break that promise."

They were angry now, the brotherhood of the dead. They let him know it in no uncertain terms.

"Silence," he cut them off again. "Let me finish. I have given my promise and cannot withdraw it. But there is one who may choose. I leave the choice to that one.

His bandaged arm rose, his white-swathed hand pointed at Linda. "Choose, you. Is it bride you will be, or—" That pointing arm swept outward to the black figure, waiting just before the distant skull with his lash. "Choose! Which shall it be?"

Which should it be? Linda Loray peered across the green glow to that snaking whip, coiling and avid for her flesh. Her head turned.

She saw Henry Fulton, read his wax-white face, read the meaning of his drooling, lascivious mouth. Even if he were living ... She shuddered, and her eyes went back to the other, terrible shape.

"What is your choice, Linda Loray? Bridal bed or the lash?"

The man down there at the other end of the crypt moved. His head tossed back, as if to fling back a shock of hair as black but more lustrous than the hairless cloth that covered it …

That gesture was unmistakable. It was Holt who stood there! Holt Carst! Somehow he had managed to get in here, somehow managed to overcome Ninita's helper where he had been waiting for her summons. Disguised, he had thus contrived to get in here, and now he had let her know who he was!

"I choose the lash," Linda announced, hard put to it to keep her elation out of her tone.

The red-headed girl's death had made her rescue easy. Holt would wait for her there, only a few paces from the door. When she reached him they would both dash out. Before any of the League of Lazarus could get to them they would be away...

"Come then, my duckling!" Ninita cackled. "Come, my gosling."

"Go!" Lazarus commanded.

Linda stepped out of her coffin. She went past the chuckling, relieved hag. She went past the flaming skull. She went steadily across the stony floor that was slimy with the blood of the two mad girls who had fought there to the death. There was joy in her heart.

Holt drew the lash lingeringly between his black-gloved fingers. He seemed to gather himself together. His acting was superb.

The place was so still the silence beat at Linda, pressed against her the shroud that was to have been her bridal gown. She was near to Holt now, near enough to whisper.

"Sweetheart! You are so brave. So very brave!"

"You don't know how brave, Linda," his whisper came back to her. "You don't know …" His arm lifted the short handle of his whip. His wrist circled a bit, so that its long lash coiled in wide, lazy circles about his head. He was gaining every instant of time that he could, every instant that would be so precious when they dashed at last for safety …

The lash struck out at Linda! It slashed across her side, cut through the shroud-stuff and wealed her shrieking skin!

"Holt!" she screamed. "Holt!" And then she was screaming no longer. Her arms were flung up to protect her eyes. Her head was bowed, and the whirring, biting whip was playing around her, was slashing at her. With infinite cruelty it flicked, just flicked her garment, tearing the shroud wisp by wisp, stripping her naked with its cruel bite.

"You fool!" Holt's voice was harsh. "This is what I brought you here for!"

She was nude, entirely nude. She darted away. The lash curled about her waist, brought her back to her tormentor, to her lover turned torturer. It made a thorny web about her, a web through which she could not pass. It bit at her skin, stung her flesh. It had stripped her, and now it was flaying her …!

Her mind was caught in that tortuous mesh, wishing only—and vainly—for the release of death …

A deafening detonation exploded about Linda. There were screams somewhere, shouts. There were shots …

The whip was no longer whirring about her, no longer licking at her. She went to her knees. Twisting as she fell, Linda saw a tossing, uproarious chaos involve the slanting amphitheatre from which the League of Lazarus had watched its saturnalia. She saw uniformed men swarming among the corpses, saw a club lift and fall on one grisly skull …

And a face, a grizzled, staring-eyed, but human face, appear from within it!

Fingers clutched her throat from behind, fingers cloth-covered. "I'll make sure you won't talk," Holt's voice grated in her ears. The fingers closed, hard upon her larynx, cutting off her breath. A knee dug into her spine, garroting her. "I'll get away and they won't know I've ever been here."

The fight was so fierce, up at the other end of the crypt that no one saw what was happening at this end. Linda knew she was about to die …

Footfalls pounded out of the darkness. The strangling fingers were suddenly gone from Linda's throat, the torturing knee from her backbone. She collapsed to the floor, but the veil lifted from her eyes. She saw a fist rise and fall on a black-swathed head, saw the face of the man whose fist it was.

Youthful, but no longer grey-hued, no longer brooding—Dan Thilton!

"I must have lain there in the cellar a long time," Dan Thilton said, "after you knocked me out. When I came to I crawled out through the hole under the porch. I telephoned for the state cops; then I followed the tracks of the so-called dead men. They were plain in the graveyard, leading right to the tomb that was the entrance to that place where they carried on their mumbo jumbo. By the time I found the entrance the state cops came driving into town, and we went right to work breaking that door down. I guess we got down into the underground chamber just in time to save you."

They were in the room where Linda had first awakened to terror. She was clothed now. A grey dawn was pressing against the window through which she had climbed, and from the lobby beneath came the noises that told of the police-detail lining up those of their prisoners who were still alive, getting them ready for the bus that was to take them to jail.

"How did you know to look for me in the cellar?" she asked.

"I was on the porch roof, trying to get to you and talk some sense into you, so I saw what happened to you when you fell. I had to wait until the bunch that were dressed up as corpses went back to the graveyard, and then I went downstairs to find you. Carst was in the lobby, looking for you, I guess, and he jumped me. I knocked him out, tied him up, and went on down to the cellar."

"He said he had been arousing the people of Torburg to fight the League of Lazarus. He said it was he who got Lije and Jed here to fight them."

"That's right. He got them here and he gave them the shotguns too, loaded with blanks so they weren't any good. Lije and Jed and I weren't scared enough of his outfit to suit him, and he was afraid we were going to make trouble, so he took that way to get rid of us. But I was up here watching your room. You see, when you came in and said he'd wired you to come here tonight, it made me sure of what I'd already suspected—that there was some connection between him and what was going on. Because those other girls came here to marry Holt Carst, too! They vanished right away. Queer thing was, they were all insured in his name."

"Insured ...! I remember ... He did get me to sign a paper, just before he left. Said it was an application for a marriage license, but it may have been an application for insurance. I trusted him."

Linda opened her suitcase. She had already taken out of the wardrobe the frilly, glamorous garments that, tired as she had been last night, she had carefully hung up because they were to have been her trousseau. As she started to fold them into the bag, she glimpsed out of the corner of her eye. Thilton's gaunt frame, silhouetted against the window out of which he was staring with grim bleakness.

"Sure it was an insurance application," he said. "Carst played both ends against the middle. Getting the insurance on these girls was the final business. In the first place, he got the girls for that bunch of rich old libertines that paid him plenty for a new kind of thrill. Lazarus' was the richest; his name doesn't matter now that he's dead. And Carst is through, too. Yankee juries work fast. He's through and Torburg's clean again."

"I'm glad," Linda breathed. "It seemed such a nice village from the little I saw of it last night."

"Nice isn't just the right word for it. It's grand. Carst and his gang came from outside, and they soiled our town for a little while, and now they are gone. But the hills were here before they came, and will be here long after they are forgotten. The wooded hills, the green and pleasant valleys, the white houses where friendly people live …

"Friendly people," Linda breathed, thinking of the cold grey city to which she was returning. "Neighbors... Yes, it's a lovely town. I'd like to stay here …"

Thilton looked at her, hope dawning in his eyes. "Do you mean that? I wish you would. I was thinking I'd have to move to Boston if I wanted to see you any more—and I do … I love you, Linda."

As he came toward her slowly, shyly, Linda knew that she had learned more about this man in a few hours of terror than she could have learned in years of just living.

"I love you, too," she answered. Her voice was low, but joy was in her heart. She thought. "It's funny, I did come here to get married—and that's what I'm staying for!" She smiled. But she didn't say it aloud—just then. She couldn't, for she could not talk and be kissed at the same time. And by now she was being thoroughly kissed …

Corpses on Parade

By Edith and Ejler Jacobson

Chapter 1: Dues Payable to Death

THEY buried Andy Carter on one of those bleak February mornings when the sun forgets to shine. He had a big turn-out; and I wasn't surprised to see every society editor in town at St. Anne's, dressed in mourning, with note-books and pencils constantly in hand, jotting down the notables present.

I guessed at the paragraph they'd give me: "Barry Amsterdam, New York's play-boy and thrill-seeker Number One, was grieving at the loss of his erstwhile playmate, the fabulously wealthy heir to the Carter utility millions, whose untimely death—" and so forth.

I only hoped they'd leave it at that. Because I *knew*, and so did others, that Andy Carter hadn't died of pneumonia. He had died of whatever it was that had made him a ghost-faced stranger the last time I'd seen him alive.

Or could you call that—life? That cringing shadow of a man who'd whimper as he pulled his hand from my clasp, refused to answer the natural questions a best friend would ask?

We didn't speak of it to each other, we who were the monied fraction of New York, but it was there, behind every bland mask of a face at the fashionable funeral. Andy Carter had died of stark, grisly terror!

"YOU LOOK like the prelude to several long drinks Barry, my boy," said a slow voice at my elbow. It was Duke Livingstone, city editor of the Chronicle, and in times past, friend enough to squash some of my snappier high-jinks before they reached the headlines. Tall and baldish, with eyes like an owl's, and a mouth that was sometimes like a kid's and sometimes like a professor's. He was humorous; he had to be. A grimmer man might have gone crazy, knowing the things he knew about people and their shortcomings.

"I feel like the tail end of a bad life," I told him. "And what brings you here? Poor old Andy wasn't that important."

Duke put a long finger against his thin nose and wagged it. "Poor old Andy," he said, "died without explaining a few things that might be interesting to the press. For instance, what happened to the Carter money? Andy didn't live long enough to spend four million—"

"Duke, skip it," I urged. "Skip it as an editor, anyway. Don't hurt the Carters any more than you can help it."

Duke's owlish eyes followed my gaze to a brave erect little figure, black-veiled, at the front of St. Anne's. "And that's another thing," he drawled. "I have a hunch Bonny Carter knows more about her brother's death than any of us. Don't worry. I won't interrupt her grief—yet. You're a little sunk on her, aren't you?"

Sure. I was sunk on her. Until Andy's —well, we called it illness—we'd been talking Armonk every night of the week. Duke knew it, so I didn't bother telling him. And I guess he knew I didn't want him around, just then, because he vanished, like the good fellow he was.

There was something about Bonny Carter, even in the stark shock of sudden loss, that made a man think of the way spring felt when he was a kid. She was—well, perfect. Violet eyes, tawny hair, flawless skin; that was only a part of it. You could feel something underneath that, a kind of beautiful purity that made you want to help her and protect her.

I don't know what she saw in me, except that I loved her; but I knew, from the way she reached out her hands to me the minute she saw me, that if anyone could comfort her in this tragedy, it was I. I swore silently to myself that I'd live up to her trust in me. God, how little we know our own follies! In spite of myself, through my very efforts to save her, I was to add to her sorrows!

"Barry," she whispered, "has he gone? That newspaper man, I mean?"

I held her fingertips, reverently. "Yes, he's gone," I said. "I asked him to. Duke's not a bad sort."

"No, he isn't. But I'm wary of reporters." She was a little breathless, and it was not the breathlessness that comes from tears. Her glance darted about unhappily, and then she beckoned me into a side aisle.

"I have to talk to you before we go to the cemetery," she said. "Barry, I don't know what I'll be like afterward. I've been so worried! We don't have a cent, Mother and I, and we don't know what's happened to it. Andy's club was awfully decent about paying for the funeral. But the living should pay for their own dead."

I tried to tell her that it would be all right, that the sweetest thing she could do for me would be to let me take care of her and her mother forever. But she retreated from me in a kind of appalled daze—and then I saw a look in those violet eyes that made me wish I'd died before I saw it.

It was the same look that had been on Andy's face the last time I saw him alive ... a look that made you think terror, like a huge cancer, was amok in a living being, feeding on it and slowly causing its death.

She wasn't looking at me. She was looking at the pall-bearers, six black figures, moving with Andy's coffin down the aisle. Was it the candle-light, or the tragic occasion that made them seem what they were, that sad sextet? Or was it—my mind recoiled toward sanity from the thought—that same expression of panic gone hopeless that turned those faces, so familiar to cameramen around the town's hot-spots, into death's-heads of despair?

I DIDN'T see Bonny at the cemetery, nor after the burial, for the very good reason that the burial ended in a near-riot. I remembering thinking, then, that life had turned into a crazy caricature of death. I didn't know, you see, that I was as yet only in the hinterland of a horror that would blacken my world, later ...

It was just after the first spadeful had been flung against the coffin. Grant Anders, the leading pall-bearer, stood very straight and gaunt at the edge of the grave, his loose black coat flapping in the February wind like the wing-humming of the Grim Reaper. Grant's family had come over on the Mayflower; he was an old classmate of mine. I thought that he was not looking too well.

Suddenly high, mirthless laughter pierced the reverent silence. It was Grant's voice. There was a sharp cracking sound. Grant faltered, and then plunged into the open grave, his dead fingers still linked around a smoking revolver.

I suppose I must have taken charge in the panic that followed, because when Sergeant Connor put a heavy hand on my shoulder, it seemed I had pushed eight men away from the body, and was engaged in slapping a middle-aged matron out of hysteria.

"I'm a friend of the Carters," I explained. "I know all these people. I tried to keep them from running wild."

"Ye've been doin' a bit of runnin' wild yerself, m'boy," said the sergeant, not unsympathetically. "However, I'm glad ye let no one touch the body." He beckoned to a comrade in brass-and-blue, and they hoisted poor Grant out of the pit. "Suicide," they observed pithily.

Grant had been a great one for thrills when I knew him, and he was willing to pay for them whenever they offered. Consequently, he'd usually carried at least a century on him, generally more.

Yet, when we examined his pockets in that vain half-blind search for motive that follows every tremendously wrong human act, we found—a nickel, two pennies, a clean handkerchief, and one slip of paper in the otherwise empty wallet. It was a notice, from the Quadrangle Club that dues, amounting to ninety dollars quarterly, were payable on the first of February.

I thought dully, and it was a thought that clicked 011 an empty cartridge, that members of the Quadrangle Club seemed to be showing a singular mortality. First Andy—now Grant Anders. I was occupied with a resentment against Kitty Anders. Grant had married her on a dare, and it worked out as such marriages usually do. Grant had been good sport enough to stick it, but I was sure Kitty, with her erratic expensive tastes, had brought my former classmate to this pitiable end.

What a difference there is in women! I thanked God for the sweet sanity of my Bonny—little realizing that when I saw' her next, she would seem far from sane.

I gave the sergeant my name, address and twenty dollars for being helpful. The funeral guests were gone; and what was left of Andy and Grant was in hands fit to deal with remains. Suddenly, after all the excitement, I began to feel a little sick—and more than anything in the world, I wanted to see Bonny.

NEITHER SHE nor her mother were at the town apartment when I got back to Manhattan. I floundered into an easy chair, and gritted my teeth over a Scotch and soda. At ten-minute intervals, I phoned the Carters. By five in the afternoon, they were still out. I had just about decided to go over there and wait for them, when Suki, my manservant, announced a visitor.

It was the city editor of the Chronicle. He helped himself to a Corona, and asked for a drink, and then his mouth that was humorous as a kid's came out with a bombshell.

He said, "Kitty Anders has just jumped out of the window." And then he sighed, and blew the kind of contented smoke rings you see in bedroom slipper ads.

When it penetrated, I shouted, "You're crazy! Or else everyone else is!"

"I always knew about everyone else," Duke answered. "You learn about them in my racket. Now, lad, I've done you a turn or two in our time. You knew the Anders better than I did. Would you say Kitty was the sort of woman who'd kill herself out of grief at the loss of a husband?"

I laughed, not happily. "Hardly. She's dead then?"

Duke nodded. "Most messily dead. It's a shame. She was a pretty woman. Say, didn't I tell you earlier you needed a drink? Keeps a man's stomach down. Swallow one, and I'll take you over for a look at the corpse. There's some kind of cop who says you know the answer."

I damned Sergeant Connor in my private thoughts, and went to the Anders' apartment on East Seventy-third in a press car. I'd avoided that apartment since Grant's marriage—it was gaudy, and there seemed to be a price tag on everything, screaming expense. I dreaded, too, the habitual reek of over-applied Oriental perfumes that had been a perfect expression of Kitty.

I needn't have. No hint of bottled flowers was in that air. Instead, a sultry foulness, faint but undeniable, hit us the moment we entered. Duke's long nose wrinkled in distaste. I wasn't imagining it.

In the bedroom, surrounded by gewgaws she would never enjoy again, lay Kitty Anders, and for salon she had the coroner, the press and the law. And now I placed that odor of corruption; it proceeded from the dead woman's decently shrouded body.

I said, "She's been dead for days!" and the coroner looked at me curiously and shook his head ...

"Take yerself a look," said Sergeant Connor, pulling the sheet from Kitty's face. I looked—and something in me froze. I'm not a coward;

I've been in some tough spots in my time and laughed afterward, but this was different. In the first place, with the removal of the sheet, the stench became almost overpowering—as though Kitty had been pregnant with death before she died!

And on the dead face was that unnamable expression of hopeless despair that I had seen on too many faces that day. That was it—she had carried death within her like an unborn evil—I turned away, half-sick with a fear I dared not name to myself.

"Ye wouldn't know what makes the poor girl smell so horrible, would ye?" asked the sergeant.

I said, "The living don't smell like that, nor fresh corpses ...

The coroner straightened, and looked at me. He was haggard and perplexed "Of course not. But we have sworn testimony that Mrs. Anders was alive this morning, that she shouted a warning to passers-by before she jumped ..." he shrugged, and went into the next room. Duke followed him, hoping, I suppose, to get a more complete report. The sergeant was busy with Kitty's effects.

I don't know what kept me in that tomb-smelling room, unless it was fear of the haunting uncertainty of the thing. Some malign fate seemed amok among my friends; tomorrow, unless I learned its source of power, it might strike nearer home ...

No one else had seen the small white thing clutched by those stiff white fingers. No one saw me as I stooped to wrest the thing from their clasp.

The fingers were soft to the bone, pulpy as though maggot-ridden. I forced myself to delve there ... and the woman's hand turned to putty in mine, like a squashed putrescent fruit! I was a man; I didn't get sick on the spot. That would come later.

In her hand had been a membership card to the Quadrangle Club.

Chapter 2: One Ticket To Hell

"SNAP OUT of it," Duke kept telling me, on the way back. "You're white, Barry. Well, do you know any more than I do? The sarge seemed to think you might. I'd like to get it into a six o'clock extra."

I didn't answer, because I was swallowing to keep my stomach where it belonged. Besides, what was there to say? Duke had a nose; he knew as much as I did.

Was it true, or was my imagination playing tricks on my memory? That last time Andy had retreated from me, at the Antler Bar, hadn't I thought, "What ghastly shaving lotion the lad uses!" For there *had* been a super-abundance of scent about him, a scent with sickly-rancid undertones ... God, it was true! Whatever they died of, these ill-fated things, they'd been dying of it for a long time before! Some loathsome disease, that rotted all of them, heart and brain last ... I swallowed, harder than ever, and managed to talk. "Looks like the dissolution of the upper classes. The snootiest club in town is really getting something to turn its nose." And I showed him the rumpled card I'd torn from those rotted fingers.

"Shut up," Duke said sharply. "You're letting it get you. Come back with me while I put the Chronicle to bed. She'll run an article on the Quadrangle Club that ought to stop the slaughter. You might have two cents to put in."

I said, "No," because I remembered, with tightening heart muscles, that I hadn't located Bonny all day. And she had told me that morning that she owed the cost of Andy's funeral to—the Quadrangle Club! No wonder she had looked as though doom were a little way off, watching her helpless struggle with malevolent and unfathomable eyes! It was enough to drive a man mad, that sinister shadow whose substance I could not perceive!

There was no need to phone. I knew when I saw the mink coat and black hat on a couch in the foyer, that I had a most welcome guest. I heard the automatic playing the Pathetique symphony.

Bonny crouched, head buried in her elbows, in a big chair. Her small, black- robed body swayed mournfully to the third movement. God, I was glad to see her—and not to—to smell her!

She was pure, thank God, and untainted. Still had the same faint toilet water scent about her, woodsy with lavender ... she winced when I put my hands on her shoulders.

"Bonny, where have you been all day?" I asked anxiously.

She turned to me a white face in which the violet eyes looked like great bruises. "Dodging reporters," she answered. "Barry, I have to stay here tonight."

"You can't," I answered, with a sharpness that was as much reproof to myself as to her. "There aren't enough rooms. And—" I added, laughing feebly—"no chaperone."

"Chaperone!" She laughed with me, but it was a high, uncomfortable laugh that made my flesh creep. "Bitter music," she commented, and then: "What do I need with a chaperone? I want protection, just for tonight."

I shook her, for she was still laughing in that bitter, almost hysterical way, but it had no effect. "Bonny, you've got to tell me! What are you afraid of?"

She shuddered. "Everything—even you. You've been wicked in your time, haven't you, Barry? Awfully wicked ... but I love you."

That wasn't like Bonny. I'd told her all about myself, and the lowlights of my past, and she'd been pretty magnanimous about it. She wasn't one to rake up old ashes. Suddenly I hated that poignant music; like a crossed child, I snatched the record. I heard the needle whine once, and then the third movement of the symphony was in a hundred fragments on the floor.

"I felt that way—once," Bonny told me. She had stopped laughing. Her voice was flat, hopeless. "Now it doesn't matter. Can I stay tonight, Barry? It may be the last time I'll ever be near you ..."

I shouted, "For God's sake, talk straight! If you'd only tell me what's terrifying you—you can't stay here. Think, Bonny. We buried Andy this morning. You don't want to go to hell tonight, do you?"

She had resumed her rocking back and forth, in the cradle of her own arms. "Andy this morning," she crooned. "Tomorrow—Kitty. And the day after—who knows ? Maybe Bonny. Poor Kitty. Poor Bonny."

I couldn't bear the picture her insane sing-song conjured in my mind. Bonny with her tawny hair to die like Kitty! I slapped my sweetheart, hard. She whimpered—and laughed!

I remember pleading and haranguing alternately, but nothing shook Bonny from her mad mood. I shot questions about the Quadrangle Club at her, but she kept crooning and laughing to herself, in the ghastly mockery of a lullaby. Finally I said, "I'm calling up your mother. She'll spank you for this."

"Mother's gone," said Bonny. "Poor Mother!" A telephone call to the Carters' proved she was right, for the time being, anyway.

I'd had enough skirting on the edge of nerve-strangling mystery. I could think of only one man who might know something—a very little something—and if I pooled my knowledge with his, we might together find a ray of blessed light.

"Suki," I shouted, forgetting that there were still human ears left not deafened by madness. "Take care of Miss Carter. Don't let anyone in. I'll be back in an hour." I handed the boy my gun. He blinked, and nodded. Suki was a good boy, loyal and intelligent.

Bonny laughed as I walked out into the night.

DUKE WASN'T at the office when I got there. They told me he'd gone to check some material for a special article on the Quadrangle Club, featured for front page release in the morning. I groaned, fell into Duke's swivel chair, and waited.

There wasn't much humor in Duke's face when he came in, at eleven-thirty. He took one look at me, and said, "When did you eat last?"

"I don't know. Maybe this morning."

"Let's step across the street. I won't say what I have to say to a guy with an empty stomach."

I didn't like the ham and eggs. I wouldn't have liked nectar and ambrosia, at that point. But Duke sat over me sternly, making me gulp the stuff down anyhow, and he only relaxed over my half-finished cup of coffee.

"I've been over to the Quadrangle Club," he said harshly. "An empty layout; big brownstone front, thick curtains, and a stuffed butler at the door. Couldn't get in, though. God knows how they've kept the cops out after today's high-jinks. They sponsored the funeral, didn't they? Well, you need a ticket from the Social Register to crash. I didn't want to waste time."

I said I'd heard all that before. The Quadrangle Club had been one of those things in the background all my life, like the Horse Show.

"My lad," said Duke, his face one long grimace from the bald spot on his brow to the cleft in his narrow chin; "do you know whom I saw in the lobby, just past the butler?"

"No. You look as though it might have been a ghost."

"Correct," said the Duke. "It was Andy Carter."

There are points beyond which the mind cannot go, discrepancies of evidence which only the insane may enter and live. I knew, as soon as Duke told me that *I believed him*. And I know, too, that something snapped in my brain. It had to. I started moving, and moving fast.

First, I drove through every red light on the route to my own apartment. I wasn't surprised to find Suki blubbering and frantic, and Bonny gone. That was part of the grotesquely hideous nightmare.

"Miss Carter get telephone call. I not can stop her. She say—" Suki paused, and there was stark fear in his face—"her brother want her, she go. Is not Miss Carter's brother dead this morning?"

Dead! Kitty Anders must have been dead a week before she stopped moving about in the land of the living! What was to keep a corpse from rising then, if the dead forgot to die?

It was only after I got to the Quadrangle Club that the horror stopped. I put one finger on the doorbell and kept it there. The door opened to the width of a man's arm. Something bright flared astoundingly in my face, and blinded me. I didn't see or feel whatever it was that smashed down on my skull and sent me into oblivion with a burst of shooting stars.

I FELT my head going round and round, just before I opened my eyes, I expected to wake up in hell, but they'd canceled that trip, apparently, because I was in my own bed, with Suki's worried brown face bending over me, and Duke Livingstone's back between me and the window.

Duke's mouth puckered as he turned. "Still with us?" he said. "When I found you in the gutter, you looked as though you had been done in for good." He paused and then exploded: "Nuts. What a set-up! The cops won't even touch it!"

My mouth was dry, and there was a weight on top of my head, where I'd been cracked, that seemed a truckload. I said, "I'm not so sure," and reached for the phone. Sergeant Connor told me cheerily that everything was under control.

"Then why the hell don't you raid that place?" I told him.

The Sergeant answered, his cheer considerably shaken, "Now, me boy, we can't raid a respectable private club because of a coincidence."

"A damned peculiar coincidence!"

His voice dropped to a whisper. "We got orders—not to touch it!" When I expostulated, there was a soft click ...

"Barry, there's only one way," Duke's voice was weary, as though he'd been up every night for a million years. "You've got that ticket I haven't got. You're a Social Register lad. Get in touch with the Quadrangle Club, and apply for membership."

It was a ticket, all right. A ticket to hell. But maybe I'd find Bonny in hell ...

A brisk secretarial voice at the other end of the wire told me I would be investigated, and if I furnished the customary references, my membership would be considered ...

Duke's article on the front page of the Chronicle that morning was one of those brave damn-fool things that only cub reporters and veteran editors have the nerve to do. He told his story simply, starting with Andy's funeral. There was Grant's suicide, and Kitty's. He stated flatly that Kitty hadn't killed herself for Grant's sake. "The popular young matron," said he, "was anything but a faithful and loving wife."

He hauled over the Quadrangle Club, briefly mentioning its history as a tony haven for the best people of the Eighties; and he posed the question, reasonably enough, "Why has the ha-cha generation of bluebloods joined the brownstone tradition? Can it be that behind those venerable portals there is a stimulus for those jaded appetites; a pleasure so exhaustive that its ending leaves nothing but self-loathing and desire for death?"

Duke grinned at me when I looked up at him, like a small boy who has made an offensive precocious remark and expects to be told how bright he is.

I said, "Nice work, Duke. I'm glad you left your latest hunches about the Carters out of it. That was decent."

"A newspaperman is never decent. I left that out because I may not have proof."

"Proof!" I howled. "You can't prove anything. The Chronicle's going to run into the biggest libel suit in history."

Duke smiled his sad, crooked, smile. "Maybe. But it won't go to trial tomorrow. And by the time we get our day in court, I'm gambling we'll have proof enough to halt the whole blamed mess."

I was finishing the second cup of black coffee. "And where would you be getting it?" I said.

Duke didn't answer, just kept looking at me.

"I know," I said. "You think I'm going to get it for you. God, I hope I can! I hope I can find Bonny—" I didn't dodge his whimsical blow to the chin. It was his way of bucking me up.

"You'll find her," he assured me. "If there's anyone who can crack the story, it's you. If you want an expense account on the Chronicle ..."

I said, "No. I'm on my own."

"Got to be going," said the Duke. "Think it over, Barry. A big paper has resources. Files of information, contacts ... it can send you inside places you couldn't crack yourself. It's a help."

I agreed with him. It was the brightest ray of light I'd seen yet. Duke gave me a press card, informing the police that Barry Amsterdam was working for the New York Chronicle, and left me to my own devices.

Chapter 3: Doom Cracks Its Whip

JUDGE RAINEY told me that afternoon in his office, "If I hadn't known your uncle, Barry, I'd throw you out! What do you mean, I'm blocking police investigation! Why would I do a thing like that? Why, I don't even belong to the damned club!"

"But," I insisted, "you're the only political force in town that could. The others don't come from your kind of family." The Judge, a big man with a magnificent silver head, forgot that he'd known my uncle. He threw me out ...

It seemed hopeless, hopeless. It might be three weeks before I'd pass that brown-stone front myself, and in the meantime, Bonny ... I felt dry in the throat every time I thought of Bonny. It was like the thirst of a dying man lost in the Sahara.

Something made me look up as I walked through the front lobby of the office building. Something indescribably vile ... and familiar. An odor of the charnel-house ...

A woman, swathed to the eyebrows in silver fox, had just passed me. I recognized her at once as Judge Rainey's young and beautiful second wife. I ran after her, and grabbed her arm. She turned, and ...

I—I had known Thea Rainey as one of the town's huskier young glamor girls, seen her cantering an hour after dawn, heard her throaty alive laugh ... and now I saw her with the cancer of death almost victorious in her wasted frame!

"Barry Amsterdam," she said, and then she laughed—but what a laugh! The ghost of her youth, chuckling in hell ... and, God help her, she stank. Under the heaviness of her perfume, there was a rank odor of decaying flesh ...

I had dropped her arm, but she retrieved mine. I shuddered at the touch, and she knew it, and licked her lips.

"They'll get you too," she whispered. "You're a nice lad, Barry. Once—you didn't know it, did you?—I fancied I loved you. They'll bring you to me in death, Barry ... they'll let me kiss you ...

I went back to Thea's apartment with her. It took every ounce of stomach I had, but I went. She promised she'd talk, if we were alone ... she even seemed to know where Bonny was ...

Her butler served us sandwiches and highballs. She touched neither. When I had pleaded with her for agonizing minutes, she rose. Her chalky face assumed an expression of terrible despair.

"You want to know what they do to us?" she whispered, tensely, crazily. "I'll show you!" Before I could stop her, she had zipped her dress open from throat to hem. She stepped out of it.

I cried, "Stop!" but she didn't stop. She stepped out of her slip, and I saw the white diaphragm below her brassiere, gleaming uncleanly ... she tore off the brassiere, and the silk shorts. In hideous nudity, she advanced one step toward me. Her breasts, her hips, seemed half-decomposed … and the smell! It was like the fumes that might arise from a city's garbage lying for hours under an August sun …

And then I was engulfed in a putrefaction that had been the beauty of Thea Rainey. Her arm, white as the underside of a fish belly, twined about my neck, she pressed her naked body to me, she darted her face close to mine.

I felt the kiss of loathsome death, and when I would have withdrawn, she pressed closer. Then—I've read about lips melting in an embrace, but I'll never read it again without being sick. For that was exactly what Thea's lips did. They squashed, with the same hideous *plosh* of rotten fruit that had marked the disintegration of Kitty's hand …

I didn't turn to look. I ran. My mouth felt ghoulishly filthy, as though I were a cannibal epicure. I ran right to the Chronicle office.

"Duke," I said, "I know why the police won't touch it. It's not Rainey. It's Rainey's wife …"

And then I was suddenly very sick.

THEA RAINEY'S funeral was held next day at St. Anne's. Society was there; but it was a weirdly changed society from the polite group that had met two days before at Andy Carter's funeral. In fifty hours, the upper crust of Manhattan had been transformed to a cowering half-idiocy… no one mentioned the haste of the burial. We were thinking of other things. Each of us seemed menaced by some unholy destruction. We did not speak to each other.

More, by two score, were the faces that wore an expression of hopeless despair. And we knew, we who had escaped so far, that they were the doomed … they told us nothing, though they had been our friends, and our loved ones.

There was a great wreath of flowers from the Quadrangle Club. But its roses and lilies were not enough to combat the mingled odor of strong perfumes that rose from those who had come to honor the dead. Perfumes that covered a vague but unmistakable odor of decay. Thea Rainey had been embalmed cleverly; they had drained her blood and replaced the broken features with wax. But for her friends, the dying, no such service had been rendered.

I didn't go to the burial. I needed fresh air. I walked aimlessly about town that forenoon. I wasn't quite sane, I think. A dozen times, I followed some woman simply because she had red hair … but she was never Bonny.

Bonny! Had the thing touched her yet, the filthy disease that a doctor in Thea's case, had despairingly named heart disease? Why hadn't she been at the funeral? Was she stolen, or killed?

I saw the last cars of Thea's cortege winding southward on Park. Dully I watched them; they were bound for a cemetery in Brooklyn.

But the last—was that a glimpse of tawny hair I caught behind the curtained window—made a U-turn, and headed north. North! They had buried Andy in Westchester ... and Bonny had said she was going to—her brother!

I taxied to my garage, took my car, and stamped on the accelerator. It wasn't clever, half-blinded with dread as I was; for by the time I'd located Sergeant Connor, and had him explain me out of traffic court in Yonkers, it was three-thirty. I was at Hawthorne by five ... and when I came to the cemetery night was on me. Night without a moon....

The gates were locked, so I clambered over the wall. In the darkness the tombstones were a glimmering reproach to one who would discover their secrets. I crept along stealthily to Andy's grave. Once I saw a swinging lantern, and I ducked behind a monument, hugging the dank cold earth that was nourished on death.

But there were no lights where we had left Andy. *There was a pile of fresh earth where his stone had been, and the grave-pit yawned wide open.* With the cold sweat pouring down my face, I peered from behind the dirt-pile....

Two hooded figures stood on either side of the unlidded coffin. And lying within, her pale hands crossed over the embalming sheet, her violet eyes alive with mad fear, was Bonny!

They were lifting the lid, ready to put it into place ... I jumped toward the nearest figure, caught him in a frantic half-Nelson, and pushed. Like a frightened ghost, the other figure leapt away.

"Barry, you don't know what you're doing!" shrieked Bonny. I didn't listen. I kept pushing. Beneath the black robe, I felt that familiar puttiness.

Bonny stood up in the coffin, her hair falling over her shoulders, pure as a dream of heaven in her white dead-dress. "Barry, let me die ... This isn't a hard death! It's over so soon ... not like the others ... Let me save you, Barry!"

DIMLY, through the wild hate that throbbed in my brain, I knew that she was giving her life for my salvation. I didn't want that, God, no! I pushed, a little harder ... and the brain of the hooded thing splashed out of the rotted skull. I dropped the body. It fell with a soft whoosh against the coffin. When I snatched off the hood, I saw no face, only battered brain and bone …

Bonny screamed. I turned, and saw the other hooded thing reaching down on me with the butt end of a revolver. No time to duck … I took it.

Later, I would remember as though in a dream, that a black devil had carried Bonny away. But it would be no dream, because when I awoke, just before dawn, I was to find myself lying, cold and aching, across an open coffin in an open grave.

When I got back to town that morning, Suki handed me a single thing that had come by mail. It was a neat little invitation, black on white, asking me to attend my initiation at the Quadrangle Club that night, with the polite reminder, "Formal," in a lower left-hand corner. I looked at it till the letters danced—and fell into a drugged sleep of nervous exhaustion.

I awoke toward evening. Suki had laid out my soup and fish. I felt fresher, freer to think for the first time in days. That card … they'd rushed it, I thought … and I wondered if there were not some connection between last night's episode at the grave, and this morning's invitation. Either last night I had blundered on too much, or else … and another thought made me pause … or else the whole thing had been deliberate, that glimpse I'd caught of Bonny, luring me to witness a witless scene in a graveyard.

Too many horrors had forced themselves on my awareness in the immediate past. As I dressed, I thought how incredible it should be that I was going to the Quadrangle Club to unearth the grisliest of imaginable horrors … the Quadrangle Club that had been for fifty years a guarded haven of wealth and prestige. It was almost insane, but then, my world had been insane for days.

Even as I drove over, the thought persisted that I was going on a fool's errand. I wondered why … somewhere at the back of my head a gap persisted, something I should have known, that eluded my dulled senses.

I pulled myself together, and went through the brownstone portals.

Old-generation tone. Cut-glass chandeliers, and the gentlemen taking their port in the card room. That was the Quadrangle Club. I recognized most of the members of my own set, the moderns and their would-be modem mammas and papas.

But we were stiff and strange with each other. Incense burned almost overpoweringly everywhere, but it was not enough to hide that other smell ... Half the faces were chalky and tragic, the other half like polite masks over real terror. Nowhere did I see Bonny.

"So you've joined too, Barry," Mona Wells said to me. She was a charming kid, lithe and dark and vibrant, recently married to a friend of mine, Martin Wells. But here, for a reason I could not fathom, her brown eyes were pools of sorrow.

I said, "Where's Mart? Haven't seen him around for a while."

The wine-glass in her fingers cracked at the stem. Her eyes grew mad. "Martin's been ill," she whispered. Then, "He shot himself at seven this evening. I left him lying in his blood."

"My God, Mona! What are you doing at—a party?"

"Party!" Her voice was the voice of an animal being tortured. "It was my invitation to join ..."

When I tried to follow her, she lost herself among the guests.

IT WAS all I could do to keep from running berserk among the guests, shaking them like rats to get the information I wanted. They were all people in whose families there had been recent tragedy— like Mona. Had Martin told her before he died? Was that why he died? And where was Bonny? Did she know ... too much, too?

Music came from the dim hallway, and in the glittering drawing-room, guests were dancing. What a dance that was! Like the slow waltz of decaying corpses, who had entered hell in evening dress!

I stood and watched vainly among them for a girl with tawny hair. I felt a light tap on my shoulder, and there stood the portly butler, with Mona Wells, white and shaken, at his side.

"Mr. Amsterdam, if you please, I've received word that the initiation is to begin. Won't you come upstairs for your interview?"

We followed him up the winding old-fashioned staircase, Mona still refusing to look at me. At the end of a corridor, the butler swung open a door, and deferentially waited for me to enter. "In here, sir ..." I paused, for the room was in darkness. Then I shrugged my shoulders. Nothing much was left to lose ... I passed the obsequious figure and went into darkness.

I heard the click of a lock behind me, and footsteps fading down the hall.

I found a wall by groping, and leaned against it.

A voice, muffled as though it came through a filtered microphone, said, "That will do nicely, Barry Amsterdam. You may stand as you are."

I answered, "Who the hell are you?" My voice sounded grim, as though it were echoing from wall to wall of that small room, as though the room were a catacomb....

"I am Justice, if you like a name." The voice, I told myself, in spite of the stiffness of those short hairs at my nape, must be human. Again that pestering gap! It was a joke.... I said as much.

"This is not a joke," the voice went on. "Justice has long been due to you and your kind—parasites, despoilers, fatteners on the land! There is in each of your lives, or in the lives of those you pretend to love, some crime too ugly for public knowledge. But Justice knows!"

Of course it was a human voice! Damnably human! That pestering thought at the back of my head was beginning to click ... in a moment, I'd have my finger on it. I said, "What is this? Blackmail?" As though it had not heard me, the muffled voice continued, "And you, Barry Amsterdam ... we have waited for you a long, long time! Too long you have escaped the fate you merit, but you will not escape now."

The thing had clicked. *I knew the name of the man behind that voice.* It had been so evident, all along, that I'd missed it! Exultantly I realized that at last I was one step ahead of him, because I knew who he was, and he didn't know I knew it. I couldn't blurt it out now. It might have been my death sentence.

To keep my voice steady, I yelled, "So what?"

"You will mail to the Quadrangle Club in the morning a check for one hundred thousand dollars. You will shun the society of friends. You will do our bidding, come at our call, and respond out of your generosity to any further call for funds."

"The hell I will!"

"You will do these things, or else the death that rots before it kills will come to Bonny Carter."

I shouted, "You dirty perverted murderer!" I wanted to hit something, hard, but you can't hit at a voice.

"We are glad to accommodate with proof," the voice slurred on. Then I *had* to grab at the wall, because the floor started tilting under me, like one of those crazy things at Coney Island. I felt myself slipping, gently, to a lower level in the building where there was light.

Chapter 4: The Scent of Burning Flesh

I BLINKED a little. I was in a sort of cage, constructed by driving iron bars in a semicircle from floor to ceiling of a stone-walled room. The back wall of the cage was the section of the floor that had just swung down. At a height of ten feet there was a gap in the rails, through which I had fallen; and a sort of gate in front of me, latched on the outside.

The room beyond my cage was large and rectangular and had a platform extending across the far end. A big machine, something like a gigantic searchlight, occupied the left side of it. Wide cracks of light in the long wall to my left indicated a shut door.

There was a chair just in front of the camera-thing, a wooden chair, with leather straps about the legs and back. I peered, trying to find a sign of life in the purplish dimness.

Far to the left, in the shadows, two figures gleamed, luminously white. I cried out in sheer horror at the sight of them ... they were women, nude, bound upright to stone pillars.

One of them was Bonny. Bands of adhesive covered her mouth.

Had I found her—too late? I went crazy mad, tried to force the steel bars that kept me from her, shouted insane challenges to the thing that had done this to us.

Two black-robed figures stepped from behind the machine. One of them stood guard over the helpless women; it was hooded, and I recognized it as the thing that had spirited Bonny out of her brother's coffin, that had taunted me a few minutes ago in the dark room.

I was cold with despair, because I *knew* who he was. I *knew*, but my knowledge had come too late—I could do nothing. And Bonny in deadly danger....

The other figure was not hooded—it was the club's butler! He descended from the platform and walked toward me, coming to a stop just out of reach of my arms. His robe fell open a little and I caught a glimpse of the heavy automatic that nestled in its holster under his shoulder. God! I thought. If I could only get my hands on that gun for thirty seconds!

The butler said, "Sir, the master wishes you to witness an exhibition. He trusts it will bring you around to his way of thinking." He retreated, and while my heart went berserk in my throat, I saw him unbind one of the struggling nude figures, and strap her to the plain wooden chair.

Not Bonny, thank God! The girl facing that evil-looking machine was Mona Weils. Like a demon lecturer explaining his lantern slides, the butler continued suavely, "Mrs. Wells has also refused to accede to our wishes. She has one more chance before we accomplish her end—a little prematurely, to be sure."

Mona shrieked in horror, "I won't do it! You can't make me, you murdering fiends! You got Martin, didn't you? Well, you can send me after him!"

As though it were a step in a routine, the butler opened that door on the left wall ... light flooded the chamber. There, behind a network of iron bars, like the door to a prison, their foul white faces mad with hatred of the fiend who had destroyed them, stood the legion of the cursed—the rotting! Beyond them, I saw the sad but still-human faces of the others.

"Mrs. Wells," said the butler, "will do nicely for your education, Mr. Amsterdam." He stepped behind the machine. I heard a whirring sound, and there was a sudden, blinding flash of light accompanied by the sickening smell of burnt flesh. Mona shrieked again. God, I'll hear those shrieks in a dream the night before I die!

It had happened! That was all it took; a whirring sound, a flash of light, and you—started to rot! I joined her shrieks. Over and over again I screamed at the hooded monster and the inhuman butler: "You damned swine! You damned swine!"

Mona's voice died to a whine, and became silent. She slumped in her bonds. The butler undid her straps and led her back to the pillar and tied her up again. Her head slumped forward on her chest—she was unconscious. I hoped that she was dead.

The butler glanced at her once and then came over and stood near my cage—a little nearer than before. I could have almost reached out and touched him. A sudden inspiration flashed through my mind. It was a slim and desperate chance ... but it *might* work! If only I could get him one step closer ...

The rotting corpses who once were my friends were silent now behind their bars —silent with hopeless terror and despair.

THE HOODED figure turned toward me. An unholy chuckle escaped from under the hood. "Do you see your friends now, Barry Amsterdam? Do you see them as they are? As you will be soon? Their bodies are rotting now even as their souls rotted long ago. It is Justice and they are afraid of Justice. They are afraid of me! Those who have not yet felt the power of my—for want of a better name, shall be call it Radium X-Ray?—treatment, know that their time to face it will surely come.

"They don't know me, Barry Amsterdam, these sons and daughters of the four hundred. I am only one of the forty million. But they are afraid of me! They know that they are safe only so long as they obey me. They cannot escape, for no matter where they go, I can follow them

—because they don't know who I am. I can sit beside them on the train or drink with them at their houses, and they will not know that Justice has overtaken them. They will never know—until it is too late and their souls are roasting in hell!"

He stopped suddenly and gestured toward Bonny. "Perhaps another demonstration will convince you, Barry Amsterdam, that it is better to submit to me. She no longer has any money, so she can no longer obey my commands. It is time for her to meet the death her rotten soul deserves."

It had come! I could wait no longer. The single card I held must be played—a slim, last, desperate hope....

I shouted:

"No one else may know you now ... but I know you—Duke Livingstone!"

The hooded figure uttered a roar of rage and sprang toward his fiendish machine. The butler, his face white with sudden fear, took an involuntary step toward me—started to draw his pistol.

This was what I had hoped for! At the same moment I had shouted Duke Livingstone's name, I thrust my arms through the bars of my cage. My hands clasped behind the butler's neck and with the strength of a madman, I jerked his head toward me. There was the sodden crunch of flesh and bone meeting hard iron and the butler's form went slack in my arms.

Duke Livingstone had halted momentarily in astonishment at my sudden action, and that hesitation was all I needed. Holding the unconscious butler against the bars with one arm, my other hand darted to his half-drawn automatic. I fired two quick shots.

Duke spun heavily, reeled back a half-dozen paces, and slumped to the floor. I fired three more shots into his twitching body. It jerked convulsively and then was still....

As the echoes of the shots died away there was absolute silence for a few seconds. I heard a high-pitched voice scream. "The butler has the keys!" and then all hell broke loose. Shrieking imprecations and crying for me to free them so that they might tear their former tormentors to pieces, the mob of living corpses beat frantically at the iron bars of their prison, while the yet untainted were almost hysterical with joy.

I found the keys, but before freeing the others I released Bonny and held my coat about her head as we hurried from that hellish room so that she could not see the sickening and ghoulish fate of Duke Livingstone and the butler....

"I SUPPOSE it drove him crazy," I explained to the reduced group of friends who had survived. "He was always saying that it got him, knowing the things he knew about people."

"He was a devil!" moaned Jane Anders, Grant's sister. "He got Judge Rainey's wife, to keep the police off us. He played husband against wife, mother against child. He was a ghoul!"

"We mustn't talk about it," Bonny whispered. "Barry, take me home."

She nestled against me in the car. "Barry, I tried to save you. That's why, yesterday, when I caught a glimpse of you from the car, I showed myself, hoping you'd follow me. If you couldn't rescue me at once, I thought at least you'd see that the mess was far too loathsome for you to bother with."

My arm wound tighter about her. "You thought that would keep me away! Bonny, didn't you know I loved you?" I thought for a moment of the inanity of women, and of the courage of this one. "But Bonny," I said, "why did you leave my apartment the night I left you with Suki?"

She shuddered slightly. "Duke Livingstone called and told me Andy was alive, that he'd seen him. He seemed to think I knew more about it that he did, so I didn't think anything was wrong, 'til I found myself his prisoner. He kept me gagged most of the time …

I swore softly at the dead … "If I'd only realized what I should have realized a little earlier! I might at least have saved poor Mona Wells. It kept bothering me, what the tie-up was between the Quadrangle Club and the horrors. I was helpless before it dawned on me that Duke was the tie-up. He had to be the man. It was he who'd suggested it to me in the first place. If it hadn't been for Duke, there just wouldn't have been a tie-up—either in my mind or in the newspapers. I wonder why he didn't try to keep it a secret?"

"Duke wanted his scheme to have publicity, because, I imagine, he was about ready to close operations in New York. With Thea Rainey dead, he couldn't stave off an investigation much longer. And when the investigation started, he'd be out from under. Then he meant to give the horror as much front page space as possible, so that when he started operations elsewhere under the same disguise, people would be afraid of him.

"He meant to use you, Barry, either as a victim or an ally. If you'd been frightened off at the graveyard—if you hadn't come to the Club—you'd have been his chief character witness at an investigation. But you came, Barry—and you saved all of us who were left to save."

I had been nodding as she explained, and suddenly I felt that my head wasn't going to nod any more at my volition. I was really faint. I pulled up to a curb, explained, and let Bonny take the wheel.

"Dearest, what's the matter?" she asked anxiously.

I said, "That darned clout on the head I took last night. Wonder if I should have it X-rayed."

"No!" She almost shrieked at me. "Don't—even—think of that word again!"

I HAD it X-rayed, nevertheless, but there wasn't anything wrong except a bump. Bonny doesn't know about that. Our home life is about as harmonious as things human can be, but—I hope and pray neither of us needs an X-ray again! Because I still remember the look in Bonny's violet eyes, when I mentioned the word....

Pigeons from Hell

By Robert E. Howard

Chapter 1: The Whistler in the Dark

GRISWELL AWOKE suddenly, every nerve tingling with a premonition of imminent peril. He stared about wildly, unable at first to remember where he was, or what he was doing there. Moonlight filtered in through the dusty windows, and the great empty room with its lofty ceiling and gaping black fireplace was spectral and unfamiliar. Then as he emerged from the clinging cobwebs of his recent sleep, he remembered where he was and how he came to be there. He twisted his head and stared at his companion, sleeping on the floor near him. John Branner was but a vaguely bulking shape in the darkness that the moon scarcely grayed.

Griswell tried to remember what had awakened him. There was no sound in the house, no sound outside except the mournful hoot of an owl, far away in the piney woods. Now he had captured the illusive memory. It was a dream, a nightmare so filled with dim terror that it had frightened him awake. Recollection flooded back, vividly etching the abominable vision.

Or was it a dream? Certainly it must have been, but it had blended so curiously with recent actual events that it was difficult to know where reality left off and fantasy began.

Dreaming, he had seemed to relive his past few waking hours, in accurate detail. The dream had begun, abruptly, as he and John Branner came in sight of the house where they now lay. They had come rattling and bouncing over the stumpy, uneven old road that led through the pinelands, he and John Branner, wandering far afield from their New England home, in search of vacation pleasure. They had sighted the old house with its balustraded galleries rising amidst a wilderness of weeds and bushes, just as the sun was setting behind it. It dominated their fancy, rearing black and stark and gaunt against the low lurid rampart of sunset, barred by the black pines.

They were tired, sick of bumping and pounding all day over woodland roads. The old deserted house stimulated their imagination with its suggestion of antebellum splendor and ultimate decay. They left the automobile beside the rutty road, and as they went up the winding walk of crumbling bricks, almost lost in the tangle of rank growth, pigeons rose from the balustrades in a fluttering, feathery crowd and swept away with a low thunder of beating wings.

The oaken door sagged on broken hinges. Dust lay thick on the floor of the wide, dim hallway, on the broad steps of the stair that mounted up from the hall. They turned into a door opposite the landing, and entered a large room, empty, dusty, with cobwebs shining thickly in the corners. Dust lay thick over the ashes in the great fireplace.

They discussed gathering wood and building a fire, but decided against it. As the sun sank, darkness came quickly, the thick, black, absolute darkness of the pinelands. They knew that rattlesnakes and copperheads haunted Southern forests, and they did not care to go groping for firewood in the dark. They ate frugally from tins, then rolled in their blankets fully clad before the empty fireplace, and went instantly to sleep.

This, in part, was what Griswell had dreamed. He saw again the gaunt house looming stark against the crimson sunset; saw the flight of the pigeons as he and Branner came up the shattered walk. He saw the dim room in which they presently lay, and he saw the two forms that were himself and his companion, lying wrapped in their blankets on the dusty floor. Then from that point his dream altered subtly, passed out of the realm of the commonplace and became tinged with fear. He was looking into a vague, shadowy chamber, lit by the gray light of the moon which streamed in from some obscure source. For there was no window in that room. But in the gray light he saw three silent shapes that hung suspended in a row, and their stillness and their outlines woke chill horror in his soul. There was no sound, no word, but he sensed a Presence of fear and lunacy crouching in a dark corner ...

Abruptly he was back in the dusty, high-ceilinged room, before the great fireplace.

He was lying in his blankets, staring tensely through the dim door and across the shadowy hall, to where a beam of moonlight fell across the balustraded stair, some seven steps up from the landing. And there was something on the stair, a bent, misshapen, shadowy thing that never moved fully into the beam of light. But a dim yellow blur that might have been a face was turned toward him, as if something crouched on the stair, regarding him and his companion. Fright crept chilly through his veins, and it was then that he awoke—if indeed he had been asleep.

He blinked his eyes. The beam of moonlight fell across the stair just as he had dreamed it did; but no figure lurked there. Yet his flesh still crawled from the fear the dream or vision had roused in him; his legs felt as if they had been plunged in ice-water. He made an involuntary movement to awaken his companion, when a sudden sound paralyzed him.

It was the sound of whistling on the floor above. Eerie and sweet it rose, not carrying any tune, but piping shrill and melodious. Such a sound in a supposedly deserted house was alarming enough; but it was more than the fear of a physical invader that held Griswell frozen. He could not himself have defined the horror that gripped him. But Branner's blankets rustled, and Griswell saw he was sitting upright. His figure bulked dimly in the soft darkness, the head turned toward the stair as if the man were listening intently. More sweetly and more subtly evil rose that weird whistling.

"John!" whispered Griswell from dry lips. He had meant to shout—to tell Branner that there was somebody upstairs, somebody who could mean them no good; that they must leave the house at once. But his voice died dryly in his throat.

Branner had risen. His boots clumped on the floor as he moved toward the door. He stalked leisurely into the hall and made for the lower landing, merging with the shadows that clustered black about the stair.

Griswell lay incapable of movement, his mind a whirl of bewilderment.

Who was that whistling upstairs? Why was Branner going up those stairs? Griswell saw him pass the spot where the moonlight rested, saw his head tilted back as if he were looking at something Griswell could not see, above and beyond the stair. But his face was like that of a sleepwalker. He moved across the bar of moonlight and vanished from Griswell's view, even as the latter tried to shout to him to come back. A ghastly whisper was the only result of his effort.

The whistling sank to a lower note, died out. Griswell heard the stairs creaking under Branner's measured tread. Now he had reached the hallway above, for Griswell heard the clump of his feet moving along it. Suddenly the footfalls halted, and the whole night seemed to hold its breath. Then an awful scream split the stillness, and Griswell started up, echoing the cry.

The strange paralysis that had held him was broken. He took a step toward the door, then checked himself. The footfalls were resumed.

Branner was coming back. He was not running. The tread was even more deliberate and measured than before. Now the stairs began to creak again. A groping hand, moving along the balustrade, came into the bar of moonlight; then another, and a ghastly thrill went through Griswell as he saw that the other hand gripped a hatchet—a hatchet which dripped blackly. Was that Branner who was coming down that stair?

Yes! The figure had moved into the bar of moonlight now, and Griswell recognized it. Then he saw Branner's face, and a shriek burst from Griswell's lips. Branner's face was bloodless, corpse-like; gouts of blood dripped darkly down it; his eyes were glassy and set, and blood oozed from the great gash which cleft the crown of his head!

Griswell never remembered exactly how he got out of that accursed house. Afterward he retained a mad, confused impression of smashing his way through a dusty cobwebbed window, of stumbling blindly across the weed-choked lawn, gibbering his frantic horror. He saw the black wall of the pines, and the moon floating in a blood-red mist in which there was neither sanity nor reason.

Some shred of sanity returned to him as he saw the automobile beside the road. In a world gone suddenly mad, that was an object reflecting prosaic reality; but even as he reached for the door, a dry chilling whir sounded in his ears, and he recoiled from the swaying undulating shape that arched up from its scaly coils on the driver's seat and hissed sibilantly at him, darting a forked tongue in the moonlight.

With a sob of horror he turned and fled down the road, as a man runs in a nightmare. He ran without purpose or reason. His numbed brain was incapable of conscious thought. He merely obeyed the blind primitive urge to run—run—run until he fell exhausted.

The black walls of the pines flowed endlessly past him; so he was seized with the illusion that he was getting nowhere. But presently a sound penetrated the fog of his terror—the steady, inexorable patter of feet behind him. Turning his head, he saw something loping after him—wolf or dog, he could not tell which, but its eyes glowed like balls of green fire. With a gasp he increased his speed, reeled around a bend in the road, and heard a horse snort; saw it rear and heard its rider curse; saw the gleam of blue steel in the man's lifted hand.

He staggered and fell, catching at the rider's stirrup.

"FOR GOD'S sake, help me!" he panted. "The thing! It killed Branner—it's coming after me! Look!"

Twin balls of fire gleamed in the fringe of bushes at the turn of the road. The rider swore again, and on the heels of his profanity came the smashing report of his six-shooter—again and yet again. The fire-sparks vanished, and the rider, jerking his stirrup free from Griswell's grasp, spurred his horse at the bend. Griswell staggered up, shaking in every limb. The rider was out of sight only a moment; then he came galloping back.

"Took to the brush. Timber wolf, I reckon, though I never heard of one chasin' a man before. Do you know what it was?"

Griswell could only shake his head weakly.

The rider, etched in the moonlight, looked down at him, smoking pistol still lifted in his right hand. He was a compactly-built man of medium height, and his broad-brimmed planter's hat and his boots marked him as a native of the country as definitely as Griswell's garb stamped him as a stranger.

"What's all this about, anyway?"

"I don't know," Griswell answered helplessly. "My name's Griswell. John Branner—my friend who was traveling with me—we stopped at a deserted house back down the road to spend the night. Something—" at the memory he was choked by a rush of horror. "My God!" he screamed. "I must be mad! Something came and looked over the balustrade of the stair—something with a yellow face! I thought I dreamed it, but it must have been real. Then somebody began whistling upstairs, and Branner rose and went up the stairs walking like a man in his sleep, or hypnotized. I heard him scream—or someone screamed; then he came down the stair again with a bloody hatchet in his hand—and my God, sir, he was dead! His head had been split open. I saw brains and clotted blood oozing down his face, and his face was that of a dead man. But he came down the stairs! As God is my witness, John Branner was murdered in that dark upper hallway, and then his dead body came stalking down the stairs with a hatchet in its hand—to kill me!"

The rider made no reply; he sat his horse like a statue, outlined against the stars, and Griswell could not read his expression, his face shadowed by his hat-brim.

"YOU THINK I'm mad," he said hopelessly. "Perhaps I am."

"I don't know what to think," answered the rider. "If it was any house but the old Blassenville Manor—well, we'll see. My name's Buckner. I'm sheriff of this county. Took a prisoner over to the county-seat in the next county and was ridin' back late."

He swung off his horse and stood beside Griswell, shorter than the lanky New Englander, but much harder knit. There was a natural manner of decision and certainty about him, and it was easy to believe that he would be a dangerous man in any sort of a fight.

"Are you afraid to go back to the house?" he asked, and Griswell shuddered, but shook his head, the dogged tenacity of Puritan ancestors asserting itself.

"The thought of facing that horror again turns me sick. But poor Branner—" he choked again. "We must find his body. My God!" he cried, unmanned by the abysmal horror of the thing; "what will we find? If a dead man walks, what—"

"We'll see." The sheriff caught the reins in the crook of his left elbow and began filling the empty chambers of his big blue pistol as they walked along.

As they made the turn Griswell's blood was ice at the thought of what they might see lumbering up the road with a bloody, grinning death-mask, but they saw only the house looming spectrally among the pines, down the road. A strong shudder shook Griswell.

"God, how evil that house looks, against those black pines! It looked sinister from the very first—when we went up the broken walk and saw those pigeons fly up from the porch—"

"Pigeons?" Buckner cast him a quick glance. "You saw the pigeons?"

"Why, yes! Scores of them perching on the porch railing."

They strode on for a moment in silence, before Buckner said abruptly: "I've lived in this country all my life. I've passed the old Blassenville place a thousand times, I reckon, at all hours of the day and night. But I never saw a pigeon anywhere around it, or anywhere else in these woods."

"There were scores of them," repeated Griswell, bewildered.

"I've seen men who swore they'd seen a flock of pigeons perched along the balusters just at sundown," said Buckner slowly. "Negroes, all of them except one man. A tramp. He was buildin' a fire in the yard, aimin' to camp there that night. I passed along there about dark, and he told me about the pigeons. I came back by there the next mornin'. The ashes of his fire were there, and his tin cup, and skillet where he'd fried pork, and his blankets looked like they'd been slept in. Nobody ever saw him again. That was twelve years ago. The blacks say they can see the pigeons, but no black would pass along this road between sundown and sunup. They say the pigeons are the souls of the Blassenvilles, let out of hell at sunset. The Negroes say the red glare in the west is the light from hell, because then the gates of hell are open, and the Blassenvilles fly out."

"Who were the Blassenvilles?" asked Griswell, shivering.

"They owned all this land here. French-English family. Came here from the West Indies before the Louisiana Purchase. The Civil War ruined them, like it did so many. Some were killed in the War; most of the others died out. Nobody's lived in the Manor since 1890 when Miss Elizabeth Blassenville, the last of the line, fled from the old house one night like it was a plague spot, and never came back to it—this your auto?"

They halted beside the car, and Griswell stared morbidly at the grim house. Its dusty panes were empty and blank; but they did not seem blind to him. It seemed to him that ghastly eyes were fixed hungrily on him through those darkened panes. Buckner repeated his question.

"Yes. Be careful. There's a snake on the seat—or there was."

"Not there now," grunted Buckner, tying his horse and pulling an electric torch out of the saddle-bag. "Well, let's have a look."

He strode up the broken brick walk as matter-of-factly as if he were paying a social call on friends. Griswell followed close at his heels, his heart pounding suffocatingly. A scent of decay and moldering vegetation blew on the faint wind, and Griswell grew faint with nausea, that rose from a frantic abhorrence of these black woods, these ancient plantation houses that hid forgotten secrets of slavery and bloody pride and mysterious intrigues. He had thought of the South as a sunny, lazy land washed by soft breezes laden with spice and warm blossoms, where life ran tranquilly to the rhythm of black folk singing in sunbathed cotton fields. But now he had discovered another, unsuspected side—a dark, brooding, fear-haunted side, and the discovery repelled him.

The oaken door sagged as it had before. The blackness of the interior was intensified by the beam of Buckner's light playing on the sill. That beam sliced through the darkness of the hallway and roved up the stair, and Griswell held his breath, clenching his fists. But no shape of lunacy leered down at them. Buckner went in, walking light as a cat, torch in one hand, gun in the other.

As he swung his light into the room across from the stairway, Griswell cried out—and cried out again, almost fainting with the intolerable sickness at what he saw. A trail of blood drops led across the floor, crossing the blankets Branner had occupied, which lay between the door and those in which Griswell had lain. And Griswell's blankets had a terrible occupant. John Branner lay there, face down, his cleft head revealed in merciless clarity in the steady light. His outstretched hand still gripped the haft of a hatchet, and the blade was imbedded deep in the blanket and the floor beneath, just where Griswell's head had lain when he slept there.

A momentary rush of blackness engulfed Griswell. He was not aware that he staggered, or that Buckner caught him. When he could see and hear again, he was violently sick and hung his head against the mantel, retching miserably.

Buckner turned the light full on him, making him blink. Buckner's voice came from behind the blinding radiance, the man himself unseen.

"Griswell, you've told me a yarn that's hard to believe. I saw something chasin' you, but it might have been a timber wolf, or a mad dog.

"If you're holdin' back anything, you better spill it. What you told me won't hold up in any court. You're bound to be accused of killin' your partner. I'll have to arrest you. If you'll give me the straight goods now, it'll make it easier. Now, didn't you kill this fellow, Branner?

"Wasn't it something like this: you quarreled, he grabbed a hatchet and swung at you, but you dodged and then let him have it?"

Griswell sank down and hid his face in his hands, his head swimming.

"Great God, man, I didn't murder John! Why, we've been friends ever since we were children in school together. I've told you the truth. I don't blame you for not believing me. But God help me, it is the truth!"

The light swung back to the gory head again, and Griswell closed his eyes.

He heard Buckner grunt.

"I believe this hatchet in his hand is the one he was killed with. Blood and brains plastered on the blade, and hairs stickin' to it—hairs exactly the same color as his. This makes it tough for you, Griswell."

"How so?" the New Englander asked dully.

"Knocks any plea of self-defense in the head. Branner couldn't have swung at you with this hatchet after you split his skull with it. You must have pulled the ax out of his head, stuck it into the floor and clamped his fingers on it to make it look like he'd attacked you. And it would have been damned clever—if you'd used another hatchet."

"But I didn't kill him," groaned Griswell. "I have no intention of pleading self-defense."

"That's what puzzles me," Buckner admitted frankly, straightening. "What murderer would rig up such a crazy story as you've told me, to prove his innocence? Average killer would have told a logical yarn, at least. Hmmm! Blood drops leadin' from the door. The body was dragged— no, couldn't have been dragged. The floor isn't smeared. You must have carried it here, after killin' him in some other place. But in that case, why isn't there any blood on your clothes? Of course you could have changed clothes and washed your hands. But the fellow hasn't been dead long."

"He walked downstairs and across the room," said Griswell hopelessly. "He came to kill me. I knew he was coming to kill me when I saw him lurching down the stair. He struck where I would have been, if I hadn't awakened. That window—I burst out at it. You see it's broken."

"I see. But if he walked then, why isn't he walkin' now?"

"I don't know! I'm too sick to think straight. I've been fearing that he'd rise up from the floor where he lies and come at me again. When I heard that wolf running up the road after me, I thought it was John chasing me—John, running through the night with his bloody ax and his bloody head, and his death-grin!"

His teeth chattered as he lived that horror over again.

Buckner let his light play across the floor.

"The blood drops lead into the hall. Come on. We'll follow them."

Griswell cringed. "They lead upstairs."

Buckner's eyes were fixed hard on him.

"Are you afraid to go upstairs, with me?"

Griswell's face was gray.

"Yes. But I'm going, with you or without you. The thing that killed poor John may still be hiding up there."

"Stay behind me," ordered Buckner. "If anything jumps us, I'll take care of it. But for your own sake, I warn you that I shoot quicker than a cat jumps, and I don't often miss. If you've got any ideas of layin' me out from behind, forget them."

"Don't be a fool!" Resentment got the better of his apprehension, and this outburst seemed to reassure Buckner more than any of his protestations of innocence.

"I want to be fair," he said quietly. "I haven't indicted and condemned you in my mind already. If only half of what you're tellin' me is the truth, you've been through a hell of an experience, and I don't want to be too hard on you. But you can see how hard it is for me to believe all you've told me."

Griswell wearily motioned for him to lead the way, unspeaking. They went out into the hall, paused at the landing. A thin string of crimson drops, distinct in the thick dust, led up the steps.

"Man's tracks in the dust," grunted Buckner. "Go slow. I've got to be sure of what I see, because we're obliteratin' them as we go up. Hmmm! One set goin' up, one comin' down. Same man. Not your tracks. Branner was a bigger man than you are. Blood drops all the way—blood on the bannisters like a man had laid his bloody hand there—a smear of stuff that looks—brains. Now what—"

"HE WALKED down the stair, a dead man," shuddered Griswell. "Groping with one hand—the other gripping the hatchet that killed him."

"Or was carried," muttered the sheriff. "But if somebody carried him— where are the tracks?"

They came out into the upper hallway, a vast, empty space of dust and shadows where time-crusted windows repelled the moonlight and the ring of Buckner's torch seemed inadequate. Griswell trembled like a leaf. Here, in darkness and horror, John Branner had died.

"Somebody whistled up here," he muttered. "John came, as if he were being called."

Buckner's eyes were blazing strangely in the light.

"The footprints lead down the hall," he muttered. "Same as on the stair—one set going, one coming. Same prints—Judas!"

Behind him Griswell stifled a cry, for he had seen what prompted Buckner's exclamation. A few feet from the head of the stair Branner's footprints stopped abruptly, then returned, treading almost in the other tracks. And where the trail halted there was a great splash of blood on the dusty floor—and other tracks met it—tracks of bare feet, narrow but with splayed toes. They too receded in a second line from the spot.

Buckner bent over them, swearing.

"The tracks meet! And where they meet there's blood and brains on the floor! Branner must have been killed on that spot—with a blow from a hatchet. Bare feet coming out of the darkness to meet shod feet—then both turned away again; the shod feet went downstairs, the bare feet went back down the hall." He directed his light down the hall. The footprints faded into darkness, beyond the reach of the beam. On either hand the closed doors of chambers were cryptic portals of mystery.

"Suppose your crazy tale was true," Buckner muttered, half to himself. "These aren't your tracks. They look like a woman's. Suppose somebody did whistle, and Branner went upstairs to investigate. Suppose somebody met him here in the dark and split his head. The signs and tracks would have been, in that case, just as they really are. But if that's so, why isn't Branner lyin' here where he was killed? Could he have lived long enough to take the hatchet away from whoever killed him, and stagger downstairs with it?"

"No, no!" Recollection gagged Griswell. "I saw him on the stair. He was dead. No man could live a minute after receiving such a wound."

"I believe it," muttered Buckner. "But—it's madness! Or else it's too clever—yet, what sane man would think up and work out such an elaborate and utterly insane plan to escape punishment for murder, when a simple plea of self-defense would have been so much more effective? No court would recognize that story. Well, let's follow these other tracks. They lead down the hall—here, what's this?"

With an icy clutch at his soul, Griswell saw the light was beginning to grow dim.

"This battery is new," muttered Buckner, and for the first time Griswell caught an edge of fear in his voice. "Come on—out of here quick!"

The light had faded to a faint red glow. The darkness seemed straining into them, creeping with black cat-feet. Buckner retreated, pushing Griswell stumbling behind him as he walked backward, pistol cocked and lifted, down the dark hall. In the growing darkness Griswell heard what sounded like the stealthy opening of a door. And suddenly the blackness about them was vibrant with menace. Griswell knew Buckner sensed it as well as he, for the sheriff's hard body was tense and taut as a stalking panther's.

But without haste he worked his way to the stair and backed down it, Griswell preceding him, and fighting the panic that urged him to scream and burst into mad flight. A ghastly thought brought icy sweat out on his flesh. Suppose the dead man were creeping up the stair behind them in the dark, face frozen in the death-grin, blood-caked hatchet lifted to strike?

This possibility so overpowered him that he was scarcely aware when his feet struck the level of the lower hallway, and he was only then aware that the light had grown brighter as they descended, until it now gleamed with its full power—but when Buckner turned it back up the stairway, it failed to illuminate the darkness that hung like a tangible fog at the head of the stair.

"THE DAMN thing was conjured," muttered Buckner. "Nothin' else. It couldn't act like that naturally."

"Turn the light into the room," begged Griswell. "See if John—if John is—"

He could not put the ghastly thought into words, but Buckner understood.

He swung the beam around, and Griswell had never dreamed that the sight of the gory body of a murdered man could bring such relief.

"He's still there," grunted Buckner. "If he walked after he was killed, he hasn't walked since. But that thing—"

Again he turned the light up the stair, and stood chewing his lip and scowling. Three times he half lifted his gun. Griswell read his mind.

The sheriff was tempted to plunge back up that stair, take his chance with the unknown. But common sense held him back.

"I wouldn't have a chance in the dark," he muttered. "And I've got a hunch the light would go out again."

He turned and faced Griswell squarely.

"There's no use dodgin' the question. There's somethin' hellish in this house, and I believe I have an inklin' of what it is. I don't believe you killed Branner. Whatever killed him is up there—now. There's a lot about your yarn that don't sound sane; but there's nothin' sane about a flashlight goin' out like this one did. I don't believe that thing upstairs is human. I never met anything I was afraid to tackle in the dark before, but I'm not goin' up there until daylight. It's not long until dawn. We'll wait for it out there on that gallery."

The stars were already paling when they came out on the broad porch. Buckner seated himself on the balustrade, facing the door, his pistol dangling in his fingers. Griswell sat down near him and leaned back against a crumbling pillar. He shut his eyes, grateful for the faint breeze that seemed to cool his throbbing brain. He experienced a dull sense of unreality. He was a stranger in a strange land, a land that had become suddenly imbued with black horror. The shadow of the noose hovered above him, and in that dark house lay John Branner, with his butchered head—like the figments of a dream these facts spun and eddied in his brain until all merged in a gray twilight as sleep came uninvited to his weary soul.

He awoke to a cold white dawn and full memory of the horrors of the night. Mists curled about the stems of the pines, crawled in smoky wisps up the broken walk. Buckner was shaking him.

"Wake up! It's daylight."

Griswell rose, wincing at the stiffness of his limbs. His face was gray and old.

"I'm ready. Let's go upstairs."

"I've already been!" Buckner's eyes burned in the early dawn. "I didn't wake you up. I went as soon as it was light. I found nothin'."

"The tracks of the bare feet—"

"Gone!"

"Gone?"

"Yes, gone! The dust had been disturbed all over the hall, from the point where Branner's tracks ended; swept into corners. No chance of trackin' anything there now. Something obliterated those tracks while we sat here, and I didn't hear a sound. I've gone through the whole house. Not a sign of anything."

Griswell shuddered at the thought of himself sleeping alone on the porch while Buckner conducted his exploration.

"What shall we do?" he asked listlessly. "With those tracks gone there goes my only chance of proving my story."

"We'll take Branner's body into the county-seat," answered Buckner. "Let me do the talkin'. If the authorities knew the facts as they appear, they'd insist on you being confined and indicted. I don't believe you killed Branner—but neither a district attorney, judge nor jury would believe what you told me, or what happened to us last night. I'm handlin' this thing my own way. I'm not goin' to arrest you until I've exhausted every other possibility.

"Say nothin' about what's happened here, when we get to town. I'll simply tell the district attorney that John Branner was killed by a party or parties unknown, and that I'm workin' on the case.

"ARE YOU game to come back with me to this house and spend the night here, sleepin' in that room as you and Branner slept last night?"

Griswell went white, but answered as stoutly as his ancestors might have expressed their determination to hold their cabins in the teeth of the Pequots: "I'll do it."

"Let's go then; help me pack the body out to your auto."

Griswell's soul revolted at the sight of John Branner's bloodless face in the chill white dawn, and the feel of his clammy flesh. The gray fog wrapped wispy tentacles about their feet as they carried their grisly burden across the lawn.

Chapter 2: The Snake's Brother

AGAIN THE shadows were lengthening over the pinelands, and again two men came bumping along the old road in a car with a New England license plate.

Buckner was driving. Griswell's nerves were too shattered for him to trust himself at the wheel. He looked gaunt and haggard, and his face was still pallid. The strain of the day spent at the county-seat was added to the horror that still rode his soul like the shadow of a black-winged vulture. He had not slept, had not tasted what he had eaten.

"I told you I'd tell you about the Blassenvilles," said Buckner. "They were proud folks, haughty, and pretty damn ruthless when they wanted their way. They didn't treat their slaves as well as the other planters did—got their ideas in the West Indies, I reckon. There was a streak of cruelty in them—especially Miss Celia, the last one of the family to come to these parts. That was long after the slaves had been freed, but she used to whip her mulatto maid just like she was a slave, the old folks say... . The Negroes said when a Blassenville died, the devil was always waitin' for him out in the black pines.

"Well, after the Civil War they died off pretty fast, livin' in poverty on the plantation, which was allowed to go to ruin. Finally only four girls were left, sisters, livin' in the old house and ekin' out a bare livin', with a few blacks livin' in the old slave huts and workin' the fields on the share. They kept to themselves, bein' proud, and ashamed of their poverty. Folks wouldn't see them for months at a time. When they needed supplies they sent a Negro to town after them.

"But folks knew about it when Miss Celia came to live with them. She came from somewhere in the West Indies, where the whole family originally had its roots—a fine, handsome woman, they say, in the early thirties. But she didn't mix with folks any more than the girls did. She brought a mulatto maid with her, and the Blassenville cruelty cropped out in her treatment of this maid. I knew an old man years ago, who swore he saw Miss Celia tie this girl up to a tree, stark naked, and whip her with a horsewhip. Nobody was surprised when she disappeared. Everybody figured she'd run away, of course.

"Well, one day in the spring of 1890 Miss Elizabeth, the youngest girl, came in to town for the first time in maybe a year. She came after supplies. Said the blacks had all left the place. Talked a little more, too, a bit wild. Said Miss Celia had gone, without leaving any word. Said her sisters thought she'd gone back to the West Indies, but she believed her aunt was still in the house. She didn't say what she meant. Just got her supplies and pulled out for the Manor.

"A month went past, and a black came into town and said that Miss Elizabeth was livin' at the Manor alone. Said her three sisters weren't there any more, that they'd left one by one without givin' any word or explanation. She didn't know where they'd gone, and was afraid to stay there alone, but didn't know where else to go. She'd never known anything but the Manor, and had neither relatives nor friends. But she was in mortal terror of something. The black said she locked herself in her room at night and kept candles burnin' all night... .

"It was a stormy spring night when Miss Elizabeth came tearin' into town on the one horse she owned, nearly dead from fright. She fell from her horse in the square; when she could talk she said she'd found a secret room in the Manor that had been forgotten for a hundred years. And she said that there she found her three sisters, dead, and hangin' by their necks from the ceilin'. She said something chased her and nearly brained her with an ax as she ran out the front door, but somehow she got to the horse and got away. She was nearly crazy with fear, and didn't know what it was that chased her—said it looked like a woman with a yellow face.

"About a hundred men rode out there, right away. They searched the house from top to bottom, but they didn't find any secret room, or the remains of the sisters. But they did find a hatchet stickin' in the doorjamb downstairs, with some of Miss Elizabeth's hairs stuck on it, just as she'd said. She wouldn't go back there and show them how to find the secret door; almost went crazy when they suggested it.

"When she was able to travel, the people made up some money and loaned it to her—she was still too proud to accept charity—and she went to California. She never came back, but later it was learned, when she sent back to repay the money they'd loaned her, that she'd married out there.

"Nobody ever bought the house. It stood there just as she'd left it, and as the years passed folks stole all the furnishings out of it, poor white trash, I reckon. A Negro wouldn't go about it. But they came after sunup and left long before sundown."

"What did the people think about Miss Elizabeth's story?" asked Griswell.

"Well, most folks thought she'd gone a little crazy, livin' in that old house alone. But some people believed that mulatto girl, Joan, didn't run away, after all. They believed she'd hidden in the woods, and glutted her hatred of the Blassenvilles by murderin' Miss Celia and the three girls. They beat up the woods with bloodhounds, but never found a trace of her. If there was a secret room in the house, she might have been hidin' there—if there was anything to that theory."

"She couldn't have been hiding there all these years," muttered Griswell. "Anyway, the thing in the house now isn't human."

Buckner wrenched the wheel around and turned into a dim trace that left the main road and meandered off through the pines.

"Where are you going?"

"There's an old Negro that lives off this way a few miles. I want to talk to him. We're up against something that takes more than white man's sense. The black people know more than we do about some things. This old man is nearly a hundred years old. His master educated him when he was a boy, and after he was freed he traveled more extensively than most white men do. They say he's a voodoo man."

Griswell shivered at the phrase, staring uneasily at the green forest walls that shut them in. The scent of the pines was mingled with the odors of unfamiliar plants and blossoms. But underlying all was a reek of rot and decay. Again a sick abhorrence of these dark mysterious woodlands almost overpowered him.

"Voodoo!" he muttered. "I'd forgotten about that—I never could think of black magic in connection with the South. To me witchcraft was always associated with old crooked streets in waterfront towns, overhung by gabled roofs that were old when they were hanging witches in Salem; dark musty alleys where black cats and other things might steal at night. Witchcraft always meant the old towns of New England, to me—but all this is more terrible than any New England legend—these somber pines, old deserted houses, lost plantations, mysterious black people, old tales of madness and horror—God, what frightful, ancient terrors there are on this continent fools call 'young'!"

"Here's old Jacob's hut," announced Buckner, bringing the automobile to a halt.

Griswell saw a clearing and a small cabin squatting under the shadows of the huge trees. The pines gave way to oaks and cypresses, bearded with gray trailing moss, and behind the cabin lay the edge of a swamp that ran away under the dimness of the trees, choked with rank vegetation. A thin wisp of blue smoke curled up from the stick-and-mud chimney.

He followed Buckner to the tiny stoop, where the sheriff pushed open the leather-hinged door and strode in. Griswell blinked in the comparative dimness of the interior. A single small window let in a little daylight. An old Negro crouched beside the hearth, watching a pot stew over the open fire. He looked up as they entered, but did not rise. He seemed incredibly old. His face was a mass of wrinkles, and his eyes, dark and vital, were filmed momentarily at times as if his mind wandered.

Buckner motioned Griswell to sit down in a string-bottomed chair, and himself took a rudely-made bench near the hearth, facing the old man.

"Jacob," he said bluntly, "the time's come for you to talk. I know you know the secret of Blassenville Manor. I've never questioned you about it, because it wasn't in my line. But a man was murdered there last night, and this man here may hang for it, unless you tell me what haunts that old house of the Blassenvilles."

The old man's eyes gleamed, then grew misty as if clouds of extreme age drifted across his brittle mind.

"The Blassenvilles," he murmured, and his voice was mellow and rich, his speech not the patois of the piney woods darky. "They were proud people, sirs—proud and cruel. Some died in the war, some were killed in duels—the menfolks, sirs. Some died in the Manor—the old Manor—" His voice trailed off into unintelligible mumblings.

"What of the Manor?" asked Buckner patiently.

"Miss Celia was the proudest of them all," the old man muttered. "The proudest and the cruelest. The black people hated her; Joan most of all. Joan had white blood in her, and she was proud, too. Miss Celia whipped her like a slave."

"What is the secret of Blassenville Manor?" persisted Buckner.

The film faded from the old man's eyes; they were dark as moonlit wells.

"What secret, sir? I do not understand."

"Yes, you do. For years that old house has stood there with its mystery. You know the key to its riddle."

The old man stirred the stew. He seemed perfectly rational now.

"Sir, life is sweet, even to an old black man."

"You mean somebody would kill you if you told me?"

But the old man was mumbling again, his eyes clouded.

"Not somebody. No human. No human being. The black gods of the swamps. My secret is inviolate, guarded by the Big Serpent, the god above all gods. He would send a little brother to kiss me with his cold lips—a little brother with a white crescent moon on his head. I sold my soul to the Big Serpent when he made me maker of zuvembies —"

Buckner stiffened.

"I heard that word once before," he said softly, "from the lips of a dying black man, when I was a child. What does it mean?"

Fear filled the eyes of old Jacob.

"What have I said? No—no! I said nothing."

"Zuvembies," prompted Buckner.

"Zuvembies," mechanically repeated the old man, his eyes vacant. "A zuvembie was once a woman—on the Slave Coast they know of them. The drums that whisper by night in the hills of Haiti tell of them. The makers of zuvembies are honored of the people of Damballah. It is death to speak of it to a white man—it is one of the Snake God's forbidden secrets."

"You speak of the zuvembies," said Buckner softly.

"I must not speak of it," mumbled the old man, and Griswell realized that he was thinking aloud, too far gone in his dotage to be aware that he was speaking at all. "No white man must know that I danced in the Black Ceremony of the voodoo, and was made a maker of zombies and zuvembies. The Big Snake punishes loose tongues with death."

"A zuvembie is a woman?" prompted Buckner.

"Was a woman," the old Negro muttered. "She knew I was a maker of zuvembies—she came and stood in my hut and asked for the awful brew—the brew of ground snake-bones, and the blood of vampire bats, and the dew from a nighthawk's wings, and other elements unnamable. She had danced in the Black Ceremony—she was ripe to become a zuvembie—the Black Brew was all that was needed—the other was beautiful—I could not refuse her."

"Who?" demanded Buckner tensely, but the old man's head was sunk on his withered breast, and he did not reply. He seemed to slumber as he sat. Buckner shook him. "You gave a brew to make a woman a zuvembie—what is a zuvembie?"

The old man stirred resentfully and muttered drowsily.

"A zuvembie is no longer human. It knows neither relatives nor friends. It is one with the people of the Black World. It commands the natural demons—owls, bats, snakes and werewolves, and can fetch darkness to blot out a little light. It can be slain by lead or steel, but unless it is slain thus, it lives forever, and it eats no such food as humans eat. It dwells like a bat in a cave or an old house. Time means naught to the zuvembie; an hour, a day, a year, all is one. It cannot speak human words, nor think as a human thinks, but it can hypnotize the living by the sound of its voice, and when it slays a man, it can command his lifeless body until the flesh is cold. As long as the blood flows, the corpse is its slave. Its pleasure lies in the slaughter of human beings."

"And why should one become a zuvembie?" asked Buckner softly.

"Hate," whispered the old man. "Hate! Revenge!"

"Was her name Joan?" murmured Buckner.

It was as if the name penetrated the fogs of senility that clouded the voodoo-man's mind. He shook himself and the film faded from his eyes, leaving them hard and gleaming as wet black marble.

"Joan?" he said slowly. "I have not heard that name for the span of a generation. I seem to have been sleeping, gentlemen; I do not remember—I ask your pardon. Old men fall asleep before the fire, like old dogs. You asked me of Blassenville Manor? Sir, if I were to tell you why I cannot answer you, you would deem it mere superstition. Yet the white man's God be my witness—"

As he spoke he was reaching across the hearth for a piece of firewood, groping among the heaps of sticks there. And his voice broke in a scream, as he jerked back his arm convulsively. And a horrible, thrashing, trailing thing came with it. Around the voodoo-man's arm a mottled length of that shape was wrapped, and a wicked wedge-shaped head struck again in silent fury.

The old man fell on the hearth, screaming, upsetting the simmering pot and scattering the embers, and then Buckner caught up a billet of firewood and crushed that flat head. Cursing, he kicked aside the knotting, twisting trunk, glaring briefly at the mangled head. Old Jacob had ceased screaming and writhing; he lay still, staring glassily upward.

"Dead?" whispered Griswell.

"Dead as Judas Iscariot," snapped Buckner, frowning at the twitching reptile. "That infernal snake crammed enough poison into his veins to kill a dozen men his age. But I think it was the shock and fright that killed him."

"What shall we do?" asked Griswell, shivering.

"Leave the body on that bunk. Nothin' can hurt it, if we bolt the door so the wild hogs can't get in, or any cat. We'll carry it into town tomorrow. We've got work to do tonight. Let's get goin'."

Griswell shrank from touching the corpse, but he helped Buckner lift it on the rude bunk, and then stumbled hastily out of the hut. The sun was hovering above the horizon, visible in dazzling red flame through the black stems of the trees.

They climbed into the car in silence, and went bumping back along the stumpy train.

"He said the Big Snake would send one of his brothers," muttered Griswell.

"Nonsense!" snorted Buckner. "Snakes like warmth, and that swamp is full of them. It crawled in and coiled up among that firewood. Old Jacob disturbed it, and it bit him. Nothin' supernatural about that." After a short silence he said, in a different voice, "That was the first time I ever saw a rattler strike without singin'; and the first time I ever saw a snake with a white crescent moon on its head."

They were turning in to the main road before either spoke again.

"You think that the mulatto Joan has skulked in the house all these years?" Griswell asked.

"You heard what old Jacob said," answered Buckner grimly. "Time means nothin' to a zuvembie."

As they made the last turn in the road, Griswell braced himself against the sight of Blassenville Manor looming black against the red sunset. When it came into view he bit his lip to keep from shrieking. The suggestion of cryptic horror came back in all its power.

"Look!" he whispered from dry lips as they came to a halt beside the road. Buckner grunted.

From the balustrades of the gallery rose a whirling cloud of pigeons that swept away into the sunset, black against the lurid glare …

Chapter 3: The Call of Zuvembie

BOTH MEN sat rigid for a few moments after the pigeons had flown.

"Well, I've seen them at last," muttered Buckner.

"Only the doomed see them perhaps," whispered Griswell. "That tramp saw them—"

"Well, we'll see," returned the Southerner tranquilly, as he climbed out of the car, but Griswell noticed him unconsciously hitch forward his scabbarded gun.

The oaken door sagged on broken hinges. Their feet echoed on the broken brick walk. The blind windows reflected the sunset in sheets of flame. As they came into the broad hall Griswell saw the string of black marks that ran across the floor and into the chamber, marking the path of a dead man.

Buckner had brought blankets out of the automobile. He spread them before the fireplace.

"I'll lie next to the door," he said. "You lie where you did last night."

"Shall we light a fire in the grate?" asked Griswell, dreading the thought of the blackness that would cloak the woods when the brief twilight had died.

"No. You've got a flashlight and so have I. We'll lie here in the dark and see what happens. Can you use that gun I gave you?"

"I suppose so. I never fired a revolver, but I know how it's done."

"Well, leave the shootin' to me, if possible." The sheriff seated himself cross-legged on his blankets and emptied the cylinder of his big blue Colt, inspecting each cartridge with a critical eye before he replaced it.

Griswell prowled nervously back and forth, begrudging the slow fading of the light as a miser begrudges the waning of his gold. He leaned with one hand against the mantelpiece, staring down into the dust-covered ashes. The fire that produced those ashes must have been built by Elizabeth Blassenville, more than forty years before. The thought was depressing. Idly he stirred the dusty ashes with his toe. Something came to view among the charred debris—a bit of paper, stained and yellowed. Still idly he bent and drew it out of the ashes. It was a note-book with moldering cardboard backs.

"What have you found?" asked Buckner, squinting down the gleaming barrel of his gun.

"Nothing but an old note-book. Looks like a diary. The pages are covered with writing—but the ink is so faded, and the paper is in such a state of decay that I can't tell much about it. How do you suppose it came in the fireplace, without being burned up?"

"Thrown in long after the fire was out," surmised Buckner. "Probably found and tossed in the fireplace by somebody who was in here stealin' furniture. Likely somebody who couldn't read."

Griswell fluttered the crumbling leaves listlessly, straining his eyes in the fading light over the yellowed scrawls. Then he stiffened.

"Here's an entry that's legible! Listen!" He read:

"'I know someone is in the house besides myself. I can hear someone prowling about at night when the sun has set and the pines are black outside. Often in the night I hear it fumbling at my door. Who is it? Is it one of my sisters? Is it Aunt Celia? If it is either of these, why does she steal so subtly about the house? Why does she tug at my door, and glide away when I call to her? Shall I open the door and go out to her? No, no! I dare not! I am afraid. Oh God, what shall I do? I dare not stay here—but where am I to go?'"

"By God!" ejaculated Buckner. "That must be Elizabeth Blassenville's diary! Go on!"

"I can't make out the rest of the page," answered Griswell. "But a few pages further on I can make out some lines." He read:

"'Why did the Negroes all run away when Aunt Celia disappeared? My sisters are dead. I know they are dead. I seem to sense that they died horribly, in fear and agony. But why? Why? If someone murdered Aunt Celia, why should that person murder my poor sisters? They were always kind to the black people. Joan—'" He paused, scowling futilely.

"A piece of the page is torn out. Here's another entry under another date—at least I judge it's a date; I can't make it out for sure.

"'—the awful thing that the old Negress hinted at? She named Jacob Blount, and Joan, but she would not speak plainly; perhaps she feared to—' Part of it gone here; then: 'No, no! How can it be? She is dead—or gone away. Yet—she was born and raised in the West Indies, and from hints she let fall in the past, I know she delved into the mysteries of the voodoo. I believe she even danced in one of their horrible ceremonies—how could she have been such a beast? And this—this horror. God, can such things be? I know not what to think. If it is she who roams the house at night, who fumbles at my door, who whistles so weirdly and sweetly—no, no, I must be going mad. If I stay here alone I shall die as hideously as my sisters must have died. Of that I am convinced.'"

The incoherent chronicle ended as abruptly as it had begun. Griswell was so engrossed in deciphering the scraps that he was not aware that darkness had stolen upon them, hardly aware that Buckner was holding his electric torch for him to read by. Waking from his abstraction he started and darted a quick glance at the black hallway.

"What do you make of it?"

"What I've suspected all the time," answered Buckner. "That mulatto maid Joan turned zuvembie to avenge herself on Miss Celia. Probably hated the whole family as much as she did her mistress. She'd taken part in voodoo ceremonies on her native island until she was 'ripe,' as old Jacob said. All she needed was the Black Brew—he supplied that. She killed Miss Celia and the three older girls, and would have gotten Elizabeth but for chance. She's been lurkin' in this old house all these years, like a snake in a ruin."

"But why should she murder a stranger?"

"You heard what old Jacob said," reminded Buckner. "A zuvembie finds satisfaction in the slaughter of humans. She called Branner up the stair and split his head and stuck the hatchet in his hand, and sent him downstairs to murder you. No court will ever believe that, but if we can produce her body, that will be evidence enough to prove your innocence. My word will be taken, that she murdered Branner. Jacob said a zuvembie could be killed ... in reporting this affair I don't have to be too accurate in detail."

"She came and peered over the balustrade of the stair at us," muttered Griswell. "But why didn't we find her tracks on the stair?"

"Maybe you dreamed it. Maybe a zuvembie can project her spirit—hell! Why try to rationalize something that's outside the bounds of rationality? Let's begin our watch."

"Don't turn out the light!" exclaimed Griswell involuntarily. Then he added: "Of course. Turn it out. We must be in the dark as"—he gagged a bit—"as Branner and I were."

But fear like a physical sickness assailed him when the room was plunged in darkness. He lay trembling and his heart beat so heavily he felt as if he would suffocate.

"The West Indies must be the plague spot of the world," muttered Buckner, a blur on his blankets. "I've heard of zombies. Never knew before what a zuvembie was. Evidently some drug concocted by the voodoo-men to induce madness in women. That doesn't explain the other things, though: the hypnotic powers, the abnormal longevity, the ability to control corpses—no, a zuvembie can't be merely a madwoman. It's a monster, something more and less than a human being, created by the magic that spawns in black swamps and jungles—well, we'll see."

His voice ceased, and in the silence Griswell heard the pounding of his own heart. Outside in the black woods a wolf howled eerily, and owls hooted. Then silence fell again like a black fog.

Griswell forced himself to lie still on his blankets. Time seemed at a standstill. He felt as if he were choking. The suspense was growing unendurable; the effort he made to control his crumbling nerves bathed his limbs in sweat. He clenched his teeth until his jaws ached and almost locked, and the nails of his fingers bit deeply into his palms.

He did not know what he was expecting. The fiend would strike again—but how? Would it be a horrible, sweet whistling, bare feet stealing down the creaking steps, or a sudden hatchet-stroke in the dark? Would it choose him or Buckner? Was Buckner already dead? He could see nothing in the blackness, but he heard the man's steady breathing. The Southerner must have nerves of steel. Or was that Buckner breathing beside him, separated by a narrow strip of darkness? Had the fiend already struck in silence, and taken the sheriff's place, there to lie in ghoulish glee until it was ready to strike?—a thousand hideous fancies assailed Griswell tooth and claw.

He began to feel that he would go mad if he did not leap to his feet, screaming, and burst frenziedly out of that accursed house—not even the fear of the gallows could keep him lying there in the darkness any longer—the rhythm of Buckner's breathing was suddenly broken, and Griswell felt as if a bucket of ice-water had been poured over him. From somewhere above them rose a sound of weird, sweet whistling...

GRISWELL's control snapped, plunging his brain into darkness deeper than the physical blackness which engulfed him. There was a period of absolute blankness, in which a realization of motion was his first sensation of awakening consciousness. He was running, madly, stumbling over an incredibly rough road. All was darkness about him, and he ran blindly. Vaguely he realized that he must have bolted from the house, and fled for perhaps miles before his overwrought brain began to function. He did not care; dying on the gallows for a murder he never committed did not terrify him half as much as the thought of returning to that house of horror. He was overpowered by the urge to run—run—run as he was running now, blindly, until he reached the end of his endurance. The mist had not yet fully lifted from his brain, but he was aware of a dull wonder that he could not see the stars through the black branches. He wished vaguely that he could see where he was going. He believed he must be climbing a hill, and that was strange, for he knew there were no hills within miles of the Manor. Then above and ahead of him a dim glow began.

He scrambled toward it, over ledge-like projections that were more and more taking on a disquieting symmetry. Then he was horror-stricken to realize that a sound was impacting on his ears—a weird mocking whistle. The sound swept the mists away. Why, what was this? Where was he? Awakening and realization came like the stunning stroke of a butcher's maul. He was not fleeing along a road, or climbing a hill; he was mounting a stair. He was still in Blassenville Manor! And he was climbing the stair!

An inhuman scream burst from his lips. Above it the mad whistling rose in a ghoulish piping of demoniac triumph. He tried to stop—to turn back—even to fling himself over the balustrade. His shrieking rang unbearably in his own ears. But his will-power was shattered to bits.

It did not exist. He had no will. He had dropped his flashlight, and he had forgotten the gun in his pocket. He could not command his own body. His legs, moving stiffly, worked like pieces of mechanism detached from his brain, obeying an outside will. Clumping methodically they carried him shrieking up the stair toward the witch-fire glow shimmering above him.

"Buckner!" he screamed. "Buckner! Help, for God's sake!"

His voice strangled in his throat. He had reached the upper landing. He was tottering down the hallway. The whistling sank and ceased, but its impulsion still drove him on. He could not see from what source the dim glow came. It seemed to emanate from no central focus. But he saw a vague figure shambling toward him. It looked like a woman, but no human woman ever walked with that skulking gait, and no human woman ever had that face of horror, that leering yellow blur of lunacy—he tried to scream at the sight of that face, at the glint of keen steel in the uplifted claw-like hand—but his tongue was frozen.

Then something crashed deafeningly behind him; the shadows were split by a tongue of flame which lit a hideous figure falling backward. Hard on the heels of the report rang an inhuman squawk.

In the darkness that followed the flash, Griswell fell to his knees and covered his face with his hands. He did not hear Buckner's voice. The Southerner's hand on his shoulder shook him out of his swoon.

A light in his eyes blinded him. He blinked, shaded his eyes, looked up into Buckner's face, bending at the rim of the circle of light. The sheriff was pale.

"Are you hurt? God, man, are you hurt? There's a butcher knife there on the floor—"

"I'M NOT hurt," mumbled Griswell. "You fired just in time—the fiend! Where is it? Where did it go?"

"Listen!"

Somewhere in the house there sounded a sickening flopping and flapping as of something that thrashed and struggled in its death convulsions.

"Jacob was right," said Buckner grimly. "Lead can kill them. I hit her, all right. Didn't dare use my flashlight, but there was enough light. When that whistlin' started, you almost walked over me gettin' out. I knew you were hypnotized, or whatever it is. I followed you up the stairs. I was right behind you, but crouchin' low so she wouldn't see me, and maybe get away again. I almost waited too long before I fired—but the sight of her almost paralyzed me. Look!"

He flashed his light down the hall, and now it shone bright and clear. And it shone on an aperture gaping in the wall where no door had showed before.

"The secret panel Miss Elizabeth found!" Buckner snapped. "Come on!"

He ran across the hallway and Griswell followed him dazedly. The flopping and thrashing came from beyond that mysterious door, and now the sounds had ceased.

The light revealed a narrow, tunnel-like corridor that evidently led through one of the thick walls. Buckner plunged into it without hesitation.

"Maybe it couldn't think like a human," he muttered, shining his light ahead of him. "But it had sense enough to erase its tracks last night so we couldn't trail it to that point in the wall and maybe find the secret panel. There's a room ahead—the secret room of the Blassenvilles!"

And Griswell cried out: "My God! It's the windowless chamber I saw in my dream, with the three bodies hanging—ahhhhh!"

Buckner's light playing about the circular chamber became suddenly motionless. In that wide ring of light three figures appeared, three dried, shriveled, mummy-like shapes, still clad in the moldering garments of the last century. Their slippers were clear of the floor as they hung by their withered necks from chains suspended from the ceiling.

"The three Blassenville sisters!" muttered Buckner. "Miss Elizabeth wasn't crazy, after all."

"Look!" Griswell could barely make his voice intelligible. "There—over there in the corner!"

The light moved, halted.

"Was that thing a woman once?" whispered Griswell. "God, look at that face, even in death. Look at those claw-like hands, with black talons like those of a beast. Yes, it was human, though—even the rags of an old ballroom gown. Why should a mulatto maid wear such a dress, I wonder?"

"This has been her lair for over forty years," muttered Buckner, brooding over the grinning grisly thing sprawling in the corner. "This clears you, Griswell—a crazy woman with a hatchet—that's all the authorities need to know. God, what a revenge!—what a foul revenge! Yet what a bestial nature she must have had, in the beginnin', to delve into voodoo as she must have done—"

"The mulatto woman?" whispered Griswell, dimly sensing a horror that overshadowed all the rest of the terror.

Buckner shook his head. "We misunderstood old Jacob's maunderin's, and the things Miss Elizabeth wrote—she must have known, but family pride sealed her lips. Griswell, I understand now; the mulatto woman had her revenge, but not as we'd supposed. She didn't drink the Black Brew old Jacob fixed for her. It was for somebody else, to be given secretly in her food, or coffee, no doubt. Then Joan ran away, leavin' the seeds of the hell she'd sowed to grow."

"That—that's not the mulatto woman?" whispered Griswell.

"When I saw her out there in the hallway I knew she was no mulatto. And those distorted features still reflect a family likeness. I've seen her portrait, and I can't be mistaken. There lies the creature that was once Celia Blassenville."

The Man Who Loved a Zombie

By Russell Gray

Chapter 1: Zombie!

MOONLIGHT etched in shadowy outlines the motionless figure seated with its back against a tombstone. At our approach the figure rose suddenly. I heard a rifle cock, saw its muzzle point toward us.

Lou Stamm said, "Take it easy, Edgar. Don't be too quick with that gun."

The rifle lowered. Edgar Blagden came forward to meet us and peered into our faces. The moon was a white ball in a cloudless sky, and in its shimmering radiance, the graveyard seemed to be filled with weird shapes and shadows weaving in and out between the tombstones. And the face of Edgar Blagden was the color of a thing that would inhabit graveyards. There was a dead hopelessness in his eyes, as if he himself were one of the damned.

"Joey Cobb!" he whispered to me. "Why did you come back to Redwell? Didn't you know that this place is accursed? Haven't you heard that here the dead arise and walk among the living?"

"Holly wrote me about it," I answered quietly. "I came here to look after her."

Edgar Blagden laughed harshly. "What can you do? What can any mortal do but wait helplessly until she dies and then wait besides her grave until her body has rotted so that she can no longer be raised from the dead?"

The man sounded mad, but so did everybody else in Redwell. Of course, I didn't believe the fantastic stories I had heard since arriving in Redwell that morning—stories of a strange epidemic which was killing off the inhabitants, and of its victims who arose from their graves, not living but moving like the living.

Redwell was a small farming village isolated from the rest of the world by deep valleys. Few who were born there left it; few visitors came. No trains ran within fifty miles of it, and the single road which led out of the village was not much more than parallel lines of muddy ruts, making the fifty mile trip highly uncomfortable by automobile. Such a community breeds superstition, and this tale of the walking dead was one of the superstitions.

Yet Holly believed the stories, and Holly had spent a number of years at a sophisticated Northern school. And Lou Stamm, who had been my chum since childhood and was the most level-headed fellow I knew, took the stories seriously. He had brought me to the graveyard tonight to show me Edgar Blagden watching over the grave of his young wife, Maria.

Blagden's lonely vigil over the newly-made grave wasn't proof of the stories, of course. But it was proof of the terrifying hold superstition had over the natives.

I said: "Somebody in Redwood must have read something about zombies and it affected his mind and he started to imagine he saw ghosts walking."

Lou Stamm shook his head. "Not ghosts, Joey. I read up on zombies, but only after the first of the rumors started. There's something to it, just as there's something to Voodoo. There are zombies in Haiti, Joey. All my reading has convinced me of that. Intelligent men swear they have seen them. And now I, too, can swear that I have seen them."

"WHAT?" I exploded and stared at Lou. He was no superstitious yokel. He was a writer of national repute who preferred to stay in Redwell because all his tales dealt with the local color and the people of the community.

"Last night," he said in a husky voice, "I came across Gil Strong walking on the road. Gil had died three days before, and shortly after he was buried, he had disappeared from his grave. I met him last night, and if ever I saw a dead man, Gil Strong was dead. And yet he was walking. I tried to talk to him. He didn't answer. He looked at me out of dead eyes. I'm not ashamed to admit it; I became terrified and ran away."

"They'll never get Maria," Blagden mumbled. "I'll stay here till the body rots."

"That's what they do in Haiti," Lou Stamm said. "Relatives watch the grave for days lest a witch doctor turn the corpse into a zombie before it rots. Joey, why couldn't one of the witch doctors have come here from Haiti?"

"Nonsense," I told him. "You would recognize him. There are no Negroes within miles of Redwell. You would even know if a white stranger were around."

Lou nodded. "I thought of that. But why couldn't one of our natives have learned the secrets of Haitian witch doctors?"

There was no answer to that except that his premise was all wrong, that it was impossible to resurrect the dead.

Edgar Blagden had returned to the tombstone over the grave of his wife. He sat there motionless, gun over his knees, like something that was a carved part of the tombstone.

"Let's get out of here," I whispered to Lou. I was not particularly afraid of graveyards, but Lou's words had made me uncomfortable. And the way the moonlight formed flickering shadows which moved about the tombstones kept me glancing about.

On the way back to the road Lou stopped beside an open grave. Dirt was piled around it as if it had been pushed, up from below. The coffin was still in the grave, its lid open.

"That was Gil Strong's grave," Lou said.

"Ghouls," I said. "That's the explanation. And last night you met somebody on the road who resembled Strong. A stranger might have passed through at night."

"The moon was as bright as tonight," Lou argued. "I swear it was Gil Strong."

"Moonlight is deceptive," I told him.

He said nothing. He showed me several other open graves of villagers who had been buried within the last week. Then we were on the road, arguing as we walked. Nothing I said could shake his conviction that somebody in Redwell was turning dead people into zombies, and I confess that as I walked I felt increasingly uneasy. Not that for a moment would I concede to myself that such things as zombies could exist. But if people like Lou Stamm and Holly Boland were frightened, something must be happening.

The only store in Redwell was Will Shelley's general store. Usually the place was crowded with farmers who hung around gossiping and playing checkers. Tonight the place was empty save for Will Shelley. A shotgun lay on the counter—loaded, I was sure. I was at the point of making a crack about dead people being able to die only once, but I looked at his face and decided to keep my mouth shut. Shelley pushed the packs of cigarettes we asked for across the counter and scooped up the money without a word, and Shelley had a reputation of being able to talk any man's head off. He kept looking out into the night and didn't move far from the shotgun.

As we were leaving, the wall phone jangled. We paused in the doorway, knowing somehow that the phone call meant bad news.

"Jane?" Will Shelley said in the mouthpiece. "My God!"

He dropped the receiver, snatched up the shotgun and made for the door. His deeply-lined face was ashen.

I grabbed his arm. "What is it, Will? Can we help?"

"No. Nobody can help. Jane phoned she's sick. It's the epidemic. She'll die and then she'll be made into one of these zombie things!"

He snatched his arm away from me and started running down the road.

"WHAT IN heaven's name is this epidemic?" I demanded. "If Doc Hillhouse can't do anything about it, why not send for doctors who know their business?"

"It's not as simple as that," Lou replied. "There have been epidemics which have stumped the medical profession throughout the world. This may be one of them. Doc Hillhouse is a good man, even though he prefers practicing in Red- well to a big city. He had studied a lot, travelled a great deal, and writes important papers for the medical journals. And he says that there has never been anything like this sickness before. Victims simply sicken and die within two hours. He thinks it is a particularly virulent form of encephalitis, which is an inflammation of the brain."

We were walking back up the road, puffing thoughtfully on our cigarettes.

I said: "And it's the people who died of that who turn into zombies?"

"Well, nobody has died of any other cause since this hellish business started," Lou said. "I see what you're getting at. Whoever resurrects them, kills them off that way first so that their body will be unimpaired. They don't need a brain because zombies can't think, anyway. They can only obey orders."

"Say, don't get me wrong," I protested. "I don't for a moment believe this zombie nonsense."

For a time we walked in silence along the moonlit road. Half a mile away we could make out the two gables of the Boland house which stood on a slight elevation. Holly Boland was there waiting for me. For years we had waited for each other. She had been away to school; I had gone to Chicago to make my way as an engineer. Now my income was big enough to permit us to be married. And as I walked toward her home, I had a feeling that we had not surmounted the last obstacle to our marriage, that this hellish business was part of a scheme of fate or the devil to keep us apart.

Quietly I said: "As soon as it is light I'm going to take Holly away from here."

"Yes," Lou agreed. "I'll take Ivy away, too. We'll leave together in your car." Ivy Boland was Holly's cousin with whom Lou was in love.

A girl dressed in white was coming toward us in the moonlight. As we neared, I looked at her curiously. Why would a girl be walking alone at night when the belief that living-dead things were abroad kept the other villagers locked in their homes?

Lou gasped beside me and I turned my head toward him. He had stopped walking, was gaping at the girl who was now no more than twenty feet from us. His lips were working soundlessly, and then at last his voice came hollowly through them.

"It's Maria Blagden," he said.

I whirled toward the girl. I had known Maria since childhood and that girl looked like Maria—but she couldn't be! Twenty minutes ago I had seen her husband guarding her grave. Lou Stamm and Holly and others had told me of having attended Maria's funeral the day before, of having seen her in her coffin wearing the gown she had been married in. And that girl on the road was wearing a bridal gown!

She moved past us as if we didn't exist. Her eyes swept over us, but they didn't see us.

I leaped toward her, grabbed her arm. "Maria!" I said. "Where are you going?"

At my touch she ceased walking as obediently as if she had been a robot and I had pressed the proper button. I looked into her eyes, and what I saw there hit me with a kind of cold, clammy physical impact. Because they were the eyes of a dead person. No soul was mirrored in them, no intelligence, no emotion.

"Maria!" I said. "You know me. I'm Joey Cobb."

"My God!" Lou whispered. "Look at her face. It's the face of a corpse. She is a corpse, Joey. She's dead."

And still I couldn't bring myself to believe that the dead could walk. "It's a trick," I cried, and I grasped her by both shoulders and shook her. Her head bobbed back and forth as if on hinges; but her face remained set in that death mask. No word, no human sound, came from her lips. With a thin cry of horror I dropped my hands from her.

Chapter 2: The Walking Dead

A SHRILL whistle came from the side of the road. Maria Blagden turned her head slowly until her eyes were staring in the direction whence the whistle had come. No, her eyes weren't staring. They were simply fixed in that direction, sightless yet seeing, just as she was dead yet living. Then she started to move toward the woods with stiff, mechanical steps.

Perhaps Lou and I should have stopped her. But we were too overcome by horror to do anything but gape incredulously until her white-clad form disappeared among the trees. She was gone for a minute or two before we roused ourselves as from a nightmare.

"You see!" Lou cried. "Now do you believe?"

I didn't answer. Whether or not I believed, I did not know. But I did know that I was more frightened than I had ever been before in my life.

I said: "What happened to Edgar Blagden? He was guarding her grave. We've got to investigate."

Lou nodded and we started back down the road.

We walked quickly, not saying anything, each of us fighting down the reluctance to return to the graveyard. On the way back from the general store we had passed the graveyard a quarter mile down the road. We reached it in a few minutes.

And we found Edgar Blagden still sitting with his bade against the tombstone of his wife's grave and the shotgun across his knees.

He did not rise to meet us. He would never rise again. Or if he did walk the earth once more, he would not be of the living. The grave of his wife, Maria, was open.

I bent over the still form of Edgar Blagden. "Dead," I said in a hollow voice. "Yet there seems to be no mark of violence on him. His shotgun wasn't fired."

Lou tugged impatiently at my sleeve. "Come on, Joey, let's get out of here."

"I suppose we shouldn't take the body with us," I said. "He was murdered and you're not supposed to move a murdered body until the police arrive, or what passes for the police in Redwell. We can phone the constable from the Boland house."

Lou was already in motion. "Yes, yes. But hurry. Whether we leave him or take him with us, it won't make any difference. He'll become a zombie like the others."

We were on the road now, hurrying to the Boland house. Fear for Holly gnawed at me. I must get her out of Redwell as soon as possible. I was no longer debating with myself whether it was possible for the dead to walk. That was no longer important. The fact was that Holly and I and all the rest in Red- well were menaced by something so horrible that the mind could not contemplate it and remain sane.

AS WE neared die white, freshly painted colonial structure, we saw that nearly all the lights were on in the house. There was something comforting about those lights, something that spoke of security and civilization. Holly and her cousin Ivy were waiting for us on the porch. They ran to our arms, and I held Holly's lovely, vibrant form close to me.

"Dr. Hillhouse just phoned," she said in a voice tinged with hysteria. "There's been another victim of the epidemic—Jane Shelley."

"So soon!" I exclaimed. "While we were in the general store, less than half an hour ago, she phoned her husband that she was sick."

"And now she's dead," Ivy wailed. "We'll all die, and, worse, we won't stay dead. What will become of us?"

The door of the house opened and four people came out on the lighted porch. They were Ivy's parents, Cosmo and Dora Boland, Saul Moyer, the village constable, and Henry Yates.

Aside from Yates, Cosmo Boland was the most prosperous individual in Redwell. He was the holder of most of the mortgages on the neighboring farms. Tall, grey-haired, hawk-faced, he had a reputation for utter heartlessness in his business dealings. His wife, on the other hand, was a sweet, plump little bundle of goodness who devoted her energies to the charities made necessary by her husband's ruthlessness.

Henry Yates was a comparative newcomer to Redwell. He was some sort of power in Wall Street and did all his business by telephone. He had built himself a great stone house which looked something like a medieval fortress on a hill overlooking all of Redwell. Here he lived alone with two male servants. He said that he had come to Redwell because he wanted quiet and peace, and he certainly had gotten it—until the last few days.

Saul Moyer, a wizened little man, held the position of constable more as an honor than for any practical reason. There hadn't been a crime in Redwell in ten years, and the little wooden jail was used only as a storage shed for surplus hay. But now he had something to do, and there seemed to be nothing he could do about it.

"Edgar Blagden has been murdered," Lou Stamm exclaimed as soon as the four appeared on the porch. "He was watching his wife's grave. And she, Maria—we met her on the road—a zombie!"

Holly moaned and trembled against me. Everybody started talking at once, and then Moyer's voice shrilled above the others.

"Edgar murdered! Now maybe the State police will do something. I put in a call for them, but all I could tell them was that people were dying of what appeared to be a mysterious sickness. They said what we needed were doctors, not police. Then I told them about the zombies and they laughed at me. Now, by God, they'll have to come."

Slowly Lou Stamm said: "Edgar Blagden was murdered and so were the others who died. Murdered so they could be turned into zombies. But you won't be able to prove that Edgar was murdered. There's no mark on him."

Suddenly Lou straightened up. "He was killed by Voodoo. That's it. The zombie business comes from Haiti and so does Voodoo. Whoever learned the secrets of the Haiti witch doctors of how to resurrect the dead, also learned how to cause people's death by Voodoo curses. They make a tiny figure of the intended victim, molding into it a strand of his hair or a paring from his fingernail. Then they do something like sticking pins into it or throttling it, or perhaps in this case muttering a death-dealing incantation over it, and the victim, however far away, dies."

A HEAVY, choking silence descended on us. Holly clung even more tightly to me. If there were zombies, then there could be Voodoo curses which could kill, and even flight would not save us.

Henry Yates laughed harshly. "I'm surprised at you, Mr. Stamm. A writer, believing these superstitious tales!"

"But I've seen the zombies," Lou protested. "They were dead and now they walk about. And people are dying without cause."

Cosmo Boland cleared his throat noisily. "Whatever the cause of these horrors, we have to take steps to protect our loved ones. I shall take my family away from this place as soon as it is light."

"Right!" I agreed heartily. "I don't believe in zombies and I don't believe in Voodoo curses, but I believe that none of us will be safe if we remain in Redwell."

Saul Moyer said: "My duty is here. Right now I'm going to the graveyard to fetch Edgar Blagden's body and see if I can find out how he died. Will one of you come with me to give me a hand with the body?"

I VOLUNTEERED and reluctantly Lou Stamm offered to come along, too. We went in my car. As I stepped on the starter, I turned to look at Holly standing on the porch. A slight breeze stirred her brown curls. She was all I ever wanted in a woman—lovely to look at and to hold in my arms, and so excitingly alive. She waved her arms and smiled bravely and something happened to my heart as I thought that she might become like Maria Blagden.

It was a very short ride to the graveyard. We said nothing as we made our way between the tombstones. And a hundred feet from the grave where Maria's corpse had lain we stopped suddenly.

Edgar Blagden's body no longer leaned against the tombstone.

With a choked cry I rushed forward. Moyer's and Lou's feet pounded behind me. The open grave was there just as we had left it. But Edgar Blagden's body was gone.

"There he is!" Lou cried.

He pointed to where the trees closed in on the graveyard two hundred feet away. A man—or what had once been a man—was moving slowly in the moonlight. We could see only his back, but there was no mistaking that wiry frame. And we could make out the shotgun he carried under his arm.

"He's dead," I muttered. "I felt for his pulse and there wasn't any. His flesh was cold. He's dead, I tell you. He can't be walking there."

But he was. And as we watched he stepped in among the trees.

"Come on," the constable yelled and started running.

We wanted to go away from that frightful thing, not toward it. Moyer was almost to the trees before Lou and I had regained sufficient self-control to move after him. The moon penetrated eerily through the branches. We tramped about, searching, but we were not too eager. Suppose we did find him—what then?

After ten minutes we gave up the search and returned slowly and silently to my car.

Chapter 3: Hell's Farmers

WE HURRIED back to the Boland house. Holly and her aunt and uncle and cousin were still on the porch; Henry Yates had evidently departed. Lou Stamm, jabbering like a frightened school boy, blurted out our experience.

I said: "There's no sense waiting until tomorrow. Let's leave at once."

"What's the use?" Lou wailed. "Voodoo magic can follow you to the other side of the globe. If any of us are marked for death, there is no way we can escape."

"Shut up, Lou!" I snapped, restraining myself with difficulty from taking a sock at him. "I'm getting the girls and Mr. and Mrs. Boland away from this cursed place at once." I asked Holly: "How soon can all of you be ready?"

Holly turned a strained white face up to me. "Can't we wait until daylight? I feel safer in the house than traveling on that lonely road in the dead of night."

Cosmo Boland said: "I think Holly's right. We'll be safer tonight behind locked doors than in a car on a lonely road."

Well, there was something to that. Henry Yates drove away in his rickety car and the rest of us went into the house and locked every window and put every light on. I whispered to Holly: "I'll be back in a little while; I want to fix some-thing on my car," and slid out of the house.

Outside the house I paused in indecision, then got into my car and started it. As I shoved the gears into first, a white face appeared at the window on my left. I jumped, then said with relief: "Holly, what are you doing here?"

"Don't go, Joey," she pleaded. "There's danger out there."

I tried a laugh, a pretty feeble effort. "But you don't even know where I'm going," I protested.

"You are going to search for the ouanga packets or whatever they are, and destroy them."

"Ouanga packets?" I echoed. "Never even heard of them."

"I've read some of Lou's books on Voodoo. They're the charms made up by Voodoo witch-doctors. Often they are death charms. There is one for each person marked for death, and the only way we can save ourselves is to get hold of the ouanga meant for us and destroy it. Otherwise, one by one, we'll die the way the others have and later we'll be made into zombies."

"Surely you don't believe that?" I scoffed.

Her eyes were wide. "I don't know what to believe. It has to be something like that. Why have so many died so mysteriously ? And you yourself have seen dead people come to life."

My teeth clenched. "I intend to see one of them at close range. I'm sorry we let Maria and Edgar Blagden get away."

"It's dangerous, Joey."

I shrugged. "From the little I know of zombies, they're harmless. And if there is anything to these ouangas, one isn't safe anywhere. Death is induced without violence or any dramatic waylaying in the woods. According to you and Lou, it's done purely through remote control, so no place is less dangerous than any other."

MY TONE was bantering, but when I saw the fear that flitted over her face I felt like kicking myself. Now she wouldn't even think that she was safe behind locked doors. And to try to assure her that this business of ouangas and zombies was the sheerest superstitious nonsense wouldn't have done any good, for it didn't much matter which way death came, whether through sorcery or disease or the machinations of a human fiend.

She moved around to the other side of the car, opened the door and got in beside me. "If the danger is equal everywhere, then I'm going with you."

My protests were futile. Finally I started the car. Perhaps, after all, she would be better off at my side where I could keep an eye on her. I didn't trust anybody. Even Lou Stamm, who had given in all the way to primitive superstition, admitted that a human agency was behind it all. Perhaps it was Lou himself or even Cosmo Boland. Yes, she might be safer with me.

For some time we bumped over the narrow, stony little side roads which branched off the main road to the various farms. Holly sat with one hand gripping the door, her frightened eyes searching the moonlit night. She was afraid that we would find what we had come to look for—and I must confess that to some extent I was, too. I recalled how I had dropped my hands in horror from Maria Blagden's living-dead body. Would I have more courage if I again met her or another like her?

The farmhouses we passed were dark and silent. Well, the farmers went to bed early; but there was something about each house we passed that gave me an impression that it had been uninhabited for a long time. Even the dogs, which always outraged the night with their yelping at the approach of any car, were all silent tonight.

Near a low, freshly painted farmhouse I stopped the car. Lights shone from every window.

"Well, here are signs of life at any rate," I said. "Whose house is that? It was built after my time in Redwell ... Holly, what's the matter?"

A spine-chilling moan had come from her lips. I swung my head toward her. She was staring at that house as if it were a ghost.

"Holly, what is it?"

Her voice came in a thin whisper. "That's Edgar and Maria Blagden's house. They're the only ones who lived there, and they're both dead."

I said: "And you think that Maria and Edgar have returned to live in their home, even though they're not living?"

"Yes, Joey."

"What nonsense!" I said. "They might be in there all right, but I'll wager that they are as much alive as you and I. I'm convinced now that the explanation for all this zombie business is that the dead people weren't really dead."

I threw the door open. Whatever fear had been in me had now given way to anger. Somebody was perpetrating a monstrous hoax on the simple folk of Redwell, and I'd be damned if I'd be taken in by it.

Holly grabbed my arm. "Don't go, Joey. I'm afraid to stay alone."

"Then come with me."

"No."

I cursed myself for having let her accompany me. Alone I could have seen this thing through.

I said: "All right, I'll take you home." In ten minutes time I would return and get to the bottom of the hoax if I had to choke the explanation out of those phony corpses.

The door of the farmhouse flew open and a man appeared carrying a hoe on one shoulder. Even at that distance it was easy to recognize him.

"You see!" I cried triumphantly. "That's Edgar Blagden, there's no mistaking that. By God—" Again I pushed open the door of the car.

"Wait!" Holly wailed. "Look, somebody is coming behind him. Oh, God, that's Maria! She's dead. I saw her dead. I saw her in her coffin and then lowered into her grave. And you said you were sure Edgar was dead!"

I STARED at the house. More people were coming out of the door. Gil Strong who, Lou had told me, had died several days ago. And Jane Shelley who had died earlier that evening, according to Dr. Hillhouse. And three or four others whom I recognized as natives of the village.

Holly was moaning crazily at my side. I threw my arms about her, holding her trembling body in a fierce grip.

"Cut it out, Holly!" I snapped. "There's a reasonable explanation for this. There has to be. I'm going out there and—"

"No!" Holly shrilled. "Look, Joey, they're going out to the tomato field. Each of them has a hoe. You know that zombies are raised from the dead in Haiti to be cheap labor in the fields. Because they're dead they don't get tired and they hardly eat anything. They're zombies and they're going to work the fields just the way they do in Haiti. Oh, God, Joey, I'm going mad!"

I forced myself to slap her sharply across the face. It was the only way I could snap her out of her hysteria. A tremor shook her body; then she subsided in my arms, trembling and weeping.

That dread procession was moving toward the tomato field in single file. They must have seen my car, but they paid no attention to it. Their feet hardly lifted; their shoulders were bowed, they glanced neither to the right nor left but kept their eyes straight in front of them. When they reached the field, they spread out and began to hoe between the rows of tomatoes, their arms rising and falling slowly, automatically, like those of automatons.

Gently I said to Holly; "I'm going out there. It's a hoax, I tell you. It has to be. If we leave here now with the conviction that those people are dead, we'll never sleep another moment in our lives. Don't you see that we have to make sure?"

She lifted her tear-stained face to me. She nodded. "Yes, you're right I'll go with you."

"No. You wait here and lock yourself in the car."

I helped her raise the windows, and when I was sure that all four doors were locked I set out toward the tomato field. I hated to leave her there, but what else could I do? Flight with her would have been easier; but I feared what would come after that. This scene would haunt us forever unless we discovered the truth.

The truth? What was it, really? Suppose I found out that those things in the field were really dead ...

Fear again ran riot within me, though

I forced myself forward, I found myself wishing I had a gun. But if they were dead, what good would a gun be?

Boldly I strode between two rows of tomato vines. None of the workers looked up at me. Their hoes rose and fell as if they would go on doing that forever.

The first one I came to was Gil Strong. "Gil," I said, "stop hoeing."

He obeyed me. His face turned toward me and I wanted to cry out. Those eyes were absolutely empty, lifeless. The features were without character, utterly blank.

The next word I had to force past my throat. "Hoe."

He started to hoe. It was utterly horrible the way he obeyed my commands. I told him to take three steps forward, then three steps back, and he did precisely as I commanded.

Feeling my senses tottering, I went to the next person—or thing. It was Hal Harvey, a local farmer. And he, too, obeyed every word I uttered, and always listlessly, lethargically, as if he were an empty shell in human form which gained whatever strength it had from a hellish outside force.

I ran to the next worker, Maria Blagden. She still wore that white bridal gown which was now ripped and spattered with dirt. I grasped her arm, twisted it almost out of its socket. She made no outcry; no slightest grimace of pain contorted her face.

I felt that I was going mad. "Maria!" I screamed. "I'm hurting you and I'm going to hurt you more. Aren't you afraid?"

She simply stood there.

I slapped her face, dug my nails into her arms. Nearby her husband continued to hoe. He did not even look at what I was doing to his wife. In a frenzy I turned and swung a punch at his jaw and he sprawled among the tomatoes, and lay there until I ordered him to get up. It wasn't a man I had struck. It was something inanimate, which yet had the power of motion when directed to move. It was a thing whose soul had fled and whose brain had died when its body had died.

I went completely berserk. I ran among the creatures, knocking them down, cursing them, sobbing at them. They offered no resistance. I could have tom them apart bit by bit and there would have been no word from them, no gesture of defense.

Perhaps I would have gone truly mad there in the tomato field if a sharp clear voice hadn't called out from the road. "Joey! For God's sake, Joey!"

I whirled. Holly was running toward me. She had seen the whole horrible thing from the car.

"Stay there!" I shouted and raced toward her. Halfway between the field and the car we met.

"Joey, what is it? I saw you fighting with them."

"No, not fighting," I gasped. "Come back to the car."

I didn't want her to get too near to them. It was bad enough that I had seen them at close range.

"They're dead!" she whimpered as we ran to the car. "They're zombies, Joey. You found that out."

"I don't know," I sobbed. "I wish to heaven I did."

Chapter 4: The Death of Holly

LESS THAN an hour later we were fleeing from Redwell.

The story Holly and I had babbled on our return to the Boland house had caused fear to give way to panic. We decided not to wait until daylight, but to leave then. We had nothing to fear from the night or from the zombies, as I had found out. What we had to flee was the menace of becoming zombies ourselves.

The Bolands were throwing clothes into bags while I waited impatiently on the porch. Lou Stamm was with me.

Morbidly Lou said. "You can't escape from Voodoo sorcery, but we might as well try it. It's better than just sitting around and waiting for death and what will follow."

"Once we're out of Redwell we're safe," I yelled at him. "I admit now that I don't know what it's all about, but I'm sure this cursed business is limited to this place. If this thing could spread—why, man, everybody in the nation could be changed into a living-dead creature."

"Yes," Lou said in a strange voice. "That's what I'm afraid of. Oh, I'm afraid for Ivy and myself and the rest of us, but our fate will mean nothing compared to what might happen."

I stared at him. But I no longer laughed at his words. I had seen those things in the field and I was ready to believe anything. I rushed into the house and urged them to hurry.

Holly and I sat in the front seat of my sedan; Ivy and Dora and Cosmo Boland in back. Lou stood with one foot on the running-board.

"Come on in front with us," I said.

He shook his head. "I'm not going. I suppose I ought to be with Ivy, but I can do more good here. Our only chance is to get at the root of the thing, to find out who the witch doctor is and kill him."

Ivy started to wail protests, begging Lou to come with us.

Lou said, "My place is here," and strode off abruptly. I hesitated. Perhaps I should remain behind with him and fight these horrors at their source. But Holly needed me more. I had to get her and her family away from here at all cost.

So I started the car and roared down the rutted road. In almost no time I was doing sixty, although that was no sane speed over so bad a road. We streaked past the graveyard, past the general store. In a couple of minutes we would be outside the boundaries of Redwell.

I skidded around a bend in the road on two wheels—and then I saw the two figures standing motionless in the middle of the road less than a hundred feet away.

Everybody in the car screamed at once. I came down on the brake with all my strength, yet instead of slowing down, the car hurtled forward still fester. I glimpsed the vacant faces and empty staring eyes of the two zombies as they stood there apparently waiting to be mowed down by the car. It did not occur to me that they were dead anyway and that the lives of the five of us in the car were all that mattered. Instinct caused me to swing the wheel.

The car swerved onto the grassy side of the road. We flashed past the zombies, and my breath came back to me as I realized that I had succeeded in avoiding them. But when I tried to swing the car back on the road, nothing happened. The wheel turned in my hand, but the car kept rushing straight ahead.

I saw a tree loom up before us. Frantically I clawed at the useless wheel and I was screaming and cursing and everybody else in the car was screaming and I felt Holly clutching at my sleeve. Then we struck the tree.

My chest went forward against the wheel; then I was sliding down as the car toppled over on its side. The whole car seemed to crash down on my head and I continued falling for a long time, going down and down in a bottomless void.

SUDDENLY I was back in the car and as from a far distance I heard a moan. I drew a breath and agonizing fire stabbed into my chest. Beneath me I felt soft flesh, and all at once complete consciousness flooded back.

It was Holly under me. I yelled her name, tried to draw the weight of my body away from her. Pain shot through the arm with which I tried to lift her and I had to let her limp form sag.

In the back of the car the moaning went on. I twisted my head and Ivy's dead-white face hung a few inches from my own. Her eyes were shut, her lips apparently motionless, but the moan came from her. Above her, pressing into her ribs with one shoulder, was Cosmo Boland. His head hung in a queer, limp position; his neck was broken. Dora Boland was somewhere out of sight in the wreck.

I turned my attention to Holly. In spite of the pain in my chest and arm I fought the door above me open. The car was on its side. I made my way out to the running-board and straddled it. Then I pulled Holly up. How I managed it I do not know. Every motion meant unendurable agony. Finally Holly was half out of the car, half in, with my one good arm holding her up under her armpits. Blood poured down one side of her face, ran down her neck, stained her dress.

I dropped my ear down to her heart, and I cried out with joy as I heard the faint flutter of life.

I continued to pull her up through the door. When she was almost out, her weight became too much for me. I started to go over backward. Weakened with pain, I couldn't hold onto her. Her body slipped from my grip and slid back into the wrecked car. Frantically I groped with my injured arm for support, and the sudden wrenching pain drove me into unconsciousness even before I fell off the running board and hit the ground.

After a while I heard people talking and I mumbled: "Holly, is that you? Holly, somebody tampered with my car and I couldn't get out of the way of the tree. Holly—Holly ..."

I opened my eyes and tried to sit up. Something sharp jabbed into my chest and I fell back on my shoulders.

Dr. Hillhouse was kneeling over me, his lined intelligent face creased with worry. "Take it easy, Joey," he said gently. "I think you have a rib or two broken and you broke your arm, but you'll be all right in no time."

But I was not concerned about myself. "Holly?" I asked. "How is she, Doc?"

His eyes shifted away from mine. I looked past him and saw Henry Yates and Saul Moyer standing behind him. Their eyes turned away from me, and a cold hand closed over my heart.

"Holly!" I shrieked and sat up. There was pain, I suppose, but now I didn't feel it.

"Easy, son," Dr. Hillhouse said, placing a restraining hand on my shoulder. "There's nothing you can do about it. You're lucky you came out of it alive."

I brushed his hand away and stood up. Four bodies were lying on the ground near the wrecked car. The moonlight shone on them—the cruel, white moonlight showing four upturned dead faces. And one of those faces was Holly's!

I stood numb, not feeling anything, not saying anything. Constable Moyer said: "My God, all four Bolands at one clip!" Then there was a silence.

SLOWLY I went toward the bodies and dropped down beside Holly's. My hand dropped to her smooth flesh; it was already cold. In death she was as beautiful as she had ever been in life, except that now there was no color in her face.

I looked up at the three men. "But she can't be dead. She was alive in the car. Ivy was, too. Cosmo Boland was dead and maybe Dora was, but not the girls."

Dr. Hillhouse shook his head. "They might have lived a few minutes. When we got here you were the only one alive."

With my good hand I pulled a handkerchief from my pocket and tenderly wiped the blood from Holly's face. I kissed her. Her lips were like ice.

Then I went to pieces. Ignoring my broken arm, I gathered her lifeless body to me, implored her to speak to me, and raved wildly of vengeance. Moyer and Dr. Hillhouse tore me away from her and led me to the doctor's car and drove me to Moyer's house which was nearest.

While Dr. Hillhouse set my arm and placed it in a splint and bandaged my rib, Moyer and Yates fetched the four bodies in their cars. They laid out the bodies on the floor of a bedroom. And all the time I spoke crazily of vengeance.

"He didn't want us to leave Redwell, whoever is behind these zombies," I said. "He wants to kill everybody in the village so that he can turn them into zombies. I'll find him and kill him. He's the one who did something to the steering wheel and the brakes of my car while I waited for the Bolands to get ready. He had those zombies waiting on the road, knowing that I would try to avoid them and that I wouldn't be able to straighten the wheel out or stop the car. He—"

I stopped talking suddenly. I stood up.

Dr. Hillhouse came toward me. "Sit down, Joey. You'd better lie down for a while. You need plenty of rest."

I went past him toward the door. Dr. Hillhouse tried to stop me and I knocked him down with my good hand. Moyer and Yates went for me. I slammed through the door and started running. As I headed for trees, I heard them behind me, calling for me. It wasn't hard losing them in the woods.

After a while I stopped to rest, then went on again. My broken arm didn't bother me, and my rib, being bandaged, wouldn't be much trouble. Once in college I had played through forty minutes of a savage football game with a broken rib, and nobody, not even myself, had known about it until the game was over.

Anyway, there wasn't room for me to feel pain. There wasn't room for anything but the conviction that I had to kill Lou Stamm.

Chapter 5: Army of the Dead

A LIGHT went on in Lou Stamm's cottage as I approached it. I pushed the door open and strode in. Lou was bringing a lighted match up to a cigarette in his mouth. He looked worn and tired. The match fell from his fingers.

"Joey! What are you doing here? Where are the others?" His eyes fell on my arm in the sling. "What happened to you?"

I went toward him slowly, the fingers of my good hand opened and closing.

"You know," I said hollowly. "You were around the Boland house while I was inside. You tampered with the steer-wheel and brakes of my car. And then you gave us some silly excuse for not coming with us because you knew we were going to our death."

He stared at me. "Where's Ivy? Is she all right?"

"You're not fooling me," I told him. "You followed us to where you had instructed the zombies to stand so that I'd swing the car off the road. Holly and Ivy and maybe Dora Boland were still alive when you got there. You killed them, and you were about to kill me too when the arrival of Moyer and Yates and Doc Hillhouse scared you away."

"Ivy's dead?" he whispered. "No, it can't be true."

I lunged at him, got my hand on his throat and threw all my weight against him. We went down, myself on top. I was bigger than Lou, but I had only one hand and the accident had weakened me. He managed to squirm out from under me, and then he got his knees on my good arm and held me down.

"Joey, for God's sake!" he gasped. "If they're dead I don't blame you for losing your head, but—" His voice broke. "Ivy can't be dead. No!"

"You know she is, damn you!" I spat up at him. "You killed her."

He rose to his feet like a man moving in a dream. His voice came from deep inside of him. "Would I have killed the woman I loved? Does that make sense? I would as soon have killed her as you would have killed Holly!"

Maybe it made sense and maybe it didn't. He knew about zombies and about Voodoo. Once he had started on that diabolical business there was no stopping. Love and all the rest ceased to mean anything ... In a sudden frenzy of hatred I got up and flew at him again. He knocked me into a chair.

"Where are the bodies?" he demanded. "Are they zombies yet?"

"You know they're in Saul Moyer's place," I burst out, and for the third time I threw myself at him. It struck me suddenly that I had to keep him from going to their bodies. The least I could do for them now was to see that they remained decently dead.

This time he did not take the trouble to fight back. He turned and ran and I went after him. He outdistanced me easily. I ran until my bursting lungs forced me to slow down to a walk. Saul Moyer's house was more than a mile away. When at last I reached it, all the lights were out. I put on lights behind me until I was in the bedroom where the bodies had been laid out.

Only one corpse lay on the floor now—that of Cosmo Boland with its grotesquely twisted neck. I had come too late! Lou Stamm had arrived here sufficiently ahead of me to change the three women into zombies. Moyer and Yates and Dr. Hillhouse must have left shortly after I had, and so Lou had been able to go about the diabolical resurrections without interruption.

I slumped down on the bed, overcome with weariness and a sense of futility. Holly and her cousin and her aunt were now one of the walking dead. I had to find them and do something to them so that they could rest decently and in peace. I didn't know what. How can one kill the dead?

After a while I rose and searched the house for a gun. I couldn't find anything more deadly than a butcher's knife, so I took that. I was determined to kill Lou Stamm. Perhaps if he died, his influence over the zombies would die.

I left the house and walked along the road. Much had happened that night, but I could tell by the moon that it was only an hour or two after midnight. I left the road and walked across the fields, through woods. I wasn't sure where I was going, what I would do when at last I found the zombies. Presently I came to the Shelley farm where I had seen the zombies working in the tomato field. There was no sign of them now. The Shelley house was empty.

I WAS standing outside the house, wondering where I could go next, when I heard the first of the shots. Before the echo had died away, there came another shot, and then a burst of firing. It sounded like a machine-gun. I set off at a trot in the direction from which the shots seemed to come.

After a few more bursts the shots ceased. I wasn't thinking much as I trotted across fields; perhaps my mind was too dazed with sorrow and horror to be capable of clear thought. I didn't wonder why a machine-gun should be in Redwell or what the shots might signify. The shots were no doubt tied up in some way with the zombies and so I moved in that direction.

I was climbing steadily uphill, and after a while I saw the stone walls of Henry Yates' house.

Yates did no farming. The eccentric Wall Street speculator had enclosed the ground surrounding his house with a high wall of massive grey stones which made the place look like a fortress. In front of the wall some ten acres of flat ground had been cleared like a parade ground in front of a medieval castle.

And as I stopped just inside a line of trees' which fringed the clearing, I saw troops marching across that parade ground.

For a minute or two I was too overcome with horror for my brain to receive the message of my eyes. Little by little I understood the frightful significance of what I saw, and then I was convinced that this was a nightmare or that I was stark raving mad.

For it was the zombies that marched. An army of the dead! Yet each had across its shoulder the deadly weapon of the living—a modem rifle with bayonet fixed!

There were about twenty in that hellish army, marching in rows of four. It was a naked army, or nearly naked, half men, half women, and all were clad only in loin-cloths. The dead have no use for clothes and the dead have no sex, so that at first it did not seem unnatural that they were nearly naked.

They were marching toward the wall of the house, in perfect step, yet without the snap and military precision of soldiers. There was that listlessness, that unutterable weariness in their movements of the dead who desire to return to the eternal peace of their graves, yet cannot.

And Holly was among them!

I could have picked her out at once, and yet for a time I fought against seeing her. At last I could not help but look at her. She was marching between Gil Strong and another farmer, with her heavy rifle carried firmly on her tender, naked shoulder. Only a short while ago I had held her dead body in my arms— and now she walked with the other dead of Redwell. Moonbeams glistened on the soft curves of her body, on her splendid rounded breasts; yet in some diabolically intrinsic way she lacked sex. She had ceased to be a woman; she was simply a corpse.

Behind her marched Ivy, her child-like, delicate form looking as if it could not hold up that heavy gun. And I saw Dora Boland too, and Jane Shelley and Edgar and Maria Blagden and Hal Harvey and all the others who had recently died in Redwell.

Suddenly a machine-gun started barking and then another. Great God, they were shooting at the zombies from the wall! And suddenly I understood. The zombies were attacking the house, and Yates and his servants were desperately trying to defend themselves.

Bullets whined all around me. I heard them among the leaves overhead. Holly was in the path of those bullets. For one wild moment I forgot that she was already dead. With a cry of anguish I started to run toward her.

I hadn't taken more than a step or two when a pair of arms wrapped themselves around my legs from behind, throwing me heavily to the ground. The jolt ripped my broken arm like a sharp knife. The wind was knocked out of me and I hadn't the strength to fight the hands which dragged me back to the shelter of the trees.

"You damn fool!" Saul Moyer said. "Another minute and you'd have been killed. You're no zombie—yet."

MOYER WAS crouched on one side of me, Lou Stamm on the other. I just lay there looking up at Lou, saying nothing. Had I been wrong about him? If he were the master of the zombies, wouldn't he be out there directing the attack?

Both Moyer and Lou were staring toward Yates' house. "My God, I can't believe it!" the constable muttered. "The machine-gun can't miss them at that distance, yet not one of them is felling."

I sat up. The machine-guns were going like mad, yet that army of the dead continued to move on, without hurrying, without slowing down; it approached that wall relentlessly, inexorably, like death itself. And not one fell, not one faltered.

Suddenly both machine-guns stopped at the same time. Had the defenders on the wall, recognizing the futility of resistance, fled? And then I realized that the zombies had stopped within a hundred feet of the wall. They stood perfectly motionless, rifles on their shoulders, the moonlight gleaming on their naked backs.

"Something is going to happen," Lou whispered hoarsely. "They're waiting for further orders."

A form stepped into the clearing at our right. Even by the light of that bright moon he was too far away for us to distinguish his features. He lifted his right hand and barked a single word of command.

"Charge!"

THE ZOMBIES went into motion again, this time with their rifles held at ready. Moonbeams glinted on cold steel. They did not run, did not hasten their pace, but their naked torsos were bent forward as if ready to spring with out-thrust bayonet as soon as a living opponent appeared.

"We've got to get him," I cried. "The one who gave the order. He's the witch doctor, the leader of the zombies."

I started to my feet. The machine-guns were going again, and stray bullets were whining through the air all about us. Lou grabbed my arm and pulled me down again.

"Don't be a sap, Joey. He's disappeared again. And if we move from here, we can hardly miss being hit."

The zombies had reached the gate. I couldn't see what the ones in front did, if anything, but all at once, the gate swung open. They marched through. The machine-guns swung away from the clearing. There was a desultory burst, then the guns went silent. A single, high-pitched scream rent the air, followed by other screams.

"We've got to do something," I yelled. "We can't just stay here while—"

I couldn't finish the sentence. The picture my unfinished words brought up was too horrible. I visualized Holly and the others ripping open living bodies with cold, jagged steel—killing methodically, mercilessly, like so many robots.

Saul Moyer was almost sobbing. "What can we do? Guns are no good against them. They can't be killed. God in heaven, do you know what this means? This is the beginning of an army of zombies. Nothing will be able to withstand them. They'll overrun the world; the army will grow larger and larger with the additions of the ones they kill, until all the world will be controlled by the dead."

The screams had stopped. The house was terribly silent.

"Lou!" I cried. "You know about these things. There must be a way that zombies can be fought."

Lou lifted his head from his hands. "I've read that if you feed them salt they return to their graves."

"Salt!" I stared at Lou and then at Moyer and I shook my head to clear my brain. Suddenly my mind was back to normal for the first time since the accident. It must have been the mention of something as ordinary and as common as salt that did it.

I said: "We've seen things we can't explain, but that doesn't mean they're not explainable. We've assumed that those people are dead, but how do we know?"

"I've seen a lot of corpses in my day," Moyer replied. "I know a corpse when I see one. You yourself know that Holly is dead."

"Do I?" My heart beat with a strange excitement. "Sometimes even doctors are mistaken, or a body may appear to be dead and yet not be permanently dead. Perhaps some form of catalysis. Look—didn't all those who were turned into zombies die from the strange disease which Doc Hillhouse can't diagnose."

"Not all," Lou said with a catch in his throat. "Ivy and Holly and Mrs. Boland were killed in an accident."

"But they weren't," I exclaimed. "Now I see it. Holly and Ivy and probably Mrs. Boland were alive immediately after the accident. Only Mr. Boland had been definitely killed—his neck was broken, unmistakably. And of those four only three were resurrected into zombies. Mr. Boland was left dead."

THEY LOOKED at me. "That's right," Lou agreed slowly. "When I reached Saul's house, Mr. Boland's body was still there and the others were gone." He shook his head sadly. "But suppose what you imply is true, that only those who died of the unknown disease can be turned into zombies. It alters nothing. They are dead just the same, or the machine-gun bullets would have killed them."

I subsided hopelessly. What mattered how they had died if they were dead, for they had walked directly into that ma-chine-gun barrage without any effect on them.

"Wait!" I said suddenly. "The person responsible for this, the witch doctor or whatever he is, is alive and vulnerable. He commands the zombies; we saw it ourselves. If we kill him, the horrors will end."

"If we knew who he was," Lou muttered bitterly.

I turned to Moyer. "Saul, were you the first to reach the scene of the accident?" "No. Doc Hillhouse was there first. Yates and I were driving in my car. Doc had already pulled all the bodies out and he was working on you. He said all were dead but you."

"Lou, you know something about Doc Hillhouse's travels," I said. "He's been all over the world. Was he in Haiti?"

"Yes. Two years ago he—" Lou broke off, mouth open. "That's it! Doc Hillhouse is the one. When people became sick, he was the one called. He gave them something or did something to them which made them die, or appear to die, in such a way that he could later resurrect them. He did that to Ivy and Holly and Mrs. Boland, and he was going to do the same to you when the arrival of Saul and Yates interrupted him."

"And after you, Joey, ran out of my house half-crazy, we scattered to look for you because we were afraid you'd run amok or something," Moyer put in. "Then Doc must have sneaked back to my place and made zombies out of the three Boland women. He was the one we saw ordering the zombies to charge."

All three of us rose to our feet. There was a terrible intensity in my voice as I said, "The zombies are still in the Yates house. Hillhouse must be with them. Let's go."

"The zombies will kill us," Moyer protested. "We haven't a chance in the world against them."

"I don't care," I said. "The devil himself won't keep me from Hillhouse. If they're really zombies, we've got to stop them before they get too strong, and Hillhouse's death might do that. If they're not really zombies, there's a chance for them. Are you coming with me, Lou?"

He nodded. Moyer muttered: "Don't count me out so quickly." Moyer had his rifle. I remembered the butcher knife I had taken from Moyer's house. I had dropped it when Lou had tackled me when I had been about to run to the zombie army. I fetched it. Lou picked up a stout branch. Then the three of us set out.

Chapter 6: The Master of Death

WE DID not go directly across the clearing but skirted the edge of the woods until we came to the side wall which was only about ten or twenty feet from the trees. Silently we moved along the shadow of the wall to the front gate. From within the walls there came no sound. The gate was open and we went through it.

My heart was thumping and I suppose my face looked as bad as the faces of Lou Stamm and Saul Moyer. Worse than the fear of death was the thought that the creatures who might attack me were dead things against which there was no possible defense.

Lou raised a cry. "Good Lord, look at that? It was a massacre!"

Moonlight revealed the bodies lying in the court—the bodies of the defenders who had been mercilessly slain by the army of the dead. My stomach turned over. Holly had been one of the murderers—adorable, gentle Holly who in life wouldn't have harmed a fly, had become a living-dead monster that slew without conscience!

Moyer and Lou stayed just inside the gate, transfixed by horror, as I moved toward one of the bodies. I stared at it, dropped to my knees, plunged my good arm inside the clothes. Sardonic laughter rattled in my throat. I ran to another of the forms, to a third, a fourth. The other two, watching me, must have thought I had gone mad. All were straw dummies dressed in the clothing of men and women, and all had been ripped and gashed by bayonets.

Where were the men who had manned the machine-guns? Who had uttered the screams we had heard as the zombies had burst through the gate?

A low voice said: "Good-evening, gentlemen."

I stiffened. The words had not been addressed to me. My inspection of the dummies had taken me close against the wall, out of sight of the man who now confronted Lou Stamm and Saul Moyer. The newcomer's back was to me, but I knew at once who he was.

"We thought we would find you here, Doc," Lou said quietly.

He gripped the branch in his hand. Moyer was leaning on his rifle. Dr. Hillhouse shifted a little and I saw a revolver in his hand.

"Looking for me here, gentlemen?" Dr. Hillhouse said. "Why?"

Dr. Hillhouse would shoot the two down in cold blood. He would have to in order to protect himself, and Moyer hadn't a chance of getting his rifle up in time. Tightly gripping the butcher knife, I stole up behind the doctor.

"Why do you think?" Moyer blurted. "You devil!" And he started to bring up his rifle.

Rage at the sight of the bodies which the constable thought were real corpses had made him lose his head. Both he and Lou would have been dead in a couple of seconds if at that moment I had not thrown myself at Dr. Hillhouse. With all my strength, I thrust my knife into his back. He collapsed so suddenly that I went down on top of him.

By the time Moyer and Lou lifted me to my feet Dr. Hillhouse was dead. "Good work, Joey," Moyer said. "Thanks. What do we do now?"

"We look for the zombies," Lou said. "Perhaps Hillhouse's death liberated them. They must be in the house."

As we went silently toward the house, I told them that the bodies were straw dummies. They didn't believe me until they inspected the dummies themselves.

Moyer scratched his head. "Now what's the meaning of that?"

Just then a voice barked out inside the house: "Forward march!" The sound of bare feet padding rhythmically on a hard floor came to us.

We froze in our tracks. "They're coming for us!" Moyer gasped.

The voice in the house said: "Company halt!" The feet stopped.

"They're being drilled in the house," Lou whispered and he started forward. We followed. Crouching beneath a window, we stared into the enormous living room of the house.

All the furniture had been removed. The army of the dead stood in double file in what was supposed to be attention, though there was a listless, lifeless droop to the nearly naked bodies which was utterly unsoldierly. But they were more deadly and more savage than any soldiers the world had ever known.

"Present arms!"

Rifles rattled. Their movements were so terribly lethargic and yet so precise. My eyes shifted to the one who had issued the commands.

"It's Henry Yates!" I whispered incredulously. "Oh, God, I've just killed an innocent man!"

STANDING AGAINST the farther wall were Yates' two male servants. One was short and thin, the other tall and thin, and both had brutal, crafty faces. They were looking at Yates with unconcealed amusement as he strutted pompously back and forth before the army of the dead.

"See how they obey me," he boasted to his servants. "Did you see how they ripped into those straw dummies. They would have done the same if those dummies had been men. No army in the world will be able to withstand them. The machine-guns didn't stop them. Nothing on earth will stop them." He thrust a hand out in front of him and slowly brought the fingers together. "Caesar and Napoleon had only mortal legions to lead. I shall have an invincible army."

"He's mad!" Saul Moyer breathed into my ear.

The attack of the zombies had been only a rehearsal. Next time it would not be dummies into which they would thrust their bayonets, but living people. The screams had been simulated by the servants to give the attack a semblance of reality. But the bullets the servants had fired at the zombies through the machine-guns had been real enough; I had heard them falling around me. Yates had been testing his soldiers' vulnerability, and now, knowing that they could not be killed, there would be no stopping him.

"The world shall be mine," Yates went on. "I shall be the greatest man in the history of mankind."

The servants looked at each other and smiled. They knew that he was mad, yet they obeyed him. Then their eyes moved over the zombies, stopped at one, and lust flared in their eyes.

Like me, they were looking at Holly. Living or an undead monster, standing there in only that brief loin-cloth with the ceiling light shining down on her loveliness, she was something to look at.

Hatred burned in me. I forgot about the innocent man I had just murdered; I could think only of more killing. Lou Stamm, his body close to mine, was breathing heavily. He had eyes only for Ivy. As one, we started from the window.

"Where are you going?" Saul Moyer asked.

"In there of course," Lou told him.

"No," Moyer protested. "I can pick Yates off from here." He straightened up and thrust the rifle through the open window.

At that moment the tall servant looked in the direction of the window. He screamed a warning, Moyer's rifle roared and I saw Yates' body leap in the air. Then the servants had automatics out and were shooting at the window.

Lou and I raced around to the door. Unarmed as we were, it was a foolhardy thing to do, and even had we been armed we would have been helpless against the zombies. But the sight of the girls we had loved had done something to us. We wanted only to get to the girls, feeling certain, somehow, that they would not attempt to harm us.

As we ran, we continued to hear the sound of guns. Moyer was shooting back at the servants. We went through a front door, entered a foyer, and then plunged into the living room. In the doorway we stopped abruptly.

The firing had ceased. The tall servant was motionless on the floor. Yates was on the floor, too, wounded but still alive. The short servant was facing the window, automatic in hand. He didn't see us, but Yates did.

The army of zombies was motionless, standing stiffly with guns held in front of them and their vacant faces showed no interest in what was happening in the room.

Yates screamed: "Charge! Kill them I Charge! Kill!"

His words galvanized the zombies into motion. They moved forward.

"Holly!" I yelled. "It's me, Joey!" But her face remained dead, empty, as she advanced toward me with out-thrust bayonet along with the others.

THE SHORT servant whirled and screamed. He started to run toward us, tripped, and the wave of zombies swept over him. Yates was shrieking like a woman, trying to crawl out of the way. But they made no distinction between leader and victims. They could only obey orders, and they had learned how to use their bayonets on the dummies. I glimpsed Edgar Blagden thrusting his bayonet down at Yates, I heard Yates' dying shriek—then Lou and I turned and fled.

In the foyer Lou went one way, I another. Too late I realized my mistake. Lou had gone out the front door, I toward the back of the house. The zombies were bursting into the foyer. I found myself at the foot of the staircase. There was nothing to do but go up the stairs.

I was halfway up the stairs when I heard bare feet padding up after me. Glancing over my shoulder, I glimpsed a white form. Only one was pursuing me, but that was enough. I ran down the hall, pulled open a door, slammed it behind me. Frantically I fumbled for the key to lock myself in. There was none!

I ran to the window. It would be only a one-story drop to the ground. But as I looked down I saw three or four of the zombies below. I was trapped!

The door opened. This is the end, I thought, and swung around.

It was Holly.

Instinctively I emitted a cry of relief. "Holly, thank—"

I broke off. She had the face and form of Holly, but the soul and mind of Holly were gone. There was no recognition in her face at the sight of me; nothing but a vast emptiness as, bayonet fixed, she advanced toward me.

"Holly!" I said. "I'm Joey Cobb, the man you love. You don't want to kill me. You love me."

My words meant nothing to her. She had been given an order and she had to carry it out. The point of the bayonet was only a foot or two from me when I leaped.

I hurled my body under the bayonet. She was too slow to thrust the bayonet down before my shoulder struck her just below the knees. It was the shoulder of my bad arm which hit her, and the impact felt as if I had come up against a brick wall. She went over backward, the rifle dropping from her hands. A black cloud of pain and dizziness swept over me. I knew that I had done something to my broken arm and perhaps to my broken rib and that I was slipping into unconsciousness. If she got to that gun again I was through.

Somehow I managed to fight through the black cloud, got my good hand on her thigh, tried to keep her down by dropping my shoulders on her squirming body. I couldn't hold her. I brought back my fist, and with every remaining ounce of strength I drove it toward her chin. The moment after my fist struck bone I slid off into unconsciousness ...

THE FIRST thing that penetrated my awareness when I opened my eyes was the dawn streaming in through the window. I was lying fully dressed on a bed and looking down at me I saw Lou Stamm's anxious face.

"What happened?" I asked. "The zombies—Holly—are they—"

"Everything is under control," Lou replied. "When the zombies chased me, I climbed up on the wall and barked: 'Company attention.' That did the trick. It seems it doesn't matter much who gives the orders; they know only how to obey. That's why when Yates told them to kill, they made no distinction between him and his servants and us. After Saul Moyer and I had herded them all into a room and locked them in, I came up here and found both you and Holly unconscious. She's down there now with the others." "And she's—none of them have returned to normal?"

Lou shook his head miserably. "No. If Doc Hillhouse were living he might have told us how to bring them out of it"

"Doc Hillhouse?" I said. "Where did he fit in? Didn't I murder an innocent man?"

"No. He was the one behind it all. Yates was simply a dupe. One of Yates' servants lived long enough to give us an idea of what it was all about. Yates, as you know, was wealthy. He had made his money manipulating companies and even human lives on the stock exchange.

The lust for power must have touched his mind in the same way as every dictator must be more or less mad. Dr. Hillhouse knew of this and saw of a way of separating him from his wealth. He told him he could create an invincible army, an army of the dead, with which Yates would be able to conquer the world.

"Dr. Hillhouse did create the army we saw, enough of one to convince Yates. He must have turned most of his fortune over to Dr. Hillhouse, because Yates thought he was buying power over all the world. The demonstration last night of that army attacking against a machine-gun barrage was to prove beyond doubt the invulnerability of the zombies. The machine-guns fired real bullets, all right, but Dr. Hillhouse had bribed the servants. They fired above the attackers' heads."

I sat up. "Then that means that Holly—the others—are not really zombies—not dead at all—because otherwise there would have been no need to fire above their heads."

Lou nodded. "Yes, they're not dead. But—they're still the way they were and perhaps we will never bring them out of their state. In that case it would be better if they were—dead."

I slid off the bed. With Lou's help I managed to get downstairs. Everybody in Redwell was in the house or outside. The zombies were in the library. They were clothed now land their guns had been taken away from them. They sat on chairs or on the floor, motionless as statues, their eyes vacant, their faces lifeless.

I approached Holly who sat on her legs in a corner of the room. She did not look at me.

"Holly, don't you know me?"

Her face turned to me. There was nothing in it. I burst into tears and wept like a baby.

At noon the state police arrived and doctors from the nearest city. My arm was reset and I was ordered to go to bed, but they couldn't get me away from the Yates house. The doctors examined the zombies, held whispered conferences, shrugged, and shook their heads.

Toward evening Lou Stamm rushed out on the porch where many of us whose relatives or loved ones were among the mindless creatures had sat wordlessly for hours.

"Something's happening," Lou cried. "Ivy recognized me."

We pounded into the library. I went straight to Holly, put my good arm around her. She looked up at me and light slowly entered her eyes. I was trembling violently as I kept repeating her name. She frowned, then smiled.

"Joey, darling, why are you looking at me like that?" she said. She passed a hand over her forehead. "What am I doing here? I feel as if I've been asleep a long time."

I shouted with joy. The spell was broken. All about me others were laughing and weeping ...

THREE MONTHS have passed. Holly and I are now living in Chicago. We had a big double wedding—Holly and I, Lou and Ivy.

We were never to learn just what Dr. Hillhouse had done to those twenty in Redwell to make them into living dead creatures. Sometimes, remembering that night of terror, I am almost convinced that they had really died and had been resurrected. For Holly had been dead in my arms after that accident.

Yesterday I read in a newspaper about a Dr. Corbin, professor of sociology, who had spent a year in Haiti studying Voodooism and zombies. I went to visit him and we had a long talk. He was, of course, profoundly interested in what had occurred at Redwell.

HE SAID: "Frankly, Mr. Cobb, I have not been able to find a zombie, although many Haitians have sworn to me that they have seen them. I am convinced that zombies exist. Not actually living-dead persons, but something which approximates such a state, perhaps induced by a combination of unknown drugs and hypnotism. Even the government of Haiti recognizes the existence of zombies."

He removed a volume from a bookshelf. "Can you read French? This is the Criminal Code of the Republic of Haiti."

I knew enough college French to be able to freely translate the section. It read somewhat as follows:

"The use of drugs which, without causing actual death, produce a lethargic coma more or less prolonged, shall be considered attempted murder. If the person has been buried after the administration of such drugs, the act shall be considered murder no matter what result follows." I thanked him and left. That evening I told Holly what I had learned. She nodded abstractly and stared into space. I sat deep in an armchair, looking at her. A minute or two passed and she had not moved.

"Holly!" I cried in sudden terror and rushed to her.

She started. "What's the matter?"

I sank down at her side with a sigh of relief and gathered her in my arms. "Nothing, sweetheart. I guess I'm still jittery."

But we were both afraid.

While Zombies Walked

By Thorp McCluskey

THE PACKARD ROADSTER had left the lowland and was climbing into the hills. It was rough going; this back road was hardly more than two deep, grass-grown ruts—the car barely crawled. Overhead the vivid greenery of the trees nearly met, shrouding, intensifying the heat.

Eileen's letter had brought Anthony Kent down the Atlantic seaboard, his heart leaden, his thoughts troubled. There had been a strangeness in Eileen's brusque dismissal.

"Tony," the letter had read, "you must not come to see me this summer. You must not write to me anymore. I do not want to see you or hear from you again!"

It had not been like Eileen—that letter; Eileen would at least have been gentle. It was as though that letter had been dictated by a stranger, as though Eileen had been but a puppet, writing words which were not her own ...

"Back in the hills aways," an emaciated, filthy white man, sitting on the steps of a dilapidated shack just off the through highway, had said sourly, in answer to Tony's inquiry. But Tony, glancing at his speedometer, saw that he had already come three and seven-tenths miles. Had the man deliberately misdirected him? After that first startled glance there had been a curious flat opacity in the man's eyes ...

Abruptly, rounding a sharp bend in the narrow road, the car came upon a small clearing, in the heart of which nestled a tiny cabin. But at a glance Tony saw that the cabin was deserted. No smoke curled from the rusty iron stovepipe, no dog lay panting in the deep shade, the windows stared bleakly down the road.

Yet a planting of cotton still struggled feebly against the lush weeds! This was the third successive shack on that miserable road that had been, for some strange reason, suddenly abandoned. The peculiarity of this circumstance escaped Tony. His thoughts, leaden, bewildered, full of the dread that Eileen no longer loved him, were turned too deeply inward upon themselves.

It had been absurd of Eileen—throwing up her job with the Lacey-Kent people to rush off down here the instant she heard of her great uncle's stroke. Absurd, because she could have done more for the old fellow by remaining in New York.

And yet old Robert Perry had raised his dissolute nephew's little girl almost from babyhood, had put her through Brenau College; Tony realised that Eileen's gesture had been the only one compatible with her nature.

But why had she jilted him?

The woebegone shack had merged into the forest. The road, if anything, was growing worse; the car was climbing a gentle grade. Now, as it topped the rise, Tony saw outspread before his eyes a small valley, hemmed in by wooded hills. A rambling, pillared house, half hidden by mimosa and magnolias, flanked by barns, outbuildings, and a tobacco shed, squatted amid broad, level acres lush with cotton.

At first glance the place seemed peculiarly void of life. No person moved in the wide yard surrounding the house; no smoke curled from the field-stone chimney. But as Tony's gaze swept the broad, undulating fields he saw men working, men who were clad in grimy, dirt-greyed garments that were an almost perfect camouflage. Only a hundred feet down the road a man moved slowly through the cotton.

Tony stopped the car opposite the man.

"Is this the Perry place?" he called, his voice sharp and distinct through the afternoon's heat and stillness.

But the grey-clad toiler never lifted his gaze from the cotton beneath his eyes, never so much as turned his head or paused in his work to signify that he had heard.

Tony felt anger rising in him. His nerves were taut with worry, and he had driven many miles without rest. At least the fellow could leave off long enough to give him a civil answer!

But then, the man might be a little deaf. Tony shrugged, jumped from the car and ploughed through the cotton.

"Is this the Perry place?" he bawled.

The man was not more than six feet from Tony, working toward him, with lowered head and shadowed face. But if he heard, he gave no sign.

Sudden, blind rage swept Tony. Had his nerves not been almost at snapping point he would never have done what he did; he would have let the man's amazing boorishness pass without a word, would have turned back to his car in disgust. But Tony, that day, was not himself.

"Why you—" he choked. He took a sudden step forward and jerked the man roughly erect.

For an instant Tony glimpsed the man's eyes, grey, sunken, filmed, expressionless as though the man were either blind or an idiot. And then the man, as if nothing had occurred, was once more slumping over the cotton!

"God Almighty!" Tony breathed. And suddenly a chill like ice pressing against his spine swept him, sent his mind swirling and his knees weakly buckling.

The man wore a shapeless, broad-brimmed hat, fastened on his head by a band of elastic beneath his chin. But the savage shaking Tony had given him had jolted it awry.

Above the man's left temple, amid the grey-flecked hair, jagged splinters of bone gleamed through torn and discoloured flesh! And a greyish ribbon of brain-stuff hung down beside the man's left ear!

The man was working in the cotton—with a fractured skull!

TONY'S THOUGHTS were reeling, his mind dazed. How that man could continue to work with his brains seeping through a hole in his head was a question so unanswerable he did not even consider it. And yet, dimly, he remembered the almost miraculous stories that had come out of the war, stories of men who had lived with bullet-holes through their heads and with shell fragments imbedded inches deep within their brain-cases. Something like that must have happened to this man. Some horrible accident must have numbed or destroyed every spark of intelligence in him, must have bizarrely left him with only the mechanical impulse to work.

He must be taken to the house at once, Tony knew. Gently Tony grasped his shoulders. And in the mid-afternoon's heat his nerves crawled.

The stooping body beneath the frayed cotton shirt was snake-cold!

"Lord—he's dying—standing on his feet!" Tony mumbled.

The man resisted Tony's efforts to direct him toward the car. As Tony pushed him gently, he resisted as gently, turning back toward the cotton. As Tony, gritting his teeth, grasped those cold shoulders and tugged with all his strength, the man hung back with a strange, weird tenaciousness.

Suddenly Tony released his grip. He was afraid to risk stunning the man with a blow, for a blow might mean death. Yet, strong as he was, he could not budge the man from the path he was chopping along the cotton.

There was only one thing to do. He must go to the house and get help.

Stumbling, his mind vague with horror, Tony made his way to the car, and sent it hurtling the last half-mile down the narrow road to the house.

Only subconsciously, as he plunged up the uneven walk between fragrant, flowering shrubs, did he notice the strange discrepancy between the well-kept appearance of the fields and the dilapidation of the house. His mind was too full of the plodding horror he had seen. But the windows of the house were almost opaque with dirt, and at some of them dusty curtains hung limply while others stared nakedly blank. The screens on the long low porch were torn and rusted as though they had received no attention since spring; the lawn and the shrubbery were unkempt.

Three or four dust-grey wicker chairs stood along the porch. In one of those chairs sat a man.

He was old, and sparsely built. Had he been standing erect he would have measured well over six feet, but he lay back in his chair with his legs extending supinely before him. Tony knew instantly that this was Eileen's great-uncle, Robert Perry.

As he plunged up the dirt-encrusted steps Tony exclaimed hoarsely, "Mr. Perry? I'm Tony Kent. There's a man—"

The old man was leaning slightly forward in his chair. His blue eyes in his deeply lined face suddenly flamed.

"Have you got a gun?" The words were taut and low.

"No." Tony shook his head impatiently. His mind was full of the horror he had seen working back there in the field. A gun! What did he want with a gun? Did old Robert Perry think he would be dangerous—the story-book rejected lover type, perhaps? Nonsense. Urgent, staccato words tumbled from his lips as he ignored the question.

"Mr. Perry—there's a man back there with the whole top of his head split open. He's stark mad; he wouldn't speak to me or come with me. But—he'll die if he's left where he is! It's a wonder he isn't dead already."

There was a long silence before the old man answered. "Where did you see this man?"

"Back there—back in the cotton."

Old Robert Perry shook his head, spoke in a muttered whisper, as if to himself, "Die? He can't—die!"

Abruptly he paused. The screen door leading into the house had opened. Two Negroes and a white man had come out on the porch.

The two Negroes were nondescript enough—mere plantation blacks. But the white man!

He was tall and wide as a door. He was so huge that any person attempting to guess his weight would have considered himself lucky if he got the figure within a score of pounds of the truth; he was bigger than any man Tony had ever seen outside a sideshow. And he was not a glandular freak; he was muscled like a jungle beast; his whole posture, his whole carriage silently shrieked super-human vitality. His gargantuan face, beneath the broad-brimmed, rusty black hat he wore, was pale as the belly of a dead fish, pale with the pallor of one who shuns the sunlight. His eyes were wide-set, coal-black, and staring; Tony had glimpsed that same intensity of gaze before in the eyes of religious and sociological fanatics. His nose was fleshy and well-muscled at the tip; his lips were thin and straight and tightly compressed. Garbed as he was in a knee-length, clerical coat of greenish, faded black, still wearing a frayed, filthy-white episcopal collar, he looked what he must have been, a pastor without honour, a renegade man of God.

He stood silently there on the porch and looked disapprovingly at Tony. His thin, weak, reformer's lips beneath that powerful, sensual nose tightened. Then, quietly, he spoke, not to Tony but to the paralytic old man:

"Who is this—person, Mr. Perry?"

Tony's fists clenched at the man's insolence. His anger turned to astonishment as he heard the old man answer almost cringingly: "This is Anthony Kent, Reverend Barnes—Anthony Kent, from New York City. Anthony—the Reverend Warren Barnes, who is stopping with us for a while. He has been very kind to us during my—illness."

Tony nodded coldly. The funereal-clad colossus stared for a long moment at this unexpected guest, and Tony could feel the menace smouldering in him like banked fires. But when he spoke for the second time his words were innocuous enough.

"I'm temporarily in charge here." His voice was vibrant as a great hollow drum. "Mr. Perry's mind, since he suffered his most unfortunate stroke, has not always been entirely clear, and Miss Eileen too. I am temporarily without a pastorate, and I am glad to help in any way that I can. You understand, I'm sure?" He smiled, the sickeningly pious smile of the chronic hypocrite, and ostentatiously clasped his hands.

Again Tony nodded. "Yes, I understand, Reverend," he said quickly although some obscure sixth sense had already warned him that this man was as slimy and dangerous as a water moccasin—and as treacherous. But—that man in the field, working in the cotton with the brain-stuff hanging down behind his ear! Hurriedly, Tony went on, "I spoke to Mr. Perry when I came up the steps—something must be done at once—there's a man working out there in the field beside the road with something seriously wrong with his head. My God, I looked at him, and it looked to me as though his skull was fractured!"

With surprising swiftness the colossus turned upon Tony. "What's that you say? It looked as though *what?*"

Tony rasped, "A man working in the field with a fractured skull, Reverend! His head looks staved in—bashed open—God knows how he can still work. He's got to be brought to the house."

The giant's too brilliant, too intense black eyes were suddenly crafty. He laughed, patronizingly, as though humouring a child or a drunkard. "Oh, come, come, Mr. Kent; such things are impossible, you know. A trick of the light, or perhaps your weariness; you've driven a long distance, haven't you? One's eyes play strange tricks upon one."

He peered at Tony, and suddenly the expression on his face changed. "But if you're worried, we'll convince you, put your mind at ease. You go and get Cullen, Mose and Job. Jump smart, niggers!" He pointed up the road. "Jump smart; bring Cullen back here; Mr. Kent's got to be shown." His thin lips curled scornfully.

The two Negroes "jumped smart." The Reverend Warren Barnes calmly seated himself in one of the wicker chairs near paralytic old Robert Perry and waved carelessly toward a vacant chair. Tony sat down—glanced inquiringly at Eileen's uncle. But the aged man remained silent, apathetic, indifferent. Obviously, Tony thought, his mind *was* enfeebled; in that, at least, the Reverend Barnes had been truthful.

Almost diffidently, Tony addressed the white-haired old paralytic.

"I've come here to speak with Eileen, Mr. Perry. I can't believe that she meant—what she wrote in her last letter. Regardless of whether or not her feelings toward me have changed, I must speak to her. Where is she?"

When the old man spoke his voice was flat and hard. "Eileen has written to tell you that she wished to terminate whatever had been between you. Perhaps she has decided that she would prefer not to become too deeply involved with a Northerner. Perhaps she has other reasons. But in any case, Mr. Kent, you are not acting the gentleman in coming here and attempting to renew an acquaintanceship that has been quite definitely broken off."

The words were brutal, and not at all the sort of speech Tony would have expected, a moment ago, from a man whose mind had dimmed through age and shock. A sharp, involuntary retort surged to Tony's lips. Suddenly, then, the Reverend Barnes guffawed loudly.

"There, Mr. Kent!" he chuckled. It was a sound utterly unministerial, utterly coarse, sardonic and evil. "There—coming down the road. Is that the man you saw working in the cotton—with the fractured skull?"

Walking into the yard between the two Negroes was the white man Tony had encountered earlier. He was plodding along steadily almost rapidly, with no assistance from his coloured companions. The straw hat was set tightly down upon his head, shading his face and covering his temples. There was no bit of greyish stuff hanging down beside his left ear.

The three men halted before the porch. The Reverend Barnes, grinning broadly, showing great, yellowed, decaying teeth, stood up and put his hands on the porch rail. Abruptly he spoke to Tony

"Is this the man, Mr. Kent?"

Tony, his mind numb with amazement, answered, "It's the man, all right."

The Reverend Barnes's grin deepened. "Are you all right, Cullen? Do you feel quite able to work? Not ill, or anything?"

There was a long, long pause before the man answered. And when at last he spoke, his voice was curiously cadenceless, as though speech were an art he seldom practised. But there was no doubt about what he said.

"Ahm all right, Reverend Barnes. Ah feels good."

The big man chuckled, as though in appreciation of some ghastly joke.

"You haven't any headache?" he persisted. "No dizziness from the sun, perhaps? You don't want to knock off for the rest of the day?"

After a moment the reply came.

"Ah ain' got no haidache. Ah kin work."

The Reverend Barnes smiled pontifically. "Very well, then, Cullen. You may go back to work."

"Wait!" Tony exclaimed. "Tell him to take off his hat."

The big man wheeled slowly; slowly his right hand lifted, like that of some mighty patriarch about to pronounce a benediction—or a damning curse. For an instant Tony glimpsed murder in his eyes. Then his hand fell, and he spoke smoothly, quietly to Cullen.

"Take off your hat, Cullen."

With maddening, mechanical slowness the man lifted his hat, and Tony saw a mat of iron-grey hair, caked with dirt.

"Put your hat back on, Cullen. You may go back to work."

The man turned, was plodding slowly from the yard. And in that instant, striking vaguely against his dazed consciousness, the realisation came to Tony that only the hair on the left side of the man's skull was matted with ground-in dust—the hair above his right ear was relatively clean! He opened his lips to speak. But the Reverend Barnes, as if anticipating him, was saying with amused, contemptuous finality:

"He's gone back to work. Dirty fellows, aren't they—these poor white trash?"

And Tony, wondering if his own reason were tottering, let the man go …

The big man settled comfortably back in his chair.

"You thought you saw something you didn't," he said. His voice was soft now, soft and tolerant as silk. "Eye-strain, nervousness that's very close to hysteria. You must look after yourself."

For an instant Tony cradled his face in his hands. Yes, he must get hold of himself; his mind was overwrought. He raised his head and looked at the old man. "Eileen," he said doggedly. "I must see her."

Old Robert Perry opened his lips to speak. And suddenly the big man turned in his chair to stare deeply into the aged paralytic's eyes.

"You would like to see Miss Eileen?" he asked Tony, then, with grave courtesy, "But certainly, Mr. Perry. He's come such a distance; it would be a pity—"

"Whatever you say."

The Reverend Barnes rose from his chair, smiled sorrowfully and pityingly toward Tony.

"Job, Mose," he said to the two Negroes, "stay here on the porch, in case Mr. Perry has one of his spells." He nodded significantly to Tony. "I'll call Miss Eileen. Such a lovely, sweet girl!"

Leisurely, moving on the balls of his feet like some magnificent jungle beast, he rose and stalked across the porch, opened the rusty screen door and disappeared within the house.

Mr. Perry did not speak; neither did Tony. There was something in the air that eluded him, Tony knew—some mystery that even Mr. Perry himself concealed, some mystery that seemed as elusive as the breeze stirring the magnolias.

FOOTSTEPS WITHIN the house, and Eileen Perry, small, slender, with the wistful beauty of a spring flower, came onto the porch. Behind her, as if carelessly, his face overspread with a pious smirk, lounged Reverend Barnes.

Tony started up eagerly.

"Eileen!"

For a moment she did not speak. Only her splendid eyes looked at him hungrily, with ill-concealed terror rising in their depths.

"You shouldn't have come, Tony," she said then, simply.

The words were a rebuff. Yet Tony fancied that he had seen her hands lift toward him. He took a single step forward. But, as if to elude him, she stepped swiftly to the rail, stood with her back toward him.

"I *had* to come, Eileen," Tony said. His voice sounded oddly choked. "I love you. I had to know if you meant—those words you wrote, or if it was some strange madness—"

"Madness?" She laughed, and there was sudden hysteria in her low contralto voice. "Madness? No. I've changed, Tony You may think what you please about me; you may think that I'm fickle, or that I'm insane—whatever you will. But—above everything else in the world I did not want you to come here. Is that plain enough for you? I thought I tried to tell you that in my letter. And now—I wish that you would go."

As a man who dreams a nightmare, Tony heard his own voice, muttering, "But don't you *love me*, Eileen?"

For a moment he believed that she would speak, but she did not. She turned, and, without a backward look, walked into the house.

The giant, Reverend Barnes, was rubbing his hands together—an incongruous, absurd gesture in a man of his physique. And then, after a moment, he laughed, a hoarse, obscene guffaw. But Tony, heartbroken, heard the insulting sound as no more than a disquieting rumble that had no meaning. His lips quivering, his eyes misty with the sudden tears he could not restrain, he walked slowly across the porch.

Then, as though the longing in them could bring her back to him, his tear-dimmed eyes gazed into the emptiness where Eileen had stood, looked unseeingly across the flowering mimosa, stared downward for a second at the porch rail.

A single word had been written on that rail, written in dust with a fingertip. Tony's mind did not register the significance of that word; it was transmitted only to his subconscious. But, as if mechanically, his lax lips moved.

The somberly clad giant suddenly tensed, took a step forward.

"What was that you said, Mr. Kent?"

Mechanically Tony repeated the word.

The big man's eyes swept the rail. The grin had abruptly gone from his face; his muscles knotted beneath his rusty black coat.

And then he leaped. And simultaneously leaped the two Negroes who had lingered, diffidently, down the porch.

Monstrous, spatulate, pasty-white hands clenched into Tony's throat. Abruptly fighting, not with his numbed brain, but with a primitive, involuntary instinct of the flesh for self-preservation, Tony sent his fists lashing into the pair of black faces before him. But the giant renegade minister was on his shoulders like an albino shrouded leopard; the Negroes were tearing at his arms. His knees were buckling.

Like a slender tree stricken by the woodsman's axe, he wavered and plunged headlong. There was a cascade of darting light as his head crashed against the dusty pine boards. Then came oblivion.

ANTHONY KENT awoke to swirling, throbbing pain. His skull beat and hammered; the dim walls of a small room, barren save for the straw-mattressed cot on which he lay, swooped and gyrated before his eyes.

Slowly he recalled what had occurred. The Reverend Barnes, that magnificent jackal, had struck him down as he stood on the porch. He was in some long-disused room, presumably a servant's bedchamber, within the old Perry house.

A word was struggling upward from deep within his brain. What was that word? Almost he remembered it. It was the word Eileen had written in dust on the porch rail, a word repulsive and hideous.

Eileen had been trying to tell him something, trying to convey some message to him. Eileen, then, loved him!

What was the word?

There was a small, square window in the room, through which a feeble, yellowish light struck high up on the opposite wall. The sun was setting, then; he had been unconscious for hours. But it was not at the window that Tony glanced despairingly. It was at the two-by-six pine beams nailed closely together across that small square space!

Tony stumbled to his feet, reeled to the window and shook those wooden bars with all his strength. But they were solid white pine, and they had been spiked to the house with twenty-penny nails.

Through the narrow apertures between the beams Tony could see the broad, level fields, and the road, sloping gently upward to disappear within the encircling forest.

People were coming down that road now; grey, dusty people who plodded toward the house. They appeared almost doll-like, for the room in which Tony was imprisoned was on the side of the house, and long before the road swung in toward the yard they passed beyond his vision. But as Tony watched them his nerves crawled.

They walked so slowly, so listlessly, with dragging footsteps! And they stumbled frequently against one another, and against the stones in the road, as though they were almost blind. Almost they walked like soldiers suffering from shell-shock, but recently discharged from some hospital in hell.

For many were maimed. One walked with a deep, broken stoop, as though his chest had been crushed against his backbone. Another's leg was off below the knee, and in place of an artificial limb he wore a stick tied against the leg with rope, a stick that reached from twelve inches beyond the stump to the hip. A third had only one arm; a fourth was skeleton-thin.

In the Name of God whence had these maimed toilers come?

And then a soundless scream rattled in Tony's throat; for, coming down the road alone, walking with the same dragging lifelessness as did the others, was another of the grey toilers. And, as the man turned the wide sweep in the road that would lead him to the house and beyond Tony's vision, Tony glimpsed, in the last yellow rays of the setting sun, the horror that had once been his face!

Had once been his face! For, from beneath the ridge of his nose downward, *the man had no face!* The vertebrate whiteness of his spine, naked save for ragged strings of desiccated flesh, extended with horrid starkness from the throat of his shirt to merge with the shattered base of a bony skull!

HIDEOUS MINUTES passed, minutes through which Tony fought to retain some semblance of sanity. At last he staggered weakly to the door, only one thought in his mind—to escape that mad place and take Eileen with him.

But the door, like the bars across the window, was made of heavy pine. From its resistance to his assault Tony knew that it was secured by bars slotted through iron sockets. It was impregnable.

Darkness was within that room now. Night had come quickly with the setting of the sun, velvety, semi-tropical night. The window was a purplish square through which a star gleamed brilliantly; the pine bars were invisible in the gloom. Tony was engulfed in blackness.

Yet, in a corner near the floor, there was a lessening of the darkness. Tony, crouching there, saw that the light came through a quarter-inch crack between the planks. Throwing himself down, he glued his eyes to that crack.

He could see only a small portion of the room beneath him, a rectangle roughly three feet by twelve, yet that was enough to tell him that the room was the dining room of the old house. The middle of an oaken table, littered with dishes and scraps of food, bisected his field of vision.

At that table, his back toward Tony, sat the apostate Reverend Barnes. A little way down the table a black hand and arm appeared and disappeared with irregular frequency. The rumble of voices floated upward through the narrow slit.

"God!" Tony thought. "If only I had a gun!"

He remembered, then, that the old paralytic had asked him if he had a gun.

From the mutter of voices Tony guessed that there were three men seated about that table; the two Negroes were talking volubly yet with a low, curious tenseness; the Reverend Barnes interrupting only infrequently with monosyllabic grunts. All three seemed to be waiting.

Beside the big man's pallid white hand, on the naked oaken table, sprawling disjointedly amid soggy bits of bread and splotches of grease and chicken bones, lay an incongruous object, a little doll that had been wretchedly sewn together from various bits of cotton cloth. It possessed a face, crudely drawn with black grease or charcoal, and a tuft of kinky hair surmounted the shapeless little bag that represented its head. Obviously it caricatured a Negro.

From time to time, hunching over the table like a great gross idol, his shiny, worn clerical coat taut across his massive shoulders, the renegade minister would pick up the little rag doll, flop its lax arms and legs about, and put it down again.

Suddenly, then, a door, invisible to Tony, opened and closed. The conversation of the two Negroes abruptly ceased. Two black men shuffled slowly across the dining room floor, came close to the table, opposite the colossus. Tony could see them both.

The face of one was rigid and grim, and he held his companion firmly by the arm. The second Negro was swaying drunkenly. His lips were loose and his eyes bleared. Yet there was terror in him.

The Reverend Barnes hunched lower over the table. Tony could see the big muscles in his back ribbing beneath his rusty coat, and the big brass collar-button at the back of his pillar-like neck. "You're here at last, nigger?" he asked softly. "You're late. What delayed you? They came from the cotton a long time ago, we have already eaten supper."

The drunken man mouthed some reply that was unintelligible, terror-ridden.

The giant's shoulders seemed to tighten into a ball of muscle. "You're drunk, nigger," he said, and his voice trembled with contemptuous loathing. "I smell com liquor on your breath.

It stifles me; how any man can so degrade himself—'Look not upon the wine when it is red.'" He paused. "You fool; I told you not to drink. How can you stay down the road and watch for strangers if you're drunk? You can't be trusted to wave the sheet when you're drunk. You failed today. What have you to say for yourself?"

Words tumbled from the man's slobbering mouth. "Ahm not drunk. Ah tuk de cawn foh toofache—"

The giant shrugged. "A stranger came up the road today before we could hide them in the cotton. You're drunk, nigger. I have forgiven you twice. But this is the third time."

He picked up the little doll.

"This is you, nigger. This is made with your sweat and your hair—"

A scream burst from the man's throat. He had begun to shake horribly.

"Hold him, niggers," the giant said imperturbably. "I want to study this; I want to watch it work."

Black hands grasped the writhing, shuddering man.

The Reverend Barnes picked up a fork. He was holding the little doll in his left hand, looking at it speculatively. And it seemed to Tony—although it may have been a trick of the light—that the lifeless doll writhed and moved of itself, in ghastly synchronisation with the trembling and shuddering of the terror-maddened human it caricatured.

Carefully, the Reverend Barnes stuck a prong of the fork through a leg of the doll. There was a slight rending of cotton.

The shuddering wretch screamed—horribly! And the colossus nodded his head as if in satisfaction.

Again the fork probed into the doll. But this time the big man jabbed all four tines through the little doll's middle. And this time no scream, but only a gasping, rending moan came from the Negro so firmly held by the strong hands of his kind. And suddenly he was hanging limply there, like a slaughtered thing …

The Reverend Barnes pulled the fork from the doll, tossed the torn doll carelessly on the floor.

"He's dead, niggers," he said then, callously. "He's stone dead."

As Tony lay sprawled on that rough pine flooring, peering down with horrified fascination into the room below, the incredible realisation grew and grew in him that he had witnessed the exercise of powers so primitive, so elemental, so barbaric that descendants of the so-called higher civilisations utterly disbelieve them.

God! Was this voodoo? Perhaps, but the Reverend Barnes was a white man; how had he become an adept? Was it something akin to voodoo but deeper, darker? Had that wretched Negro died through fright, or had there really been some horrible affinity between his living body and the lifeless doll?

What of the thing without a face, walking down the road?

The word that Eileen had written in the dust on the porch rail was hammering at Tony's consciousness. Almost he grasped it, yet it eluded him. An unfamiliar word, reeking of evil ...

For a long time there was only silence from the room below—silence, and a thickening haze of bluish smoke. The Negroes, Tony guessed, were smoking, although the big man almost directly beneath his eyes was not. Abruptly, then, the Reverend Barnes rose to his feet. Tony heard him walk across the floor; there was the sound of a door opening, and then a deep, throaty chuckle.

"No need for you to do the dishes tonight, Miss Eileen. Just leave them where they are; we don't need them anymore. Come with me; I'm going to take you back to your room."

Tony heard the man padding heavily yet softly across the floor, and Eileen's reluctant, lighter footsteps. The dining room door opened and closed.

Tony stumbled to his feet, then shook the door with a despair that was almost madness. Exhausted at last, he clung limply to the iron latch, panting.

Minutes passed—minutes that seemed hours.

Suddenly, from close to his ears, Tony heard muffled sounds of sobbing. Eileen, crying as though her heart was broken, was imprisoned in the next room!

"Eileen!"

Abruptly the sobbing ceased.

"Tony!" The girl's voice came almost clearly into the room, as though she had moved close to the wall. "You didn't—escape them, Tony?"

"They ganged me," Tony said grimly. "I think they were going to let me go, but that big two-faced rattlesnake saw what you wrote on the porch rail, and then they jumped me."

There was a gasp from beyond the wall and then a long silence. At last Eileen said, softly and penitently, "I'm sorry, Tony. I thought that you would read it and—understand—and come back later with help. I'm sorry that I got you into this, Tony. I tried to keep you out. But when you came here I—I loved you so, and I wanted so terribly to escape. I had a wild hope that when you got safe away, even though you didn't understand, you would ask someone who knew and could tell you what zombies meant—"

Zombies! That was the word she had written in dust on the porch rail! And instantly, with kaleidoscopic clarity, there flashed across Tony's brain a confusion of mental images he had acquired through the years—an illustration from a book on jungle rites—a paragraph from a voodoo thriller—scenes from one or two fantastic motion pictures he had witnessed ...

Zombies! Corpses kept alive by hideous sorcery to work and toil without food or water or pay—mindless, dead things that outraged Nature with every step they took! These were zombies, the books glibly said, grim products of Afro-Haitian superstition ...

The men who wrote those books had never suggested that zombies might be real—that the powers which controlled them might be a heritage of the blacks exactly as self-hypnotism is a highly developed faculty among the Hindus. No, the books had been patronisingly written, with more than a hint of amused superiority evident in them; their authors had incredibly failed to understand that even savages could not practise elaborate rites unless there was efficacy in them. . . .

"Zombies!" Tony muttered dazedly. And then, eagerly, "But—you love me, Eileen, I knew it; I knew you couldn't mean those things you wrote—"

"He made me write them," Eileen whispered. "He—came here in the spring, Tony. Uncle thinks that they ran him away—from wherever he was—before. He brought four Negroes with him.

"Uncle was old, Tony, and he didn't keep much help here—only six or seven coloured men. The place was run down, Tony; after Uncle had put me through college he didn't have much incentive for keeping it up; he's always told me that I could have it for a sort of country home—after he died.

"But then—this man who said he had been a minister came, and saw all these unworked acres and how isolated the place was.

"He went to Uncle, and told Uncle that he would furnish extra help if Uncle would give him half the crop.

"It was after the—help came that Uncle's Negroes left. Some of them even moved out of their shacks—out of the county. And this man—this Reverend Barnes, had already made a little doll and told Uncle that it was supposed to represent him. He tied the little doll's legs together with Uncle's hair and told Uncle that with stiff legs Uncle wouldn't be able to run away and get help. He told Uncle that any time he wanted to, he could stick a pin through the little doll and Uncle would die.

"And—Uncle can't move his legs! It's true, Tony, every word he said. That man, that—devil, can do anything he says.

"He read all my letters to Uncle, and all of Uncle's letters to me, too, before he sent them down to the post office. He tried to keep me from coming here.

"And when I did come he made another doll, Tony, to represent me. It's stuffed with my hair, Tony; they held me while he cut my hair. He's got little dolls that represent everyone here; he keeps them in a bag inside his shirt.

"He can kill us all, Tony, whenever he pleases!"

Hysteria had begun to creep into her voice. She paused for a moment. When she went on, her voice was calmer.

"He keeps one of his coloured men as a lookout in a tree at the top of the hill. The man can see way down to the main road. When he sees anyone turn up this way he opens out a big sheet and they hide the—*helpers*—"

Tony chuckled grimly.

"He didn't open out the sheet today," he muttered. "He was drunk." He tried to make his voice sound confident. "Eileen, sweetheart—we'll have to get out of this. It shouldn't be impossible, if we can only keep calm and try and think."

There was a silence. Then Eileen's words came back with quiet, hopeless finality.

"We can't break out of these rooms, Tony. The house is too strongly built. And—I think that tonight he's going to do something dreadful to us. I think that he's afraid to stay here any longer. But before he leaves this place he's going to—Tony, I know that man! He's ruthless, and he's—mad. Sometimes I think that he was really a minister. But not now, not now. He's pure devil now!"

HOW LONG Tony and Eileen, with the terrible earnestness of despair, talked to each other through the wall that night, neither ever knew. But it must have been for hours, for they talked of many things, yet never of the horror that menaced them. And they spoke calmly, quietly, with gentle tenderness …

Why should the doomed speak of that which they cannot evade?

Both knew that they were utterly in the giant madman's hands to do with, save for a miracle, as he pleased. Both knew that the apostate minister was merciless ...

There was no moon. But it must have been close to midnight when Tony heard the footsteps of several men on the stairs, the grating of the locks on Eileen's door, the sound of a brief, futile struggle, and then Eileen's despairing cry, "Good-bye, Tony, sweet—"

Frothing like a rabid beast, he hurled himself at the door, at the barred window, at the walls, beating at them with his naked fists until his knuckles were raw and numb and sweat poured in rivulets from his body.

Grim minutes passed. And then the footsteps returned. There was the sound of pine bars being withdrawn. Tony waited, crouching.

When they entered he leaped. But there was no strength in him—only a terrible, hopeless fury. Quickly they seized his arms, bound his hands firmly behind him with rope, dragged him, struggling impotently, down a steep flight of stairs, through the ground floor hall, and down a second flight of stairs, musty and noisome.

Here they paused for a moment while they fumbled with the latch of a door. At last the door swung open, and they dragged Tony forward into an immense, dimly lit chamber. The door swung shut; the old fashioned iron latch clicked.

This was the cellar of the plantation house, an enormous, cavernous place, extending beneath the whole rambling structure. Once designed for the storage of everything necessary to the subsistence of the householders living on the floors above, its vast spaces were broken by immense, mouldy bins. An eight-foot cistern loomed gigantically in a dark corner; wine shelves extended along one entire wall. The whole monstrous place had been dug half from the clayey soil and half from the solid rock; the floor underfoot, rough and uneven, was seamed and stratified rock.

Two oil lanterns, hanging from beams in the cobwebby ceiling, lighted no more than the merest fraction of that great vault; the farther recesses were shrouded in blackness.

The three Negroes—Mose, Job, and the man who had brought in the drunken lookout—waited expectantly, their black hands strong on Tony's arms. And suddenly Tony was a raging fury, tearing madly at those restraining hands ...

There in the centre of the old cellar, kneeling over a small, fragile form lying still and motionless on the mouldy rock, was the gigantic, black-clad Reverend Barnes!

That still, fragile form was Eileen!

At the sound of Tony's struggles the giant looked up, stood erect. Great beads of perspiration bedewed his unnaturally pallid forehead—yet there was a pursy, significant grin on his face.

"Hard work, this, Mr. Kent," he said genially. "Much harder work than you would think."

"What are you doing to her!"

There was exultant triumph in the booming reply.

"I am binding her with a spell, so that she will always do what I say. This is powerful obeah, Mr. Kent. I never dreamed—" He paused, while a swift dark shadow overspread his huge face, so strong and yet so weak. But the shadow passed as swiftly as it had come, and once again his eyes blazed with evil. "Within a few moments I shall put the same spell on you, also, so that you too will always do what I say."

Chuckling, he spoke to Tony's guards.

"Tie his feet securely and pitch him there by the wine-bin. I'll not want him until later."

With both his hands and feet tightly bound, the three Negroes dumped Tony down on the jagged rock beside the wine-bin. Tony's face was turned toward where the fallen minister squatted beneath the lanterns, a monstrous, Luciferian image.

"Sit down on the floor, niggers," he said slowly. "Relax and rest; there's no need to stand." The deep, resonant voice throbbed with kindliness. "I must think."

Obediently, the three squatted in a row on their haunches and sat looking with silent expectation at this white conjure-man who was their master.

The frock-coated figure shook its head slowly, as though its brain were cobwebby. Then, slowly, it opened the front of its filthy linen shirt, baring the grey-white of its chest—the chest of a powerful and sedentary man, who yet had always shunned the healthful sunlight—the chest of a physical animal whose warped brain had, perhaps through most of its years, abhorred the physical as immoral and unclean. A bag hung there at the figure's chest, suspended by a cord around its neck. Two big hands dipped into that gaping pouch …

Tony was struggling, struggling; rolling his body back and forth in straining jerks, trying to loosen the ropes that bound his feet and hands.

That bag of cotton dolls! One of those dolls represented Eileen.

Tony's shoulder crashed against the beams beneath the wine-bins, leaped with pain as an exposed nail tore the flesh. But the ropes held …

The big man's forearms, beneath the shiny black coat, were suddenly bulging—and in that instant the three Negroes who had been squatting on their haunches were rolling and writhing on the floor, their hands clawing at their throats, their bodies jerking and twisting, their faces purpling, their eyes bulging!

Slow minutes passed. And still the giant, renegade minister crouched there, motionless, his big forearms knotted, his face drawn into a sardonic grimace.

The struggles of the three were becoming feebler. Their arms and legs were beating spasmodically, as though consciousness had gone from them. And at last even that spasmodic twitching ceased and they lay still.

Yet the Reverend Barnes did not stir.

But then, after it seemed to Tony that an eternity had passed, he withdrew his hands from the bag. In his left hand he held by the throat two little cotton dolls, in his right hand, one. With a careless gesture he tossed them to the floor, rose to his feet, and stood slowly flexing and unflexing his fingers. At last he stooped over the three motionless Negroes and grunted with satisfaction.

"Fools, to think that I would ever keep you after your work was done!" He was swaying slightly. Seemingly he had forgotten Tony.

But Tony was stealthily, warily sawing his bound hands back and forth, back and forth across the bit of nail that jutted from the base of the wine-bin. Strand by strand he was breaking the half-inch hemp.

The Reverend Barnes had returned to his position beside Eileen, was once more squatting beside her. She had not moved. But she lay unbound; the colossus was very sure of his sorcery!

For long minutes he sat motionless, his shoulders drooped, his muscles flaccid. At last, with a deep sigh, he raised his head and looked at Eileen.

"Beautiful, beautiful womanhood!" he whispered softly. "All my life I've wanted a woman like you—"

He reached out a big, splayed and unhealthily colourless hand, touched Eileen's body. Beneath his gentle touch she stirred and moaned.

And suddenly Tony was cursing him wildly.

"Damn you; you hound of hell in priest's clothing!"

The Reverend Barnes's huge hand paused in its caressing.

"You feel jealousy, Mr. Kent?"

Tony could not see the expression on the man's face; he was a black-robed bulk against the lantern light. But there was a terrible gentleness in his voice.

"You filthy—" Tony choked. Words would no longer come to him; his rage was beyond words.

"Mr. Kent," the big man said softly, and Tony sensed that a slow, utterly evil smile was stealing across his face, "in a little while—such a little while—you'll no longer care what I do with her. You'll be beyond caring."

He swung about to face Tony.

"But—before I—dispose of you," he continued, with startling unexpectedness, "I'm going to tell you the—truth about myself. Why? Perhaps because I want to explain myself, to justify myself to myself. I don't know. Perhaps, in this moment, I have a sudden clear premonition of God's inevitable vengeance—for I am damned, Kent; I know full well that I am damned.

"I have been a preacher for twenty years,

Kent. Not the soft-spoken, politically minded type that ultimately lands the rich city churches; sin was too real to me for that; I fought the Devil tooth and claw.

"Perhaps that was the trouble. My ecclesiastical superiors were never certain of me. They thought of me as a sort of volcano that might explode at any time; I was unpredictable. And they suspected, too, I think, the devil in me— the physical lustiness and the desire for material things I fought so hard to stifle. They gave me only the poorest, backcountry churches, they' starved me; I was hungry for a mate and I could not even afford a wife. I think they hoped that I would fall into sin, so that they might thus be circumspectly rid of me.

"My last church was a pine shack twenty miles deep in a swamp. My parishioners were almost all Negroes—Negroes and a few whites so poverty-stricken that not one had ever seen a railway train or worn factory-made shoes. And inbreeding, in that disease-ridden country, was the rule, not the exception; you have no idea ...

"I worked, there in that earthly hell, like a madman. There was something there, something tangible, for me to fight—and I have always been a literal man. It was a shaman—what you would call a medicine-man or witch doctor. He was, of course, a coloured man.

"It may sound incredible, but I *competed* against that man for almost a year. We were exactly like rival salesmen. I sold faith, and enforced my sales with threats of hell-fire and damnation; he manufactured charms and love potions, prophesied the future and healed the sick.

"Of course I went after him hammer and tongs. I blasted him in church; I ridiculed him;

I told those poor ignorant people that his salves and his potions and his prophecies were no good. Eight months after I arrived there I began to feel that I was winning …

"After about a year had passed he came to see me. We knew each other, of course; I will describe him—a very gentle old man, very tall, very thin and grey. He told me that he wanted me to go away. I think that he knew my weakness, the bitterness in me, better than I knew it myself.

"He raised no religious arguments; in fact, I don't think there were ever any really fundamental differences between us. You know that Holy Writ speaks of witches and warlocks and demons, and my chief objection to this man lay in my private conviction that he was a faker, a mumbo-jumbo expert pulling the wool over the eyes of fools. And, even though I am a fundamentalist, still, this is the twentieth century. The upshot of it was that I laughed at him and listened.

"He merely told me that if I would go away he would teach me his power. What power? I said. I should have known that he was trying to trap me—to strike a bargain. He looked at me. 'Among other things, to raise the dead, that they may do your bidding,' he said, very slowly and seriously, 'although I have never myself done this obeah, because there has never been the need.'

"I laughed at him very loudly then, and for a long time.

"'Well,' I told him, after I got my breath back, 'I am a pretty poor preacher—if the calibre of my parish offers any criterion whatever. Perhaps I am not destined for the life of a minister, after all. Certainly my superiors don't think so. Therefore, if you will teach me these things of which you speak, and if they work, I will never preach another word as long as I live. But, if they do not work, you will come to church on Sunday, and proclaim yourself a faker before the entire congregation.'

"I felt very sure of myself, then, and I expected him to attempt to avoid the showdown. But he only answered me, quietly and gravely, 'I am the seventh son of a seventh son. I will teach you the obeah my father taught me, and if it works you will go away.'

"So—and I will tell you that I kept my tongue in my cheek all the while—I learned the rituals he taught me, learned them word for word, and wrote them down, phonetically, on paper to his dictation.

"But—he had not lied!"

The black-clad giant paused, and Tony saw that he was trembling. Presently the trembling passed, and, in a quiet, colourless monotone, the apostate minister added, "I knew, then, that I was eternally damned."

Tony shook his head. "No. Give up this—madness. No man has ever had the power to—condemn his own soul!"

The colossus shook its head; Tony could see a sneer hardening on its lips.

"I'll—pay! Because I have, now, what I have always wanted—power! Power over other men—and women! Shall I tell you what I am presently going to do with you? I'm going to make you so that you will forget everything; you will walk and talk only when I tell you to; you will do only what I say. You have money; I will make you take your car, and drive Miss Eileen and me to New York. There you will go to the bank, or wherever it is you keep your money, and draw everything out for me. Then, once again, you will get in your car and drive, but this time you will be alone, and while you are driving I will stick a pin into a little doll. 'Heart failure,' the doctors will say."

For a moment Tony did not speak. Then with a strange steadiness, he asked: "But—Eileen?" The big man chuckled. "You ask that question of a man who has denied himself women through all his life? Eileen will belong to me." Abruptly, ignoring the bound, suddenly raging man on the floor beside the wine-bin, he turned away. But now, when again he squatted close to Eileen, he did not remain motionless. From somewhere about his clothing he produced a needle and thread, and bits of cloth, and he was sewing. And as he sewed he muttered strange words to himself, in a tongue Tony had never heard before, muttered those words in a cadenceless monotone, as though he himself did not understand them, but was repeating them by rote, as perhaps, they had been taught to him by some aged coloured wizard ...

Tony's bound wrists rubbed back and forth, back and forth across the nail. Suddenly the strands binding his hands loosed.

Slowly, inch by inch, Tony hunched along the wine-bin, drawing up his feet. Warily he watched the big, crouching man; at any moment the Reverend Barnes might notice ...

But seemingly, the colossus was too preoccupied.

In furtive, small strokes, Tony's ankles sawed across the nail.

Suddenly the apostate minister stood up. He was looking at his handiwork, a grotesque little thing of odds and ends, crudely sewn yet unmistakably, with its limp, flopping appendages, a doll. And then he grunted approvingly, came toward Tony with the doll in his left hand.

"I'll have to take a few strands of your hair," he said grimly. His right hand reached downward toward Tony's scalp.

And then Tony's hands lashed from behind his back, clutched the pillar-like legs, strained. Abruptly the colossus sprawled his length on the uneven rock, his hands outsplayed. The little doll slid unheeded across the cold stone.

Jack-knifing his bound feet beneath him, Tony hurled himself across the floor. And with that tremendous effort the frayed ropes about his ankles ripped away.

Instantly he was atop the big man, his fingers sunk deep into the pasty white throat, his legs locked about giant hips.

But his antagonist's strength seemed superhuman. Only a half hour before those spatulate hands, as surely as though they had been about black throats, had simultaneously strangled three men. Rope-like torso muscles tautened; powerful hands tore at Tony's forearms.

The powerful hands lifted, tightened about Tony's throat. And as those huge talons flexed, a roaring began in Tony's ears, red spots danced madly before his eyes, the dim cellar swirled and heaved.

The colossus, hands still locked about Tony's throat, surged slowly to his feet. Contemptuously he looked into Tony's bloodshot, staring eyes, hurled him reeling across the rock-gouged vault.

And in that instant something hard and sharp split the base of his skull like an intolerable lightning. Bright sparks spun crazily before his eyes—flickered out in utter blackness. He felt himself falling, falling into eternity ...

Old Robert Perry, his eyes blazing with inhuman hate, stood above the Reverend Barnes's sprawling corpse, watching the red blood dim the lustre of the axe-blade he had sunk inches deep into the giant's skull!

"That hellish paralysis!" he was babbling, inanely. "That hellish paralysis—gone just in time!"

Old Robert Perry wheeled. In the feeble yellow light beneath the lantern he saw Eileen, awake now, huddled on the floor, pointing—her eyes pools of horror. And, following with his gaze her outstretched hand, he saw them, coming from the dark bins, the dead things the fallen minister had torn from their graves to toil in the cotton! They came pouring from those great bins with dreadful haste, their faces no longer stony and still, but writhing and tortured. And from the mouths of those that yet possessed mouths poured wild wailings.

Old Robert Perry was trembling—trembling.

"God!" he mumbled. "Their master's dead, and now they seek their graves!"

Dimly, as one who dreams in fever, he saw them passing him, no longer with stumbling, hopeless footsteps, but hurriedly, eagerly, crowding one another aside in their haste to escape into the night and return to their graves. And the flesh on his back crawled, and loosed, and crawled again ...

The zombies, dead things no longer beneath the fallen giant's unholy spell, twisted, broken, rotted by the diseases that had killed them, seeking the graves from which they had been torn!

"God!"

And then they were gone, gone in the night, and the sound of their wailing was a diminishing, scattering thinness in the distance ...

Old Robert Perry stared dazedly about, at Eileen, huddled on the floor, sobbing with little, half-mad cries that wrung his heart—at Tony, staggering drunkenly to his feet, stumbling blindly toward his beloved.

"Eileen!"

The name reached out from Tony's heart like the caress of strong arms. Reeling, he followed that cry across the floor to her, dropped to the rock beside her, gathered her in his arms.

DAWN WAS near when at last old Robert Perry and young Anthony Kent trudged wearily through the purple night toward the plantation house.

The belated moon, preceding the sun by only a few hours, glimmered in the east, a golden, enchanted shield; the woods were still.

The two men did not speak. Their thoughts were full of the horror that had been, of the great pit they had dug in the night and filled with the bodies of the giant renegade and his followers.

Yet, as they drew closer and closer to the rambling old house that nestled, moonbathed and serene, in the valley beneath them, words came at last.

"Anthony Kent," the old planter said earnestly, "I have, lived on this land through near four generations. I have heard the Negroes talk—of things like this. But I would never have believed—unless the truth had been thrust in my face."

Tony Kent shifted his spade to his left shoulder before he replied.

"Perhaps it's better," he said slowly, "that men are inclined to scepticism. Perhaps, as time goes on, these evil, black arts will die out. It may all be part of some divine plan."

Their footsteps made little crunching sounds in the road.

"Thank God that the fiend and his niggers were strangers hereabouts!" the old man said fervently. "They won't be missed. Nobody, of course, would ever believe—what really happened."

"No," Tony said. "But it's all over, now. Those dead things have gone—back to their graves."

They were close to the house. On the long walk, before the low screened porch, a small white-clad figure waited. And then it was running swiftly, eagerly toward them.

"Eileen!"

The name was a pulsing song. And then she was locked in Tony's arms, and he was kissing her upturned, tremulous lips.

The Song of the Slaves

By Manly Wade Wellman

GENDER PAUSED AT the top of the bald rise, mopped his streaming red forehead beneath the wide hat-brim, and gazed backward at his forty-nine captives. Naked and black, they shuffled upward from the narrow, ancient slave trail through the jungle. Forty-nine men, seized by Gender's own hand and collared to a single long chain, destined for his own plantation across the sea ... Gender grinned in his lean, drooping mustache, a mirthless grin of greedy triumph.

For years he had dreamed and planned for this adventure, as other men dream and plan for European tours, holy pilgrimages, or returns to beloved birthplaces. He had told himself that it was intensely practical and profitable. Slaves passed through so many hands—the raider, the caravaner, the seashore factor, the slaver captain, the dealer in New Orleans or Havana or at home in Charleston. Each greedy hand clutched a rich profit, and all profits must come eventually from the price paid by the planter. But he, Gender, had come to Africa himself, in his own ship; with a dozen staunch ruffians from Benguela he had penetrated the Bihe-Bailundu country, had sacked a village and taken these forty-nine upstanding natives between dark and dawn. A single neck-shackle on his long chain remained empty, and he might fill even that before he came to his ship. By the Lord, he was making money this way, fairly coining it—and money was worth the making, to a Charleston planter in 1853.

So he reasoned, and so he actually believed, but the real joy to him was hidden in the darkest nook of his heart. He had conceived the raider- plan because of a nature that fed on savagery and mastery. A man less fierce and cruel might have been satisfied with hunting lions or elephants, but Gender must hunt men. As a matter of fact, the money made or saved by the journey would be little, if it was anything. The satisfaction would be tremendous. He would broaden his thick chest each day as he gazed out over his lands and saw there his slaves hoeing seashore cotton or pruning indigo; his forty-nine slaves, caught and shipped and trained by his own big, hard hands, more indicative of assured conquest than all the horned or fanged heads that ever passed through the shops of all the taxidermists.

Something hummed in his ears, like a rhythmic swarm of bees. Men were murmuring a song under their breath. It was the long string of pinch-faced slaves. Gender stared at them, and mouthed one of the curses he always kept at tongue's end.

"Silva!" he called.

The lanky Portuguese who strode free at the head of the file turned aside and stood before Gender. "*Patrao?*" he inquired respectfully, smiling teeth gleaming in his walnut face.

"What are those men singing?" demanded Gender. "I didn't think they had anything to sing about."

"A slave song, *patrao*." Silva's tapering hand, with the silver bracelet at its wrist, made a graceful gesture of dismissal. "It is nothing. One of the things that natives make up and sing as they go."

Gender struck his boot with his coiled whip of hippopotamus hide. The afternoon sun, sliding down toward the shaggy jungle-tops, kindled harsh pale lights in his narrow blue eyes. "How does the song go?" he persisted.

The two fell into step beside the caravan as, urged by a dozen red-capped drivers, it shambled along the trail. "It is only a slave song, *patrao*," said Silva once again. "It means something like this: 'Though you carry me away in chains, I am free when I die. Back will I come to bewitch and kill you.'"

Gender's heavy body seemed to swell, and his eyes grew narrower and paler. "So they sing that, hmm?" He swore again. "Listen to that!" The unhappy procession had taken up a brief, staccato refrain:

"Hailowa – Genda! Haipana – Genda!"

"Genda, that's my name," snarled the planter. "They're singing about me, aren't they?"

Silva made another fluid gesture, but Gender flourished his whip under the nose of the Portuguese. "Don't you try to shrug me off. I'm not a child, to be talked around like this. What are they singing about me?"

"Nothing of consequence, *patrao*, Silva made haste to reassure him. "It might be to say: 'I will bewitch Gender, I will kill Gender.'"

"They threaten me, do they?" Gender's broad face took on a deeper flush. He ran at the line of chained black men. With all the strength of his arm he slashed and swung with the whip. The song broke up into wretched howls of pain.

"I'll give you a music lesson!" he raged, and flogged his way up and down the procession until he swayed and dripped sweat with the exertion.

But as he turned away, it struck up again:

"Hailowa – Genda! Haipana – Genda!"

Whirling back, he resumed the rain of blows. Silva, rushing up to second him, also whipped the slaves and execrated them in their own tongue. But when both were tired, the flayed captives began to sing once more, softly but stubbornly, the same chant.

"Let them whine," panted Gender at last. "A song never killed anybody."

Silva grinned nervously. "Of course not, *patrao*. That is only an idiotic native belief."

"You mean, they think that a song will kill?"

"That, and more. They say that if they sing together, think together of one hate, all their thoughts and hates will become a solid strength—will strike and punish for them."

"Nonsense!" exploded Gender.

But when they made camp that night, Gender slept only in troubled snatches, and his dreams were of a song that grew deeper, heavier, until it became visible as a dark, dense cloud that overwhelmed him.

The ship that Gender had engaged for the expedition lay in a swampy estuary, far from any coastal town, and the dawn by which he loaded his goods aboard was strangely fiery and forbidding. Dunlapp, the old slaver-captain that commanded for him, met him in the cabin.

"All ready, sir?" he asked Gender. "We can sail with the tide. Plenty of room in the hold for that handful you brought. I'll tell the men to strike off those irons."

"On the contrary," said Gender, "tell the men to put manacles on the hands of each slave."

Dunlapp gazed in astonishment at his employer. "But that's bad for blacks, Mr. Gender. They get sick in chains, won't eat their food. Sometimes they die."

"I pay you well, Captain," Gender rumbled, "but not to advise me. Listen to those heathen." Dunlapp listened. A moan of music wafted in to them.

"They've sung that cursed song about me all the way to the coast," Gender told him. "They know I hate it—I've whipped them day after day—but they keep it up. No chains come off until they hush their noise."

Dunlapp bowed acquiescence and walked out to give orders. Later, as they put out to sea, he rejoined Gender on the after deck.

"They do seem stubborn about their singing," he observed.

"I've heard it said," Gender replied, "that they sing together because they think many voices and hearts give power to hate, or to other feelings." He scowled. "Pagan fantasy!"

Dunlapp stared overside, at white gulls just above the wavetips. "There may be a tithe of truth in that belief, Mr. Gender; sometimes there is in the faith of wild people. Hark ye, I've seen a good fifteen hundred Mohammedans praying at once, in the Barbary countries. When they bowed down, the touch of all those heads to the ground banged like the fall of a heavy rock. And when they straightened, the motion of their garments made a swish like the gust of a gale. I couldn't help but think that their prayer had force."

"More heathen foolishness," snapped Gender, and his lips drew tight.

"Well, in Christian lands we have examples, sir," Dunlapp pursued. "For instance, a mob will grow angry and burn or hang someone. Would a single man do that? Would any single man of the mob do it? No, but together their hate and resolution becomes—"

"Not the same thing at all," ruled Gender harshly. "Suppose we change the subject."

On the following afternoon, a white sail crept above the horizon behind them. At the masthead gleamed a little blotch of color. Captain Dunlapp squinted through a telescope, and barked a sailorly oath.

"A British ship-of-war," he announced, "and coming after us."

"Well?" said Gender.

"Don't you understand, sir? England is sworn to stamp out the slave trade. If they catch us with this cargo, it'll be the end of us." A little later, he groaned apprehensively. "They're overtaking us. There's their signal, for us to lay to and wait for them. Shall we do it, sir?"

Gender shook his head violently. "Not we! Show them our heels, Captain."

"They'll catch us. They are sailing three feet to our two."

"Not before dark," said Gender. "When dark comes, we'll contrive to lessen our embarrassment."

And so the slaver fled, with the Britisher in pursuit. Within an hour, the sun was at the horizon, and Gender smiled grimly in his mustache. "It'll be dark within minutes," he said to Dunlapp. "As soon as you feel they can't make out our actions by glass, get those slaves on deck."

In the dusk the forty-nine naked prisoners stood in a line along the bulwark. For all their chained necks and wrists, they neither stood nor gazed in a servile manner. One of them began to sing and the others joined, in the song of the slave trail:

"Hailowa – Genda! Haipana – Genda!"

"Sing on," Gender snapped briefly, and moved to the end of the line that was near the bow. Here dangled the one empty collar, and he seized it in his hand. Bending over the bulwark, he clamped it shut upon something—the ring of a heavy spare anchor, that swung there upon a swivel-hook. Again he turned, and eyed the line of dark singers.

"Have a bath to cool your spirits," he jeered, and spun the handle of the swivel-hook.

The anchor fell. The nearest slave jerked over with it, and the next and the next. Others saw, screamed, and tried to brace themselves against doom; but their comrades that had already gone overside were too much weight for them. Quickly, one after another, the captives whipped from the deck and splashed into the sea. Gender leaned over and watched the last of them as he sank.

"Gad, sir!" exclaimed Dunlapp hoarsely.

Gender faced him almost threateningly.

"What else to do, hmm? You yourself said that we could hope for no mercy from the British."

The night passed by, and by the first grey light the British ship was revealed almost upon them. A megaphoned voice hailed them; then a shot hurtled across their bows. At Gender's smug nod, Dunlapp ordered his men to lay to. A boat put out from the pursuer, and shortly a British officer and four marines swung themselves aboard.

Bowing in mock reverence, Gender bade the party search. They did so, and remounted the deck crestfallen.

"Now, sir," Gender addressed the officer, "don't you think that you owe me an apology?"

The Englishman turned pale. He was a lean, sharp-featured man with strong, white teeth. "I can't pay what I owe you," he said with deadly softness. "I find no slaves, but I smell them. They were aboard this vessel within the past twelve hours."

"And where are they now?" teased Gender. "We both know where they are," was the reply. "If I could prove in a court of law what I know in my heart, you would sail back to England with me. Most of the way you would hang from my yards by your thumbs."

"You wear out your welcome, sir," Gender told him.

"I am going. But I have provided myself with your name and that of your home city. From here I go to Madeira, where I will cross a packet bound west for Savannah. That packet will bear with it a letter to a friend of mine in Charleston, and your neighbors shall hear what happened on this ship of yours."

"You will stun slave-owners with a story of slaves?" inquired Gender, with what he considered silky good-humor.

"It is one thing to put men to work in cotton fields, another to tear them from their homes, crowd them chained aboard a stinking ship, and drown them to escape merited punishment." The officer spat on the deck. "Good day, butcher. I say, all Charleston shall hear of you."

Gender's plantation occupied a great, bluff- rimmed island at the mouth of a river, looking out toward the Atlantic. Ordinarily that island would be called beautiful, even by those most exacting followers of Chateaubriand and Rousseau; but, on his first night at home again, Gender hated the fields, the house, the environs of fresh and salt water.

His home, on a seaward jut, resounded to his grumbled curses as he called for supper and ate heavily but without relish. Once he vowed, in a voice that quivered with rage, never to go to Charleston again.

At that, he would do well to stay away for a time. The British officer had been as good as his promise, and all the town had heard of Gender's journey to Africa and what he had done there. With a perverse squeamishness beyond Gender's understanding, the hearers were filled with disgust instead of admiration. Captain Hogue had refused to drink with him at the Jefferson House. His oldest friend, Mr. Lloyd Davis of Davis Township, had crossed the street to avoid meeting him. Even the Reverend Doctor Lockin had turned coldly away as he passed, and it was said that a sermon was forthcoming at Doctor Lockin's church attacking despoilers and abductors of defenseless people.

'What was the matter with everybody?' savagely demanded Gender of himself; these men who snubbed and avoided him were slaveholders. Some of them, it was quite possible, even held slaves fresh from raided villages under the Equator. Unfair! ... Yet he could not but feel the animosity of many hearts, chafing and weighing upon his spirit.

"Brutus," he addressed the slave that cleared the table, "do you believe that hate can take form?"

"Hate, Marsa?" The sooty face was solemnly respectful.

"Yes. Hate, of many people together." Gender knew he should not confide too much in a slave, and chose his words carefully. "Suppose a lot of people hated the same thing, maybe they sang a song about it—"

"Oh, yes, Marsa." Brutus nodded. "I heah 'bout dat, from ole granpappy when I was little. He bin in Affiky, he says many times dey sing somebody to deff."

"Sing somebody to death?" repeated Gender. "How?"

"Dey sing dat dey kill him. Afta while, maybe plenty days, he die—"

"Shut up, you black rascal." Gender sprang from his chair and clutched at a bottle. "You've heard about this somewhere, and you dare to taunt me!"

Brutus darted from the room, mortally frightened. Gender almost pursued, but thought better and tramped into his parlor. The big, brown-paneled room seemed to give back a heavier echo of his feet. The windows were filled with the early darkness, and a hanging lamp threw rays into the corners.

On the center table lay some mail, a folded newspaper and a letter. Gender poured whisky from a decanter, stirred in spring water and dropped into a chair. First he opened the letter.

"Stirling Manor," said the return address at the top of the page. Gender's heart twitched. Evelyn Stirling, he had hopes of her ... but this was written in a masculine hand, strong and hasty.

> *Sir:*
> *Circumstances that have come to my knowledge compel me, as a matter of duty, to command that you discontinue your attention to my daughter.*

Gender's eyes took on the pale tint of rage. One more result of the Britisher's letter, he made no doubt.

> *I have desired her to hold no further communication with you, and I have been sufficiently explicit to convince her how un-worthy you are of her esteem and attention. It is hardly necessary for me to give you the reasons which have induced me to form this judgment, and I add only that nothing you can say or do will alter it.*
> *Your obedient servant,*
> *JUDGE FORRESTER STIRLING*

Gender hastily swigged a portion of his drink, and crushed the paper in his hand. So that was the judge's interfering way—it sounded as though he had copied it from a complete letter-writer for heavy fathers. He, Gender, began to form a reply in his mind:

> *Sir:*
> *Your unfeeling and arbitrary letter admits of but one response. As a gentleman grossly misused, I demand satisfaction on the field of honor. Arrangements I place in the hands of ...*

By what friend should he forward that challenge? It seemed that he was mighty short of friends just now. He sipped more whisky and water, and tore the wrappings of the newspaper.

It was a Massachusetts publication, and toward the bottom of the first page was a heavy cross of ink, to call attention to one item. A poem, evidently, in four-line stanzas. Its title signified nothing—"The Witnesses." Author, Henry W. Longfellow; Gender identified him vaguely as a scrawler of Abolitionist doggerel. Why was this poem recommended to a southern planter?

> *In Ocean's wide domains,*

Half buried in the sands,
Lie skeletons in chains,
With shackled feet and hands.

Once again the reader swore, but the oath quavered on his lips. His eye moved to a stanza farther down the column:

These are the bones of Slaves;
They gleam from the abyss;
They cry, from yawning waves …

But it seemed to Gender that he heard, rather than read, what that cry was.

He sprang to his feet, paper and glass falling from his hands. His thin lips drew apart, his ears strained. The sound was faint, but unmistakable—many voices singing.

The Negroes in his cabins? But no Negro on his plantation would know that song. The chanting refrain began:

"Hailowa – Genda! Haipana – Genda!"

The planter's lean mustache bristled tigerishly. This would surely be the refined extremity of his persecution, this chanting of a weird song under his window sill. It was louder now. *I will bewitch, I will kill*—but who would know that fierce mockery of him?

The crew of his ship, of course; they had heard it on the writhing lips of the captives, at the very moment of their destruction. And when the ship docked in Charleston, with no profit to show, Gender had been none too kindly in paying them off.

Those unsavory mariners must have been piqued. They had followed him, then, were setting up this vicious serenade.

Gender stepped quickly around the table and toward the window. He flung up the sash with a violence that almost shattered the glass, and leaned savagely out.

On that instant the song stopped, and Gender could see only the seaward slope of his land, down to the lip of the bluff that overhung the water. Beyond that stretched an expanse of waves, patchily agleam under a great buckskin- colored moon, that even now stirred the murmurous tide at the foot of the bluff. Here were no trees, no brush even, to hide pranksters. The singers, now silent, must be in a boat under the shelter of the bluff.

Gender strode from the room, fairly tore open a door, and made heavy haste toward the sea. He paused, on the lip of the bluff. Nothing was to be seen, beneath him or farther out. The mockers, if they had been here, had already fled. He growled, glared and tramped back to his house. He entered the parlor once more, drew down the sash and sought his chair again. Choosing another glass, he began once more to mix whisky and water. But he stopped in the middle of his pouring.

There it was again, the song he knew; and closer.

He rose, took a step in the direction of the window, then thought better of it. He had warned his visitors by one sortie, and they had hidden. Why not let them come close, and suffer the violence he ached to pour out on some living thing?

He moved, not to the window, but to a mantelpiece opposite. From a box of dark, polished wood he lifted a pistol, then another. They were dueling weapons, handsomely made, with hair-triggers; and Gender was a dead shot. With orderly swiftness he poured in glazed powder from a flask, rammed down two leaden bullets, and laid percussion caps upon the touch- holes. Returning, he placed the weapons on his center table, then stood on tiptoe to extinguish the hanging lamp. A single light remained in the room, a candle by the door, and this he carried to the window, placing it on a bracket there. Moving into the gloomy center of the parlor, he sat in his chair and took a pistol in either hand.

The song was louder now, lifted by many voices:

"Hailowa – Genda! Haipana – Genda!"

Undoubtedly the choristers had come to land by now, had gained the top of the bluff. They could be seen, Gender was sure, from the window. He felt perspiration on his jowl, and lifted a sleeve to blot it. Trying to scare him, hmm? Singing about witchcraft and killing? Well, he'd show them who was the killer.

The singing had drawn close, was just outside. Odd how the sailors, or whoever they were, had learned that chant so well! It recalled to his mind the slave trail, the jungle, the long procession of crooning prisoners. But here was no time for idle reverie on vanished scenes. Silence had fallen again, and he could only divine the presence, just outside, of many creatures.

Scratch-scratch-scratch; it sounded like the stealthy creeping of a snake over rough lumber. That scratching resounded from the window where something stole into view in the candlelight. Gender fixed his eyes there, and his pistols lifted their muzzles.

The palm of a hand, as grey as a fish, laid itself on the glass. It was wet; Gender could see the trickle of water descending along the pane.

Something clinked, almost musically. Another hand moved into position beside it, and between the two swung links of chain.

This was an elaborately devilish joke, thought Gender, in an ecstasy of rage. Even the chains, to lend reality ... and as he stared he knew, in a split moment of terror that stirred his flesh on his bones, that it was no joke after all.

A face had moved into the range of the candlelight, pressing close to the pane between the two palms.

It was darker than those palms, of a dirty, slatey deadness of color. But it was not dead, not with those dull, intent eyes that moved slowly in their blistery sockets ... not dead, though it was foully wet, and its thick lips hung slackly open, and seaweed lay plastered upon the cheeks, even though the flat nostrils showed crumbled and gnawed away, as if by fish. The eyes quested here and there across the floor and walls of the parlor. They came to rest, gazing full into the face of Gender.

He felt as though stale seawater had trickled upon him, but his right hand abode steady as a gun-rest. He took aim and fired.

The glass crashed loudly and fell in shattering flakes to the floor beneath the sill.

Gender was on his feet, moving forward, dropping the empty pistol on the table and whipping the loaded one into his right hand. Two leaping strides took him almost to the window, before he reeled backward.

The face had not fallen. It stared at him, a scant yard away. Between the dull, living eyes showed a round black hole, where the bullet had gone in. But the thing stood unflinchingly, somehow serenely. Its two wet hands moved slowly, methodically, to pluck away the jagged remains of the glass.

Gender rocked where he stood, unable for the moment to command his body to retreat. The shoulders beneath the face heightened. They were bare and wet and deadly dusky and they clinked the collar-shackle beneath the lax chin. Two hands stole into the room, their fish-colored palms opening toward Gender.

He screamed, and at last he ran. As he turned his back, the singing began yet again, loud and horribly jaunty—not at all as the miserable slaves had sung it. He gained the seaward door, drew it open, and looked full into a gathering of black, wet figures, with chains festooned among them, awaiting him. Again he screamed, and tried to push the door shut.

He could not. A hand was braced against the edge of the panel—many hands. The wood fringed itself with gleaming black fingers. Gender let go the knob, whirled to flee into the house. Something caught the back of his coat, something he dared not identify. In struggling loose, he spun through the doorway and into the moonlit open.

Figures surrounded him, black, naked, wet figures; dead as to sunken faces and flaccid muscles, but horribly alive as to eyes and trembling hands and slack mouths that formed the strange primitive words of the song; separate, yet strung together with a great chain and collar-shackles, like an awful fish on the gigantic line of some demon-angler. All this Gender saw in a rocking, moon-washed moment, while he choked and retched at a dreadful odor of death, thick as fog.

Still he tried to run, but they were moving around him in a weaving crescent, cutting off his retreat toward the plantation. Hands extended toward him, manacled and dripping. His only will was to escape the touch of those sodden fingers, and one way was open—the way to the sea.

He ran toward the brink of the bluff. From its top he would leap, dive and swim away. But they pursued, overtook, surrounded him. He remembered that he held a loaded pistol, and fired into their black midst. It had no effect. He might have known that it would have no effect.

Something was clutching for him. A great, inhuman talon? No, it was an open collar of metal, with a length of chain to it, a collar that had once clamped to an anchor, dragging down to the ocean's depths a line of shackled men. It gaped at him, held forth by many dripping hands. He tried to dodge, but it darted around his throat, shut with a ringing snap. Was it cold ... or scalding hot? He knew, with horror vividly etching the knowledge into his heart, that he was one at last with the great chained procession.

"*Hailowa—Genda! Haipana—Genda!*"

He found his voice. "No, no!" he pleaded.

"No, in the name of—"

But he could not say the name of God. And the throng suddenly moved explosively, concertedly, to the edge of the bluff.

A single wailing cry from all those dead throats, and they dived into the waves below.

Gender did not feel the clutch and jerk of the chain that dragged him along. He did not even feel the water as it closed over his head.

The Forbidden Trail

By Jane Rice

I SIGNED the bar check, picked the frosted silver goblet off the-tray, my fingers leaving smudgy highways among the beaded wetness, and nibbled one of the sugared mint leaves experimentally.

"Hm-m-m," I said with appreciative approval"

"Dat'll put a kink in youah haih, Mistah Rutherf'd." Sam gave me a toothy grin, took the proffered half dollar, polished it on his sleeve and pocketed it—also with appreciative approval.

"Yass *suh*, boss," he said emphatically and walked away, thumping his tray happily.

Scrounging down on the back of my neck, I lifted the julep, in the direction of the open window, with its panoramic view of lower Manhattan, and quoth, "Here's to New York. Good, old New York." I drank deeply. A delicious sensation passed along my alimentary canal.

"Ahh-h-h-h-h," I sighed in a long drawn-out exhalation of peace and contentment.

"Holy, jumping catfish!" a voice squawked behind me. "As I live and breathe, Tarzan of the Apes! Tony Rutherford! When did you get back?"

My first impulse was to get down on my hands and knees and crawl under the rug; in fact, I think I would've on my second impulse, too, if I hadn't been so busy preserving not only my own equilibrium but that of my glass while undergoing a succession of thwacks on my vertebrae that felt as if they were being delivered with the flat of a meat ax. But they were, as I knew, administered by Allan Pomeroy. Those, zestful, outdoorsy accents and the subsequent pummeling could have been authored by but one person—the club bore.

"Hold it, and sit down and I'll listen to how you could've won the tennis tournament if—" I said patiently and not too grammatically.

Pomeroy came round and perched athletically on the arm of a chair. Rangy, good-looking in a curly-haired, sunburned way, with eyes the color of, and with just about as much depth as, a Dresden china doll's.

"Mag home, too?" he asked.

Mag. I must remember to tell Mag. Nothing made her madder than to be called "Mag"—like a witch with poisoned apples, or a sway-backed mare with its ears poking out of a straw hat, she'd say, stamping her size 3B pumps.

"No," I replied wearily; "I traded her to a Maisai tribesman for a bolt of calico and a cotton umbrella. And it's *Meg*."

For a moment Pomeroy's blue eyes grew very wide and then he chirruped brightly, "Oh, you're pulling my leg.

A bolt of calico ... oh, I say, that's very good," and he burst into roars of laughter while I sipped my drink and tried mental telepathy—go away—go away—go away—go away.

"Whose pictures did you take this time?" he queried, having with an immense effort subsided. "Monsieur

Lion? Madame Tiger? Frau Hippopotamus?"

"I didn't bring back any pictures," I said.

"Nothing?!"

"Nothing."

"Oh, come now, Rutherford, you're holding out on me. Whatever it is, it must be a dinger. You didn't trek through the Liberian wilderness without clicking a lens."

"Nothing." I said.

"Empty-handed?"

"Empty-handed."

"Not even a unicorn or a couple of albino gorillas?"

"No."

"You *are* holding out on me. Must be spectacular." Allan wrinkled his forehead in musing concentration. "It wasn't by any chance a zombie was it? An authentic dyed-in-the-wool zombie with a brass nose ring and bones in its hair? I've always wanted to see a picture of a zombie. Such scrumptious horror appeal. How's about it? Any zombie snaps?"

And, all at once, I was back in that God-forsaken clearing with the silence thick as guava paste and the creepers twining over everything like sightless green snakes and the dusk closing in a purple shroud, over the thatched roofs of that deserted Guere village.

"Nothing." I repeated-doggedly.

"No zombies." Allan said sadly.

"No." I said hoarsely.

Allan sat up and observed me intently. "Ah-ha," he said, "I'm on the right track." He smacked his palms together and said waggishly, "I've got it. You brought one back alive à la Frank Buck. You defied the immigration authorities. You probably stuffed him in the bottom of your trunk under a mess of collapsible canoes and things to get him by the officials without a passport and now you're going to spring him on—"

"I'll tell you what I brought back,"

I interrupted him savagely. "I brought back my sanity. Now for the love of God, leave me alone. LEAVE ME ALONE!"

Allan gawped at me as if I had suddenly sprouted horns and cloven feet and, as I got in several more violent leave-me-alones in rapid succession, he stammered a phrase about something or other in the locker room and made a hasty exit.

I RESUMED my julep sipping and gazed morosely out the window. But the julep tasted as though it had been concocted with woodash instead of bourbon and the skyscrapers seemed to have moved closer together, as if seeking protection from the very sky they strived to pierce, and even it appeared less cerulean. A boat edged up the Hudson, fearfully, it seemed to me, as if peering over its shouldered scarf of smoke belching from a red funnel. And the smoke itself looked frightened, dissipating as quickly as possible in tattered yellow streamers. Yellow as a dead man's face. A dead man who wasn't dead. And who wasn't alive. And whose features had the flabby colorlessness of a bled pig. With a muttered curse, I banged the unfinished drink down on the table, jammed on my hat and clumped out.

I told Meg about it over dinner and Meg crinkled her pug of a nose at me until the freckles ran together like golden-brown waffle crumbs and said, "You might as well face it, Tony. You're scared."

"Scared!" I ejaculated. "Me?"

"You," she answered, surveying me levelly over a forkful of mashed potatoes. "Scared. S-c-a-r-e-d—scared." She plopped the potatoes in her mouth and chewed them ruminatively. "The trouble with you is, m'love, you have a mathematical mind. To your way of thinking, two and two make four. Always has. Always will. And when, like a bolt from the blue, two and two add up to six, or eight, or a minus thirteen, you get the screaming meemies even if you won't admit it.

"Now, me," she went on insouciantly, "I have an imaginative mind. I'm gullible. If Minnie came in and said, 'There's a goblin in the garden, Mrs. Rutherford,' I'd say, 'Well, give it some porridge and see that the cat doesn't bother it.' You'd say, 'Don't be absurd!'"

"But it *would* be absurd," I began, "and besides, I'm not talking about goblins. I'm talking about Murchison and those … those … the … the—"

"I'm not talking about goblins, either, darling." Meg broke in. "Not really. I'm talking about your mind. It's all shut up tight like a little locked box with something horrible in it. And the longer the box remains scaled the more hideous that something is going to become, until after a while people will begin to whisper, 'What's wrong with Tony? Has Rutherford gone off his bat? Unsociable devil and such a swe-e-e-e-et wife.'" Meg made a moue at me and started on her salad.

"But, Meg, there's no such thing as a … as a … as what we saw!" Meg put down her fork and faced me squarely.

"There's no such thing as a dodo," she said, "or a dinosaur, or a land called Atlantis, but once there was. And I haven't the slightest doubt that when Lazarus was raised from the dead, there were any number of intelligent souls that rent their garments and ran about with ashes on their heads, vowing never again to guzzle gin slings or their biblical equivalents.

"Now you're certainly aware Liberia is no Forty-second Street. Civilization hasn't even made a nick in it. It's hot, steaming, fertile jungle. It's tom-toms and witch doctors and grigris. It is, I think, like the earth when the earth was young and hadn't begun to cool and crack and settle down to a smooth rotation on its axis." She gave me a beseeching glance. "You *do* follow me?"

"I'm trying."

"Well, who are we to deny the presence of powers, heretofore unknown to us, that may exist, possibly have existed since the beginning of time, in this last far-flung outpost of … of virgin world? You know, yourself, that if Wahla, black scamp that lie was, God love him, saw a neon sign, he'd have a hissy. Look at our bearers. How terrified they were of our phonograph, at first. Wahla threw himself flat, remember, and Dmigne drew a symbol in the dust as a sort of protective cabalistic barrier between him and the machine, while the rest of the tribe took to their heels and had to be coaxed back with beads and mirrors and gewgaws. It works both ways. Why should we refuse to believe certain astounding facts that *they* accepted?"

"Meg, do you honestly think that Langdon was capable of giving life back to the dead?" I asked.

There was a long pause while Meg stirred her coffee around and around so that it had a miniature whirlpool in the center.

"I don't think anything," she said at last, resting the spoon in the saucer. "That is, I'm not casting my vote in favor of the ayes or nays. All I know is that, for some reason, all the wild life had vanished beyond that Forbidden Trail, and that Langdon was mad, stark, staring mad and that Murchison, or the thing we called Murchison, had the bony, segmented limbs of a skeleton. That's all I actually *know*.

Minnie came in with some hot rolls.

"Mr. Rutherford," she clucked reprovingly, eyeing my plate, "you ain' et a thing. Not airy thing."

"Thunderation!" I bellowed at her. "That's all I hear. You ain' et a thing. Morning, noon, and night, I ain' et a thing and, furthermore, I ain' going to. You take care of the kitchen, I'll take care of my diet!"

Minnie thumped the rolls down on the table and, with prim lips and switching skirt, flounced pantryward.

"You see," Meg said, when the door had stopped swinging, "you've got as pretty a case of jitters as ever I saw. If you keep this up, in another month you'll be doing occupational therapy and bleating stuff like hehehewahanojibber jibberjibber to a bunch of white-coated orderlies at Bellevue."

"Alright," I gritted, "what do I do about it?"

"If I were you darling," Meg said, taking up where she had left off on the potatoes, "I'd write it down with pen and ink and, after I was sure all the "I"s were dotted and the "T"s were crossed, I'd read it over thoroughly and then put it in the bottom of the cedar chest, along with your high-school diploma and the picture of the basketball team and that old pair of sculling oars." Meg's countenance lighted with a seraphic smile arid her eyes got that sort of distant, hazy expression in them that makes all males past the stage of three-cornered pants palpitate visibly, and which usually means her mental machinery is all set to pop a piston.

"On second thought," she said dreamily, "whyn't you make a story of it, say around ten thousand words, and send it in to a magazine? There's a flame chiffon, with yards and yards of frilly skirt and the cutest sequined bolero in a shop uptown, and I think it's worth about ten thousand words. Maybe, you'd better, make it twelve thousand to be on the safe side." She beamed at me and I melted like so much warm butter and beamed back.

"You," I chuckled, "are a lulu. You are a beautiful, gorgeous hunk of luluness. You are the original La Belle Dame Sans Merci. And, if I know you, the flame chiffon is only a come-on for a black velvet wrap, with ermine tails and one of those do-funnys that hang down like a limp hat in back."

"Why, Tone-e-e-ey," Meg said reproachfully, letting me have the complete battery of those violet eyes full strength.

"WE OUGHT to be there soon, oughtn't we?" Meg slapped at a mosquito and pushed up her helmet to mop her forehead, pearled with drops of sweat and plastered with damply curling tendrils of taffy hair. "These mosquitoes certainly have the will to succeed, haven't they?"

"Right you are about both things," I said. "The mosquitoes are practically carnivores and here comes Wahla springing along on the balls of his feet and dripping importance. He's sighted the government compound."

Wahla had. I'll spare you the italicized gibberish that, as a rule, runs rampant through most jungliographies. You know the kind of thing, Wahla, my Swahili boy, cried excitedly, *"Idyen keyna ollan mayre olketyi yo!"* As a matter of fact, that's exactly what Wahla cried, and it meant the compound was about three hours distant. But from now on, you and Wahla and I are going to talk in English and nuts with all this tribal-language folderol. It'd have to be translated, anyway, so why bother with it? If you're interested in learning to speak Swahili, come, around any afternoon between four and four-five and I'll teach it to you. Really, the only words you have to know in any language are: water, food, stop, go, and help.

Sure enough, we sighted the compound not long after and evidently news of our approach had filtered through in some inexplicable manner, for we were met by a band of chattering black children, most of them naked as the day they were born, with round, bulging stomachs and eyes as bright and shiny as bilberries. The elders greeted us more gravely, nodding and bowing and, when they thought we weren't noticing, poking our paraphernalia with skinny inquisitorial fingers.

Colonel Mayhew was hospitality itself. Meg and I have trekked around in out of the way places long enough to know that these guardians of territorial outposts, hacked bodily from the ever-threatening jungle, are tickled silly to see white faces and to hear Anglicized voices. But, somehow, Mayhew was too effusive. Like a child, whose departure up a dark and gloomy stairwell to bed is delayed by the arrival of company—or as Meg put it, whose "company" does his arithmetic problems for him.

Which hit the nail right spang on the noggin. Because it developed, over the rice and curried chicken, that Colonel Mayhew wanted us to investigate an incident, a rather odd incident, concerning his assistant Murchison and also a man named Langdon who had a rubber plantation adjacent to the Cavally River. For some unknown reason the blacks in the Bandigara section had fled their villages on the Cavally and Murchison, getting wind of it, had gone to see Langdon who, so Colonel Mayhew said, was apparently the cause of the general exodus. Murchison had left a fortnight ago and Murchison had neither returned nor sent a message which, I gathered, was extremely un-Murchisony.

"But we're en route to Grand Bassam on the Ivory Coast" I demurred. "That's directly away from the Cavally River."

The colonel refilled my cup with palm wine and said he had heard there were some extremely fine panthers in the Bandigara section.

We had enough panther pictures, I said. We were, you might say, panther poor.

And how were we fixed on hamadryads, the colonel inquired.

Reptiles didn't go over so well, I explained. Not in America, anyway. Americans wanted orangutans, and bull elephants and wild dogs, and lions, and native ceremonies, and bushmen, and head hunters, and queer, tribes with decorated jowls and such.

How did Americans react to cannibals?

Just as they reacted to saber-toothed tigers, I replied. Good stuff, but, extinct.

I knew, of course, the Bandigara section was peopled with Guere?

Sure, I said, and so what? Since the government had taken over, there hadn't been a roast "long pig" in twenty years. Nowadays, what meat the Gueres ate came from rope snares or out of government tins.

But, didn't I think it odd the warlike Gueres were fleeing their villages? They had, so he had been told, even erected a forbidden barrier leading into their sector as a warning to others.

Well, I said, swigging my wine, it might be odd and then again it mightn't. Perhaps this Captain Langdon believed in a rawhide whip in lieu of pay. Some of those rubber fellows were the devil's own brood. Usually wound up with a staved-in skull, or had their heads nicely shrunk for hanging in a chieftain's hut. Then, I wouldn't be interested?

Emphatically not. No hard feelings or anything, but, in my opinion, the Gueres weren't born yesterday. If cannibalism was being practiced on the sly, all they had to do was report it and the government would land on the offenders like a Mills bomb. And the Gueres knew it. Nope, the colonel could take it from me, Langdon was pulling some sort of shenanigans. Give him plenty of rope, I said sententiously, tilting my chair on its two back legs, and the Gueres would see he got throttled with it.

AT THIS JUNCTURE, Meg spoke up in a sweet voice and said, "Now zombies would be a different story. Colonel Mayhew. The Americans just *love* zombies. They even have a cocktail named The Zombie. Three of them and you don't know whether you're dead or alive—or care. There wouldn't, by some quirk of circumstance, be any zombies in Bandigara, would there?"

The colonel choked, sprayed a gulp of palm wine all over the front of his linen coat, snorted, had to be pounded on the back, caught his breath, wheezed mightily, coughed and said through a frog in his throat, "I wasn't going to mention it, but since you brought it up"—he wiped his brimming eyes—"that's the crux of the situation."

"No!" Meg said, and the surprise was so thick I looked at her suspiciously. Meg is *never* surprised about anything.

"Zombies?" I said incredulously.

"Zombies," Colonel Mayhew echoed soberly, "leastways that's the tale that's filtered in to us."

"You don't believe it!"

"I don't know," he said slowly. "I don't know."

"Have you seen any?

"No-o-o-o. But the blacks have the wind up pretty badly. And the Gueres are a fearless lot. They'd stick anything. Except death. That kind of death. Walking death."

"But, man alive, that's incredible. There's no such thing as a zombie. It's the prime native ghost story, that's all. The choice cut, as it were.

They tell of zombies as we tell of women in white, rattling chains, and wall tapping."

"I'm not so sure, Rutherford. If it were one zombie or two, I wouldn't be so apt to credit it. From what I hear, there's supposed to be a, whole village of them."

"A whole village!"

"Yes."

"Poppycock. There's been an epidemic of catalepsy, or something. A whole, village of zombies," I hooted.

The colonel flushed. "Murchison thought it was funny, too. He left here laughing his head off at me for being an old woman." The colonel held his cup at the level of his eyes and regarded it somberly. "And Murchison hasn't come back."

"Oh, see here," I interposed hurriedly, "I didn't mean to intimate you had swallowed an old tale, hook, line, and sinker. If I thought for a moment I could get a reel of a zombie, just one, I'd be off like a shot. But I don't think there—"

"Rutherford," Mayhew said, "I give you my word that something out of the ordinary is happening on Langdon's plantation. Something that is beyond mortal understanding. And *I* think it's zombies. Take it or leave it."

The silence lengthened and grew around the table. The fragrance of frangipani was borne in on the night breeze and somewhere, away in the tangle of jungle beyond the stockade, a wah wah began its haunting, plaintive song. A black rhinoceros beetle bumped its head against the lamp, its frustrated buzz sounding unnaturally loud in the stillness.

I let my chair down with a thud and said, "I'll take it."

"Stout fella," Mayhew said and filled my cup to the top.

"To Bandigara."

"To Bandigara." I drank and smashed my cup against the wall and instantly felt like a melodramatic idiot.

There, was a second smash. Meg had thrown hers.

"I've always hankered to do that," she said and added wistfully, looking at my jersey, "I wish Dartmouth had had old school ties."

WE GOT under-way early, the next morning after a hearty breakfast that would have done justice to a mob of Kansas field hands during the wheat harvest. Mayhew saw us off with much joviality and hearty handshaking, but below his bushy brows, his eyes weren't jovial and he passed up breakfast, saying he'd eaten earlier, which was an out-and-out lie, as I'd seen his cook laying the fire in the godown not twenty minutes before the breakfast gong rang. Incidentally, the cook, a mixture of Irrut and Swahili, had seen *me* and had dropped his bundle of sticks and had beaten a Paavo Nurmi exit out the back door. He hadn't served us, either. The meal was all laid out on tin plates and waiting for us and, though Mayhew beat the gong and even stomped out in the kitchen, making a splendid noise in his English boots, we served ourselves. Mayhew was most apologetic and said the cook hadn't been feeling well, too much rice beer, and the other servants had gone to the fields early. But we weren't fooled. They knew where we were heading for and they wanted none of us.

This became quite apparent when we left. For the compound was empty. Far from being on deck to receive the bounty that it is customary for "guests" to bestow on their departure, the blacks were nowhere in evidence. True, one ebony tike, with a fat little paunch like a dusky tub of butter, came dashing out of a doorway, his chunky hands outstretched greedily for baksheesh but, before he'd gotten more than two paces in our direction, his mother hove into view behind him, fetched him a looping clout on the ear and bore him wailing back into the hut.

Mayhew tried to prevail on Meg to stay behind. And Meg said "Ha."

We turned at the bend and waved at Mayhew, who gave, us a military salute. "There ought to be, a bugler blowing taps," Meg said. Only, somehow, it didn't sound very funny.

Our Swahilis remained as impassive as ever, but for the first time in many moons, Wahla didn't sing. It was his wont to trot along the line of safari, chanting in a singsong voice: "Move, you white-tailed baboon, you liverless hyena, you blistered he dog with the legs of a kangaroo, move, move, before the anger of the white Tuan shrivels your skins, move, hiyeh!" The song varied and at some points I venture to say it would have brought a blush to the jaded cheek of a habitué of Montparnasse. Meg and I delighted in it. But, that day Wahla trudged along like a deaf mute. If we were at the head of the march, Wahla tagged in the rear and if we waited and swung in behind, he unobtrusively pushed on ahead. Once I stayed behind and sent Meg ahead and Wahla quietly idled until he had slipped halfway between. It was disturbing and yet it whetted my insatiable appetite for the mysterious. For I felt that Wahla had an inkling of what lay before us and that he was expressing his misgivings as politely as possible.

His disquiet and unease had penetrated through to the Swahilis by camp time and contrary to their usual habit of gathering in a circle after supper for chit chat or pebble throws, they withdrew and sat in clumps of three and four, silent and apparently communicating by mental telepathy. At least so far as I could ascertain, nobody said anything and yet, shortly six of them had, so they lamented, developed horrendous internal symptoms and begged to be dismissed. I gave the six castor oil and soothed them down as best I could.

In the morning they were gone.

By nightfall of the next day, ten more pleaded extreme illness and one, the sole bearer with a spark of imagination, exhibited a mashed toe that prevented his walking a step farther and couldn't possibly have been mashed by anything other than a deliberate pounding with our iron skillet.

After we made camp and were fed, Meg and I went into a huddle. It was obvious we couldn't continue on with dissatisfaction running rampant through the porters and those porters intent on getting back to where they'd started from as quickly as possible. We decided to take one camera and sufficient food to last a week. Get Wahla to hand pick two reliable bearers to carry the supplies and allow the remainder to go on to Grand Bassam under the wing of Wahla's "second lieutenant," Dmigne. Dmigne being given our Victrola, for which his admiration was intense, to insure the safe arrival of our equipage at the post.

This being agreed, we called in Wahla and explained the situation to him. Wahla was as inscrutable as a basilisk and told us gently that the signs and portents were unfavorable.

"Bosh," I said, only in Swahili and a whole paragraph of it.

"Muungu," Wahla insisted, "blew the wood smoke close to the ground which was an infallible omen of ill luck."

"Muungu was just blowing a little hard," I said.

Wahla shrugged and gazed at us with blank eyes, and popped his ankles, and spat betel juice with unerring accuracy through the tent flap.

Meg said, "All right, what do *you* want? Dmigne gets the Victrola," Wahla's expression immediately became suffused with animation and he said elaborately and at great length that, while Muungu was god of the fetishes and was all-powerful and while he wouldn't cast aspersions on Muungu for anything and hoped Muungu wouldn't misinterpret what he was about to say, that I, the white Tuan, had powerful grigris. Namely, the mirror, clear as water, that made big of little, and the watch that does not tick but tells where the true path lies.

"He means the magnifying glass and the compass," I said to Meg. "We need the compass, so we'll give him the glass" and started to say "all right" when Meg stopped me.

"Maybe, we'd better give him the compass," she said haltingly and did her darnedest to override my protestations.

After much arguing, back and forth, about the importance of the compass and its indispensability, I finally got it out of Meg that she had given the magnifying glass to Mayhew's house boy.

"Why!" I said, "why, in the name of Merry Christmas, did you have to give the glass? Why didn't you give one of those tin flashlights? God knows we have a trunk full of them. You *know* Wahla has had his eye on that glass since we entered Liberia. You *know* he thinks that and the compass are potent magic. You *know*—"

"I know it's not going to do any good to rant about it," Meg said. "Give him the compass. He'll be with us, so it won't make any difference."

"But why did—"

"Because he wanted it," Meg said exasperatedly. "My goodness, we'd, never have heard about those zombies if I hadn't lugged them in to the conversation by main force. You'd have had us in Grand Bassam snug as bugs in a rug, with all those zombies cluttering up Bandigara, and a swell opportunity shot to hell."

"You gave Mayhew's house boy the glass as a bribe to tell you exactly what was going on among the Gueres?"

"Yes"

"Then you knew all along."

"Yes."

"Why didn't you say so?"

"Because I've been your bridge partner often enough to know that a two forcing bid from me makes you sit and sniggle like an inmate of a feeble-minded institution, but that if somebody else makes a two forcing bid, you'll jump in "feet first," determined to get the bid or bust. So far, you haven't busted."

Wahla got the compass.

THE FOLLOWING morning we bade good-bye to Dmigne and the porters, saw them on their way and then we set forth, Meg and I, two huskies, their necks straight with balancing haversacks on their kinky craniums, and Wahla proudly leading the decimated parade, the compass slung under his arm in true grigris fashion.

We made swift progress, unhampered as we were by superfluous baggage. Overhead, the sun seemed to hang stationary, a glowing, brassy ball in an inverted blue bowl. Several times we passed close enough to zebra to catch a whiff of their horsy smell, which never ceases to amaze me, and twice we caught glimpses of giraffe and saw two rhinoceros evidently lost in some rapt prehistoric memory of their own, as oblivious to us as they were to the tick birds pecking daintily at their armored exteriors.

Those explorers who describe the veldt as an unbroken expanse of tan, breast-high grass have made the mistake of visiting Liberia and its neighbor, East Africa, during the dry season. We, ahem, know better, which sounds egotistical and probably is, but we have found pictures have a better market when they're teeming with broad-leaved plantains, and shrubs, and brilliant flowers, and color splashed Toucans, and sleek, well-fed beasts and such, than when they're backgrounded with parched greenery and lions with countable ribs and shabby manes who, no matter how ferocious they actually are, look on the screen like so many left-over circus props. Besides, in the dry season the animals get downright ravenous, and I'm a poor shot and Meg is no good at all in broken field running.

The landscape shimmered before and around us and imperceptibly the clumps of trees and the spiky pampas gave ground to denser foliage and lush undulating terrain. Vines began to make their appearance, creeping snakewise up the trees to join in a thick network above our heads. Bright-plumaged birds, like Byzantine jewels, flew among the branches, and mammoth butterflies, resting on the lichens and fungi, opened and closed their feathery wings as if to have us admire their ravishing splendor. Monkeys scolded us from the safe, distance of-the treetops and here and there a mischievous chap, emboldened by our lack of response, pelted us with fruit hulls. Say what you will, wild and trackless as it is, with its one law—kill or be killed, eat or be eaten—Liberia, with all its barbarity, is a paradise. A lost paradise, unbelievably beautiful and as insidious a drug as opium.

We came to the barrier at noon and I sizzled out an oath that I hadn't had sense enough to go on ahead of the march and tear it down before our blacks saw it. As barriers go it was no great shakes. A fringe of withered vine strands tied around two tree trunks, so that it blocked our barely definable path, it could have been scattered to the winds by a baby's hand. But, as far as the Swahilis went, it was as solid as a wall of reinforced cement, studded with broken glass and topped with barbed wire and Gatling guns.

I've seen these barriers before—these Forbidden Trails. As a rule, they are placed, only on secluded paths that lead to the haunts of witch doctors or hogouns, or to the shelters where young boys are segregated to undergo various rites on reaching manhood. The natives believe that to enter a Forbidden Trail is tantamount to spitting in Muungu's face, and Muungu is noted for his vindictiveness. One quick squint at my inky cohorts showed me they hadn't the slightest intention of budging from the It WASN'T as foolhardy as it seems, spot in any direction, except backward.

If you're wondering why I didn't tear the curtain to shreds right then and there and push on with a manly shout "Yoicks," or "Onward, Upward Excelsior," or something, all I have to say is, don't be silly. If a twig falls the wrong way in Liberia, the fetishes have to be consulted, and there's no point in trying to hurry matters. And a Forbidden Trail loomed as large in proportion to a twig as a milk combine to a Hereford cow. If you follow me. I hardly do myself.

Anyway, I was adamant in my determination to proceed and reserved an aloof attitude while Wahla, with the help of a number of crinkly hairs from his head and a brace of crushed ants, asked the fetishes what they thought about it. The fetishes said, no dice.

Now, I am sure, that somewhere in my arteries and veins courses the blood of a billy goat for, when Wahla directed the abject blacks to collect our belongings and forthwith began to retrace his steps without so much as a by-your-leave. I saw red. I stopped him, took away the compass like a sergeant stripping a corporal of his rank, and gave him a verbal lacing. He was, I told him, a yellow-bellied jackal, a brainless parrot, a chicken with the spine of an angle worm, and I was glad I'd found him out. I, who had consorted with warriors, with the bravest of the brave wouldn't defame myself by traveling in close proximity with the shadow of a suckling pig whose entrails were made of lizard droppings.

I took, snatched really, the camera from one of the Swahilis, turned oh my heel and brushed through the curtain, Meg trotting happily by my side.

IT WASN'T as foolhardy as it seems. We were, I knew, at the most half a day's distance, from the rubber plantation and I felt reasonably sure the thread of a path we were traveling, would soon grow larger and probably be bordered by small villages. It did. And it was. Three villages in all and deserted and all as quiet as tombs. We poked our heads in a couple of the huts. Empty. In one a crude pot with some ground maize in it attested to the precipitous flight of its inhabitants.

"Do you feel it?" Meg asked, after we had passed the last village.

"Feel what?"

"The silence. It's like a ... like a weight. A heavy, dragging weight."

"It is sort of still, isn't it?"

"Do you realize we haven't seen a bird, monkey, or even one of those scampering, fork-tailed scorpions? And what is most astonishing, not a single, solitary insect. I haven't had a tick bite for over four hours, and that's a record."

"Getting spooky?"

"Kind of. Are you?"

"Hm-m-m. Want to turn around?"

"Uh-huh. Do you?"

"Uh-huh."

The words were no sooner out of my mouth when Meg clutched my arm and hissed, "What was that?"

We both stood stock-still in our tracks, listening as hard as we could. Something was following in our wake. Carefully, I trained my gun on the trail behind us, annoyed to find my palms were moist.

The undergrowth moved, parted, and Wahla stepped forth. Without a word, he took the camera from me and assumed the lead. We walked on silently, the only sound being the snap of branches swishing back into place after our passage.

After a while, Meg took the compass and returned it to Wahla, who beamed all over and said, "How do you do," which, being the only English he knew, was the essence of politeness.

WE REACHED the rubber plantation as the sun, in fiery glory, shed one final, mighty glare upon Liberia and sank, an angry red, behind the horizon.

The rubber trees began at the border of the village and extended fan wise to the edge of the sluggish Cavally, lazing against its mangrove banks. Some of the sap catchers, I noted, had fallen away from their moorings and creepers were investigating with waving tendrils their woven intricacies. The underbrush had sent up offshoots along the ground among the trees, and on a good many of the brown, smooth trunks, unhealthy clots of fungi clung like exposed brains.

With a few notable exceptions, the plantation was but a replica of the Guere villages we had traversed. One exception that smote the eye at once was an incongruous frame dwelling, around which the fiber huts were arranged symmetrically in a circle. And even more incongruous than the dilapidated clapboard house, was a mud-baked brick addition, like a sort of igloo, that quite evidently had been added as an afterthought. Another odd feature that had me stumped was the chicken wire. Every window in that fallen-to-pieces house was literally swathed in chicken wire. I don't think a mosquito could have wriggled through without skinning its wings.

Not a wreath of smoke came from any of the thatched roofs, not a chicken clucked, not a child called. Over everything hung the presence of decay and the slow, inexorable encroachment of the jungle. There was only our breathing and the *slap, slap, slap* of the river against the mossy pilings of a lopsided boathouse, its roof caved in and a creeper sticking from a window whose splintered frame stuck out stiffly like a broken finger.

It was uncanny. A row of goose-bumps made a prickly excursion along the back of my neck, and I was conscious that each one of my hairs had a separate and distinct root.

"I don't know about you," Meg said in a small voice, "but my stomach keeps clanking against my wisdom teeth."

"Well, I don't see any zombies," I responded gruffly and, showing a fearlessness entirely foreign to my actual mental state, I shoved off, chest well thrust out like a copy book print of an intrepid explorer, and lifting my feet high to escape the entangling vines, crossed the clearing, rosy in the afterglow. I nearly fell through one of the rotted steps leading up to the porch of the wooden house. Some of the two-by-fours in the flooring were missing and, looking down, I saw an ant hill, its cone blunted and crumbling into dust. Where had its busy occupants gone? And why? Above all, *why?* Why had everybody gone? Everything. Every living, crawling creature.

Raising my hand, I rapped vigorously with my knuckles on the bleached door. The sound, horribly loud in the gathering dusk, echoed away to the ends of the earth, it seemed, and the tip of a weed, sticking like a serpent's tongue through a hole in the porch, bobbed up and down as if chuckling at some diabolic secret of its own.

Then I heard footsteps inside coming closer and closer, with a reluctant obbligato played by the squeaking planks over which they trod. They came right up to the door and stopped, and once more silence spread its hooded skirts over everything. I fancied I could *hear* someone listening beyond that weathered, partition, which shows how jumpy I was.

I knocked again. "Open up," I said. "Rutherford to see Captain Langdon."

"What do you want?" came the muffled and toneless question through the flaking wood.

"I have a message from Colonel Mayhew of Rhordon."

"Mayhew?"

"Yes, of the government compound at Rhordon. Open up, will you?"

"How many are you?" asked my invisible conversationalist.

"Three."

Silence again and finally the rattle of chains and the rusty creak of a bolt sliding back. The door swung wide on protesting hinges. The whole performance was so damned eerie I think I fully expected to see something in the nature of a Boris Karloff or a Bela Lugosi in full regalia. What actually confronted me was a fly-blown edition of Adolphe Menjou in dirty pajamas, whose mustache, instead of being neat and soigné, was scraggly and tobacco-stained and whose eyes, instead of being world-weary and sophisticated, were, as Meg so succinctly put it, like two burned holes in a blanket.

"MY NAME is Rutherford, sir," I began. "Colonel Mayhew, of the Rhordon post, requested that I"—my voice petered out under the unwavering scrutiny of those bloodshot orbs and I swallowed audibly—"deliver a message to his assistant, name of Murchison," I finished.

The beggar was clearly ill. No doubt that explained the entire situation. Some sort of plague or pestilence, as I had prophesied to Mayhew. But if it were a plague, where was the funeral pyre? And the wild life? Animals and birds and reptiles and insects aren't susceptible to plague. My thoughts ran around inside my head like so many squirrels on a treadmill.

"You are, perhaps, Murchison?" I ventured.

"No," the man replied, and he essayed an unpleasant grin, affording me a glimpse of snaggled stumps of teeth. "I am not," he said. "Murchison, indeed!" Cackling laughter welled up from his throat and choked off as abruptly as it had begun.

As I peered at him closely in the thickening gloom, my subconscious began pedaling furiously for home and mother, even while my conscious said crisply, "We have no wish to intrude, Captain Langdon. I assume you *are* Captain Langdon."

"I am."

"My message from Colonel Mayhew is for his assistant. If Mr. Murchison is unoccupied at present, I would like very much to see him,"

"Why did your friends not come with you? Why do they linger behind?"

"We thought the village singularly quiet. I, as head of the party, deemed it wise to investigate first."

"Halo-o-o-o-o," Meg's voice floated across to us.

"There is a woman?"

"Mrs. Rutherford," I answered him and shouted a return halo-o-o-o to Meg.

"The other?"

"A Swahili bearer."

"No porters?"

"Our porters are waiting for us back on the trail."

"I see." Langdon made a conciliatory gesture. "Pray, have them come in. I shall make a light."

"Halo-o-o-o-o," Meg called again, nearer.

"All clear," I yelled. "Come ahead," and bounded down the steps to meet the dim shapes of Meg and Wahla stumbling through the carpet of creepers across the clearing.

Night was settling down in earnest. In the tropics the nights fall with startling suddenness. There is no twilight, no hazy gloaming. When the sun goes down, it goes *down*, as if it were plunged into a Brobdingnagian pail of water. Already the heavens were spangled with the first great luminous stars and all the shadows were merging together into an almost tangible solidity. And nowhere was there a sound.

"Listen," I said hurriedly on reaching Meg, "it looks on the up and up but it doesn't jell. Not with me. Langdon is one of those hermit types. Thought I was going to have to produce my birth certificate before he'd let us in. Queasy sort. Keep your eyes peeled and your trap shut. Not a word about zombies. Got it?

"Murchison?"

"He's here, all right At least Langdon was familiar with the name. Here we go. Watch the second step. It's a shell of its former self."

"So'm I," Meg said. "Way down in my innards there's a three-bell alarm going off a mile a minute. Lord, what a swell place for a seance."

"Stow it. Here comes Langdon."

FAR DOWN a narrow hall, a sickly light bobbed toward us and so murky was the interior beyond the door it seemed to be drifting along all by itself in midair.

Langdon set the lamp on a table and came forward to greet us—if you can call the abrupt inclination of a head a greeting. He closed the door behind us, locked it, bolted it, and fastened a heavy chain across it. Then he shuffled over to a window, peered out through the wire screening, grunted to himself, approvingly as it were, rubbed his bands together, turned and said, "Sit down, sit down, sit down, si—" He broke off as his eyes lighted on our tripod and camera. "What's this?" he said sharply.

"A camera," I said.

"Why would you bring a camera here?"

"We're ... we're connected with the Good Will Ambassadorial Missions for Historical Inquiry," I invented. It seemed as pompous a name as any. "We … we take pictures of out-of- the-way places to show in … ah … other out-of-the-way places to promote … er … good will and … ah … fellowship." I spread my hands placatingly.

"It's as much a part of him as his Bible," Meg said demurely and sank onto a suspiciously gray settee that was bursting at the seams and leaned drunkenly to starboard.

Langdon mulled this over in his mind a few moments, darted a flickering glance at each of us in turn and, apparently satisfied with our bland countenances, subsided into a shabby Morris chair, leaking springs and sawdust.

Wahla squatted on his haunches and I selected a rickety wooden affair, with traces of gilt showing through the dirt and tested it gingerly before lowering myself into it.

"About Murchison," I began. "His superior is rather concerned over his continued absence."

Langdon flicked a speck off his filthy pajamas and said nothing.

"He thought, perhaps, he had been stricken with the fever."

Langdon merely waited.

"So, if I could see him—" My voice trailed off and I felt like a six-year-old who has been caught by an eagle-eyed teacher in the covert act of throwing a spitball.

"Unfortunately, Mr. Murchison is indisposed." The words fell like cold pellets from the thin lips.

"Then he *does* have the fever," I made a *tch-tching* noise with my tongue. "And your rubber workers? They, too, I suppose, have been—" Again my voice trailed away. Limped, rather.

The captain raised his eyebrows. "You are most inquisitive for a missionary."

"The eternal, requisite of a godly man, captain." I said didactically and, slapping my knees in the manner of one who gets on with the business at hand, I stood up and said, "Now, for a look at Murchison and we'll be on our way."

Langdon made no effort to rise.

"I said Murchison was indisposed."

"Oh, come, surely he'll want to hear news of Rhordon. Perk him up a bit. Nothing like a spot of cheer, for the bedfast."

"I'm sorry."

"He must be *quite* ill."

"He is."

"Well, in that case I'd *better* have a look at him. He may be sicker than you realize."

"And if he were?"

"Why, I'd ... I'd take him back to the compound where he'd get good care."

"Tonight, my dear Rutherford?"

"If he were able,"

"But if he were able, then he couldn't be sicker than I think, could he?"

Whereupon I got mad—my County Cork ancestry cropping out.

"See here," I said brusquely, dropping all pretense, "are you holding Murchison incommunicado?"

"Why should I?"

"I'm asking *are* you."

Langdon looked at me with glittering, reptilian eyes.

"Yes," he said quietly, "I am."

"O. K.," I said. "At last we know where we stand. There's just one other thing I want to know. Where are the villagers?"

"Where else but in the villages?" the captain replied with sardonic amusement.

"The villages are deserted, and you know it," I said.

"Not entirely. There are enough blacks left for my needs." He stressed the word "needs" ever so slightly.

"Your plantation is a shambles. It hasn't been worked for four months or more. You, my dear captain, are a liar."

"And you," he said evenly, "are a fool of a doubting Thomas. You wish to see, touch, and taste." He essayed a hobgoblin smile. "By Jehovah, you shall! Look."

LANGDON HEAVED himself out of his chair, went over to the window and pulled up the wooden-slatted blind. He gave a low whistle—two loon-like noises. The moon had risen and the clearing lay, a silver platter, on which the squat-thatched huts resembled the tumbled heads of so many John the Baptists. Beyond, the rubber trees were etched in black and white, with the Cavally slipping along, a silken skein in the moonlight. Beyond that was jungle, a dense wall of impenetrability soaking up the star-shine like a great, dark blotter.

Langdon whistled again. The notes throbbing away into the silence. I caught my breath. There were shadows on the clearing. Moving shadows. A score or more. Some gliding smoothly from sheltering hut to sheltering hut and others ground close, creeping, crawling, wriggling, as if they were blind or maimed. And there was a humming sound as if a thousand bees were fanning their wings in unison. The sound grew in volume, louder and clearer as the shadows approached. Wahla recognized it for what it was before I, and shrank back from the window with a terrified-whimper. And then I got it. It was a Guere word repeated over and over.

"Meat, meat, meat, meat, meat, meat."

The first of the oncoming figures whirled into the shaft of light from the lantern and I reeled as if I had been struck. With a curse, I ripped the cord from Langdon's grasp and the shade rattled down with a clatter, but not before I was able to ascertain that, as far as eye could see and without exception, the motley horde cavorting outside was composed of the most misshapen and mutilated creatures on God's green earth. And not only that, but their hair was braided in a fashion I, in my innocence, had thought outmoded, with bones and dried reptile skins. So Mayhew was right. Cannibalism still flourished! But zombies? No. Lepers, I thought, lepers! And my blood congealed and ran backward for the space of three full seconds. Then I clapped my hand to my hip.

"Don't bother reaching for your gun," Langdon said. "I have just had the pleasure of relieving you of it."

I stared down into the blue nose of my own Luger. If ever a man felt like a complete dunderhead, that man was I. To have played into Langdon's hands with such utter lack of forethought! I called upon my Maker in no uncertain, terms and with lurid, detailed instructions.

Meg, huddled against the sofa, looked almost transparent.

"Is it *them?*" she asked, her eyes like round delft saucers.

"Them?" Langdon queried.

"The zombies," Meg said and immediately put her hands over her mouth as if to push the words back in again.

"So," Langdon said. "Missionaries!" And his voice sounded like the wet, slimy chains of a windlass coiling up front the dank pit of a well. "You came here to steal my experiments. You came deliberately to take what is mine." His voice rose shrilly. "Mine! You would sneak, with trickery and lies, and pilfer a lifetime of research." A knotted vein pulsated in his temple.

I thought, "Here goes nothing," and braced myself for the tearing rip of a soft-slugged bullet. But, as abruptly as Langdon's passion had flared, it died.

"You will go upstairs," he said calmly, "and wait until I am ready." He lifted the outer corners of his lips in a mirthless smile. "I assure you, you will not wait long."

"Just a minute," I said. "*Are* those zombies?"

"Zombies!" The captain spat at my feet. "They are guinea pigs who have served to further a discovery that will make medical history for all time. An experiment that will rock the world and shake the foundations of empires. My name will go down in indelible letters of gold throughout the length and breadth of every land." He wiped his mouth with the back of his hand. "And you would filch it from me." A chuckle started in his throat and burst in a gurgling bubble from between his twisted lips. "You, also, shall further the cause of science. Come, my guinea pigs." He picked up the lamp and motioned us ahead with the gun.

NUMBLY, as in a dream, we were prodded up some dismal stairs and down a wretched hall from, which ancient newspapers hung in dangling strips like imitation seaweed, showing underneath the plastered ribs of the derelict house. The hungry, whining, chant of the savages outside resounded in our ears.

Langdon pushed open a warped door and proceeded to light the chipped twin of his lantern. The flame sputtered, grew steady, and, emitted a bilious glow that didn't reach anywhere near the corners, which were shrouded in dusty obscurity and festooned with ropy cobwebs. A tarnished brass bed, with a greasy ticking atop it, hugged one wall and a cane-bottomed chair, the seat splintered and sagging, hugged the bed. A once-white china pitcher hugged a paintless wash stand. And Meg hugged me. Wahla his skin the color of weak cocoa, kept as far away from the captain as the confines of the room would permit.

Langdon encompassed our "living statuary" tableau with a gloating leer that would have turned Charles Laughton a deep shade of envious chartreuse.

"I wouldn't attempt escape," he said. "It would be most unhealthy. My villagers are quite, *quite* hungry." Softly he closed the door. There was a clank as a bolt was shot home, hard. His footsteps scraped away and clopped down the clacking board stairs.

I disengaged myself from Meg's embrace and began taking the bed to pieces and hefting the assorted lengths of brass to see which was the heaviest.

"Tony," Meg said, "will zombies obey just anybody or only one person?"

"They're not zombies," I said. "There's no such thing as a zombie. They're lepers."

"Oh."

There was a long pause and then, in a tiny voice, Meg said, "Is it catching?"

"I don't know," I said, weighing a rod experimentally and rejecting it. "I've never met anybody, up until now, that had it."

"What do you think Langdon's 'research' is?"

"I don't know. Some cure for leprosy, I'd guess."

"What do you think he's going to do with us?"

"Meg, for Heaven's sake, *I don't know*."

"Well, I just asked."

A long while later Meg said, "If ... if we shouldn't manage to get out from under this one, you wouldn't ... I want you to ... that is ... what, I mean is you'll see they don't get me ... alive ... won't you?"

"You mean you want me to conk you on the bean? Sure thing," I said absently, selecting a good-sized chunk of brass and swishing it like a baseball bat.

"You're certainly nonchalant about it," Meg said. "You almost act as if you were pleased at the Heaven-sent opportunity. Do you prefer a rear view while striking, or will a profile be more effective?"

Wahla, in the corner whimpered and with one extended, quivering finger, pointed to the door. Meg's mouth formed a frozen "O" and my rebuttal to her last verbal sword thrust remained forever unborn. My eyes glued themselves fast to the doorknob which turned ever so slowly and was released.

In a flash, I was pressed against the peeling wood.

"Who's there?" I called softly.

There was no reply. Only the painful inching back of the bolt on the other side.

"Who's there?" I tried again in the slurred guttural accents of Guereian. And, inch by inch, I could hear the bolt sliding back.

"We are friends," I said, "we bring many gifts."

There was a sharp snick as the bolt was released and then a kind of plop as if something had dropped down.

"Stay as you are," I cautioned Meg and Wahla and, grasping my brass blackjack tightly, I stepped close to the jamb, flattening myself against the wall.

The door opened a crack, widened, and Wahla, with an inarticulate moan, buried his face in his hands while Meg went "peep"—just like that—under the impression that she was screaming.

THE THING that crept over the sill into the room was beyond my powers of description. Even now, sitting here in the study, surrounded by familiar objects and with a crackling log fire scattering cheer across the rugs and burnishing the paneling into a satiny patina, I find my flesh crawling and have to fight down a well-nigh irresistible desire, panic if you will, to peer under the tables. I concentrate on the ivory fish, the crystal horns of plenty on the mantelpiece, spilling their delicate tracery of ivy, and I mash out another cigarette in an ashtray already full to overflowing and wonder if I'll *ever* be able to erase the memory of that grotesque caricature of a man worming across the musty floor in the pale glow of the smoking lantern.

I'll give it to you quick. Short, snappy sentences and be done with it. His face was a sickly yellow and sort of drifted to leeward, as if it had become unfastened from the bony, structure underneath. That is, the skin itself was pendulous appearing to hang supported from the temples alone. He was clad in a tattered pair of trousers. No shirt. From the elbows down his arms were bone. Just bone. I'll not put down what it was like *above* the elbows. And what I could see of his legs below the faded pants were bone. Just bone. And those bones moved. They coordinated. They scratched against the boards of the floor and one white-jointed finger made a: quieting motion. Two agonized eyes, very blue, looked straight up into mine.

I closed the door. Murchison relaxed. For that thing *was* Murchison. I knew it for a deadly certainty. He moistened his cracked lips with a swollen tongue and spoke. Have you ever heard, speech attempted by anyone who has just had his tonsils removed? That was it. A hollow, ghost of a voice that lent the impression the windpipe itself was scraped raw. The words were spaced far apart and were few. This is what he said.

"Solutions ... in ... cabinet. Destroy. Paper ... burn papers."

"What cabinet?" I asked, kneeling and subjecting that loathsome form to a searching scrutiny.

"In ... lab—" The grisly fingers tapped on the floor. "Lab

Gritting my teeth, I picked up one of those arms and flexed it. The head rolled flabbily from side to side.

"Burn ... papers ... don't ... wait."

I pushed up the man's pants and examined his legs. Carefully, then, I pulled the trousers down and stared for a long moment at the walls.

"Don't look like that," Meg said, "Don't, Tony."

"I'll be back," I said and rose.

"What is it? Where are you going? Don't leave me. Tony, don't leave me," Meg cried and ran to throw her arms around me. "I won't be left here, I won't, I won't," she said over and over.

There was no time to argue. I gathered that thing up off the floor, spoke swiftly to Wahla, telling him to stick close, and carrying Murchison as if he were a child—and truly he weighed little more—I made for the stairway. Meg, holding the lantern aloft, almost tread on my heels.

WE WALKED in a yellow pool of light and the darkness retreated before us only to close in behind as we passed. Vaguely I knew we were making a hell of a lot of noise lumbering down the shaky stairs and over the dried-out boards in the hallway beneath, but my brain was in such a turmoil and was so overwhelmingly full of a sickening dread into which I dared not probe, that I didn't care. I felt as if I were walking in a charmed circle that not even Langdon could break, and I made my way unerringly in the direction of the discordant brick addition that had attracted our attention from the clearing.

Silence held the house in thrall. We traversed the corridor, without challenge, made a right-angled turn and were brought up short by a heavy door made of plated sheet iron. This, then, was the lab. By some stroke of fortune almost too good to be true, the door was ajar. I strode inside, still carrying my hideous burden, Meg and Wahla crowding in behind.

"Stand where you are, don't move," Langdon said from his hiding place behind the half-opened door.

It *had* been too good to be true. I had stepped into a trap. A trap baited with Murchison. My arms went slack and Murchison slipped to the earthen flooring, groveling in the dirt like a craven beast. Covering us with my Luger, Langdon kicked the door shut with his heel.

"So nice of you to cooperate," he said tonelessly. "I would have hated an attempted break on the stairs which would have necessitated shooting one, or two, or maybe the three of you. Sudden, violent death would have hampered my schedule. This way I will have all three of you safe and sound of mind and limb, with no repairs to be made before rigor mortis sets in." And, without raising his voice, "You will kindly throw your brass bludgeon in the far corner."

I did. And pushed, Meg behind me.

"Langdon." I said, "we're going to have this out. Now. What hellish thing have you stumbled on ?" I motioned toward Murchison squirming across the hard clay floor toward the door. "That's not leprosy."

"I didn't say it was."

"Then, in Heaven's name what is it?!"

"You shall soon know," Langdon said. "And I see no harm in explaining." It was plainly evident that he was enjoying himself hugely. "It's quite simple, really. So long as the blood stream is unimpaired and the organs are not diseased or injured, a body lives. Therefore"—Langdon stabbed the air with a grimy forefinger—"it follows that, if caught in time, in time, mind you, and split seconds count, a dead, body with a diseased organ can be returned to full vigor *if* that organ is replaced with a healthy one."

"Are you trying to tell me Murchison and those Guere natives have had some vital organ replaced after death and have been successful]v resuscitated!"

"I am not trying to tell you. Rutherford. I *am* telling you."

"I don't believe it," I said flatly.

LANGDON jerked Murchison off the floor by the scruff of his neck and yanked back the flaccid head. Those fleshless limbs twitched spasmodically like a dog with chorea and then, blue eyes glistening with hate, Murchison held himself still, as if by so doing he would avoid abuse, while Langdon indicated a scar at the base of Murchison's throat.

"A Guere windpipe is in there," he said.

"What happened to Murchison's windpipe?"

"Unfortunately, it was torn from his throat by the teeth of one of those natives you hear, if you listen closely, outside the building."

"How? Or, should I say, why?"

"Why? Because he underestimated his running ability and refused to believe me when I told him my Gueres were very, very hungry." He flung Murchison down and wordlessly the man began again his patient, sinuous twisting along the floor toward the door.

"I hardly think, captain, your discovery will be hailed with great fanfare and conclave if your ... your clients will have, the appearance of Murchison. He is not what you might call in 'good condition.' Nor are your Gueres. Quite the opposite, in fact."

"That, I will overcome eventually," Langdon said. "Rome, wasn't built in a day."

"These so-called solutions of yours, then, are not perfected."

Langdon smote a lopsided roll-top desk, whose pigeonholes bristled with papers.

"They are!" he snarled. "It's this blasted climate that eats the tissues off their bones and bloats them up with rot. It's the infernal miasma off those mangrove swamps and the bloody heat, heat, *heat*. Day in, day out. Heat. Death and heat. Death and heat. He stopped, blinked his eyes and said, "But you shall see for yourselves. Each of you."

"What do you propose to do?"

"I intend to kill you. Carefully, ever so carefully, so as not to spoil you."

"And you think we shall stand calmly by and let you?"

"You will have no alternative,"

"But to be forced into shooting us would ruin your plans. You said so yourself."

"Not ruin. Hamper. You forget Mr. Murchison's Guere windpipe. I have, should necessity arise, five or more blacks in a fairly normal state of preservation and they would do as patchwork."

"You realize, of course, that if we fail to report to Rhordon, Mayhew will leave no stone unturned to get to the bottom of this."

"Mayhew be damned. *I* am the law, here."

"The government thinks differently."

"The *government* be damned."

Watching us, he edged over to a steel cabinet against the wall and pulled out a drawer with his free hand. Bottles clinked together and he withdrew two filled with a foamy, liverish liquid. With a Bunsen burner, he lighted a small sterilizer such as you see in doctor's offices and, never relaxing his guard, proceeded to fill it with—of all things—cotton in perforated boxes.

"It is of the utmost importance to stuff all the openings of the body," he said.

"What are we going to do?" Meg breathed down my neck.

"I play tackle, you run."

"It won't do to try a break for the door, Mr. Rutherford," Langdon said, "if that's what you're mumbling about. I'm an excellent shot. And this is, so I have ascertained, a repeater."

"Murchison made it, I see," I said, nodding at the two pony feet sliding out the door.

"Murchison sleeps under the cook-stove." He laughed shortly. "It keeps his bones warm."

"When he lowers the lid on the sterilizer," I said out of the comer of my mouth to Meg, "don't look, just run."

LANGDON put the two bottles side by side, in a metal bracket and attached the bracket to the Bunsen burner. The liquid began to clear. He lowered the top of the sterilizer.

"Now!" I yelled to Meg and dove for Langdon's legs. At that moment I wouldn't have traded my backfield training at Dartmouth for all the Greek or Latin that has ever been written.

A bullet sang past my cheek and I had Langdon's thin shanks in my grip with all my weight behind it. A keen pain pierced my shoulder simultaneously with a bark from the Luger and then Langdon and I were rolling on the floor, struggling for a vulnerable hold.

I was conscious of a little, half-stifled cry from Meg.

"Run," I shouted, digging Langdon's thumbs out of my eyes.

She did. Straight for us. Reached us. And whacked her lantern across Langdon's head. It had about as much effect as a mosquito bite. But the lantern broke with a pop like a split electric bulb. Kerosene sprayed and a thin trickle slipped in eddies and whirls across the floor to a straw, mat spread under the swivel chair by the roll-top desk.

A blue tongue of fire danced its way, along that oily stream, licked at the matting. The tongue became a red bush, blossomed up the sides of the desk. The pigeonholed papers began to curl inward. Langdon wrenched himself free and staggered to the desk, beating at the flames with his bare hands. Sparks swirled like angry lightning bugs and the grass-caulked walls caught and blazed. With a gush, the whole interior of the place was an inferno and, somehow, Meg and I were out in the hallway, running like mad, Wahla's breech clout bobbing ahead of us like a rabbit's tail.

A bullet whizzed through the air over our heads. We gained the door, tore at the bolts, got them unfastened, turned the iron key and raced outside as another bullet embedded itself in the molding. And then, believe it or not, I came very near strangling with laughter. Wahla, the bearer in him still functioning on sixteen cylinders, had snaffled my camera as he breezed by and bore it aloft triumphantly, hurtling the steps in one bound.

"The river," I roared. "Make for the river."

I cast a hasty glance backward. The sightless windows were beginning to have a pinkish tinge and silhouetted against the deeper pink of the door stood Langdon. Above the crackle of flames two clear, loon-like notes floated to us, and from around the sides of the burning house poured that yelling band of savages.

"Meat, meat, meat, meat."

Another whistle resounded behind us. We'd never make it. Never in the wide world. Our boots tangled clumsily in the creepers and we tripped with every step.

I threw another look over my shoulder. And halted.

The Gueres, confused and frightened by the fire, were darting aimlessly this way and that, stumbling over the deformed bodies of their comrades who were unable to stand erect, and dragged themselves along on mutilated stumps. But more than that, my attention was centered on Langdon, who had descended the steps and was laying about him right and left with my piece of brass bed and bellowing exhortations at the natives to pursue us.

Behind Langdon, deadly purpose in every line of that tormented, writhing figure, crawled Murchison. He moved crabwise, slowly but surely, and closed the space between himself and the captain.

With a Herculean effort, he pushed himself to his knees, grabbed Langdon around the chest, pinioning his arms to his sides, and pulled him down.

"Meat, meat, meat, meat, meat," he screamed, and sank his teeth into Langdon's throat. In an instant, the two threshing figures were buried under a shrieking mass of blood-lustful black savagery.

I quelled a rising nausea and turned away to find Meg—camera tilted unsteadily on its tripod—grinding out the reel of film! And she actually kicked like a bucking, steer when I picked her up bodily and bore her away.

IT WAS Wahla who herded us to the river's edge by the wrecked hulk of the boathouse, which yielded up a logy and leaking native perahu. It was Wahla, also, who pointed the boat upstream, saying, "Wind, she not blow this way," and it was Wahla who patched up my shoulder wound with my underwear and set Meg to bailing with a rusty, dented bucket, and who got us past the mangrove snags and who, alone, deserves all the credit and the glory and the trumpeting for keeping us from being either cremated or drowned.

It took us three weeks by river to reach Haman, and another week overland to reach Grand Bassam. And there we were, received with many exclamations and much throwing up of hands and excited palaver, as it seems we had been given up for lost in the Bandigara fire.

Dmigne and his brethren had returned to their native kampongs in northern Liberia, some two hundred miles distant. Our films and equipage had never been heard of in Grand Bassam, although one greybeard, recently come from Maynad, volunteered the information that he had seen Dmigne with his own two eyes and Dmigne had had a magic box that made sweet sounds as of the sighing wind, and had, also, strings and strings, more than fingers, or toes, or pig tick bites, of snakeskin grigris and the like of which was extremely strange that rattled when it was touched.

"Our panthers, and wildebeests, and tribal customs. One hundred and fifty reels of them," Meg said resignedly. But to bolster Wahla's spirits, who seemed to take it as a personal "loss of face," she added, "But the one reel we did get is worth more than all of them."

Then came the bombshell. Wahla had, only that morning, presented *that* reel to Muungu as a reward for giving us a safe journey.

"Where was it? Quick! Where?"

"In the Gulf of Guinea, whose waters are fed by the Cavally which Muungu had chastened for our passage. The watch that did not tick but told the true path had directed him." Wahla said, "even as it had directed the Tuan before him."

We caught the first steamer home. I didn't return to Rhordon. I wrote Mayhew and gave him the details. And he wrote back and said undoubtedly my surmise was correct—Langdon had been trafficking in the smuggling of lepers away from Malai, the island colony off the Ivory Coast.

I don't know.

Do you?

MEG HAS just come in to plant a kiss on my forehead and say, "Hurry, darling, or we'll be late."

She is wearing a black velvet coat with ermine tails and one of those do-funnys that hang down like a limp hat in back. And she is looking at me with a puzzled, puckery frown, wondering what I am chortling about.

Copyrights and Permissions

Every effort has been made to determine United States copyright status for the stories in this volume. In many cases the copyrights were not renewed as required. My research indicates that, except as noted below, all of the works collected herein are in the public domain in the United States. Anyone with information otherwise is encouraged to contact the publisher.

About the Editor

Jeffrey Shanks is an archaeologist, historian, and scholar of early 20th century popular culture and speculative fiction. In particular, he specializes in the history and literature of the pulp magazines and early comic books. He has published a number of popular and scholarly articles on pulp writers like Robert E. Howard, H. P. Lovecraft, and Edgar Rice Burroughs.

He currently serves on the board of directors of the Comic Book Collectors Association and is the co-chair of Pulp Studies for the Popular Culture Association.

Most recently he has written or co-written chapters for several academic volumes including *Critical Insights: Pulp Fiction of the 20s and 30s* and *Undead in the West II: They Just Keep Coming*. His chapter "Hyborian Age Archaeology" in the book *Conan Meets the Academy: Multidisciplinary Essays on the Enduring Barbarian* won the 2013 Robert E. Howard Foundation Award for Best Article.

Jeffrey is currently co-editing the critical essay collection *Weird Tales: The Unique Magazine and the Evolution of Modern American Horror and Fantasy*.

Made in the USA
Lexington, KY
09 December 2014